Alison Roberts has been  live in the South of France recently, but is now back New Zealand. She is also for the Mills & Boon Medical line. A primary school teacher in a former life, she later became a qualified paramedic. She loves to travel and dance, drink champagne and spend time with her daughter and her friends. Alison is the author of over one hundred books!

Scarlet Wilson wrote her first story aged eight and has never stopped. She's worked in the health service for twenty years, having trained as a nurse and a health visitor. Scarlet now works in public health and lives on the West Coast of Scotland with her fiancé and their two sons. Writing Medical romances and contemporary romances is a dream come true for her.

THERAPY PUP TO HEAL THE SURGEON

ALISON ROBERTS

HER SUMMER WITH THE BROODING VET

SCARLET WILSON

MILLS & BOON

First published in Great Britain 2024
by Mills & Boon, an imprint of HarperCollins*Publishers* Ltd,
1 London Bridge Street, London, SE1 9GF

www.harpercollins.co.uk

HarperCollins*Publishers* Macken House, 39/40 Mayor Street Upper,
Dublin 1, D01 C9W8, Ireland

Therapy Pup to Heal the Surgeon © 2024 Alison Roberts

Her Summer with the Brooding Vet © 2024 Scarlet Wilson

ISBN: 978-0-263-32165-4

07/24

MIX
Paper | Supporting
responsible forestry
FSC™ C007454

THERAPY PUP
TO HEAL THE
SURGEON

ALISON ROBERTS

MILLS & BOON

For Megan

With the deepest appreciation for so many years of
your exceptional editorial skills and wisdom xxx

CHAPTER ONE

IT WAS ONE of those days.

The ones where there wasn't a minute to spare and it felt like you had to focus that much harder to ensure that no time got wasted and, more importantly, that no attempt to get as close to perfection as possible got sacrificed by taking short cuts.

The kind of day that Hugh Ashcroft liked the most. When his life was exactly the way he had worked so hard to make it. The fresh appreciation for it after the interruption of taking annual leave only made a pressured routine more enjoyable. Not that he'd been lazing around on holiday. Hugh had only flown back to arrive in New Zealand yesterday afternoon, after delivering a whirlwind lecture tour in several major cities in the United States—a world away from this children's hospital in the South Island's largest city.

It was also pleasing to find he had a new, senior registrar assigned to his team. Someone who was already following his own career pathway to becoming a paediatric orthopaedic surgeon. Even better, Matthew was someone who was particularly interested in his own subspecialty of oncology.

'So I only met this seven-year-old girl yesterday.' Hugh

broke the strings of the mask dangling around his neck and pushed open the doors to the operating theatre they were leaving after the successful pinning of the complicated fracture a teenager had given himself when his skateboarding trick hadn't quite worked. 'She fell over in the playground at school and came in late in the day because her leg was still painful. She had an X-ray, which ruled out any fracture, but I got an urgent call to ED.'

Hugh didn't mention that he had still been in his office at ten o'clock last night, catching up on the paperwork that had accumulated in his absence. It wasn't anyone else's business that his work filled the vast majority of his life, was it?

He pulled a clean gown on backwards to act as a coat over his scrubs and looped his stethoscope around his neck. 'I couldn't get a slot for CT and a PET scan until tomorrow morning and an MRI is booked for the afternoon but I managed to get a slot in Radiology to do an urgent bone biopsy under ultrasound and they'll be waiting for us now.'

'So you think it's an osteosarcoma?'

'Certainly looks like it. Huge lesion, just above her knee. Size of an orange. I can't believe she hasn't had problems before this.'

'The family must be terrified. What's her name?'

'Sophie Jacobs. And yes, the family is, of course, extremely concerned.' Hugh headed for the stairs rather than waiting for a lift, shoving open a heavy fire-stop door to the stairwell. 'Which is why we need to be able to give them answers as quickly as possible.'

He wasn't quite quick enough to shut down the echo of Sophie's mother's voice in the back of his head.

'But...but she's just passed her first ballet exam. She lives for her dancing...'

Yeah...'terrified' definitely summed up the parents' reaction he had witnessed last night but Hugh would never use such emotive language. He knew all too well just how devastating a diagnosis of cancer could be for a child and their family.

He knew that, if he let himself, he could be sucked back to a time when another young girl had received such a diagnosis. He would remember realising why the fight for life was called a 'battle' and the crippling toll it could take on everybody involved for months. Years, even. And, if he was careless enough, he might also get an unwelcome glimpse of that darkest of spaces when the battle was lost.

But that wasn't going to happen. Because Hugh also knew that his ability to avoid tapping into the emotions of personal memories was what made him so good at his job that getting asked to be a guest speaker all over the world was now a regular occurrence.

There were plenty of people available to provide the empathy and psychological support that was, admittedly, badly needed, but what seven-year-old Sophie Jacobs and her family needed even more were the specialists like him and his esteemed colleagues in the paediatric oncology team, who could provide the science and skill to follow through on tough decisions and provide the best quality of life for the child in a worst-case scenario and a complete cure in the best.

He was still moving fast as he reached the procedure room in the radiology department, which was another very familiar clinical space for Hugh. A glance at his watch told him he would most likely find his patient on the table with either her mother or father beside her and she might already be sedated and under the care of a team of medics and technicians. He pushed open yet another door and stepped into the room with Matthew hot on his heels.

And then he stopped, so abruptly that his new registrar very nearly collided with him.

Because he was staring at something he'd never seen in any procedure room.

Ever.

'Can somebody please tell me…' Hugh Ashcroft kept his voice quiet and he spoke slowly and very clearly so that nobody could miss the significance of what he was asking '…why there is a *dog* in here?'

Uh-oh…

Molly Holmes caught the gaze of the black and white dog sitting by her feet but if her border collie, Oreo, had picked up on the dangerous tone of this man's voice, she wasn't bothered. Why would she be, when she was so well trained to cope with anything that could happen in a clinical environment like this? Alarms going off, people moving swiftly, children screaming—none of it would distract Oreo from her mission in comforting and supporting a child. She didn't even move her chin from where it was resting on a towel on the edge of the bed, in just the perfect place for a small hand to be playing with her ear.

Molly, however, *was* bothered. Because this was the first time this was happening here and the last thing she wanted was for it to be a disaster. Thank goodness the clinical director of the entire hospital, Vivien Pryce, had chosen to observe what was going on this afternoon and she was smiling as she took a step closer to the person who'd just spoken. Molly would have thought twice about getting that close to someone who looked like a human iceberg but Vivien actually touched his arm.

'Oreo's here to help Sophie with her biopsy,' she said softly. 'Just give us another moment, would you please, Hugh? I can fill you in then.'

So...*this* was Hugh Ashcroft—the orthopaedic surgeon that everybody said was the best in the country when it came to dealing with any skeletal tumours? One of the best in the world, even? Of course it was. Molly had also heard that he insisted on doing any biopsies of his patients himself, rather than leaving it to the very capable radiology department's doctors and technicians.

Mr Ashcroft had been away on leave when Molly had started working here, having moved back to her home-town of Christchurch a few weeks ago after working in Australia for several years. Had no one informed him that the new programme of using therapy dogs in the children's hospital had been approved after apparently waiting in the wings for too long? Perhaps it had been Molly's arrival—with Oreo—that had finally tipped the balance in favour of getting the project under way?

The radiologist was on the point of inserting the cannula in Sophie's hand that would allow them to administer the sedation needed for this invasive procedure. The little girl was lying on the bed on her side. She hadn't even noticed the doctor peeling off a sticky patch on the back of her right hand, revealing skin that would now be numb from the anaesthetic cream that would make the insertion of a needle painless, because she was stroking Oreo's silky ear with her left hand.

'She's *so* pretty...' Sophie whispered.

'She thinks you're pretty too,' Molly whispered back. 'Look at the way she's smiling at you.'

'How do you know she's smiling?'

'It's her ears. See the way she pulls them down?' Talking was another distraction for Sophie from what was going on. 'You can see her teeth, too, and the way her tongue is hanging over them a bit. That's how a dog tells you they're happy and that they like you. They're smiling...'

Sophie was smiling too. So was the doctor, as she slipped the cannula into a tiny vein and taped it into position. A nurse handed her a syringe.

'You're going to start feeling a bit sleepy,' the doctor told Sophie. 'You'll be awake again very soon, okay?'

'Will Oreo still be here when I wake up?' Sophie's gaze was a desperate plea as she looked up at Molly. 'Like you said she would be?'

Molly wasn't completely sure about that now but she chose to ignore the waves of hostility she could feel coming from Hugh Ashcroft's back as he scrubbed his hands at a basin. A nurse was waiting with the gown and gloves he would need to wear to perform a sterile procedure.

'Yes,' she said, firmly. She even raised her voice a little. 'We promised, didn't we? We're not going anywhere.' She could see Sophie's eyes drifting shut as the medication was injected. 'Sweet dreams, darling.'

Oreo didn't move as Sophie's hand slid away from her ear. She would be quite happy to sit here beside the bed, as still as a rock, to guard Sophie while she had her biopsy taken, but when Molly moved back the dog followed instantly. Molly headed for the far corner of the room to tuck herself into a corner amongst the big metal blocks of X-ray machinery. Surely that would be acceptable so that she wouldn't have to break her promise to be here the moment Sophie began waking up again?

Vivien's nod suggested approval.

Hugh's glare did not. But he was glaring at Oreo, so Molly didn't get the full effect.

'We can discuss this later.' Hugh's tone was dismissive but his tone as he turned to Sophie's mother was noticeably warmer. 'Hi, Joanne. I'm sorry I couldn't get here any sooner.'

'It's okay.' Joanne stroked her daughter's wispy blonde curls. 'I can't believe how easy it's been with having Oreo able to be with her. Sophie just adores dogs... Dancing and dogs are her two favourite things in the world.'

'Mmm.'

The sound from Hugh was strangled enough for Molly to start feeling nervous about the upcoming discussion that she would, no doubt, be part of. She caught Vivien's glance as Hugh, now gowned and gloved, stepped towards the table and the older woman's expression was reassuring. Moments later, however, the beeping of a pager saw the clinical director reaching for the message and then mouthing an apology to Molly as she slipped out of the room.

Sorry...have to go...

Molly would have loved to have followed her but she'd made a promise to Sophie and wasn't about to break it. She knew she had Vivien's support. It had been Vivien who'd signed off on Molly using her highly trained dog for an extension of duties that went quite a long way above any simple animal therapy programme that allowed dogs to visit public areas of a hospital or even within the wards. Using medical assistance dogs, or 'dogtors' as they were affectionally known, was happening more and more overseas but Oreo was one of the first dogs in this country to be approved to enter clinical areas like this procedure room, recovery areas and even the intensive care unit to assist children. Molly had made the dog version of a gown Oreo was wearing to cover her back and the elastic topped booties for her paws, which were a smaller size of the disposable ones available for staff to put over their footwear.

Sophie was lying on her back now with an area of her upper leg being prepped. An ultrasound technician was manoeuvring her equipment into place and a nurse was uncovering the top of a sterile trolley that had all the instruments and other supplies that would be needed, including the jars to hold the fragments of bone tissue about to be collected.

'You don't have to watch this bit, Joanne, if you'd rather not.' Hugh looked away from the screen as the technician located the bone lesion. They were ready to begin the procedure. The biopsy needle would show up on the screen to let him position it so that they could be confident the samples would be coming from exactly the right spot.

'I won't watch,' Joanne said quietly. 'But I'd like to stay close. Just in case Sophie might know if I'm not here.' She turned to face the head of the bed so she couldn't see what was happening and she bent down so that she was curled protectively over her daughter, her lips touching Sophie's hair. 'Mummy's here, sweetheart. It's okay… I'm here…'

Molly blinked back a tear but she could feel herself nodding at the idea that Sophie might be aware of her mother's touch. During the later stages of Oreo's training in Australia, she'd seen children respond to the dog's presence even when they were deeply unconscious and on a ventilator in ICU. She'd seen their heart rate and blood pressure drop after just a few minutes of their fingers being in contact with the soft warmth of Oreo's body.

She couldn't see the screen of the machine monitoring Sophie's heart rate and blood pressure so Molly watched Hugh instead. He certainly seemed to know what he was doing and she knew he was so focussed he'd totally forgotten her—and Oreo's—presence in the room. He was calm and confident, making a small incision on Sophie's leg and inserting the device that placed a cannula down to bone level.

'Drill, thanks.' Hugh smoothly removed the stylet and went on to the next stage of the procedure to make an opening in the bone, his gaze on the screen to get right inside the tumour. 'This won't take much longer,' he told Joanne. 'I'm about to start collecting the samples. I'll have an eleven-gauge biopsy needle, please,' he said to his scrub nurse.

Molly could see the care he took to remove several samples of tissue and ease them into the collection jars. She knew some would be used for tissue-based diagnosis and others for molecular analysis. If this tumour was malignant, they would soon know just how dangerous it might be. Again, her heart squeezed painfully enough to bring tears to her eyes. Molly might not be a mother herself, yet, but she was an aunty to nieces and nephews whom she adored and she had chosen to become a paediatric nurse because of her love for children. The joy of sharing their journey back to health was the best feeling ever but being part of the challenge of caring for them when they faced—and sometimes lost—a battle for life was as much of a privilege as it was heartbreaking.

She could feel a tear tickling as it ran down the side of her nose. Without thinking, she reached up to wipe it away with her fingers. She knew she hadn't made a sound, like a sniff or something, so it had to be purely coincidence that Hugh Ashcroft looked in her direction at that particular moment as he stepped back from finishing the procedure.

Molly could only see his eyes between the top of the mask and the cap that was covering his hair, but that was enough to know that he was even less impressed than he had been when he'd seen Oreo in here.

The sedation for Sophie was already wearing off as a nurse put a dressing over the wound on her leg. The little girl was turning her head.

'Where's Oreo…?'

'Right here, darling…' Molly moved back towards the bed with Oreo glued to her leg. 'We're going to go back to the ward with you.'

Oreo put her chin on the edge of the mattress again. Her plume of a tail waved gently as she felt the touch of Sophie's hand on her head.

'Can she sleep with me tonight?'

A sound that was reminiscent of a growl came from Hugh's direction but maybe he was having trouble stripping off his gloves and gown. Or perhaps he was simply clearing his throat before speaking quietly to Sophie's mother about how long it would take for the pathology results to come through.

Molly had to shake her head. 'Sorry,' she said to Sophie. 'We can come back to the ward with you for a bit but there are special rules for dogs that visit in the hospital and Oreo's got to come home with me to sleep.'

Behind her, she could hear Joanne being told that an

MRI and PET scan were booked for tomorrow and her heart sank. The surgeon had to be already very confident of his diagnosis if he wanted the kind of diagnostic tests that would let them stage the cancer by checking for its spread to other parts of the body like the liver or lungs.

Molly made her tone bright. 'Hey...did I hear your mum say that you love dancing, Sophie?'

Sophie's nod was drowsy.

'So does Oreo.'

Sophie dragged her eyes open again. 'Dogs can't dance...'

'Oreo can. We'll show you when she comes to visit one day.'

'Promise...?'

Molly didn't shift her gaze but she could hear that the conversation with Sophie's mum had ended and she could feel the stare coming in her direction from the orthopaedic surgeon, who was now listening to what she was saying.

It was already clear that Hugh Ashcroft didn't like dogs. Or women crying. But it wouldn't be the first time that she'd encountered a surgeon who found it difficult to show a bit of compassion. Maybe it was because their patients were unconscious for most of the time they spent with them so it was easier to be aloof? To see them as simply patients needing surgical treatment without the complications of their own lives and families or their dreams and fears that could make a situation unbearable. And maybe it was just as well there were people like her around to balance the equation.

'I promise,' she whispered to Sophie.

She looked up as she heard another pager beeping, just in time to see Hugh Ashcroft leaving the procedure room.

* * *

He spotted her heading through the hospital foyer towards the main doors.

It wasn't hard. Not when she had that large black and white dog walking beside her. At least the animal wasn't still dressed up in a ridiculous version of a human's theatre gown and booties now. It was wearing a red coat with white writing that advertised its status as a service dog. It also had the medical logo of a heart divided by a stylised ECG trace. And…good grief…small dog paw prints beneath it?

'Excuse me…' It was a command rather than a query.

She turned. She'd been wearing a hat and mask in the procedure room so he hadn't really seen what she looked like and Hugh's first impression was of very curly dark hair that was almost shoulder length and quite uncontrolled looking. Wild, even…

He got closer. 'I'm Hugh Ashcroft,' he introduced himself.

'Yes, I know.'

She had hazel-brown eyes and he could see the flash of wariness in them, which was understandable, given that he'd heard her making a promise to a sick child that— when Vivien had heard his misgivings about the access her dog had been granted in visiting *his* patients—she might no longer be able to keep.

'I'm just on my way to find Vivien Pryce. I saw you and realised I don't actually know your name.'

'Molly,' she said. 'Molly Holmes. But I think you'll find that Dr Pryce is not available. I was supposed to meet her myself so that we could talk about our first session with a dogtor.'

'With a...*what*?'

'Medical assistance dogs. Calling them "dogtors" differentiates them from the pet therapy dogs that don't have the level of training needed to go into a clinical environment.'

The dog at her feet was looking up at Hugh and he got the strange notion that he was being approved of. Being smiled at, even? Perhaps that was because the dog was wagging its tail as it stared at him—a slow, thoughtful sweep against the polished linoleum. Its ears were pulled back as well, which made its eyes crinkle, just as a person's might if they were really happy to see someone they knew. Hugh didn't smile back. He avoided direct eye contact and stared at the dog's owner instead.

'Dogtors' was just the kind of cute title he might have expected people involved with this sort of organisation to have come up with. People who probably also spent a significant percentage of their lives helping to save whales or persuading farmers to play classical music to their cows as they got milked. People who wanted an excuse to make it acceptable to take animals into totally unsuitable environments. It was also an insult to anyone who'd gone through many years of tertiary training to earning the title of 'doctor'.

'First session...and *last*...' he heard himself muttering.

'Excuse me...?'

Molly Holmes' echo of his greeting was definitely a query. An outraged one, in fact. She wasn't nearly as tall as Hugh but she seemed to have just grown an inch or two. 'Dr Pryce might have something to say about that. She assured me that all HoDs were on board with the idea. And Christchurch Children's Hospital is now registered as an active participant in an international research trial looking at the benefits of therapy dog visits for paediatric patients.'

'We were on board with *visits*, yes...' Hugh shook off the impression that this woman seemed well spoken. Intelligent. And very defensive...? 'In a ward playroom, perhaps. Or other public areas. Not contaminating an area that needs to be as sterile as possible.'

'We were nowhere near a sterile field while the procedure was happening,' Molly snapped. 'And we follow clear protocols when it comes to hygiene. "Visits", as you call them, are certainly beneficial to sick children but these dogs can make clinical differences in the most distressing situations for children. Procedures like the one Sophie was having today. Or when they're having an anaesthetic induced or they're in Recovery. Or ICU.'

Her words were blurring. 'Recovery?' he echoed. 'ICU? *Theatre...?*'

'Only the induction room. The kind of spaces that parents are also allowed to be in.'

But Hugh held up his hand. 'This is worse than I thought. I don't want to discuss this with you any further, Ms Holmes. No doubt you'll hear more about my concerns from Vivien Pryce in due course.'

'I'll look forward to it,' she said. 'Have a good evening, Mr Ashcroft.' She turned away but then flicked a glance back over her shoulder. 'You might find you'll enjoy it more if you loosen that straitjacket you're wearing first. It might even help you to consider things from a point of view that isn't solely your own.'

Hugh found himself simply standing there, watching the pair of them walk out of the main doors of this hospital.

Shocked…?

Not so much at being told he was so uptight he might have difficulty enjoying his time away from work. He was quite well aware that people considered him to be a workaholic to the point of being antisocial and enough of a recluse for it to be a waste of time inviting him to parties. He didn't care that he might be considered selfish in thinking that his own point of view was the most important, either. It didn't matter to Hugh what they thought of him on a personal level as long as they also considered him to be the top of his field in his chosen specialty.

Which they did.

People weren't normally this rude directly to his face, however.

This was *his* patch. So it was his point of view that carried the weight here.

Any doubt that it would be worth his time and energy to influence the decision the clinical director of this hospital had made in his absence had just been removed.

Maybe Molly Holmes wasn't as intelligent as he'd thought. Did she not realise that smart remark might have just sealed the fate of both herself and her dog?

With a bit of luck, he might never have to set eyes on either of them, ever again.

CHAPTER TWO

DAWN WAS ONLY just breaking as Molly drove her classic 1960 Morris Minor van over the winding road in the hills that bordered the entrance to the city's harbour and the view was enough to make her catch her breath.

'It's going to be a gorgeous day,' she told Oreo. 'Good thing I'm on mornings this week because that means I can take you to the beach after work.'

Molly had moved into the family's much loved holiday house on her return from Australia recently and it was only a short walk to Taylors Mistake beach, which was now Oreo's favourite place to go. Or maybe the real favourite was one of the challenging walking tracks that went for miles through these hills.

No…judging by how excited Oreo was to jump out of the van at the old villa overlooking the harbour where Molly's mother, Jillian, lived, having finally moved off the family farm in the hills, it was the best place in the world to be when she couldn't be at home or with Molly. Of course it was. Molly's mum's young dog, Milo, was Oreo's new best friend and they got to play all day while Molly was at work. Not that she had time to stop and watch the joy with which the dogs greeted each other this morning. An overweight golden retriever was watching the game of chase and roll from the villa's veranda.

'I need to keep going,' Molly told Jillian. 'I want to get in early today.'

The shift handover started at six forty-five a.m. and Molly was always there early. It wasn't simply because this was a new job and she wanted to impress, it was because of her position. As a nurse practitioner, she had spent years in advanced training that gave her a scope of practice well above a registered nurse. Her authority to prescribe medications, interpret laboratory tests, make diagnoses and instigate interventions and treatments meant that she worked closely alongside the consultants and registrars in her area. She was part of every ward round and family meeting, knew every patient under their care and was sometimes the only medical practitioner available on busy days or in an emergency.

It was a position that carried enormous responsibilities and Molly was passionate about doing her job to the very best of her capabilities.

But, okay…there was that bit of extra motivation today.

Because Hugh Ashcroft was back in town and it was only a matter of time until their paths crossed again.

'No worries.' Jillian was fishing in the pocket of her apron for the small treats she always kept there. Oreo and Milo came racing to sit in front of her, being the best-behaved dogs ever.

'See?' she called as Molly was closing the gate behind her. 'Milo's got to do everything Oreo does now. He's going to be another dogtor, I'm sure of it.'

'I'll do some more training with him on my next days

off.' Molly nodded. 'See you later, Mum—and thanks so much…'

'You know how much I love providing doggy day care. Hey…how did it go with Oreo yesterday?'

'She was perfect. And the little girl who was having the biopsy just loved her. The surgeon not so much.'

'Oh? Why not?'

'I have a feeling he wasn't expecting to find us there. Or it might be that he's a control freak that would never consider bending a rule.' Molly bit her lip. 'I told him he might need to loosen his straitjacket.'

'Oh, Molly…you *didn't*…'

'Could have been worse.' Molly grinned. 'I could have told him he needed to take the stick out of his bum.'

Her mother laughed and flapped her hand to tell Molly to get going, so she turned to open her driver's door. Her brother had stored the car in a barn in the years she'd been away and the porcelain green shade of paintwork was still perfect. With the sun having risen further and now shining on the vehicle, she realised its olive-green colour was reminding her of something.

Oh…dear Lord…

It was Hugh Ashcroft's eye colour, wasn't it? An unusual shade of green in a human, which was just a bit darker than the traditional colour she'd chosen to repaint the van.

'How did he take that?' Jillian wasn't laughing any longer. 'The surgeon, I mean?'

'I'm not actually quite sure.' But Molly was also unrepentant. He'd deserved to hear that his attitude wasn't appreciated. She shrugged as she pulled the door shut. 'Guess I'm about to find out.'

* * *

It was far too early to expect to find the hospital's clinical director in her office but Hugh had sent an email message to her secretary, giving her his timetable for the morning and asking for a meeting to be set up in either her office or his own, with some urgency, but there was no reply by the time he needed to prepare for his first surgery of the day.

Hugh looked into an anaesthetic induction room where an anxious mother was holding a crying toddler. Thirteen-month-old Benji's oral sedative had clearly not been quite strong enough to make what was happening to him tolerable.

'He'll be asleep in just a minute or two, Susan,' he assured the distressed mother. 'Are you okay? Have you thought of anything else you wanted to ask me since I saw you and Benji's father yesterday?'

She shook her head. 'I just want it to be over,' she said. 'Shh…it's okay, Benji. It's not going to hurt.' She cuddled her baby harder as he shrieked in fear and writhed in her arms when the anaesthetist reached towards him with a face mask. 'This part is the hardest…' Susan was losing the battle to hold back her own tears and Hugh could feel himself backing away from the increasing tension and noise level. It was past time he scrubbed in, anyway.

'Try not to worry,' he said briskly. 'We're going to take the very best care of Benji. I'll come and find you as soon as the surgery is finished.'

Matthew was already at the sinks scrubbing his fingers with a sponge. He tilted his head towards the noise coming from the induction room, which was, fortunately, diminishing rapidly.

'Not a happy little camper next door,' he commented.

Hugh's response was a dismissive grunt. He took his watch off and dropped it into the pocket of his scrub tunic. He opened the pack with the soap-impregnated sponge but left it on the ledge while he lathered his arms with soap and used a nail pick. A pre-wash before scrubbing in for the first surgery of the day was mandatory and he rinsed off the soap suds thoroughly before using the sponge to begin a routine that was so familiar and automatic, this could be considered time out. Relaxation, even...

Or maybe not...

'He might have been happier to have that dog in there with him.' Matthew was scrubbing his forearms now. A theatre assistant was hovering nearby with a sterile towel ready. 'That bone biopsy yesterday was quite cool, wasn't it? I've never seen pet therapy used like that before.'

Hugh ignored his registrar's comment this time. He was scrubbing each individual finger now, moving from the little finger to the thumb, a part of his brain quietly counting at least ten strokes on all four anatomical sides of each digit. He had no intention of discussing an issue that had already taken up far too much of his head space. Good grief...his brain had even produced images of that impertinent woman and her scruffy dog as he'd been drifting off to sleep last night.

'So what can you tell me about our first case?'

Matthew dropped his towel and pushed his arms into the sterile gown the assistant was holding for him. 'Benji's parents noticed a bump on his collarbone when he was about four months old. It's got steadily more prominent and imaging has revealed a congenital pseudoarthrosis of the clavicle.'

'Which is?'

'A "false joint". Where a single bone, such as a clavicle or tibia, grows as two bones.'

'Cause?'

'Most likely due to a birth injury.'

'And why is it an issue?'

'The bump can become pronounced enough to be unsightly but, more importantly, it can cause pain and affect the function of the shoulder, which is what's happening in Benji's case. He's developed an odd crawling style because he's avoiding using his right arm.'

Hugh nodded. He was holding his arms under the stream of water from the tap now, letting suds run off from his fingers towards his elbows. 'And what are we going to do?'

'An open debridement of the bone ends and then fixation with clavicle plates and, if necessary, a bone graft with cancellous bone harvested from the iliac crest to fill the gap.'

'Good.' Hugh took the sterile towel from the tongs held by the theatre assistant and dried his hands carefully. 'I'll leave you to stay and see how they apply a wrap-around body and arm cast when the surgery's completed. I'll be popping down to my office on the ward for a meeting with Vivien Pryce before we get started on our second case for this morning.' He turned to put his arms through the sleeves of his gown. 'It shouldn't take long. I expect I'll be back by the time young Benji has gone through to Recovery.'

Baby Chloe giggled as Molly used a fluffy soft toy to tickle her tummy.

'What a gorgeous smile. She doesn't seem that bothered by having her legs strung up in the air like this, does she? We'll see how she goes today now that the weight on the traction's been increased.'

'I hope I can still breastfeed her.'

'It's possible. Not easy but if you can wriggle under the strings and lie sideways beside her, she'll be able to latch on. I've seen mums do it.' She smiled at Chloe's mother. 'It's amazing how you can find a way to do the things that are really important. I love that you're not giving up on the breastfeeding.'

The traction mechanism attached to each end of the cot was gradually stretching ligaments to try and position a congenitally dislocated hip so that it could then be held in the correct place by a splint for months to come.

'She's going to need surgery if the traction doesn't work, isn't she? That's why we're in this ward?'

'It's certainly a possibility.' Molly checked the baby's case notes. 'She's due for an X-ray tomorrow so we should have a better idea of how things are going after that. Would you like me to get the surgeon to come and have a chat to you before then?'

'Yes, please... I always try and hope for the best but being prepared for the worst is kind of an insurance policy, isn't it?'

'I couldn't agree more.' Molly was writing on Chloe's chart. 'I've finished my ward round so I'm going to go and leave a note for the surgeon to come and see you as soon as possible.' She flicked a page over. 'Oh...' An odd knot suddenly formed in her stomach. 'Chloe was admitted under Mr Ashcroft's team, yes?'

'Yes. I haven't met him yet, though—only his registrar. They told me he was away doing a lecture tour in America but he'd be back in time if Chloe did end up needing an operation.'

'He's back now. I met him for the first time myself yesterday.'

'What's he like? He must be very good at his job if he's asked to give international talks.'

Molly swerved the question by making a sound that could have been agreement. Or perhaps it was encouragement, as she picked up the fluffy toy to try and make Chloe giggle again.

The delicious sound of a happy baby stayed with Molly as she scribbled a note to ask Hugh Ashcroft to visit his potential patient's mother. She could have left it with the ward manager to deliver or put it in the departmental pigeonholes for mail but she was due for a break and wanted a breath of fresh air. Heading for the access to the courtyard garden that opened off the foyer area just outside the ward entrance took her very close to the consultants' offices, so she decided to put it on his desk herself. That way, she could make sure he saw it immediately.

She opened the door without waiting for a response to her polite knock because she knew he was upstairs in Theatre with a full list for the day. The shock of seeing him standing behind his desk peering at his computer screen was enough to make her jaw drop.

'Oh, my god,' she said. 'You're not supposed to be here.'

'It's *you*...' It was a statement rather than a question but he was looking as startled as she was. 'I could say the same thing,' he added, slowly. 'You're certainly not supposed to be in *my* office.'

He was staring at the scrubs she was wearing. At her hair, which, admittedly, was probably already trying to escape the clips she used to try and tame it during work hours. His eyebrows rose as his gaze flicked down to the stethoscope hanging around her neck and the lanyard that made it obvious she was a staff member. And then that gaze shifted again, to look straight at her. 'Who the hell *are* you?'

Oh…the intensity in those olive-green eyes that could be due to either suspicion or anger was…well, it was disconcerting to say the least. It had to be nerves that were pinching deep in Molly's gut right now because she knew what was coming—a well-deserved bollocking for having been so rude to a consultant surgeon yesterday?

'My name's Molly Holmes.' She lifted her chin. 'I started work here as a nurse practitioner last week.'

'But…what were you doing here yesterday? With that dog?'

'I've been involved in pet therapy for years. It's what I do on my days off.'

There was a moment's silence during which Molly noticed something was changing in that gaze she was pinned by. Was it softening? Because Hugh Ashcroft was now seeing her as a colleague and not a layperson who volunteered to bring her pet dog into a hospital occasionally? Or could he be just a little impressed that she chose to spend her days off in the same place she worked? That she cared enough about her patients to be here when she wasn't being paid to do so?

Perhaps being impressed was a bit much to expect.

But he wasn't looking angry so much. He was looking…

Puzzled…? Or curious? As if interest might be winning a battle with irritation…?

Her nervousness was receding now that it didn't feel like she was in quite so much trouble with one of her senior colleagues but, strangely, that sensation in Molly's gut wasn't going away. If anything, it seemed to have become even stronger.

He knew he was staring.

He knew it was a rude thing to do, but Hugh couldn't help himself. It almost felt as if, by keeping a steady gaze on this woman, he might be able to find his balance.

It wasn't often that something knocked him sideways but having Molly Holmes walk into his office like that had done it. He'd left the hospital yesterday quite confident that he would never see her—or her dog—again but... here she was. In his work space. His *happy* space. Not only that, she was a nurse practitioner. Someone who was highly trained enough to be filling gaps and monitoring his patients, possibly better than his more junior registrars.

Someone that he would expect to have a close working relationship with.

Vivien Pryce, the clinical director, who was going to arrive in his office at any moment, according to the email he'd just read, might not be very happy if Hugh said everything he'd been planning to say to her about yesterday's incident with the dog in his procedure room.

Hugh cleared his throat.

'About yesterday...' he began. 'About your dog...'

And then he stopped because he couldn't think of what to say next.

He was still staring. At her brown eyes that were fringed with lashes as dark as her hair. Her skin was tanned enough to make him think she spent a lot of time outdoors and…

…and she was smiling at him.

'Oreo,' she supplied to fill in the gap. 'She liked you, Mr Ashcroft.' Her eyebrows lifted as if she had found this quite surprising. 'And I have to admit that my dog is usually a very good judge of character.'

Hugh remembered the way the dog had been looking up at him yesterday and waving its tail in approval. Smiling at him… He actually shook his head to get rid of the image of those brown eyes, as warm as melted chocolate, fixed on him. Not unlike Molly's eyes, come to think of it.

The list of objections he had been more than ready to discuss with Vivien seemed to be getting less defined. Hugh found himself frowning as he tried to focus.

'It wasn't that I didn't know a pet therapy programme was being considered for our ward,' he said, a little curtly. 'But nobody said anything about allowing animals to have access to the kind of areas you mentioned, like an intensive care unit. Or a procedure room, for that matter. I was…surprised, to say the least.'

Molly was nodding. 'I'm sorry about that. And I take full responsibility. There was a meeting last week, while you were still away, and because I've already been involved with a similar programme in Australia I was invited to bring Oreo in. It was only going to be an orientation but then Radiology let us know about Sophie's appointment and Vivien asked if we could visit and it just sort of grew from there. Sophie fell in love with Oreo and asked if she could go with her for the biopsy and I said she'd love to if she was allowed and…' Molly finally paused for breath. 'Anyway... I do apologise. I can try to ensure that everyone's aware she's going to be present next time.'

Next time...? I don't think so...

Hugh wasn't aware his thought had been audible until he saw Molly's expression change. Until he saw the fierce gleam in her eyes that told him she was quite prepared to fight for whatever she was passionate about.

'There are some articles you might like to read when you have a spare moment,' she said. 'There aren't too many peer-reviewed studies that have been written up yet but anecdotal evidence is gaining quite a following. The trial that Dr Pryce has enrolled us in will be hoping to reproduce the kind of results being seen overseas, where people are reporting quite dramatic improvements in parameters like anxiety levels and pain scales in children who have animal companions in stressful medical situations. Measurable results with blood pressures and heart rates dropping, which is a pretty good indication that pain or stress levels are diminishing—'

The knock on the door interrupted her and Hugh saw her eyes widen when Vivien Pryce entered his office. He also saw the flash of something that looked very much like fear and...

...and he suddenly felt guilty because he could have caused Molly some serious problems that might have ruined the start of her new job if he'd gone ahead with his complaints.

He also felt quite strongly, and very oddly, as if he wanted to protect her, which was both very unexpected and just as unwelcome.

* * *

Oh, no...

Molly saw the apologetic expression on the clinical director's face as she entered Hugh Ashcroft's office.

'Sorry, Hugh. I've been putting out fires so far all morning and I've only got a minute or two now but my secretary said it sounded like you wanted to talk to me about something urgent.' Her sideways glance was curious. 'Is it about our first dogtor consultation yesterday? Is that why Molly's here, too?'

'No...' Molly edged towards the door. 'I just came to leave a note for Mr Ashcroft.' She hurriedly put the now rather crumpled piece of paper, asking Hugh to go and talk to Chloe's mother, on the edge of the desk. 'I'll leave you to it.'

'Don't go.' Hugh's tone sounded like a command. 'You probably need to know what I was about to say to Vivien, anyway.'

Molly bit her lip. If he wasn't about to tell Vivien how inappropriate he considered it to be to have animals in a procedure room, he was intending to tell her that their new nurse practitioner was lacking the kind of respect a senior consultant surgeon was entitled to expect.

She had to agree that he should be able to expect some privacy in his own office without having people barging in uninvited. And he certainly shouldn't have been told that he was so buttoned up he couldn't bend far enough to consider that the opinions of others might actually be as valid as his own.

But Hugh was nodding at Vivien as Molly held her breath. 'That was, in fact, what we've just been discussing,' he said. 'I was explaining that I wasn't aware there was any mention of allowing animals in areas that most clinicians wouldn't consider to be remotely suitable for pet therapy when we had that initial departmental meeting on the subject.'

'That is true. Personally, I wasn't aware of the most recent literature concerning the therapeutic benefits of allowing dogs in those kinds of areas until I was having a chat to Molly after her job application interview. It was, admittedly, an addition that should have been more widely discussed before we put it into action.'

The sound Hugh made was a cross between agreement and annoyance. Then he shrugged. 'Perhaps it's not too late. You might like to send me the links to those papers when you have a spare moment.'

Vivien flicked another glance in Molly's direction. There was curiosity in that lightning-fast glance as well—as if she was surprised that Molly had somehow defused the bomb that had been about to be hurled?

'I'll do that. But if it's more information you need, Hugh, it's Molly you should talk to. She's got far more experience in this field than anyone here. I'll also forward the memo I got from the research technician who was recording vital sign measurements on Sophie yesterday. If you compare them with the control case we monitored last week, you can see a rather startling difference. I know it's early days but I think this is going to be a very exciting trial to be part of.' She was smiling at Molly now. 'And we have our recently appointed nurse practitioner to thank for getting it off the ground.'

Hugh might have resisted the opportunity to get Molly into trouble but he wasn't about to go as far as being friendly to his new colleague. He was reaching to pick up the note Molly had put on his desk and he scanned it swiftly. 'Tell them I'll be on the ward as soon as my surgery list is complete for the day,' he said. 'That should be around four o'clock if we have no emergencies or complications to deal with. And if I'm not holding everyone up by having unscheduled meetings.' He glanced up at the clock on his wall. 'Which means I need to be scrubbed in again in less than five minutes.'

His nod signalled the end of this unscheduled meeting with Molly. He moved towards the door and Vivien turned to follow him out.

'Keep me posted on Sophie's case, would you, please, Hugh? I was thinking about how hard this is going to be for her family last night. Did you know she's the star of her ballet class? Her dad just put up a rail in her bedroom to be a barre for her to practise with.'

It was no surprise that this aloof surgeon ignored such a personal detail. Molly could hear the clinical detachment in his voice as he walked away with Vivien. 'She's scheduled for a PET scan about now. I'll forward the results...'

Molly headed back to pass on the message for Chloe's mother. The handover for the afternoon shift would be over long before Hugh was due to be back on the ward so it was very unlikely that she would see him again today, which would probably be a relief as far as Mr Ashcroft was concerned.

It was a relief for Molly as well because she was quite sure that she had, somehow, dodged a bullet.

There was no reason at all to feel disappointed. Molly had a busy few hours ahead of her dealing with whatever challenges arose in a surgical paediatric ward. Her pager was beeping right now, in fact, to alert her to a potentially urgent situation.

Moments later, she was on her way to replace an IV line that a toddler had managed to pull out. She could hear the two-year-old boy's screams already as she sped down the corridor. This could keep her occupied for quite some time but it was just the kind of challenge she enjoyed the most—winning the confidence of a terrified child and succeeding in a necessary intervention with the least amount of trauma. It was a shame she didn't have Oreo here to help, mind you.

But, by four o'clock, she would be back at her own mother's house to collect her beloved canine companion. She'd do some training with Milo before she went home but the days were lengthening nicely now that summer wasn't far away. There would be time for a walk on the beach with Oreo before it got dark.

Feeling disappointed that she wouldn't be seeing Hugh Ashcroft again today was…

…weird. That was what it was.

CHAPTER THREE

SUNSET WASN'T FAR off but there was still enough time to go and play on the beach, especially when they only had to go through the gate at the bottom of the garden and run along the track through the marram grass on the sand dunes to get past the driftwood and near the waves, where there was enough space to throw the frisbee.

Molly kicked off her sandals and got close enough for the last wash of the waves to cover her feet. She flicked the frisbee and laughed as Oreo hurled herself into the chase with a bark of delight and then leapt into the air to catch the plastic saucer and bring it back to drop at her feet. This time with her dog was a world away from the stress that could come from her work and completely different from the focus that came from the training sessions she did with Oreo and now Milo on a daily basis. It was simply hanging out. Loving each other's company.

Pure fun.

She wasn't the only person taking advantage of the last of the sun's rays to have some fun. A lone surfer, protected by a full body wetsuit, was well out to sea, waiting for a bigger wave.

For a disquieting moment, Molly was taken back in time. She was a teenager in love for the first time, watching her boyfriend and her brother out catching waves on a summer evening, and she'd never been so happy. The pain—and shock—of her first romantic disaster when she was dumped a few months later had never been forgotten.

On the positive side, the pain was never *quite* that life-shatteringly bad when it happened again.

On the negative side, it had happened too often.

Okay…sometimes it had been her decision to call time on a relationship that wasn't going anywhere but, more often, it hadn't been her choice. It was usually an amicable ending because they were great friends but, quite understandably, the guys moved on because they wanted something more in a life partner. And sometimes, it came too close to an echo of that first heartbreak.

Molly had given up trying to work out why she always seemed to be put in the 'friend zone'. The men she liked didn't seem bothered that she wasn't blonde and blue-eyed. Or that she had the solid, healthy kind of body that suited a girl from the farm. It certainly wasn't that she wasn't good company or intelligent enough to be able to have an interesting conversation.

She told herself for years that she just hadn't met the right person. That she'd know when she did and she wasn't going to settle for less. That she might be surprised to find him around the very next corner in her life. But the last break-up—the one that had persuaded Molly it was time to go home to New Zealand—was taking a bit longer to get over.

Getting settled again and starting a new job were good excuses to have no interest in even looking for male companionship but, to be honest, Molly was almost ready to embrace singledom. If she wasn't looking, maybe the 'one' would come around that corner and find her. If he didn't, it wouldn't be the end of the world. It wasn't as if she were alone, after all. She bent to pick up the frisbee Oreo had dropped hopefully in front of her and threw it again.

Oreo's joyful bark as she chased after the toy made her smile.

This was the kind of happy she could trust to last...

When she straightened up, she saw the surfer catch the wave he'd been waiting for and when he leapt to his feet, Molly found herself slowing to watch him. She didn't even notice the frisbee being dropped within easy reach.

Wow...

This guy was seriously good at surfing. Molly liked to swim in the sea but she'd never got bitten by the surfing bug. Her older brother had, though—which was how she'd met her first boyfriend—and she'd heard and seen enough over her teenage years to know how much effort and skill went into making it look this easy. This graceful.

Right from the moment he got to his feet, he was in control and there was no way Molly could look away before he reached the end of this wave. To be able to sense the power and purpose in his movement from this far away was something special. This person was passionate about what they were doing—totally oblivious to any audience, living in the moment and loving it.

He had done an aerial move within seconds, flipping his board into the air above the lip of the wave and then landing to twist and turn along the wave face. As the height and strength of the wave collapsed he even did a flashy re-entry turn off the end of it. And then he dropped down to lie on his board and paddle back out to sea, as if he couldn't wait to catch another wave. As if his life depended on it, even...

Oreo's bark made Molly realise she had ignored the frisbee for too long and she turned her attention back to the game, but as she reached the end of the beach and turned back towards home she caught sight of the surfer again—now a dark blob against the increasing colour in the sky behind him, reflecting the sunset happening on the other side of the hills. He wasn't showing off this time. He was simply poised on his board, at one with the limitless ocean he'd just been flirting with, as he rode the wave right to the wash of shallow foam so close to the beach he could step off and be only ankle deep. He picked his board up at that point, slung it under his arm and walked out of the sea...straight towards Molly.

Oreo was normally wary of strangers and stayed protectively close, often touching her legs, so Molly was astonished to see her take off and run towards the surfer. When she got close, she dropped her frisbee and then put her nose down on her paws and her bum in the air to invite the man to play. When he walked straight past her, she looked confused for a moment but then grabbed the toy and ran after the man. This time she got right in front of him before she dropped it. Molly increased her pace, ready to apologise for the annoyance her dog was creating.

But then she stopped dead in her tracks, completely lost for words.

Blindsided...

Never, in a million years, would she have guessed that the man whose longstanding passion for what he was doing on the waves showed in his level of skill and every confident, graceful movement of his body could possibly be someone who could also be so lacking in an emotional connection to other living creatures that he couldn't embrace the pure joy of being able to provide comfort to a small, scared child.

Did Hugh Ashcroft have an identical twin?

Or had she stumbled into the private life of a person who was actually the opposite of who he appeared to be in the company of others?

How—and *why*—could someone be like that?

Curiosity was quite a powerful emotion, wasn't it?

'Hullo, Molly.'

So, there was definitely no identical twin, then.

'Hullo, Mr Ashcroft...'

Even a tiny shake of his head released droplets of sea water from his hair. Hair that was very neatly cut but was so wet and full of salt, it was spiky, so even his hairstyle was utterly different.

'Call me Hugh, for heaven's sake,' he said. 'There's no need to be so formal, at work *or* away from it.'

He was staring at her, but this was very different from how it had felt when he'd given her a look of this intensity at work, when he'd demanded to know who the hell she was. He wasn't wearing his surgical scrubs, he was encased in skintight neoprene that was almost as sexy as seeing him wearing nothing at all. And he was dripping wet.

Okay...maybe it did feel pretty much the same. Because Molly could feel that curl of sensation unfolding in her gut, not unlike one of the large waves still breaking offshore, and, this time, she knew it had nothing to do with being nervous.

It didn't have anything to do with her confusion, either,

although the burning question of which person was the *real* Hugh Ashcroft wasn't about to go away.

No. This was something else entirely. Something even more powerful than that curiosity.

It had everything to do with…attraction.

Sexual attraction…

Dear Lord…she had the hots for someone she was going to be working with? Someone who had made no secret of his disapproval of her taking her dog into sacrosanct areas of the hospital. Who'd even looked vaguely disgusted when he'd caught her shedding a tear?

'Fine…' Molly was pleased to manage to sound so offhand. 'Hugh it is.'

She reached down to pick up the frisbee and flicked it towards the sea. Oreo bounced through the shallow water to catch it before it hit the waves.

'I've forgotten your dog's name,' Hugh said. He was moving again, towards where a towel had been left on the sand, neatly rolled up.

'Oreo.'

'Like the cookie? Of course…he's black and white. Great name.'

'*She*… Oreo's a girl.'

The correction sounded like a reprimand but Hugh ignored it. He wasn't really interested in her dog, was he? Or her? And that was just as well. It meant that Molly could dismiss that moment of inappropriate attraction and make sure it didn't happen again.

Oreo was back with the frisbee. Molly held out her hand but Oreo dropped it right beside Hugh's bare foot. He bent down but didn't pick up the toy. Instead, he picked up the towel and started walking again, towards the car parking area that also had a facility block.

'I'd better get a shower before I get too cold,' he said. The glance over his shoulder felt like a question.

'I'm heading that way myself.' She nodded. Oreo picked up the frisbee and followed them.

'I can only see my car,' Hugh said, a few steps later. 'Where did you park?'

'I live here,' Molly told him. 'See that little white cottage with the red roof and the big chimney up on the road?'

'You live right by the beach? Lucky you...'

'It's not exactly my house. It's the family bach. I grew up on a farm and this was where we came for holidays.'

'You still count as a local, then. I've always wondered how it got its name. Someone told me that there was a shipwreck here and that was the mistake.'

Molly laughed. 'I think getting the ship stuck on the beach was the second mistake that Captain Taylor made. The first one was thinking he was going into the harbour in Lyttleton, I believe. It was back in the early settler days of the eighteen-fifties.'

Good grief...did she think Hugh might want a history lesson? Molly didn't dare look at him. She glanced sideways at the waves, instead.

'My older brother, Jack, got into surfing when he was just a kid and was going to competitions by the time he was a teenager.' She bit her lip. 'Don't think he's as good as you are, though.'

The sudden silence made her look back to find Hugh blinking as if he was startled by the compliment but then he turned to look at the waves again himself. 'Did you surf, too?'

'No. It's always been about animals for me. I rode horses and did dog trials—you know? Rounding up sheep and getting them into a pen?'

Oreo was walking beside them, clearly resigned to the fact that the frisbee game was over for the day. Curiously, she was walking beside Hugh rather than Molly.

'I think you've got an admirer.'

'Excuse me?'

Oh, help…did he think she meant herself, after she'd told him how good he was at surfing? She tilted her head and he glanced down to follow her line of sight. Oreo looked up at him and waved her tail.

It was Hugh who broke a still awkward silence.

'Vivien sent me those articles,' he said. 'I had time to browse one of them when I went back to the ward to talk to Chloe's mother this afternoon.'

'Oh…?'

'I didn't realise quite how extensive the range of therapies is that animals can be involved with. Like physiotherapy.'

Molly nodded. The turnoff for the track up to her house wasn't far ahead of them but she didn't want this conversation to end quite yet. Not when she could talk about something that might make a real difference to how enjoyable her new job was going to be.

'I love working with physios. It's amazing how reaching out to pat a dog or taking one for a walk, even if it's just to the door of their room and back, can get them past the pain barrier of starting to move again after surgery. Oreo's good at pretending to take medicine with kids, too.

She'll drink liquid from a syringe or take a "pill" that's actually one of her treats. And it's not just beneficial to the patients. Most staff members love having a dog around and the parents and siblings of patients can get a lot of comfort out of it...' Molly sucked in a breath. She had too much she wanted to say and not enough time. 'What could be better for anyone who's having a tough time than to be able to cuddle a dog?'

'I wouldn't know.'

But Hugh's response sounded merely polite. He was looking past Molly, towards the house she'd pointed out as being where she lived. She knew he would be able to see the track leading away from the beach and, if she kept walking with him, it would be obvious that she was doing it for a reason and not simply because they were going in the same direction. Heaven forbid that it might occur to him that she'd had even a moment of being interested in him as anything other than a colleague.

'See you tomorrow, Hugh.' Molly turned away. A glance was all it took for Oreo to follow her.

'Have a good evening, Molly.'

Hugh's farewell was an echo of what she'd said to him—good heavens, was it only yesterday? Just before she told him that he might like to loosen his straitjacket. In retrospect, after seeing the way he'd moved his body in response to the force of the waves, it had been an astonishingly unfounded accusation to make. Worse, remembering what it was like watching him reminded Molly of her physical reaction to having him standing in front of her, dripping wet, in that skin-tight wetsuit. She was actually feeling that twist of sensation in her gut all over again.

And that was disturbing enough for Molly to avoid looking back at him at all costs as she walked away.

Oreo looked back, though. And when she looked up at Molly again, it felt like her dog was asking the same question that was filling her own head.

'I don't know,' she heard herself saying aloud. 'We'll just have to wait and see, won't we?'

The meeting room was full of people.

There were representatives from the paediatric oncology, radiology and surgical departments. The head of physiotherapy was here, the ward manager, Lizzie, a senior pharmacist, a senior nurse specialist and the nurse practitioner, Molly, and a child psychologist and family counsellor.

Oh, yeah...and one dog. It must be one of Molly's days off. She had probably been intending to bring Oreo into the hospital anyway but, oddly, it felt quite appropriate that the dog and her owner who'd been there at the beginning of this case were also present at such an important family meeting. Oreo was lying very still, her nose on her paws, on the floor beside Molly's foot.

It was very quiet.

Quiet enough to hear Sophie Jacobs' mother, Joanne, pull in a shaky breath, as if she was trying to control the urge to cry. Her husband, Simon, was staring at the ceiling and it was possible to see the muscles in his jaw working to keep it clenched. He was also trying not to cry in public, wasn't he? Sophie's grandmother had also been included in this meeting to discuss the diagnosis, ongoing treatment and prognosis for their precious seven-year-old girl and she had a wadded tissue pressed beneath one eye.

Hugh glanced at the paediatric oncology consultant who, along with the paediatrician who had been the admitting physician, had delivered the results of all the tests they had done and confirmed the devastating news that Sophie did, indeed, have a malignant osteosarcoma. He'd provided details of the staging process and prognosis that had, no doubt, been too much to understand at this point and would need to be talked about again, probably more than once.

The oncologist had also explained her role to care for Sophie as she received an intensive period of neoadjuvant or pre-operative chemotherapy before the surgery to remove the tumour. The pharmacist had finished an outline of the kind of drugs that would be used for the chemotherapy and answered questions about how side effects such as nausea and hair loss might be managed. The family had been warned early on in the investigations that if the tumour was malignant then amputation, rather than any limb-saving surgery, would very likely be necessary.

The oncologist met Hugh's glance and gave a discreet nod. It was the right time for him to say something about the upcoming surgery for Sophie.

There was a screen at this end of the room and Hugh tapped the mouse pad on his laptop to bring up an image.

'This was the very first X-ray we took of Sophie's leg,' he said quietly. 'And it was immediately obvious that she had something significant going on at the distal end of her femur—almost directly on top of the knee joint. We have a lot more information now, thanks to the biopsy, MRI, the PET and CT scans and all the other tests that Sophie has very bravely put up with over the last week or two.'

Joanne blew her nose. 'Thanks to Oreo,' she said. She

smiled across the table at Molly. 'I don't know how we could have coped without you.'

'It's been our pleasure,' Molly said. 'I'm going to take Oreo to visit her again in a few minutes, to let you have more time to talk to everybody today. I just wanted you to know that we consider ourselves to be part of this team and we'll be here whenever I have my days off.'

Sophie's father simply nodded brusquely.

'The good news—even though it might not seem like that at the moment—is that this is a primary osteosarcoma and not evidence of metastatic disease from somewhere else. Even better, the PET scan, amongst the other tests, has shown us that the clinical stage is early and the tumour is still intracompartmental, which means that it hasn't extended as far as the periosteum, which is the membrane of blood vessels and nerves that wraps around the bone.' Hugh was putting up images from the scans now. 'The lymph nodes are clear and there's no sign of any hot spots at all in the lungs or any other bones, which are the most likely targets for metastases. This is all really good news because it gives us confidence that the cancer hasn't spread. At all...'

Hugh paused for a moment to let that positive statement sink in. He saw the glances exchanged between Sophie's parents and, if he let himself, he knew he would be able to feel the beat of hope in the room. Not that he was going to indulge in sharing anything close to joy when he still had the hardest part of this meeting to get through.

'We still need to treat this cancer aggressively enough to try and ensure we get rid of it completely and it can't recur—or spread—and that means that the surgery Sophie is going to need *will* be amputation. The procedure that we will be recommending is the one I mentioned to you as a possibility the other day—the rotationplasty salvage procedure.'

'No...' Joanne pressed her hand to her mouth to stifle a distressed cry and her husband put his arms around her.

Hugh clicked onto a new image but as he shifted his gaze he caught the way Molly had dropped her hand to Oreo's head—as if she needed a bit of comfort herself? He could understand that the concept was confronting but it was, without doubt, the best option for Sophie.

'As I explained, what happens is that the bottom of the femur—where the tumour is located—the whole knee joint and the upper tibia are surgically removed, with the cancer and a wide clear margin around it also removed. The lower leg is then rotated one hundred and eighty degrees and attached to the femur.'

Hugh could see that Joanne Jacobs still hadn't glanced up at the image on the screen of a young boy who'd had this procedure. With no prosthesis on, he had the unusual appearance on one leg of a foot pointing backwards at knee level.

'Because the foot is on backwards, it can function as a knee joint,' he continued calmly. 'A special prosthesis is made that the foot fits into and it provides much greater mobility and stability than a full leg amputation would. It also lowers the risk of phantom leg pain.'

He put up a new image of the boy with the foot hidden inside his artificial lower leg and perhaps Sophie's father had murmured some encouragement to his wife because Joanne finally looked up as well. The next image was of the boy kicking a football—a wide grin on his face.

'The bone will continue to grow as you would expect

in a young child and, of course, the prosthesis will be adjusted to fit.' Hugh closed his laptop. 'Younger children have another real advantage in that their brains learn more easily to use their ankle as a knee and adapt their walking patterns.'

The physiotherapist at the meeting was nodding. 'I can answer any questions when you're ready to talk about it,' she said.

Joanne shook her head. She wasn't ready. She folded herself further into her husband's arms and it was obvious she was sobbing silently by the way her shoulders were shaking.

There was no point in trying to reassure these distressed parents any further at this time. Hugh caught the counsellor's gaze with a raised eyebrow and the silent communication suggested that she would stay here a little longer but, yes, it would be better for everyone else to leave and give this couple some private time to deal with their initial reactions. Others had seen the silent message and, as a group, they were beginning to leave the room.

Hugh picked up his laptop as he saw Molly and Oreo leaving. He wanted to catch a moment of the oncology consultant's time for a chat about the chemotherapy regime that would be started for Sophie, hopefully today. He had cleared a good space of time this afternoon so he would check back to see if Sophie's parents wanted to talk to him about anything, but he suspected he might be the last person they'd want to see again today.

When he walked back past the meeting room, Joanne and Simon were nowhere to be seen and the psychologist was shutting the door behind her.

'I suggested they went for a walk outside and got

some fresh air before they went to see Sophie so that she wouldn't see how upset they were,' she told Hugh. 'But we've made a plan to discuss how and when to talk to her about the amputation. I'm going to see if I can set up a meeting with the parents of that boy in your photos. I know they'll be happy to offer their support and it could be a game-changer for everybody. He's a few years older than Sophie now but maybe he'd be up for coming in to visit and show her his leg?'

'Good idea.' But Hugh's response was brisk. Everyone involved on the team assigned to this case had different roles and thank goodness there were people who were more than willing to immerse themselves in the social, psychological and emotional side of a life-changing di- agnosis like the one Sophie Jacobs had just received. His job was to make sure he gave her the best chance of, not only survival by completely removing the tumour, but the best quality of life possible, going forward, by advocating for a procedure he knew was the best option. His role was all about the surgery and the most important part of his role would be inside an operating theatre with a patient who was sound asleep and any emotional family mem- bers completely out of sight—and mind.

Just being in the tense atmosphere of that family meet- ing had been enough for Hugh to be hanging out for a bit of private time for himself to prepare for the rest of his day. He didn't need a walk in any fresh air, though. The peace and quiet of his office with the door firmly closed would be quite good enough and the close proximity of that small, personal space was too tempting to resist.

Between the paediatric orthopaedic surgical ward and the row of consultants' offices was a courtyard roof garden, opening off the foyer space that housed the stairway and bank of lifts. It wasn't huge but it provided the nice aesthetic of an open space with some lush greenery and seating. The concrete pavers were smooth enough to make it easy for IV poles to be pushed or beds to be rolled outside for a bit of sunshine.

As Hugh walked past the floor to ceiling windows to get to his office, he saw a wheelchair parked to one side of the central square of pavers. And then he saw that it was Sophie Jacobs who was sitting in that wheelchair. The wide door to the garden hadn't been completely closed so he could hear music that was being played outside. An old tune he remembered from high school discos back in the day—Abba's 'Dancing Queen'.

Sophie had a huge grin on her face and her arms were in the air as if she were dancing to the music, but she wasn't alone. Both Molly and Oreo were out there with her.

Hugh's steps slowed and then stopped. What on earth were they doing?

Skipping…that was what it was.

But it wasn't just Molly skipping. Oreo was holding up one front paw as she hopped and then the other. And then Molly made a hand signal and Oreo stood on her hind legs and went around in a circle.

Molly turned in a circle as well and Sophie clapped her hands.

Then Molly started moving in a diagonal line across the square, straight towards where Hugh was standing, but she didn't notice him. She was watching Oreo as she took long steps, her legs very slightly bent, which seemed to be a signal to the dog to go in figures of eight, her own gaze fixed on Molly's as she was weaving through the space between her legs from one side and then the other.

It was only when dog and owner paused a beat before they started skipping again in the opposite direction and he realised that it was in time to the music that Hugh remembered Molly telling her that Oreo loved to dance.

This was what she and her dog were doing, wasn't it? *Dancing...*

And obviously loving doing it as much as Sophie was loving watching it.

It was kind of cute, Hugh conceded.

But it was also...

Mesmerising?

His feet were certainly glued to the floor. His gaze was glued to Molly. To the changing expressions on her face and her hand gestures that were a language all of their own and the lithe movements of her body as she bent and twisted, reached and curled.

It was...

Okay...it was damned sexy, *that* was what it actually was.

Hugh could feel his body waking up, as fixated as his gaze had been on this woman and what she was doing. He could feel tendrils of a sensation that was both physical and mental and, while he might not have felt it to quite this degree since he was an adolescent, he knew exactly what it was.

Attraction...

Desire...?

A want that was powerful enough to feel like a need.

And the shock of that recognition was more than enough to break the spell that Hugh Ashcroft had fallen under. He could move his feet again and that was exactly what he did to escape from the disturbing realisation that he was sexually attracted to the new nurse practitioner.

Not that it was a problem. Hugh was more than capable of both keeping his own feelings completely private and making sure that something professionally awkward simply wouldn't be allowed to reappear.

But he did need the privacy and time out of his own office for a few minutes even more now than he had a few minutes ago.

CHAPTER FOUR

'I CAN'T SEE this working.' The older woman watching what Molly was doing with a young patient and his mother was shaking her head. 'It's never going to stay properly clean, is it?'

'Don't be so negative, Mum. That's why I'm getting as much practice in as I can before we take Benji home this afternoon.'

'I know it's going to be a bit of a challenge at times,' Molly conceded. 'Especially in the first week or two.' She offered the anxious grandmother a smile. 'I'm sure your help is going to be very much appreciated, Louise, but Susan is a very competent mother and I know she's going to cope brilliantly. Look at how well she's doing this nappy change.'

Susan's baby, Benji, was in an unwieldy plaster cast that wrapped around his chest and one arm to keep it completely still after the surgery he'd had to remove the false joint on his clavicle. He was also coping well with the nappy change, waving his unrestrained arm in the air, trying to grab his mother's necklace as she leaned over him.

'You're doing a great job,' Molly said. 'Tuck the edges of the first nappy right under the cast and then we'll put another one on top. We want to avoid the cast getting wet or dirty if at all possible. You may find it easier to use a smaller size than usual for the first nappy.'

'What do I do if it does get dirty or wet?'

'Use just a damp washcloth to clean it. If it's really damp, you can use a hairdryer on a cool setting to speed up the drying process or take Benji outside to get a bit of sunshine on it. Another good tip is to use a towel as a big bib when he's got food or a drink in his hands.'

'He must weigh twice as much with that cast on.' Louise sighed.

'He'll certainly be top heavy and won't be able to sit up by himself,' Molly agreed. 'He'll need to be propped up with pillows and cushions and don't let him try and walk by himself. The last thing you want is a fall, so he'll need to be carried everywhere.'

Louise made a tutting sound. 'You're going to have to be careful when you pick him up, Susie. You'll be in trouble if you put your back out again.' She turned to Molly. 'How long is he going to be in this cast?'

Molly opened her mouth to answer but stopped as she saw Benji's surgeon coming through the door of the room. Hugh Ashcroft was wearing scrubs and still had a mask dangling by its strings around his neck. Had he left his registrar to finish up in Theatre after the actual surgery was completed and ducked down to the ward for some urgent task?

Hugh acknowledged Molly with a brisk nod but his gaze went straight to Susan.

'Benji's discharge papers are signed,' he told her. 'I've reviewed the X-ray he had taken yesterday and I'm happy that he doesn't need to stay in any longer. The clavicle is exactly where it needs to be and it should heal very fast.'

He shifted his gaze to Benji's grandmother. 'In answer to your question, this cast will need to stay on for five to six weeks. We'll see Benji well before then, however, and monitor his progress in our outpatient clinic.' He was turning to leave. 'You'll find a phone number on the discharge information to call if there are any problems, so please get in touch with the team if you have anything you're worried about.'

'Thank you ever so much for everything you've done, Mr Ashcroft,' Susan said.

'Ashcroft...' Louise was staring. 'You're not Claire Ashcroft's boy, are you?'

'Ah...' Hugh had taken a step towards the door. 'Claire was my mother's name, yes...'

'You probably don't remember me. I used to work for the same house cleaning company as your mother. Spick and Span? Goodness, it must be more than twenty-five years ago. Susie here was still in kindergarten when I had that job but you would have been at primary school.'

'Ah...'

The sound from Hugh was strangled. The sudden flick of a glance in Molly's direction gave her the impression that Hugh was taken aback enough to be having difficulty deciding how to react. He looked as if he was merely going to acknowledge the information and escape but Louise kept talking.

'We only worked together until your poor sister got so sick, of course. We all understood why she had to give it up and go on a benefit to look after her.' She was making that tutting sound again. 'Such a tragedy...she never got over it, did she? Your mum? And it was so hard on you when you were just a little boy yourself...'

Molly was watching Hugh's face as Louise prattled on but when she saw his head beginning to turn as if he wanted to know if she *was* watching him, she hurriedly looked away.

'Let me help you get Benji's clothes back on, Susan,' she said, a little more loudly and firmly than she would usually. 'Or maybe your mum would like to help.'

She was hoping that Susan's mother would take the hint and stop talking. Because Molly had seen the horror washing over Hugh's face and the rigid body language that was like a forcefield being erected and it was patently obvious that this was a subject that was not only private, but it was capable of causing anguish.

Molly could actually feel that pain herself, her heart was squeezing so hard. Something else was gaining strength rapidly as well—the urge to try and protect Hugh Ashcroft.

'Louise?' This time her tone was a command. 'Could you help us with Benji, please?'

'Oh...yes, of course...' Louise looked towards Molly, then swung her head back to the door but Hugh had vanished. Louise shrugged. 'It *was* a long time ago,' she muttered. 'Maybe he doesn't want to talk about it.'

Molly's smile was tight enough to advertise that she didn't want to talk about it, either, but Louise didn't seem to notice.

'Dear wee thing, his sister, Michelle. So pretty, with her golden hair that hung in real ringlets. Until it all fell out from the chemo, of course,' she added sadly.

Molly's response was a request. 'Could you get the hoodie jacket with the zip that matches these dinosaur pants, please, Louise? That will keep Benji nice and warm and it'll be easy to get on and off.'

Benji started crying as his mobile arm got lost inside the larger size tee shirt that had been purchased to fit over the cast.

'Got cancer, she did,' Louise continued as she went to the pile of clothing in the cot. 'When she was only about three, poor kid. Can't remember what sort it was but she was in and out of hospital for years and years and then she died. Never really saw Claire after that.'

She handed the jacket top to Molly, who was showing Susan how to position her hands to lift her top-heavy baby, who was now crying loudly. Susan looked as if she might start crying herself.

'She died not that long after. There were rumours that she'd taken some kind of overdose but I reckon it was down to her heart being broken so badly.' Louise must have realised that nobody was listening and gave up. 'Rightio...let Nana help you get your jacket on, Benji. We need to get you back home, don't we?'

Molly helped with getting the baby dressed and then left the women to pack the rest of their belongings to be ready for Benji's father, who was coming to collect them.

It wasn't that she hadn't been listening to Louise. Molly was professional enough to hate gossip but she couldn't deny that she had been listening avidly to every word. It explained so much, didn't it?

That aloofness.

The way he could be a completely different person when he thought he was totally alone and doing something, like surfing, that provided such an effective escape from the real world.

She could forgive the control he kept over himself. She could understand the distance he preferred to keep from others. How could he not have learned to protect himself from getting too involved?

Molly was still thinking about what she'd heard as she went to the next patient needing her attention. Thinking about the little boy that Hugh Ashcroft had been. A child who'd had to live with a terrible tragedy? It was the kind of story that would touch anyone's heart, but Molly Holmes had always been a particularly soft touch for a sad story.

And this one had already captured her heart completely.

Hugh stayed well away from the ward for the next few hours. Until he could be completely sure that Benji's grandmother would be nowhere on the grounds of Christchurch Children's Hospital.

It helped that, after a morning of scheduled surgeries, Hugh had a fully booked outpatient clinic for the afternoon. There was no time at all to dwell on the unpleasant pull into the past that Hugh had experienced in his visit to Benji's room and plenty of cases that were complex enough to need his full focus. Concentration that worked a treat until the last patient to be ushered into the consulting room for today's clinic.

Fourteen-year-old Michael had been a patient under Hugh's care for some years now.

'You've had a bit of a growth spurt, haven't you, Mike?'

'Just over eight centimetres,' his father said proudly. 'He's going to end up taller than me at this rate.'

'It's making his scoliosis worse, though, isn't it?' Michael's mother looked pale and worried. 'Is that why he's getting so short of breath lately?'

'It is,' Hugh agreed. 'Lung function is compromised because the diaphragm and chest wall muscles can't move the way they should. Is getting short of breath interfering with what you want to do, Michael?'

The teenager nodded. 'I can't go to the gym... I can't hang out with my mates at the skate park... It's hard to even walk...'

Listening to him speak made it very clear how far his lung function had deteriorated since Hugh had last seen him.

'His brace is hurting him, too,' his mother added.

'I'm not surprised,' Hugh murmured. He clicked his keyboard to bring up scan images taken only days ago. The screen showed a spinal column distorted enough to resemble a letter S.

'See that?' Hugh talked directly to Michael. 'You've now got a sixty-five-degree curve on the top of your spine and nearly eighty degrees on the bottom. Surgery is recommended when the scoliosis is over fifty degrees and, with the effect it's having on your breathing, I think it's becoming urgent.'

Michael's nod was solemn. 'You said this might happen one day—that I'd need an operation. I'm ready for it. You have to put rods and screws in my back, don't you?'

'And maybe some bone grafts. It's called a spinal fusion and it will straighten your back enough to make it easy to breathe again. I think you'll find you can do a lot more at the gym—and on your skateboard—but you'll have to be patient while you recover properly, okay?'

'Sure...' Michael's eye contact was brief and his tone just a little off-key. 'How soon can I get it done?'

He was scared, Hugh realised, but he didn't want anyone to know—his friends, his family or even his surgeon. He was young enough to crave comfort but old enough to know that adults had to be able to look after themselves. Maybe he didn't want his mother to be any more upset than she already was.

For a moment that was even briefer than that eye contact, Hugh remembered what it had been like when he was fourteen.

Being that scared even though it was for different reasons.

And being unbearably lonely at the same time.

Dammit...

This was because of Benji's grandmother. She'd known enough to invade his privacy and make it public that his younger sister had died from her cancer. That it had broken his mother irreparably. How much more did she know? And would she think it was so long ago it didn't matter if she shared it with others?

Like Molly Holmes...?

Hugh had the horrible feeling that Molly had seen more than he would want anybody to see but he'd been ambushed, hadn't he? He hadn't even known that he might need to be ready to protect himself from what had felt like a potentially lethal attack.

Hugh squashed the thought ruthlessly. This wasn't about him.

It was never about him. Not at work or away from it.

'Let's have a look at my schedule,' he said to Michael. 'It's a four-to-six-hour operation but you'll only need a few days in hospital. It'll be a bit longer before you can go back to school, though. When do the summer holidays start?'

'First week of December. But my exams will all be over in November.'

'Sounds like a plan,' Hugh said. 'It would be nice if you were back home and well into your recovery by Christmas, wouldn't it?'

Michael's mother was reaching for her husband's hand. 'That would be the best Christmas present we could get.'

It was nearly five o'clock by the time Hugh put his last folder of patient notes on the desk for the clinic administration staff to sort out.

Benji would have been discharged hours ago.

Molly would have finished her morning shift about the same time so there was no danger of being reminded of what he'd spent the whole afternoon trying to forget. It should be quite safe to go and check on his post-op patients from this morning. He needed to see the teenager who'd torn his anterior cruciate ligament playing a game of rugby and received a hamstring tendon autograft to repair it. He was a day-surgery patient and his registrars would have been monitoring him since he came out of Theatre but Hugh preferred to see all his patients himself before they were discharged.

'Have you had a chat to the physio?' he asked him. 'Did they check your brace and size the crutches for you?'

'They made me go up and down the stairs to make sure I know how to use them.'

'Good. And you've got an orthopaedic outpatient appointment set up?'

'Yes.'

'Excellent. You can go home.'

Hugh could go home, as well. He might even have time

to get out to the beach and catch a wave or two before it got dark. Not at the beach where Molly lived, mind you. He wasn't planning to go back there any time soon.

Maybe it was because he was thinking about her that Hugh turned his head as he walked past the courtyard garden. She wasn't out there, of course, but it was all too easy to conjure up the memory of her dancing with her dog.

All too easy to feel a frisson of what he'd felt when he'd been watching her.

No. He certainly wasn't going to go back to that beach to surf again. He didn't want to meet Molly out of work hours again.

He wasn't too sure he wanted to meet her *during* work hours, in fact, so it was an unpleasant surprise to turn back from that glance into the garden to find her walking straight towards him.

As if he'd conjured *her* up along with that memory.

After this morning, he had more to worry about than a fleeting moment of attraction. She knew something about him that was personal. Something he didn't want to become common knowledge.

Hugh could feel his eyes narrowing. Because attack was the best form of defence, perhaps? 'What are you still doing here?' he demanded. 'I thought your shift finished a long time ago.'

'I stayed a bit longer,' Molly said. 'I was talking to Joanne Jacobs. Sophie's mother?'

'I know who she is.' Hugh was still watching her carefully but he couldn't see any sign that this was anything but a professional exchange. There was nothing to suggest she was interested in—or possibly had taken note of—anything personal about him at all.

'I'm just heading back to see her again. It was a pretty intense conversation. They're still struggling with the idea of the rotationplasty.'

Hugh's frown deepened. 'So I heard.'

'Well… I thought of something that might help—especially when they're talking to Sophie about it. I worked with a girl who had the procedure in Australia and she was a very keen dancer as well.'

'Oh…?'

It was there again, unbidden, in his head. A private video clip of Molly with her arms in the air, making a circle and then gracefully bending her body to bring the circle low enough for the dog to jump through.

'So… I went to print something out but then I wondered whether I should be getting this involved.' Molly was fishing in the pocket of her scrub tunic. 'Can I show you? I don't want to overstep boundaries or anything and she is your patient.'

Hugh blinked. Surely Molly had overheard what Benji's grandmother had said this morning? Was she just going to pretend it had never happened? That she wasn't aware of any personal information that was going to change their professional relationship?

Well…that was fine by him…

'What is it?' He had to admit he was curious.

Molly had rolled the sheet of photocopy paper so it didn't get creased. She unrolled it and Hugh's eyes widened.

It was an astonishing picture. A small girl—maybe eleven or twelve years old—was doing one of those ballet leaps that could make them look as if they were suspended in mid-air, with their arms and legs stretched out wide, if the photo was taken at precisely the right moment. The girl in this photo was looking straight at the camera as she jumped and she had a smile as wide as the reach of her arms, but what was truly remarkable was that one of her legs was a prosthesis.

Hugh could see in an instant, by the scarring high on her leg, that the girl had undergone the procedure of using the ankle as a new knee joint. The back-to-front foot was hidden inside the structure of the artificial leg and…there was a pale pink ballet shoe on the foot to match the one on the girl's normal leg.

'Her name's Amber,' Molly said. 'I don't feel like I'm invading her privacy because she—and her family—were so proud of this photo. Amber's the poster girl for the orthopaedic and prosthetic departments and this picture's on the website for the hospital I worked at in Australia.'

'So Sophie's family could find it themselves with an Internet search?'

'Yes…but Sophie's only seven and I thought she might like a real picture so that she could look at it whenever she wanted to.'

Hugh was having another one of those strange moments, like he'd had with Michael, when he'd been whisked back into the past to remember what it was like being a teenager. Now he was going even further back. To when his sister was so sick and she'd lost all her hair. She'd loved her ballet class, too, when she'd been well enough to attend. Would she have felt better if she'd seen a picture of a girl with no hair, doing a leap in the air like this, with the happiest smile in the world on her face?

His throat felt oddly tight. How good would *he* have felt as a big brother if he'd shown her that imaginary photograph and told her that it could be *her* doing that in the future? Michelle would have probably slept with the picture under her pillow and put it on the wall when she was in hospital, as she did with the one of Fudge—the family's chocolate brown Labrador.

Would Molly feel that good if it helped Sophie?

Hugh suspected she'd probably have to wipe a tear off her face—as he'd seen her do in that radiology room when Sophie had had her biopsy—except it might be a much happier tear this time.

He swallowed past the sudden lump in his own throat.

'I don't think you're overstepping any boundaries,' he said. 'Show it to Joanne first or perhaps the psychologist who's working with them.'

'Okay…thanks, Hugh.' Molly was rolling the paper up again.

'No…thank *you*…' he responded.

She caught his gaze, her eyes wide. 'What for?'

What for, indeed?

For going above and beyond any part of her job description—working overtime after an already long day without any financial reward for her efforts—to help the patients she was caring for on a very personal level?

For being the kind of person who would spend their days off doing the same thing by being a handler for a pet therapy programme?

Or was it deeper than that for Hugh? Was he thanking her for respecting his privacy? For making it clear she wasn't about to display curiosity, let alone try to get more information about his past?

Maybe it went even deeper than *that*.

Perhaps what Hugh was really thanking Molly for was

making him feel that she was someone who could be trusted on a personal level, because people like that were few and far between in his life.

Pretty much non-existent, in fact.

And that made Molly Holmes rather special.

Not that he was about to tell her any of that. What he did do, however, was smile at her. A smile that felt like it was coming from somewhere he hadn't been in...what felt like for ever.

From right inside his heart?

'For doing something that might make a real difference,' was all he said. 'Good job, Molly.'

CHAPTER FIVE

THE OUTPATIENT CLINIC had finished long ago.

Almost all the department's ancillary staff members—the receptionists, technicians and nurses—had already left for the day. Hugh's registrars were up on the ward doing a final ward round and sorting any clinical issues.

Julie, the charge nurse manager, poked her head around the door of the consulting room Hugh had stayed in to snatch a few extra minutes of peace and quiet.

'Haven't you got a home to go to, Hugh?'

'I've got my last case notes to update. On Benji?'

'Oh, yes…isn't he doing well? He's crawling properly now instead of scooting along on his bottom to avoid putting any weight on the other shoulder.'

'Definitely a success story.'

'I didn't envy his mum having to look after him in that cast for so long, though I guess it's not as bad as a spica cast for hip dysplasia.'

'That's certainly harder to keep clean.' But Hugh turned back to the computer on his desk to indicate that he wanted to get on with making notes about how well Benji's clavicle had healed, not discuss how well his family had coped with the recovery period.

Julie took the hint and left but Hugh was aware of a

remnant of thought about that patient interview that had nothing to do with anything clinical. Thankfully, Benji's grandmother hadn't come to this last appointment with her daughter but that hadn't stopped Hugh from remembering that encounter the day the toddler had been discharged after his operation.

And, as usual, that made him think about Molly Holmes.

He saw her all the time when she was working in his ward, mind you. He'd seen her quite often in the hospital on her days off when she brought her dog in for pet therapy sessions. He'd even seen her in the theatre suite once when she'd been with a child who was having a general anaesthetic induced and he had no problem with that. Hugh was more than happy that they were both far more comfortable around each other now than they had been when they'd first met but...

...but it was always just a bit disturbing when she entered his mind when she was not physically present in his environment.

When something reminded him that she had tapped into a space that nobody was allowed to enter by making him believe he could trust her. If anything, that feeling had grown a lot stronger because, in all the intervening weeks, Molly had never said or done anything to suggest that she intended to cross boundaries. She hadn't even given him one of those 'knowing' looks that women seemed to be so good at delivering.

It was getting less disturbing, however. Possibly because it happened so often? It was only yesterday when he'd gone to the paediatric oncology ward to see how Sophie Jacobs' latest round of neoadjuvant chemotherapy was going that he'd had a double whammy of being reminded, in fact. Sophie had that piece of A4 paper stuck onto the wall above her bed. The one Molly had printed out with the ballet dancer doing the leap with her prosthesis.

That reminded Hugh not only of that conversation they'd had about the image of someone dancing but of Molly herself dancing, with that dog. But that was exactly what Hugh needed to think of to flick the 'off' switch. Preferably before he was reminded of an attraction he had managed to gain complete control of.

He channelled that control into his fingers as he typed into the digital patient records.

The surgical intervention of the resection and excision of the clavicular pseudoarthrosis, in conjunction with bone grafting using autograft tissue from the iliac crest and then internal fixation, has resulted in a very satisfactory bone union. The cosmetic result is pleasing and the patient is rapidly gaining full function of his shoulder joint.

That summed up the consultation well, along with the radiologist's comments on the latest X-rays and notes from the physiotherapist. There was only one thing to add.

There are no indications that further follow up is needed at this point although a second surgery in the future to remove the plates may be an option if implant prominence or irritation occurs.

Hugh saved his notes, logged out of the access to medical records and closed down the desktop computer.

Closing the door of the consulting room behind him, Hugh was startled by a clattering noise coming from the reception area. Surely he hadn't taken so long it was time for the cleaners to come through the deserted department?

And then he heard something so unexpected he couldn't quite place it.

Someone coughing?

A *dog's* bark?

And, dammit…there was Molly Holmes in his head again.

He walked past the reception desk and into the waiting area and somehow he wasn't even surprised to see that she was here in a physical sense as well.

With her dog.

No…make that *two* dogs…

Milo wasn't too sure about this.

He barked again and then crouched to deliver a growl that sounded way more playful than ferocious.

Was there really something scary about the spokes on the wheelchair parked in the corner of the waiting room? Or maybe it was being in the hospital environment with all its strange smells and noises and too many people and things on wheels.

'It's okay, Milo.' Molly reached into the pouch that was attached to a belt around her waist and took out a tiny treat to give to the young dog. 'I know it looks scary but it's just a wheelchair. Look—Oreo's not bothered at all, is she?'

But when she looked up, Oreo had uncharacteristically deserted her post where she was sitting at the end of a row of chairs and was heading straight for the person emerging from the back of the department. Fortunately, Oreo didn't bounce at Hugh Ashcroft. She just stopped in front of him and waved her tail in a polite greeting. His expression, however, was reminiscent of when he'd walked into

Sophie Jacobs' bone biopsy appointment and had seen her there with Oreo.

Was this going to undo the growing ease that seemed to have developed between herself and Hugh in the last weeks? An edging closer that could possibly develop into a real friendship?

Sometimes, recently, when Hugh had smiled at her in passing, and even more when he'd caught her gaze deliberately, Molly had had moments of dreaming that something more than friendship could evolve. The way he was looking at her right now, however, suggested that any thoughts in that direction were purely one-sided.

'I'm so sorry.' Molly grimaced. 'My friend Julie told me it would be fine to bring Milo in for some training when the department was empty and before the cleaners came in. I thought today's clinics finished more than an hour ago.'

'They did. I stayed late.' Hugh stepped around Oreo without acknowledging the greeting he was being given. 'You have *two* dogs?'

'This is Milo. He's my mother's dog but I'm going to adopt him, at least for a while. Her retriever, Bella, has just had another litter of pups and it'll be too much for Milo when they get mobile. She kept him from the last litter because she thought he could be a good candidate as a therapy dog and I think she's right. He just needs to get some more exposure to clinical spaces and I knew that Orthopaedic Outpatients would have plenty of wheelchairs and walkers and crutches to make things interesting.'

While she was talking, Milo had bravely taken a step towards the wheelchair and stretched his nose out to sniff the unfamiliar object. Then he cringed and jumped back-wards. Molly bit her lip. And then she glanced at Hugh.

'Have you got another minute or two to spare?'

'Why?'

'I think the wheelchair might be less threatening if it had someone sitting in it.'

'You want *me* to sit in the wheelchair?'

'You're a stranger. It would make it more realistic. I can go out and come in again and if you encouraged Milo, he might come and say hullo and realise the chair isn't going to bite him. He's very friendly and it'll only take a min-ute.' She gave Hugh her best smile. *'Please...?'*

She saw the hesitation but she shamelessly held his gaze because instinct told her that this was an opportunity to add something much more personal to their professional relationship and that was the only way this could turn into any kind of a real friendship.

Hugh shrugged. 'Why not? I owe you a favour.'

'Why?'

'Sophie Jacobs' parents signed the consent forms for the rotationplasty today. She's going to have the moulds of her foot made in the next few days and we can sched-ule her surgery after she's recovered from this round of chemo.'

'Oh...' Molly forgot about Milo's training for the mo-ment, catching her bottom lip between her teeth again. 'That's *such* good news. And she'll be back in the or-thopaedic ward for a while. I'll have to bring Oreo in to visit again.'

'It is good news. Having a visit from a lad who had the procedure a few years ago helped the decision making but it was that picture of yours that started the ball rolling in the right direction. Did you know that Sophie said "I want to be just like her" as soon as she saw it?'

Molly nodded. 'I was there. I knew that Joanne and Simon wanted to get her through the initial chemo before making a final decision, but I had a feeling they just needed the time to get used to what Sophie's leg was going to look like.'

Hugh was walking towards the wheelchair. Molly patted her leg and Milo obediently followed her into the side corridor without pulling on his lead. Oreo's gaze was on Hugh.

'Oreo, *down*,' Molly commanded. *'Stay.'*

With an audible thump, Oreo dropped to the floor and put her nose on her paws. Hugh sat in the wheelchair. When Molly walked back in she casually approached Hugh and he clicked his fingers at Milo.

'Hullo,' he said. 'Who's a good boy?'

Milo went straight towards him, his whole body wiggling with happiness at being noticed. Molly reached for a treat but Milo didn't notice because he was poking his nose around the wheel, trying to reach Hugh's hand for a pat.

She expected Hugh to pull back but, to her amazement, he was smiling at Milo, who nudged his hand so that it was automatic to fondle the dog's head and ears and then his neck.

'It's not so scary, is it?' Hugh looked up at Molly. 'Want me to roll around?'

'If you've got time, that would be fabulous.'

Milo leapt back as the wheelchair moved and Molly just let him watch. Oreo got up as the wheelchair went past her and started walking beside Hugh but Molly didn't tell her to stay again. It felt like she was showing Milo how it was done and, when Molly gave Milo some more length on the long lead, the young dog went straight towards them and walked behind Oreo.

They both got treats a few minutes later.

'Thank you so much,' Molly said to Hugh. 'I couldn't have done that by myself.' She smiled at him. 'I won't make you hop around on crutches or use a walker.'

Hugh made a huffing sound that was almost laughter. 'I think I'd prefer to put off giving a walker a trial run.' He got up out of the wheelchair. 'I do happen to know when orthopaedic gear like this goes when it's out of date or deemed not worth repairing. Would it be helpful if you had some rusty crutches or an ancient wheelchair at home for training purposes?'

Molly nodded enthusiastically. 'That would be awesome. Let me know if there's anything available and I can pick it up. I've got a van.'

Oreo was following Hugh towards the doors that led from the outpatient department into the main corridor that joined the front foyer of the hospital.

'She really likes you,' Molly said. 'Sorry... I realise it's probably a one-sided attraction.'

Oh, *help*...had she really said that aloud? It sounded as if she was talking about herself and Hugh.

But Hugh didn't seem horrified. 'I don't dislike dogs,' he said. 'I grew up with one.' He paused and gave Oreo a pat. 'Fudge, his name was. He was a rather overweight chocolate Labrador. He lived to be fourteen, which was the same age I was at the time he died.'

'*Oh*...' Molly could feel her face scrunching into lines of sympathy. 'It must have been devastating to lose him. He'd been there for your whole life.'

Hugh was staring at her and Molly's heart sank. She'd crossed a line, here, hadn't she? Pushed herself into a personal space where she was definitely not welcome? Maybe this wasn't as bad as asking about his sister who'd died but it was pretty close. His dog would have been a huge part of his life. As important as another sibling, even...?

But Hugh's gaze dropped to Oreo again.

So did Molly's. She watched the gentle touch of his fingers as they traced Oreo's head and ear.

She could actually *feel* that touch herself and it was doing strange things to her body. No wonder Oreo's eyes were drifting shut in an expression of ecstasy.

'It was devastating enough to make me know I never wanted to do it again,' Hugh added quietly.

Molly swallowed. 'It's unbearably hard to lose dogs,' she agreed.

Hugh's hand lifted abruptly as though he'd just realised what he was doing. A look from Molly was enough to get Oreo to move back to her side and she clipped a lead onto the harness that was part of her service dog coat.

'But, for me,' she added, 'it would be even harder to live without them.'

The sound Hugh made was no more than a grunt. He was heading towards the doors again. 'I'll let you know if there's any unwanted mobility aids available.'

'Thank you. And thanks for your help. You don't owe me any more favours.' Molly wasn't sure if he could hear her as the doors swung shut behind him. 'You never did...'

He didn't owe her any more favours.

She'd told him she had a van and could collect any large items like an unwanted wheelchair. Maybe if it hadn't been a lightweight, easy-to-fold kind of wheelchair that still left space in the back of an SUV for a battered, old walking frame and some elbow crutches that had seen better days, Hugh wouldn't be driving out to Molly's house.

Except that it was something he wanted to do enough to overcome any doubts about whether or not it was something he *should* be doing.

It was a warm, late spring evening and, while it was too late to rope his surfboard to the roof rack and try to catch a wave, there was always a pull towards the beach and the sea for Hugh. Even filling his lungs with the smell of the ocean could be enough to tap into the freedom of being in the water—or, better yet, skimming the face of a wave that took him to a place where nothing else mattered.

Where there was nothing but the joy of utter freedom.

If Molly was on an afternoon shift she wouldn't be at home but that wasn't a problem. He knew which house was hers, having had it pointed out to him from the beach, and he would just leave the items on her doorstep. It might be better if that was the case, in fact, because one of the doubts Hugh had entertained—the *main* doubt—was that Molly might think he was coming on to her by turning up out of the blue.

Had that disturbing recognition of attraction not been completely quashed?

Was he coming on to her?

No. Hugh turned up the steep road that wound over the hill to Taylors Mistake beach. Of course he wasn't. The last thing he wanted was a relationship that would interfere with his life and he was confident that Molly probably felt the same way. Even if she was single, Molly had quite enough going on in her own life and, anyway—she wouldn't have the slightest interest in a man that she'd considered so uptight he might as well have been wearing a straitjacket.

So that made it feel safe.

And…it would be nice to have a friend.

Someone he could trust.

It was oddly disappointing when his knock on the door of the little white cottage with the red roof and the big chimney went unanswered but Hugh simply shrugged and went to unload the back of his vehicle. He could have a quick walk on the beach before he went home and that would make the journey more than worthwhile.

As he propped the elbow crutches inside the walking frame, however, he heard Molly's voice.

'*Yes…* Good girl, Oreo. Go… Go, go, *go…*'

It was a happy shout. There might have been some hand clapping going on as well and there was definitely an excited dog bark.

Hugh told himself he wasn't being nosy. It would simply be polite to let Molly know that he'd delivered the mobility aids, so he walked around the side of the house, stopping as he came to a long back garden that morphed into the marram grass covered sand dunes between the row of houses and the beach.

There was some kind of obstacle course laid out on the coarse grass of a beachside lawn.

Molly was still shouting.

'*Jump…* Good girl… And over the seesaw…*yes…*'

The jump was a tree branch of driftwood set on top of two wooden crates. The seesaw was a long plank of wood balanced on an empty forty-gallon drum that must have come from a farm. So had that tractor tyre that was suspended above the ground to make a hoop that Oreo had been jumping through as Hugh stopped to watch. Neither dog nor handler noticed him. Oreo raced up the thin plank of wood on the drum, stopped for a moment to let the wood tilt down on the other side and then she was off again. Over the jump from another direction, through a bending tunnel that was the only part of the course that didn't look homemade and then she was weaving through a set of poles in the ground.

Molly was as focussed as Oreo and clearly loving it just as much. She ran beside her dog, making a hand signal to encourage a jump, clapping to emphasise something good—even running with her head down herself as Oreo went flat to run through the tunnel.

She was wearing ancient denim shorts that looked like cut-off jeans judging by their frayed hems, and a tee shirt that was knotted on one side to make it fit close to her body. Her hair was loose—a wild mop of black curls—her face was pink from exertion and she was out of breath when she held out her arms to Oreo to jump into for a hug.

She was laughing as she put Oreo down and straightened, which was the moment she saw Hugh standing there.

And…it made Hugh suddenly feel as happy as he felt when he was riding a particularly good wave. As if he were flying.

As if there was nothing he needed to worry about in this moment.

As if he was free…

'Oh, my goodness… *Hugh*…?'

Oreo went straight towards Hugh and sat in front of him.

'Sorry to interrupt,' he said. 'I brought some old mobility gear for you, like the wheelchair you wanted. They're by your front door.'

'Oh, wow…thank you *so* much. That's fantastic.' Molly was pushing curls damp with perspiration back from her face. That wild hair was framing a face that clearly didn't have a scrap of makeup on it and…

…and…she looked absolutely gorgeous.

Stunning, even…

Oreo barked at Hugh as if she were trying to cut his train of thought and he was grateful enough to smile at the dog and reach down to pat her head.

'She wants to play,' Molly told him. 'She wants you to do her agility course with her.'

Hugh shook his head. 'I wouldn't know how.'

'She'll show you.' Molly was grinning at him. 'You'll love it, I promise. It's more fun than surfing.'

'Impossible.'

'You won't know until you try. Go on… I *dare* you…'

A tumble of thoughts raced through Hugh's mind. That Molly was encouraging him the way she had been urging Oreo on? That if he ever wanted a chance to prove he wasn't as uptight as Molly thought he was, this might be the best opportunity ever. That this was the kind of light-hearted stuff that friends could enjoy doing together and…

…and that smile was simply irresistible.

'Fine.' Hugh loosened his tie and pulled it off. He rolled up the sleeves of his shirt. 'Come on, Oreo.'

Molly called directions. 'Over the jump. Follow Oreo to the A frame… Now get ahead of her, point to the jump and then head for the seesaw…'

It was only Hugh who needed the directions. Oreo knew the course by heart and was so happy to be showing off to Hugh that she kept barking, even as she disappeared into the tunnel and then weaved at incredible speed back and forth through the poles.

Hugh was laughing himself by the time he got back to Molly, despite being completely out of breath.

'Hold out your arms,' Molly commanded. 'It's not finished until Oreo gets her cuddle.'

Without thinking, Hugh held out his arms and suddenly they were full of the warmth and hairiness of a large dog. He was getting licked on his neck and...this was another kind of happy, wasn't it? He hadn't been this close to a dog since he'd hugged Fudge before he went to school.

The day he'd come home to find he wasn't lying there at the gate with his ball safely between his paws, waiting for their game. And he never would be again...

Hugh crouched to let Oreo slip from his arms to the ground. Molly's smile was still doing something unusual to his brain. For the first time ever, he was thinking of Fudge and remembering the joy of being with him was overriding the sadness of losing him.

'Well...that *was* fun,' he admitted. 'But it doesn't beat surfing.'

'I can't believe you actually did that.' Molly was biting her lip as if she was trying not to grin too widely. 'I was so wrong about you...'

Her smile had faded and her gaze was fixed on his. He could see the way her bottom lip almost bounced free of her teeth and the appreciation in Molly's eyes made him want to turn back and do that obstacle course with Oreo all over again.

No...

What it *really* made him want to do was to kiss Molly.

For a long, long moment, Hugh couldn't breathe. It felt like he didn't need to because time had stopped. He couldn't look away from those golden-brown eyes, either. It was probably only for a heartbeat—maybe two, but it was long enough for something to force its way into his head.

A cloud that was dark enough to obliterate any sunshine.

Fear...?

He jerked his gaze away from Molly's. He pretended to look at his watch.

'Is that the time?' What a stupid thing to say. 'I have to go,' he added. 'I've got a lot of prep to start getting done tonight.'

'Oh...?'

Molly sounded slightly bewildered. When he sneaked a lightning-fast glance as he turned away, she wasn't looking at him.

'Yes. It's Sophie's surgery the day after tomorrow. We've got a full team meeting to plan the surgery in detail tomorrow and I want to be well prepared for that.'

'It must be a big deal. You're basically reattaching an amputation, aren't you?'

'Yes.' This was better. Professional conversation. And Hugh was on his way to escape.

'Do you have vascular surgeons involved? And neuro?' Molly asked.

'It's a huge team. And there's a lot of interest with it being an unusual procedure, so it's in the main theatre with the gallery.'

Hugh was feeling almost safe again as he got closer to

his car. He was also feeling a bit embarrassed. How rude did Molly think he was, running off like this?

'Why don't you come and watch as well, if you're not working?' he suggested. 'It's a long surgery but not something you get to see every day.'

Molly's intake of breath was an excited gasp. '*Could* I? It *is* a day off for me.'

'You're part of the extended team involved in Sophie's care and I know that this surgery might not be happening if it hadn't been for you. I can make sure there's a front row seat saved for you.'

There…the movement of time and tide were completely back to normal.

If Molly had been aware of any inappropriate and/or unwanted notions that had entered Hugh's head when he'd been staring at her like some lust-struck teenager, she had forgotten all about it now.

She was biting her lip again and her eyes were shining. 'I can't wait.'

CHAPTER SIX

HE'D ALMOST KISSED HER.

Hugh Ashcroft had actually been thinking about *kissing* her.

Oh, *my*…

As she slipped into the seat on one end of the front row in the gallery above Theatre One, the only thing Molly would have expected to be thinking about was how exciting it was going to be watching some extraordinarily rare orthopaedic surgery.

'Scalpel, please.'

Hearing Hugh's voice through the speakers on either side of the enclosed gallery area should have been enough to focus absolutely on what she could see on the screens beside the speakers, which gave a close up, 'surgeon's eye' view of what was happening below them. Having an audience was clearly no distraction for Mr Ashcroft but, even through the glass, perhaps he was aware that everyone was holding their breath, waiting for the first incision. He had to know they would appreciate every bit of detail he was able to share.

'So our first incision is longitudinal below the groin and this gives us access for the dissection of the femoral artery and vein.'

Yeah…the ultimately professional, *impersonal* tone of his voice should have made Molly sit forward and focus on what she had come to see. But what she was, in fact, thinking about as that first incision was made was that the gowned and gloved surgeon standing beside the small, draped shape on the operating table had been so close to kissing her the day before yesterday that she could still feel her toes curling.

'I'm clamping the femoral artery to prevent bleeding during the surgery and now we'll extend the incision.'

Molly needed to clamp the direction her thoughts were going in. She focussed on the screen as vessels and nerves were slowly and painstakingly revealed and the specialist microvascular surgeon working with Hugh took over, giving a commentary on everything she was doing, such as the continuous dissection of the sciatic nerve behind the leg muscle. These important structures would be kept separated and completely intact while the middle section of the leg was removed.

This was a surgery that would take from six to eight hours and there were long periods of intense and often silent work going on.

And Molly couldn't stop her gaze drifting from the close-up screen back to where Hugh had his head bent, looking into the actual operating field. He was completely covered with sterile fabric and a hat and mask and eyewear but, with his head bent like that, Molly could see a patch of skin at the back of his neck and she could feel a sensation deep in her belly as if something was melting.

She couldn't stop her thoughts drifting back to what could have ended up being a kiss.

Had she *wanted* Hugh to kiss her?

Judging by the sharp spear of sensation that obliterated the melting one, the answer to that question was resoundingly affirmative. The sexual attraction was real.

In retrospect, Molly was surprisingly disappointed that Hugh *hadn't* kissed her.

How ridiculous was that?

Even if she was ready to start looking for someone to fill the life partner-shaped gap in her life, Hugh Ashcroft would not be a contender.

Why not?

Molly ignored the little voice at the back of her mind and tuned back into what was happening on the screen. More incisions were being made and the surgical teams were discussing where to cut the bones of the upper and lower legs to leave sufficient margins to healthy tissue.

Minutes ticked on and turned into hours. People around Molly in the tiered seating, mostly wearing surgical scrubs themselves, came and went as they got paged or finished their breaks or needed to grab something to eat but Molly didn't move from her privileged spot in the front row. And, as fascinated as she was, her focus definitely faded at times.

Enough for that little voice to make another attempt.

Why not? You mean you don't believe that the right man might be just around the next corner in your life, like you keep telling yourself? Does Hugh not even make a shortlist?

No, Molly told herself.

Give me one good reason.

I can give you more than one. The first is that we work together and you know as well as I do that my last relationship was with Jonathon who I also worked with and that was the most spectacular disaster in my entire history of relationships that haven't worked out. I walked away from my job as well as that relationship. It felt like my life was completely broken.

Maybe that was because he didn't want Oreo as part of his life and that was just a cover for not wanting kids and then it turns out that he never wanted an exclusive relationship. You were just part of a harem...

Thanks for the reminder.

Molly shut the conversation down.

She didn't need reminding that she'd come home to her family and a place she loved in order to try and repair her life once and for all.

She didn't need reminding that her heart was too easy to capture.

Too easy to break.

Molly was actually scared of that happening again. What if it was the last straw and she could never put the pieces back together again?

That fear should be more than enough to silence any notion that she might want to be kissed by Hugh Ashcroft.

Besides, it was getting to the most fascinating part of this operation anyway.

'So...those are the wires in place to mark where the incisions will be made. They'll allow me to pass a suture around the exact level I want to cut the bone and we'll clamp that to the Gigli saw.' Hugh turned to his scrub nurse. 'I'll have a tonsil clamp, thanks, and then I'll be ready for the braided suture.'

Molly found she was holding her breath as she watched the absolute focus Hugh had on his task—so much so, she could sense it in every muscle of his body. She could watch his hands close up on the screen and was riveted by the precision and care he was taking to do everything perfectly and make clean cuts through both the femur and the tibia, protecting the surrounding tissue as much as possible.

And then came the most astonishing moment of this surgery as the middle section of the small leg, which contained the tumour, was lifted clear and then sent to the laboratory for examination. In the space on the table, the arteries, veins and nerves that had been so painstakingly detached from the section that contained the tumour still joined the top of the leg to the ankle and foot.

'Now comes the part that will determine the success of this surgery.' Hugh's serious tone of voice came quietly through the speakers. 'We'll rotate the foot and ankle one hundred and eighty degrees in the axial plane and then join the femur and tibia with a dynamic compression plate. I'll hand over to my microsurgery colleagues at that point to re-join the blood vessels and nerves.'

The microsurgery was fascinating to watch and Molly had no intention of leaving until everything was finished, but she found herself sneaking glances to where Hugh was assisting rather than leading this part of the surgery instead of watching only the screen where so many tiny stitches were being placed to join structures that were so small it was hard to see exactly what was happening.

It was no surprise that her attention span was getting harder to maintain. That her thoughts, along with her gaze, drifted back to Hugh yet again.

Reason number two for Hugh to not make any shortlist for a potential life partner popped into her head with startling clarity. It wasn't simply that they were colleagues that made him similar to her last spectacular error of judgement.

He didn't like dogs any more than Jonathon did.

Oh, yeah? You didn't think so when he and Oreo were having the time of their lives running around the agility course.

Molly couldn't argue with herself over that point.

Both dog and man had clearly been enjoying themselves and that had shown her another glimpse of a very different Hugh Ashcroft. Like seeing him at one with the ocean when he was surfing had done.

She was beginning to think that she might be seeing the *real* Hugh through cracks in the persona that the majority of people in his life were permitted to see.

And what about Fudge? A dog he'd lost in a vulnerable part of his adolescence and it had hit him hard enough he was never going to go there again. He didn't even want to connect with someone *else's* dog. Had Oreo sensed that? Was that why she'd been so polite—gentle, even—in her approach to Hugh? Sitting there like a canine rock when he probably didn't notice the way he was stroking her ears as he talked about Fudge?

Well…both man and dog had let go of the barriers stopping them connecting when they'd done the agility course together, hadn't they?

Had that been the reason Hugh had done something as unexpected as almost kissing her?

Oh…

There it was again…

That delicious flicker of attraction. A flame that was resisting any attempts to douse it. The sensible part of her head hadn't stopped trying, however.

I don't even know if he's single, it announced. He could be married for all I know—not everybody wears a ring. Maybe he's even got a few kids.

But the part of herself she was arguing with didn't even bother to respond. They both knew how unlikely that was. With the kind of hours Hugh worked and his dedication, it seemed far more likely that he was married only to his job. Watching him at work like this had been impressive and Molly could be absolutely certain that he hadn't been distracted for a moment by her presence in the gallery or any memory of what had—almost—happened between them.

Her interest in this surgery hadn't been exaggerated, had it?

Hugh hadn't expected Molly to stay and watch the entire operation but he'd been aware of her presence from the moment he'd entered this theatre and had seen her sitting on the end of the front row.

The awareness was far enough in the background of his consciousness to have no bearing on his focus. It was just there, like a faint hum that added something extra to his normal determination to do the best possible job that could be done. This was someone who had cared enough about this patient to have gone to the trouble of finding that picture of the girl dancing with her rotationplasty prosthesis. To happily give the time and effort that bringing her dog in to dance for Sophie had required.

This mattered to Molly.

She was still there when Hugh was checking the perfusion of the reattached foot, feeling for a palpable pulse and noting the acceptable skin colour, but she had gone when Hugh glanced up to the gallery after the final closure of the wound.

He stayed to supervise the final dressing where they would be using soft, orthopaedic wool as a thick bandage under the plaster cast to prevent too much pressure on repaired vessels and nerves as they healed. He was still there in the recovery room a while later as Sophie regained consciousness enough for him to be able to check for the first indication that nerve function was still intact. It was a very satisfying moment when the drowsy, heavily medicated little girl managed a tiny movement in her ankle joint when asked.

Hugh went to meet her anxious parents, able to tell them that the surgery had gone as well as they could have hoped for.

'She'll be taken up to the intensive care unit soon and will stay there for twenty-four to forty-eight hours.'

'Can we go and see her?'

'Of course. I'll get a nurse to take you in. The ICU consultant who'll be in charge of her care while she's in the unit is in with her now.'

'Thank you *so* much, Mr Ashcroft. You must be exhausted after being in Theatre for so long today.'

'It's what I do,' Hugh said simply. 'And when it goes this well, it's the best job in the world.'

He had to admit he *was* exhausted after so many intense hours of concentration—on his feet, and under the glare of artificial light—and Hugh knew he should really take a break after he'd done a brief ward round of his inpatients. He would have his phone by his side at all times and he'd come back in an hour or two to check on Sophie again, but she was stable enough to make any complications unlikely and there was a huge team of specialists in intensive care and paediatric oncology who had already taken over the primary care for this little girl in the post-operative phase of her treatment.

Going home to his inner-city apartment for a break wasn't attractive. Hugh needed some fresh air and whatever real daylight was left for the day. He could have headed into the centre of the city to the huge park and had a walk but, as he drove out of the hospital car park, he found himself following the line of hills on the southern city border. Heading for the place that would restore his energy levels and alertness faster than anywhere else.

He could have turned to his left a short time later to get to the beach that was closest to work but it seemed a no-brainer to turn right. To get to a beach that was far less likely to be crowded by other people shedding any stress from their working day. A beach that was his favourite but that he hadn't been back to since that surprise meeting with Molly after he'd gone surfing. And, after his visit to her little white cottage, he hadn't expected to ever come here again. Because he was sensible enough to heed an alarm when it sounded. Especially when he knew exactly *why* it was sounding.

Not that Hugh had consciously given it any thought since then, but he was well aware that if he hadn't grappled control back from the brink of losing it, he would have ended up kissing Molly Holmes completely senseless.

Because a tiny part of him suspected that she might have wanted him to?

Not that it mattered right now. Because control had been regained and he was far too drained after a marathon surgery to be remotely interested in thinking about something that would be disturbing.

Surfing would have been the best option but that wasn't possible when Hugh needed to be within earshot of his phone in case he had a call regarding Sophie's condition, but just a barefoot walk on the sand and some deep breaths of sea air should do the trick. It wouldn't take long.

Had Molly felt the same way after her long day in the gallery?

Was that why he could see the black and white shape of her dog running in the shallows as he stepped onto the beach?

But where was Molly?

Oreo was barking now and, instead of scanning the beach to look for a woman holding a frisbee, Hugh looked in the opposite direction. Thanks to following Oreo's line of sight, he could see past the break of the first wave and... good grief...was that Molly swimming? Without a wetsuit? At this time of the year the water would still be icy.

She was on her way back to shore but it wasn't until she reached the shallows and a relieved Oreo that Hugh realised how much less than a figure covering wetsuit Molly was wearing. She was in a rather scant bikini that showed off every curve of her body.

Every rather delicious curve...

She came out of the water at a run, heading straight for a crumpled towel on the sand and, even at this distance, Hugh could see how cold she looked.

Oreo was shaking water out of her coat as Molly snatched up the towel.

'Hey…' Hugh was close enough to call a greeting. 'That was brave. You must be absolutely freezing.'

'Hugh…' Molly stopped rubbing at her hair and held the towel in front of her. There were goosebumps on the skin of her arms and he saw her suppress a shiver. 'What on earth are you doing here?'

'I needed a break and some fresh air.'

'I'll bet… I was drained enough from just watching what you've been doing all day.' Molly was clutching the towel in front of her body now.

Hiding…?

But she was grinning. 'If you really want to wake yourself up, go and have a dip in those waves. It's gorgeous.'

'I haven't got anything to swim in.'

Her eyes widened in mock shock. 'Are you telling me you don't wear any undies, Mr Ashcroft?'

Nobody ever talked to him like this. Probably because he looked—and behaved—like someone who couldn't take a joke or a bit of teasing? Hugh's lips twitched. Maybe being unexpectedly teased like this was almost as good as fresh air and sunlight for getting rid of accumulated tension. But old habits died hard, as they said.

'I'm not about to put my underwear on public display,' he said.

Uh-oh…that was the kind of thing someone who was uptight enough to be repressed and prudish might say, wasn't it?

'I haven't got a towel,' he added, realising that sounded just as lame the moment he uttered the words.

But Molly was still grinning. 'I'll share mine,' she offered. 'Go on…you know you want to.'

And, astonishingly, Hugh knew she was right.

He *did* want to. He wanted to shake off the tension and stress of an extraordinarily intense day by doing something a bit crazy.

But he still shook his head. He could never be tempted enough to turn his back on the most important thing in his life. 'I can't leave my phone. I'm on call in case there are any complications with Sophie.'

'Are you expecting any?'

'No. She was looking great when I left Recovery. She could even move her ankle for me.'

'No *way*…' Molly's jaw dropped. 'That's amazing. I'm so happy to hear she's doing well. And hey… I can guard your phone and answer it if necessary. I can guarantee you won't need more than about sixty seconds in that surf to get the full recuperative benefits.'

The Hugh who'd never met Molly Holmes and her dogs would never have been so impulsive. He would have simply found another excuse not to do something as unconventional and potentially humiliating as running into the ocean in his underwear but…

…it appeared that Hugh wasn't quite the same man as he'd been a couple of months ago.

Because he handed his phone to Molly and stripped off his clothes. He didn't unbutton more than the second button of his shirt—he just yanked it over his head. Even Oreo seemed to be staring at him in disbelief but then she barked her approval and ran with him as he splashed through the shallow water until he could dive under a wave. And Molly was right, sixty seconds would have been more than enough to wash off every ounce of fatigue and pang of discomfort in overused muscles, but he stayed in twice as long, just to make sure.

If he'd stayed in any longer, he might have acclimatised to the chill water and been able to enjoy a swim, but Hugh was too conscious of needing to be near his phone so he came out of the water and got hit by the wind chill, even though it was only a mild sea breeze.

He reached for the towel Molly held out to him.

'No calls,' she told him. 'I was right, wasn't I? It was worth having a dip.'

'So worth it.' Hugh nodded.

'Better than surfing?' she suggested.

He shook his head. 'No…and I'll let you know later if it was really worth the hypothermia.'

Molly's towel was already damp so wasn't very effective in drying his skin, so Hugh was shivering uncontrollably before he'd rubbed more than half his body with the towel and Molly, who now had an oversized jumper on over her bikini, was biting her lip and looking—a little repentant?

Cute…

'You'd better come and stand under a hot shower for a minute,' she told him. 'Otherwise you'll never get properly warm again. Come on…' She didn't give him the chance to respond through his chattering teeth. Worse, she swooped on his pile of clothing and grabbed his shirt and trousers and then took off towards the sand dunes and the row of houses.

And she was still in possession of his phone!

Oreo looked torn for the space of two seconds and then took off after Molly.

There was nothing Hugh could do, other than pick up his shoes that had his socks stuffed inside them and go after them. By the time he went inside the cottage, Molly already had the shower running.

'Help yourself to shampoo or anything,' she invited. 'I'll get you a clean towel.'

The shower was over an old, clawfoot bath with just a curtain to stop the water splashing into the room. Hugh didn't peel off his sodden boxer shorts until he was safely behind the curtain, under the rain of water that felt hot enough to scald his chilled skin. He stayed under it for about as long as he'd been in the ocean and then reached to turn off the tap.

'Don't turn it off...' Molly was back in the bathroom. 'I need to jump in myself and the plumbing can be a bit temperamental. I'll put your towel by the basin, okay?'

'Thanks.' Hugh poked his head around the edge of the curtain to see Molly about to drop the towel near where she'd left his phone beside a glass that held a toothbrush and tube of toothpaste.

Her toothbrush. Hugh could suddenly imagine Molly wearing nothing but a towel herself, standing in front of that mirror to clean her teeth last thing at night. And then two things hit him like a ton of bricks.

Molly was still wearing nothing but those two rather small scraps of fabric under that jumper.

And *he* was no more than a few inches away from her and was wearing absolutely nothing at all...

No...make that three things. Because now Hugh was thinking of the gorgeous curves of her body and the perfection of her smooth, olive skin being marred by goosebumps. In retrospect, he knew he'd been wondering what it would feel like to run his fingers, oh, so lightly over those goosebumps.

Would they reappear if he helped her peel that woollen jumper off?

Oh...*help*...

In the same instant a wave of that attraction that had almost made him kiss her—something he'd thought had been dealt with and banished—washed over him with even more of a shock than plunging into the icy sea so recently, Hugh noticed that Molly was watching *him*.

In the mirror.

It still felt like direct eye contact when he met her gaze, though.

Until she turned to face him and the touch of their gazes became suddenly searing. She still had the towel in her hand and, instead of dropping it, she held it out so that he could take it before he stepped out from behind the curtain. He knotted it loosely around his waist the moment his feet hit the floor.

Because he needed to hide the reaction his body was having to that wash of attraction that had somehow morphed into a level of desire like nothing Hugh had ever experienced in his life.

Molly couldn't move.

She couldn't breathe.

The universe seemed to be holding its breath as well as she simply stood there, holding that gaze for moment after moment after moment...

Until Hugh took one step closer, slid his fingers into her salt-tangled curls to hold her head and leaned down to cover her lips with his own.

Of course he knew it was what she wanted. A whole

silent conversation had just been held in that prolonged eye contact. Questions asked...

Permission given...

No...maybe Molly had actually begged a little for this to happen...

The shower was still running behind him, which made it sound as if they were standing in a heavy rain shower, and the small room was filled with the warmth and steam of it. It was filled even more with the astonishing power of what was overwhelming every one of Molly's senses.

Hugh...

The taste of him.

The pressure of his lips.

The sliding dance of his tongue as he deepened a kiss that had already woken up every cell in Molly's body.

She felt his hands beneath the hem of her jumper now, sliding up her skin towards her breasts. Her hands followed his so that she could pull this unwanted piece of clothing off. To clear away a bulky obstacle, hopefully before he changed his mind and vanished again.

Hugh's lips and tongue were on the skin of her neck and shoulder moments later.

'You taste like the sea...'

Molly shivered. Partly because of the shaft of desire taking over her body but also because she was still wearing a damp bikini and her skin was sticky with sea salt. Chilled enough for it to be making Hugh's lips and tongue feel like flames licking her skin.

'You're cold...' Hugh's towel was falling to the floor as he took her hand. 'Come...'

He helped her step over the edge of the bath into the

rain of the hot water. He helped her peel off her bikini top and bottom. And then he kissed her again.

A fierce kiss...

A need like none she had ever experienced took over Molly's body—and mind. There was danger here but there was no turning back. The sound Hugh made as she pressed herself even closer to his body could have been one of frustration—as if he was about to make this stop because he, too, had recognised it wasn't safe?

'No...'

It wasn't really a word. More like a sound of desperate need as Molly ran her hands down Hugh's back until she found the iron-hard muscle of his buttocks and shaped them with her hands. Pulled them closer.

The sound Hugh made then was more like a sigh of defeat. Or submission?

His hands were gripping Molly's bottom now. Lifting her so that she could wrap her legs around him. Holding her so they could find their balance and rhythm and give in to the waves of desire that were building to a climax like no other.

It was over too soon.

But not quite soon enough because the hot water that Molly's cottage had available was running out and the shower was already cooling down fast.

At least that interrupted what could have been an awkward moment as Molly's feet touched the enamelled surface of the bath. Even eye contact was avoided for a few seconds as she climbed out and Hugh turned the tap off, she handed him his towel and reached for another one on a towel rail.

When they did finally make eye contact again, Molly

raised her eyebrows. She wanted to lighten what was threatening to become an atmosphere they might both find too much, too soon.

'Better than surfing?' The words came out as a husky kind of whisper.

Hugh had to clear his throat before he could speak.

'Maybe...' he said.

His smile and tone suggested that it was possible he might need to experience it again to be sure.

And Molly smiled back. She wasn't about to object.

Maybe it could have happened then. In a comfortable bed. If the sound from Hugh's phone hadn't changed everything.

'It can't be anything urgent.' He picked up his phone. 'It's only a text message.' He looked up from the screen a moment later. 'Sophie's properly awake,' he told Molly. 'She's just moved the toes on her reattached foot.'

The very personal ground they had been on was being blurred into something professional and it felt...uncomfortable? Molly was quite certain that the last thing Hugh would want to talk about now was sex.

'I'll let you get dressed,' she said quietly. 'You'll want to go in and see her.'

She let her gaze graze his as she slipped out of the bathroom to find her own clothes. Less than a split second of contact but it was enough to let her know that Hugh appreciated that she understood.

His work always came first.

CHAPTER SEVEN

MAYBE SHE'D IMAGINED that unbelievable encounter in her bathroom.

She'd certainly *re*imagined it, more than once, during the somewhat sleepless night she'd just had.

But the version of Hugh Ashcroft that Molly encountered when she took Oreo into the children's hospital the next afternoon bore no resemblance at all to the man with whom she'd had the sexiest, most passionate encounter of her life less than twenty-four hours earlier.

He was back to being the version of the distant and disapproving surgeon she'd first encountered in that radiology procedure room.

Did he regret what had happened between them?

He certainly hadn't appeared to feel like that when he'd paused long enough to place a lingering kiss on her lips before he'd left the cottage.

Was he concerned that the information might be welcomed into the gossip mill with even more fascination than what Molly already knew about his private life?

No…surely Hugh knew that any trust in her was not misplaced?

Molly was the one who should be concerned. She'd allowed this gorgeous but complicated man to capture her heart and now she'd allowed him close enough to capture her body. They had to be the most significant building blocks to falling head over heels in love with someone and Molly wasn't at all sure she was at a point where she could halt that process if—or *when*—it became a matter of self-protection.

If she had her heart broken again this soon, she might never find the courage to let someone else this far into her life. Ever.

Perhaps that look was simply because Hugh felt it was a step too far, taking Oreo into the paediatric intensive care unit where Sophie Jacobs was in the early stages of her post-operative recovery? Oreo was on her very best behaviour, thank goodness, and she had waited for a signal that it was a time no other patients in the unit or their families might be disturbed. They had probably not even noticed her arrival because the rooms that opened onto the central space with the nurses' station and banks of monitoring equipment were very private, especially when the curtains were drawn across the internal windows. The unit staff had also been consulted about this visit but...

...maybe Hugh was being reminded of the first time he'd seen a dogtor near one of his patients and maybe he was a bit shocked by how much had changed between himself and Molly since then...

Sophie was in a nest of soft pillows, her leg well supported and stable. Molly could just see an oxygen saturation probe clipped to the big toe of her reattached foot. She had electrodes on to monitor her heart and an automatic cuff to take her blood pressure. There were IV lines to deliver medications including the pain relief she was having and other tubes snaked from beneath a light, brightly coloured bed cover. With no hat on to cover her bald scalp, Sophie looked so incredibly vulnerable, it would be no surprise that some people might think it was totally inappropriate to have an animal in here who could potentially disrupt such a delicately balanced, technical set up.

But Sophie's mother was crying softly when she saw Molly and Oreo. 'I'm so glad you could come,' she said. 'Soph made me promise that she'd be able to see Oreo as soon as she woke up. I wasn't sure you'd be allowed in here but I said "yes" because that was what she wanted more than anything…'

'We can only stay for a few minutes.' Molly glanced over her shoulder, knowing that they were being carefully watched by staff members, including Hugh, who was talking to one of the intensive care consultants. 'This is the first time pet therapy has happened in the ICU here.'

She held Oreo's leash close to the clip on her harness and made sure the dog didn't get near any tubes or lines. She put a towel on the edge of Sophie's bed and tapped it to tell Oreo where to put her chin.

'Sophie?' Joanne was on the other side of the bed, stroking Sophie's head. 'Are you awake, darling? Guess who's come to see you…'

Eyelashes fluttered but Sophie was reaching out with her hand before she opened her eyes.

'Aww…' Her lips were curving into a smile. 'It's Oreo…'

The small hand had found Oreo's nose and fingers traced their way up to find her head and ears. Her dog might have been poked in the eyes on the way because Molly could see her blinking, but Oreo didn't move a muscle. She barely waved her tail and she didn't take her gaze off Sophie's face.

Molly had to fight back tears. She was *so* proud of Oreo.

She could see the emotion on Joanne's face as her daughter got the gift she'd wanted the most in this difficult time. Even Sophie's nurse, who was taking photos of this visit, was using a tissue to blot her eyes.

Molly didn't know whether Hugh had witnessed the joy. By the time Molly led Oreo quietly out of the unit a few minutes later, he could have been long gone. She didn't head straight back to her van in the car park, however. Because it had been such a short visit to the ICU, Molly thought she'd leave via her ward to see if there was another child who might like a visit from Oreo. And, when the doors of the lift slid open on the ward floor, she saw Hugh walking away from his office in the company of a very distressed looking woman.

Oreo picked up on the emotional intensity the moment she stepped out of the lift. She sat down, refusing to move any further towards the ward, and waited for Hugh to get closer.

He'd never been so relieved to be offered such an irresistible distraction.

Not only was his own mind diverted by a flash of how it had felt, albeit briefly, to be in a parallel universe with Molly Holmes yesterday evening, the distraught woman with him—Annabelle Finch—seemed to be having a reprieve from any aftermath of the awful conversation he'd just had with her.

She was veering towards Oreo.

'Oh…aren't you gorgeous?' Annabelle still had tears on her cheeks as she looked at Molly. 'Am I allowed to pat him?'

'Of course.' Molly smiled.

'She's a girl.' It was Hugh who made the correction. 'This is Oreo, Annabelle. She belongs to Molly, here, and she's trained to visit children as an assistance dog.'

He was also looking directly at Molly and had to ignore an odd squeeze in his chest as she shifted her gaze to catch his. This was definitely not the time to allow any pull to-wards what had happened between himself and Molly.

'This is Annabelle,' he said. 'She's Sam's mum. Sam is one of my patients.'

Annabelle was on her knees now, her cheek on Oreo's neck as she hugged the dog. 'Sam would love you,' she said. 'He's been begging me for a puppy for months now and…and I was planning to get one after the end of his chemo—in time for Christmas…' She turned to bury her face in Oreo's thick coat just in time to stifle a sob.

Hugh could feel his whole body tensing. Trying not to be pulled into this mother's pain. It was quite notice-ably a much harder ask than normal. Because Molly was standing so close and his body was desperate to remind him of how it felt to be even closer to her?

He cleared his throat. 'Maybe Molly's got time to take Oreo in to visit Sam for a few minutes?'

'I have.' Molly nodded. 'That's why I came down. We could only be in the ICU for a very short time so we'd both appreciate a chance to make another visit.'

Annabelle lifted her face. 'Really? You could do that?'

'Why don't you go and see how Sam feels about it?' Hugh suggested. 'Come and tell us if he's awake again and his pain levels are under better control. Otherwise, it might be a bit much for him. Check with his nurse, too?'

Annabelle nodded, but an almost smile was hovering on her lips. 'Where will I find you?'

Hugh thought fast. 'I'm sure Oreo could use a breath of fresh air. We'll just be out in the garden here.'

We...?

Did Hugh want to be alone with Molly when he'd have no chance of *not* thinking—and probably saying something—about last night?

No.

Yes...

He held the door open for Molly. 'I thought you might need a bit of background,' he said quietly.

Oreo looked delighted to be back in the garden where she'd danced with Molly and, with no one else there, she could be let off the lead for a few minutes.

Molly sat on one of the benches and Hugh sat down beside her. Close enough for his thigh to be touching hers and it was inevitable that memories of last night came flooding back in a kaleidoscope of sensations that were enough to make Hugh catch his breath.

It wasn't just the sex that had been a revelation, was it? He'd never felt like this *afterwards*, either. As if his body were watching a metaphorical clock and counting down every second until he could do it again.

Molly seemed to be avoiding catching his gaze. She'd closed her eyes, in fact, and she was taking in a slow, deep breath—as if *she* were aware of that clock as well? The thought that she might be feeling the same way he was about repeating the experience was enough for Hugh to know this definitely wasn't the time to say anything. Their body language might already be enough to catch the attention of someone walking past the windows and...

Hugh had no intention of turning his back on what had been disturbing enough to welcome the distraction that Molly and Oreo's arrival had provided.

'So...' His deep breath mirrored Molly's. 'Sam is four years old. I saw him about eighteen months ago when he fell off his scooter and broke his arm. His humerus. Like Sophie, the X-ray that was taken was the first indication that he had something serious going on.'

Molly's face was very still. Her eyes wide. She was absolutely focussed on what Hugh was saying. 'An osteosarcoma?' she breathed.

'No. In Sam's case it was a Ewing sarcoma. Rare. And incredibly aggressive. He had equally aggressive chemotherapy and radiotherapy and I did a limb-saving surgery to remove the diseased humerus and replace it with a bone graft that we took from his fibula.'

Molly didn't say anything when he paused for a breath this time, but Hugh could feel she was holding her own breath.

'He seemed to be doing well for some time. We thought we'd caught it. Annabelle told me she felt like she could finally breathe again. She's in her early forties. She chose to become a single mother and is totally devoted to Sam.' Hugh swallowed carefully. 'The first metastases showed up a few months ago and further chemo has been ineffective. The tumours are right through his body—in his lungs, bones, spine, brain...'

Hugh didn't bother continuing the list. 'Surgery's not an option unless it's palliative...which is why he's been transferred to my team. He broke his femur yesterday due to the bone damage from a fast-growing tumour. His leg is in a cast but it needs surgery to stabilise it effectively so I was consulted about whether removing the lesion and plating the fracture could significantly improve his level of comfort. I think it probably could but it's a much higher risk operation in his condition so it's got to be Annabelle's choice whether or not the risk is worth it. We're keeping a theatre slot free for later today, just in case.'

Hugh had been watching Oreo exploring the garden as he spoke quietly. Perhaps instinct had been protecting him from making direct eye contact with Molly, because now, when he turned his head, he could see a level of emotion in her face and eyes that he would never let himself feel for a patient.

Yes, this was an incredibly sad story and it was reaching an even sadder ending but that only made it vital for Hugh not to be sucked into an emotional vortex. He had to stand back far enough to offer support and make the best decisions for both Sam and his mum, Annabelle.

'So...' The word was crisp, this time. Decisive. 'If you—and Oreo—can handle it, it might be...you know...'

He didn't finish his sentence. It was too heartbreaking to think about a small child finding even a moment of joy in what could be his last days alive. Or a memory being made that his mother might treasure for the rest of her life. He didn't need to finish it...

'I know,' Molly whispered. She was blinking hard and then she lifted her chin. 'And it's precisely why I got into this in the first place. Oreo's at her best with children like Sam. My job is just to put her in the right place at the right time.'

Maybe Oreo heard her name. Or maybe she'd picked up on Hugh's tone of voice. She'd given up exploring and come to lie quietly at their feet. When the doors to the garden opened and Annabelle came out to find them, Oreo wasn't looking at the newcomer. She was gazing up at Molly, waiting for her cue.

And Molly looked down at her dog. It was a moment of silent communication. A warning perhaps that they were about to do something difficult but it would be okay because they would be doing it together.

It was a message carried on an undercurrent that felt like…

…like love. A love so strong it was palpable.

It was only between Molly and Oreo but, for a heartbeat, before he could definitively shut it down, Hugh felt as if he was included in it.

Or perhaps he'd just *wanted* to be…

Oh…*man*…

Emotional moments were part and parcel of a job working with sick kids and their families. Being with a mother who was facing the final days of her precious child's life took it to a whole new level. Adding all the feels that bringing a dog into the picture could provide made it…

…poignant enough to be a pain like no other.

How much easier would it be to be able to put up a wall to protect yourself from that kind of pain—the way Hugh Ashcroft seemed to be able to do with ease? Molly hadn't heard any wobble of emotion in his voice when he'd been filling her in on Sam's case out in the garden earlier. He'd avoided looking at her as he'd given her the clinical facts. He was concerned with weighing up the benefits versus risks of a surgical procedure and making sure the mother was able to make an informed consent. Or not.

And yes…knowing that he'd lost his sister to a childhood cancer gave her an insight into why he was like he was but…but it still didn't make sense. Not when she knew that beneath the cool, professional persona that Hugh put on in public there was a man who was capable of feeling things.

Passionately feeling things…

Things you might expect like the satisfaction of saving a young life or ensuring a better future for a child.

But unexpected things, too—like the power of the ocean.

Like the sensual pleasure of the intimate touch of another human.

It had been surprisingly hurtful to find herself shut out again, so when Molly saw Hugh also heading towards the lifts from the direction of his office, she increased her pace.

'Hugh? Have you got a minute?'

He looked up from the screen of his phone and Molly's heart sank. She could swear he was dismayed to see her and Oreo.

'Is it important?'

'I think so.' Molly tried to keep her tone calm. 'I've just come from being with Sam and his mum.'

Hugh glanced at his watch. 'Really? You've been in there for more than an *hour*?'

'Sam was so happy to have Oreo there. We let her lie on the bed beside him and he went to sleep with his arm around her. We didn't want him to wake up and find she'd disappeared.'

Because Annabelle had known he would start crying instantly. From the pain he was in and because his new friend was no longer beside him.

'We got some lovely photos.' Molly pulled her phone out. 'Would you like to see them?'

'Not right now.' Hugh was turning towards the lift. 'I've got a lot to get on with.'

'You'll probably have even more soon. Annabelle's decided that she wants Sam to have the surgery on his leg. If he gets enough analgesia to cope with the pain, he's completely knocked out.'

'Thanks for the heads-up.' Hugh was frowning now. Thinking about what might be a difficult surgery? 'Is she certain about that?'

Molly nodded. 'She said that if it could keep Sam comfortable to enjoy his favourite food or a bedtime story or even one more visit and a cuddle with Oreo, then it would be worth it.' Molly was staring at Hugh's profile. 'I've promised I'll bring her to see him every day I can, depending on my shifts. Either here, or when they get home again.'

'*If* they get home.' Hugh's words were a mutter that nobody nearby would have overheard. They would have heard the disapproving tone in his next words though. 'I don't think that's a good idea.'

Molly blinked. He didn't want to see the photos and that was fine. She understood that images of a frail child with no hair, IV lines in his arms and oxygen tubing taped to his face could be confronting for Hugh when they had nothing to do with anything medical. But to deny that child the moments of joy—of forgetting that life could be unbearably hard—that was also so apparent in those photos was…well…it was unacceptable.

'Why not?' Molly demanded.

It wasn't surprising that the challenging note in her

voice was enough for Hugh's registrar, who was stepping into the lift, to turn and stare at them. Or that Molly could see a flash of…what was it? Annoyance? Anger, even?… on Hugh's face.

'Not here,' he said coldly. 'Come with me.' He turned away from where Matthew was holding the lift door open. 'Go ahead without me,' he told him. 'I'll be there in a few minutes.

He strode back to his office, held the door for Molly and Oreo to enter and then closed it behind them, with a decisive click.

'Sam may not survive this surgery,' he said, without preamble. 'If he does, it might make him more comfortable but it will not prolong his life. He's on palliative care and Annabelle knows that the probability is very high that he won't make it home again.'

'I'm aware of that,' Molly said.

'Are you also aware that you're at risk of getting too involved in this case? On a personal level?'

'I know what I'm doing,' Molly said. 'It's not the first time I've worked with a terminally ill child, Hugh.'

He was staring at her as if she'd just stepped off a spacecraft from another planet.

'Why?' He sounded bemused. 'I don't understand how—or *why*—you would choose to get so involved in a case like this?'

'And I don't understand how *you* can avoid it,' Molly said quietly.

Maybe that was it in a nutshell. Why they could never be together, no matter how tightly Molly's feelings for Hugh had entwined themselves around her heart.

'I *learned* how. So that I could be capable of doing my

job properly, without having decisions affected by un-helpful emotional involvement with my patients *or* their families.'

Hugh met her gaze and the shutters were firmly down. It felt like Molly was being given a reprimand. That she should also do what it took to acquire this skill?

'It's better to keep an appropriate, professional dis-tance,' Hugh added as if she had somehow agreed with his viewpoint.

She stared back. It wasn't going to happen. She wasn't even going to try and make it happen.

'Distance from what? Or whom?' she asked, enunci-ating her words clearly. 'Just from the patients and their families? From your colleagues?'

Like her...?

'From *life*...?' Molly forgot that she was speaking to a senior colleague, here. Or that they were in the place they needed to be able to work together in amicably, never mind what had happened between them away from the hospital. Perhaps it was the hurt caused by realising that their time together out of hours was not significant that was making her angry. That he could have sex with her and then push her away to protect that precious distance...

Hugh opened his mouth and then closed it again, clearly unable to find the words he wanted. Oreo was pressed against Molly's leg and she could feel the shiver that ran through her dog's body. She put her hand gently on Oreo's head to let her know she wasn't the one who was doing anything wrong.

'Who's it better *for*, Hugh?' Molly wasn't done yet. 'It's never going to be better for the other person, or people, in the equation. So let me answer that, if you haven't already figured it out for yourself.' She narrowed her eyes. 'It's better for *you*. And only you. Me? I'll continue to let people know how much I care about them because...in the end, that's better for *me*.'

Molly didn't give Hugh a chance to respond. She turned and walked out of his office, Oreo glued to her side.

She knew she'd crossed a rather significant boundary line but she hadn't said anything that she didn't believe in. Being distant was never going to be better for someone like Sophie Jacobs and her family. Or for Sam and his mother, who was going through unimaginable pain right now.

And yeah...keeping that kind of distance was never going to be better for herself, either. Or Oreo. Even as they reached the staircase, Oreo was looking back towards the office they'd just stormed out of. Hoping to see the man she, for some inexplicable reason, had decided she was devoted to.

Okay...maybe it wasn't inexplicable. Because Molly's heart had been equally captured, hadn't it?

And that was when Molly changed her mind. Hugh keeping this distance he'd learned to do so well *might* actually be better in this case.

For both of them.

CHAPTER EIGHT

'SO WHAT ACTUALLY HAPPENED, Tane?'

The lanky thirteen-year-old that Hugh had been called into the emergency department to see made a face that hinted at how enormous this catastrophe could be for him.

'It was the final moments of the game, bro. I had the ball and it was the only chance for us to break the tie before the whistle went. And I did the highest jump shot ever…got it through the net…crowd goes wild…but then I landed…'

'Did you hear anything go pop or feel it snapping as you landed?'

'Felt like someone shot me in the back of my foot, you know?' He had his hand shielding his eyes now. 'They had to carry me off the court.'

Tane was still wearing the boxer shorts and singlet with his number and the name of his team.

'Can you turn over so you're on your stomach?' Hugh asked. 'Hang your feet over the end of the bed…that's it. And now relax your feet and calf muscles as much as you can.' He took hold of the calf muscle above the ankle on Tane's uninjured leg, squeezed it firmly and watched the foot move downwards. The same stimulus on the other leg provoked no movement whatsoever in the foot.

'You've definitely ruptured your Achilles tendon,' Hugh told him.

'Oh, *man*... How long am I going to be out for?'

'Depends on the severity, which we'll find out when I send you for an ultrasound and an MRI scan. If it's a minor or partial tear, you'll be in a cast or walking boot for six to eight weeks. If it's severe or a complete rupture, it'll need surgery and it will take a lot longer to heal.'

'But there's a sponsors' tournament that's part of the national team's selection series next month...'

Tane was on the verge of tears so Hugh didn't tell him he thought this injury was quite likely to be on the severe end of the spectrum. Time enough to do that when the results of the scans came through. Right now, it was time for Hugh to be somewhere else. Before the tears started.

'I'll be back to see you as soon as you've had the scans done,' he said, turning away from his patient. 'We'll talk about the next steps then.'

Sometimes, it was kinder to give people the chance to prepare themselves for bad news, but if Tane needed surgery to reattach the tendon to his heel or possibly replace part of it with a graft and it was going to take six months or more to heal, then Hugh would tell him. If the lad got tearful or angry he wouldn't let it affect him on a personal level, or change whatever management he advised.

That was what keeping an emotional distance enabled him to do. And yes, it was better for Tane as well as for himself. How would it help anyone if he sat here, holding this boy's hand and sympathising with what a disaster this was for his hopes of making the national team? Or worse, letting himself be persuaded that it might be okay to try a conservative approach with a few weeks' rest in a cast first and then finding it could be harder to achieve the best result from a surgical repair.

Molly was wrong.

His complete opposite, in fact.

Hugh was at a loss to understand why he'd been attracted to her in the first place, but at least he could be confident it wasn't going to get any more complicated. From now on, he was going to keep an emotional distance from Molly Holmes as well as his patients.

Preferably, a physical distance as well.

He hadn't even gone into the induction room the other day, when he'd learned that Molly had stayed on so that Oreo could be with Sam as he was taken to Theatre and given his anaesthetic. He hadn't seen her in the ward since that surgery despite knowing that Sam had not been discharged and it was unlikely to happen as they kept the little boy comfortable in a private room away from the main bustle of the ward.

If Molly was keeping her promise and taking Oreo in to see him every day possible, perhaps she was avoiding him as well now that it was obvious they had so little in common?

Hugh should be happy that it was going to make it easy to forget the unfortunate lapses of his normal self-control that had led to doing things as outrageous as running around an agility course with a dog.

And having *sex* in a shower?

The fact that he wasn't happy and that it was proving surprisingly difficult to forget anything about Molly was enough to give Hugh a background hum of something unpleasantly reminiscent of anger. And that only made him even *less* happy.

* * *

Mr Hugh Ashcroft wasn't looking aloof when Molly saw him walking briskly past the windows when she was giving Oreo a toilet break in the roof garden.

He was looking as if he was in a decidedly bad mood. He was actually scowling!

Thank goodness he didn't look outside and see her because that would, no doubt, make him even grumpier. They hadn't spoken since she'd unleashed on his lack of connection with his patients the other day. They hadn't even made eye contact. And...

...and Molly was missing him.

Okay, she knew perfectly well that they were totally unsuited to being with each other but that didn't change the fact that Molly's heart had been well and truly captured—even before he'd given her the best sex she'd ever had in her life.

Even now, as she saw the tall man with the scowl on his face striding past the garden, she could also see a lonely boy who had not only been grieving the loss of his sister but had lost his beloved dog as well. Molly could almost see the barriers he'd built to prevent himself feeling that much again and her heart ached for him because she knew, all too well, that those barriers were also preventing him from feeling the joy that life could offer.

She'd already pushed him too far, though, hadn't she?

She wasn't going to get another chance and that made her feel sad.

Almost as sad as she felt every time she and Oreo quietly slipped into Sam's room to spend some time with him. The sweet little boy was being kept pretty much pain free now but the complications with his lungs and heart were making his care too complex for Annabelle to be able to manage at home.

She knew she was going to be saying goodbye to her precious son in hospital within a short period of time but she was making the most of every moment she still had with him, and the way Sam's face lit up when he was conscious enough to know that Oreo was beside him was enough for Molly to make sure she came in every day. She enlisted the help of her mother one day when she was on duty to bring Oreo to the hospital to make a brief visit during Molly's lunch break and on another day she came back in the evening after she'd finished her shift.

There were many other patients needing her attention, of course.

Sophie Jacobs had gone home a week after her rotation-plasty surgery. She would need crutches and a wheelchair until her leg had healed enough to be fitted for her custom-made prosthesis and she would be spending a great deal of time with her team of physiotherapists to learn to use her ankle joint as her new knee, but she left the ward with a huge smile on her face and the picture from her wall, of the other little girl doing her ballet leap with her prosthesis, folded up and in her pocket. She gave Molly a copy of one of the photographs the nurse had taken when Oreo visited Sophie in the intensive care unit after her surgery. Sophie had been just waking up and the smile on her face as she'd been able to touch Oreo's head was enough to melt anyone's heart.

Maybe even the heart of the man who'd done Sophie's surgery?

Molly pinned the photo, with pride, to a long corkboard on the wall near the entrance to the ward. She—and her beloved canine partner—were becoming a part of the fabric of this hospital and nobody—other than Hugh—had questioned the wisdom of their frequent visits to a small boy who was dying.

Molly had been invited to attend a very sombre meeting where an end-of-life care plan was discussed for Sam. Hugh was apparently caught up in Theatre but his presence wasn't considered necessary given that Sam would not be having any further surgery. His oncologist and cardiologist were there, along with Molly representing the nursing staff and the support of Sam's grandmother and aunty for Annabelle. At the end of the meeting, Annabelle signed consent forms for a process known as Allowing a Natural Death or AND, which meant keeping Sam as comfortable as possible for as long as possible but restricting the interventions to prevent death, such as CPR including intubation or defibrillation. She also made what was, for this hospital, the first request of its kind, ever.

'I know it's a lot to ask...' Annabelle's words were choked '...and maybe it won't be possible but... I think Sam believes that Oreo is *his* puppy now. If she could be there at...at the end...'

She broke down completely then and Molly was the first to get up and go to give Annabelle a hug. She knew that any comfort Oreo could provide would be for Annabelle as much as for Sam.

'If it's possible,' she said softly, 'we'll make it happen.'

It *was* a big ask. Not because Molly wasn't willing to be there if it was at short notice or in the middle of the night but because it was quite likely that Sam's heart function or respiratory efforts could cease without any warning. What did end up happening, however, was a more gentle progression with signs that Sam's small body was giving up the fight. His blood pressure dropped and his body temperature began fluctuating. His skin became slightly mottled as his circulation slowed down and Annabelle found she couldn't tempt her son to eat, even with his favourite treats.

Molly took Oreo in during the afternoon. Assistant dog protocols meant that she had to stay in the room with Annabelle, *her* mother and her sister but, having positioned Oreo on the bed beside where Sam was being held in his mother's arms, she made herself as inconspicuous as possible in a corner of the room. Oreo looked as though she was asleep, with her eyes shut and Sam's hand just resting on top of her body and Annabelle stroking her sometimes, but, occasionally, the dog would open her eyes and her glance would find Molly's, as if seeking reassurance she was doing the right thing as she stayed there, motionless, for an hour and then another. And Molly would smile and sometimes murmur quietly, telling her that she was a good girl and to stay where she was.

Oreo still didn't move even after Sam quietly sighed and then didn't take another breath. Molly waited until Annabelle's mother and sister closed in to share the holding and grieving for Sam and then signalled Oreo, who slipped off the bed unnoticed by the family.

The charge nurse on duty, who was in the room at that point, followed Molly and Oreo out of the room.

'Are you okay?' she asked Molly.

Molly could only nod. She didn't trust her voice to work yet.

'Take Oreo home.' The charge nurse gave her a quick

hug. 'And look after yourself. You're both heroes, you know that, don't you?'

Molly tried to smile but it didn't work. It was time for her to take Oreo home and she knew that Sam's family would be well cared for and allowed to stay with him as long as they wanted to. Her own tears were making everything a bit of a blur as she walked out of the ward, but Oreo knew the route well by now and was leading Molly towards the stairwell beside the lifts. In a few minutes they would be outside and then in the familiar privacy of the old van. Maybe she knew how important it was that Molly needed to get somewhere where she could have a good cry.

She didn't see him.

She probably wouldn't have recognised him if he'd been standing right in front of her because Hugh could see that Molly was half blinded by tears.

And he knew why.

He'd been heading towards his office when someone had intercepted him and told him quietly that little Sam Finch had died. Hugh had simply nodded acknowledgement and thanked the messenger and it was then he'd spotted Molly leaving the ward with Oreo.

There was no reason not to continue to his office, where he had an article on an experimental surgical technique for bone grafting waiting for him to peer review for a leading journal of paediatric orthopaedics.

Yes, the news was sad but it was part and parcel of specialising in orthopaedic surgery for children with bone cancer and, fortunately, they seemed to be winning more and more battles these days. Hugh had learned long ago how to protect himself from being sucked too deeply into a case like Sam's.

But Molly clearly hadn't.

A short time later, Hugh found the image of her struggling to control her grief as she escaped the hospital was interfering with his focus on the article.

Where had she gone? Was she alone in that little cottage by the sea?

Was she okay?

Did she have someone to talk to?

Someone that could help her get past what could be a damaging level of emotional involvement rather than wallowing in it?

Someone like himself…?

Hugh shook the notion off and tried harder to focus on what was a well-written paper, on the advancements in biomaterials and methods for bone augmentation, but he couldn't prevent his thoughts drifting back to Molly.

He couldn't get rid of the odd tightness in his chest that was unusual enough for him to wonder if he might have an undiagnosed issue with his heart.

No. He knew what the problem was.

He was worried about Molly. He'd warned her about how unwise it had been to involve herself in this case but that didn't mean he wasn't sympathetic to her finding out the hard way that he was right.

He wasn't going to say 'I told you so'. He wasn't expecting her to take back the things she'd said about his ability to distance himself being selfish because he was the only person to benefit and that he was living less of a life than others.

To be honest, Hugh had no idea what he was going to

say or what Molly might say back to him. He just knew
he needed to see her, which was why he closed his laptop
and reached for his car keys.

This was better.

Molly had cried her eyes out at the same time as throwing the frisbee for Oreo again and again. The background
of waves breaking on the beach was soothing and a soft
evening sea breeze was enough to dry the tears on her
cheeks without becoming too cold. When Oreo was panting so hard she had to drop her toy and head into the
waves to cool off, Molly sat to simply watch for a while
and that was even better because she could feel the edges
of her sadness being softened by the comfort of being in
a place she loved.

With the dog she loved with all her heart.

Oddly, it wasn't surprising to look up and see Hugh
walking towards her. Molly knew that he would have
heard about Sam and he'd warned her how hard it might
be to have involved herself so much. But the fact he was
here told her that he wasn't being judgemental or righ-
teous because being like that would be far more effective
in their working environment. His expression suggested
that he was feeling concerned.

Concerned about her?

That was a kind of involvement on his part, wasn't it?

That meant he wasn't keeping himself as distant as he
might think.

And, for some reason, Molly felt a spark of something
that felt like…hope…?

'I thought I might find you here,' he said.

Molly just nodded.

'I thought you might like a bit of company.'

Molly nodded again and Hugh sat down on the sand beside her. For a minute or two they both watched the waves endlessly rolling in and then receding. And then Hugh spoke quietly.

'You okay…?'

Oh… Molly could hear how difficult it was for him to ask that question. He knew he was inviting a conversation that might include something emotional. Something a long way out of any comfort zone of his.

She needed to reassure him that she wasn't going to stamp on any personal ground so she managed to find a smile as she nodded slowly.

'I'm okay,' she said. 'I'm incredibly sad, of course. I'm gutted for Annabelle and her family but I don't regret my involvement. And Oreo was an absolute angel. I know she helped…'

'I'm sure she did.'

Molly had to brush away a few leftover tears. She could feel Hugh's gaze on her face and the increase of tension in his body language.

'I really am okay,' she told him. 'It's okay to feel sad sometimes, you know. And it's okay to cry…'

Oreo was still playing in the shallow water. They had the beach to themselves and the only sound was the soft wash of small waves breaking.

'I haven't cried since I was fourteen.'

Hugh's words were not much more than a whisper and Molly knew he was telling her something he had never told anyone else.

'When you lost your sister?'

Hugh was silent for so long that Molly thought she

might have crossed too big a boundary but then he spoke again and his voice was raw.

'And Fudge...' The way he cleared his throat made Molly wonder if he was close to tears himself. 'My mother had him put down a few days after Michelle died.'

Molly gasped in total shock. 'Oh, my God...what happened to him?'

Hugh was staring out to sea. 'Nothing...my mother just said he was too old. I came home from school and he... just wasn't there...'

Molly was staring at Hugh. Horrified. Imagining that boy who was dealing with the loss of his sister and having the lifelong companion who could have offered comfort like no other simply snatched away for no good reason. Her heart was breaking for fourteen-year-old Hugh. But it was also breaking for the man who was sitting beside her.

Who'd learned not to love any people—*or* dogs—because the world would feel like it was ending when you lost them.

All Molly wanted to do was to hold Hugh in her arms. To offer, very belatedly, all the understanding and comfort that *she* was able to bestow.

She knew not to touch him, however. That Hugh had stepped onto an emotional tightrope by telling her something so personal and, if he was touched in any way, verbally *or* physically, he could fall off that tightrope and she'd never be allowed this close again.

And she really didn't want that to happen.

Because it was in this moment that Molly realised just how much in love with Hugh Ashcroft she had fallen.

She knew he was never going to feel the same way. That if she didn't back off she would be setting herself up for total heartbreak but…it didn't feel like she had a choice, here. It was a bit like being with Annabelle and Sam today. There was something powerful enough to make dealing with that level of pain worthwhile.

That she—and Oreo—could help.

'I've got a spot in my garden where you can watch the sea while the sun sets,' she said, as if she were sharing something secret. Or perhaps just completely changing the subject? 'I've also got a bottle of wine in my fridge and I'd really like a glass of it but you know what they say about not drinking alone, don't you?'

Hugh nodded carefully. 'I *do*…'

'I know I'm not technically alone when I've got Oreo with me.' Molly bit her lip. And then she smiled. Properly this time. 'But she hates wine.'

The soft huff of laughter from Hugh was a surprise.

A definite win.

'I did come out because I thought you might need some company.' Hugh got to his feet and held out his hand to help Molly up. 'I didn't realise it was to drink wine but… hey… I'm willing to go with the flow, here.'

Molly put her hand in his, loving the strong grip and tug that made it so easy to get up and stay this close to Hugh.

It would have been easy to keep moving. To lean in so close it would be an invitation to be kissed.

But Molly didn't do that. Because if offering him an opportunity to get closer—to build a friendship, or even a relationship—was going to work, it had to be completely Hugh's choice how far he closed any distance between them.

Safety.

That was what this felt like.

He had been pretty sure Molly would have been filled in by Benji's grandmother about his family tragedy, but nobody had known about Fudge. That look on Molly's face when he'd dropped that emotional bomb had made him realise that this was the first time anyone understood exactly what it had been like for him.

It felt like Molly might be the only person in the universe who *could* understand that. More than understand, even. It felt like she could *feel* it herself.

And she didn't say anything. It was enough that he knew she understood. He certainly didn't want to revisit the past in any more detail and Molly seemed to get that, too.

So yeah...

Hugh felt safe. He could sit on a comfortable, old wicker chair with Oreo lying on the grass by his feet, drink a very nice Central Otago wine and still hear the waves as the day drew to a close and he could relax more than he remembered being able to do in...well...in for ever, really.

Perhaps that was why it felt okay to have Oreo's head resting heavily on his foot. Why, when he looked down and found the dog looking back up at him with those liquid brown eyes, he could feel a melting sensation deep in his chest. He didn't dare look up to where Molly was sitting, in the matching chair that was close enough to touch his, in case *she* was watching him, too.

'I was nine years old when Michelle... Shelly...got diagnosed with a brain tumour,' he said. 'She was only three so she never really remembered a life without being sick. She died at home when she was eight. Fudge stayed on the bed with her that day. He refused to get off even when I tried to take him outside for a wee. I think he knew...'

Oh, dear Lord…even mentioning that last day was taking him too close to a space he had successfully avoided for so long. He'd even managed to keep it locked away when he'd been trying to warn Molly that being with Sam at the end might have repercussions that could haunt her for life. If she said anything about Shelly now, he might lose something he could never get back.

His safe space…

'Dogs are amazing,' Molly said softly into the silence. 'They understand far more than we give them credit for and they have this astonishing ability to supply limitless, unconditional love…'

Her voice trailed away as if she felt like she'd said too much and when Hugh lifted his gaze he could see she had tears in her eyes.

'Grief is the worst feeling in the world, isn't it?' she murmured. 'I heard it said once that grief is love that has nowhere to go.'

Hugh had no words. He was lost in what he could see in Molly's dark eyes. They were sitting so close that all he had to do was lift his hand to touch her cheek. If he leaned towards her he would be able to kiss her.

Especially if she leaned a little, as well.

Which was exactly what she did a heartbeat after he'd moved. Hugh cupped her cheek with his hand, tilting her jaw as his lips found hers.

He didn't need any words, did he?

Not even to tell Molly how she had made such a difference in his world just by being there to hear him talk, even so briefly, about his beloved little sister. And his dog. To understand how devastating it had been to lose them both but not to ask him to say anything more. To allow him the dignity of maintaining control. One day he might tell her how his mother had disappeared, inch by inch, into the depression that eventually claimed her life. That *he* had largely disappeared for her over the years when her sick daughter was the total focus of her life.

But not now. All he wanted right now was to thank Molly for being here.

For understanding.

And he didn't need words.

Because he could touch her.

He could hold her face as he kissed her until they were both short of breath. He could stand up and take her hand and lead her into her little house and find her bedroom this time.

And he could touch her whole body—with his hands and his lips and his tongue. He could feel her skin against his own. He could make sure that this was as good as it could get—for both of them. And he could take his time because this was about more than simply a fierce physical attraction.

It was about being safe. In a world that only the two of them could inhabit.

Because Molly understood why he was so different.

CHAPTER NINE

As THE NURSE practitioner on duty, it was part of Molly's job to accompany the consultants and their registrars as they made their ward rounds. Prior to that, she needed to collect all the most up-to-date clinical information on the patients and be ready for the 'board round' before the ward round. This was where the team would gather around the digital whiteboard on the wall of the nurses' station, which had details of all the inpatients, and decide the order of priority. The most unwell were seen first, then the patients who were ready for discharge that day, followed by the more routine visits to everyone else for the monitoring of charts and medications, physical examinations and any adjustments to treatment plans.

It was Hugh, his registrar Matthew and two junior doctors doing their rounds this morning and Molly had been completely focussed collecting all the latest blood test results and notes from the handover, until Hugh and his colleagues walked towards the nurses' station for the board round.

Her stomach did a weird flip-flop then and, for a moment, Molly struggled to clear a sudden flash of images from her brain—like a movie on fast-forward—of last night. Of her body being...good heavens...*worshipped*...?

But that was what she had decided it had felt like later in the night, after Hugh had gone home. The focus he'd had on her... As if making this the most profound sexual experience she'd ever had was the only thing on his mind?

Maybe it wasn't images that flashed through her mind in that heartbeat of a moment. It was more like a reminder of physical sensations like none she had ever had before in her life. The sheer delight of the whispers of fingers against her skin. The delicious spears of desire. Anticipation—and need—building to a point that was actually painful and the blinding ecstasy of release.

No...it was more than that. It was like the physical form of emotions that were so intense and unfamiliar Molly couldn't even find words to describe them. And she certainly wasn't about to try right now.

This was work and Molly knew perfectly well that it came before anything else in this surgeon's list of what mattered the most. If there was a way to ensure that what had happened between herself and Hugh Ashcroft last night never, ever happened again, it would be to let it interfere with how either of them did their jobs. That dealbreaker was closely followed by putting any kind of pressure on Hugh to build on how well they knew each other, but at least that was easy to put aside, especially when Molly wasn't at all sure she was ready for even attempting a new relationship. The reminder was useful, however, because suddenly any personal thoughts evaporated.

The blip in focus had been so momentary hopefully nobody else could have noticed. Especially Hugh. Molly took a deep breath as she looked away from him and flicked open the notepad where she'd scribbled the information she needed to communicate with this team that wasn't on the whiteboard yet.

The first patient whose condition was causing some concern was twelve-year-old Gemma, who had had surgery two days ago for a slipped upper femoral epiphysis—where the ball at the top of the femur had slipped out of position due to damage to the growth plate—that had happened after a collision and fall in a soccer game.

'So, Gemma was doing very well with her crutches and was flagged for discharge today but she spiked a temperature during the night and is feeling unwell this morning,' Molly reported. 'She's got some redness and is complaining of increased wound pain. Preliminary results on the bloods and wound swab I took first thing after handover shouldn't be too far away.'

'Thanks, Molly. Is the ward pharmacist available? I'd like to run through our initial management of any infection.'

'I'll get someone to page her.'

Hugh's glance told her that he was impressed with her initiating tests that would determine the course of treatment needed to combat the surgical complication of infection.

It also told her that they were both now safely in a totally professional arena. That Hugh had no idea of that momentary lapse she'd had. But perhaps he hadn't been entirely wrong in telling her it was better to be able to keep a personal distance from others. Sometimes.

Like for the rest of this ward round. With Gemma examined, antibiotic treatment started and her family reassured that she wouldn't be discharged until this setback had been sorted, there were enough patients to keep the team busy until it was time for a morning tea break. Not that Hugh or his team stayed for a coffee in the ward staff room. They were gone, heading towards Radiology for a scheduled biopsy, a family meeting in the oncology ward for a patient who had just been diagnosed with a bone cancer and was about to start chemotherapy before surgery, and then an outpatient clinic that was apparently so packed it would keep both himself and his registrars largely unavailable all afternoon.

'I know you won't page us unless it's urgent,' he said to Molly as they left the ward.

She might have deemed the smile she received to be as aloof as she'd once thought Hugh actually was himself, but she could see past that protective barrier now. Or maybe it was just something new she could see in that graze of eye contact. Something that acknowledged there was a lot more than simply being colleagues between them but that Hugh was trusting her with much more than overseeing the care of his patients for the rest of her shift.

He was trusting her not to trespass across boundaries.

Especially at work, because this was his safe place.

Molly's smile in return was just as polite. 'Of course not,' she murmured.

He *could* trust her. On both counts. He'd never know that she had a totally *un*professional thought as he walked away from her. That, as she carried her mug of coffee out to the garden for a minute's peace and quiet, she was reminded—oddly—of a pony club camp she'd been to as a teenager, taken by a local legend in horse whispering.

At first Molly couldn't understand why her brain had

dredged up something she hadn't thought about in more years than she could count.

'Every horse lives with a mindset that's like a human with PTSD,' she remembered the course leader saying to them as he gave them a demonstration. *'They have eyes on the sides of their heads. They've always been prey, not the predators. They're hypervigilant. Always looking for danger...'*

Molly found herself catching her breath, as she slowly sat down on a bench and put her coffee down beside her. That was Hugh as far as relationships went, wasn't it? Hypervigilant. A kind of prey because a relationship was something that could hurt him. Destroy him, even.

The emotional trauma from his childhood must have left huge scars. Remembering what he'd told her about his baby sister's last day alive brought a lump to her throat that was sharp enough to be painful as she imagined how terrible that day must have been for a boy and his dog.

And how hard had those five years before that day been? All the attention would have been on the sick little girl to start with. Had that become a way of life? Had Hugh been left feeling abandoned? Molly had the odd urge to reach back through time and give that boy a hug. To make sure he knew how important he was, too. That he knew he was loved.

The unbearable heartache of losing Fudge before he'd even had a chance to process the loss of his sister was unthinkable.

So yeah...it wasn't a crazy analogy that he was like the horse running around the edges of that round pen with the trainer standing in the centre. That Hugh had learned to keep that distance from any kind of relationships that the trainer represented.

But he'd circled closer to Molly, hadn't he? Close enough to tell her a little bit about that childhood trauma. Close enough to make love to her, even if he hadn't realised that was what it was.

Just the way that horse had circled closer to the trainer when it had had time to read the signals, accept the newcomer in its life and trust that this person wasn't a threat.

'Then you can turn your back and walk away and the horse will come up behind you.' The trainer had slowed and then stopped and the horse had nudged his shoulder. *'Now I can walk away and the horse gets to choose where he wants to be and...look...he's right behind me. He wants to be with me...'*

Good grief...it was time to stop this before it got silly. Before Molly could imagine Hugh following her around like some sort of lovestruck puppy. Her coffee was too cold to be desirable now so she tipped it out into the garden behind her and stood up. It was time she went back to work now, anyway.

She did feel more at peace, she realised. She'd already known instinctively that Hugh needed the time and space to make his own choices. He'd already come close enough for it to be meaningful and that was...

...it was huge.

And very, very special.

Molly could wait. If anything else was going to happen between them, it would be well worth waiting *for*.

Working together made things so much easier.

If Hugh didn't see Molly at work, either when she was

on duty or there with Oreo to visit sick kids and sometimes with Milo as a training exercise, the pressure might
have been unwelcome.

It would certainly have been unforgivable not to make
contact with her after the evening of the day that little boy,
Sam, had died. When he'd opened a door into his personal
life that was never opened to anyone—even to himself, if
he could avoid it. The evening that had included sex that
had been somewhat disturbing in its level of intimacy.

Not that Molly had given any hint of it being a problem
for her. That next morning, when they'd met in the ward,
had made it seem like it was no big deal. That it could
have been simply an evening with a friend that had happened to end up in bed. That she didn't necessarily expect it to happen again and definitely wasn't going to let
it impinge on their professional relationship.

Gemma, who'd had the unfortunate complication of
a nasty post-op infection, had needed a bit more time in
hospital to get it under control and for her to then catch
up on the skills she needed with her crutches before she
could go home but she'd been discharged yesterday. It was
during that ward round, when Hugh had signed off on the
discharge, that he'd realised how easy this was.

It felt like he and Molly were friends now. Even better, that there was no pressure for it to be anything more
than that. He didn't have to ask her out on a formal date
or anything but he didn't have to avoid her company, either, and that was a relief.

He didn't have to give up on one of his favourite
beaches to go and catch a wave. With the days getting
longer and the weather more reliable, Hugh was hoping
to get into the sea as often as his work schedule would

allow. Because there was nothing better than surfing to escape…well…everything, really.

Except…maybe there was *one* thing better than surfing.

And, as the days ticked past and the smiles and quick chats, when his path crossed with Molly's, became something familiar and welcome, Hugh was starting to wonder if she might like to spend some more personal time together again.

He didn't want to ask because that might make it seem more significant than he wanted it to be. And, anyway, hadn't all the time they'd had together happened without any prior arrangements? When he'd discovered her in the outpatient department with Milo after hours and ended up helping with the young dog's training. When he'd taken that old equipment out to her house and ended up running around the agility course with Oreo. When he'd gone to the beach for a breath of fresh air and ended up swimming in sea that was so cold he'd needed that hot shower and…

Hugh blew out a breath. If he went too far down that mental track he might get lost in a level of desire that could ring alarm bells. But was there a theme here? He'd gone to find Molly on the beach the day Sam had died.

He'd met her away from work for the first time on that beach, come to think of it. Maybe all he needed to do was head for Taylors Mistake again to find out what fate had in store for him?

Whether Molly *did* want more of what had happened the last time he'd gone in that direction? No pressure, of course. On either side. And definitely no strings attached either.

* * *

No...

It couldn't be.

Which was a silly thing to think because this was exactly where she'd met Hugh Ashcroft more than once and, like the very first time, he was wearing his skintight wetsuit again and that was enough to know exactly who he was given that Molly was taken straight back to that first wave of the sexual attraction she had felt for this man. The one that had been powerful enough to make her stomach curl and her knees weak.

Both Oreo and Milo had recognised him as well and were running towards the figure with the surfboard slung under his arm but the curl in Molly's gut this time felt very different from a wash of attraction.

It felt more like...trepidation...?

It felt as though he was walking right into the middle of her life this time.

Which, in a way, he was. The Holmes family was celebrating the birthday of Molly's niece, eight-year-old Neve. Christchurch had turned on one of its spring evenings that felt far more like summer so they were all on the beach, including the dogs, having some playtime with the children before going back to the house for a barbecue dinner.

Molly was sitting on the sand, making castles by filling a moulded bucket and turning it upside down so that her youngest niece could flatten it with a toy spade. She paused, with the bucket in mid-air, as she took in the moment Hugh recognised the dogs and then realised she was part of this family group.

Even from this distance, she could feel the eye contact.

She could feel how torn he was and that made it feel like this was a very significant moment.

A make-or-break kind of moment?

Hugh had obviously come to do some surfing but it was quite possible—probable, even—that he'd been hoping that he would find her here. Molly's heart sank as she wondered if this was the moment she'd been waiting patiently for—when Hugh felt safe enough to make the choice to be with her because it was something he wanted as much as she did?

Would this be the end of any such opportunity? Hugh was cautious enough of a one-on-one relationship. Would the dynamics of a whole family be his worst nightmare? Molly could understand, all too easily, why he was taken aback. He was probably considering turning back to the car park and escaping but she knew he wouldn't do that.

How much courage had Hugh had, as a child, to face up to what life had thrown at him?

He'd learned to get through anything, no matter how hard it was.

And he'd learned to do it alone.

Molly's heart took another dive. Not just because it was aching for someone who possibly didn't even know how much it helped to *not* be alone when facing the tough stuff in life, but because Hugh didn't know the worst of what he was walking into right now. He didn't yet have any idea that her niece was celebrating her birthday.

Her eighth birthday.

Neve was now the same age as Hugh's sister, Michelle, had been when she died...

Molly got to her feet, knocking over the half-filled

sandcastle bucket in her haste. The toddler beside her waved her toy spade.

'More…' she demanded. 'Aunty 'olly…*more…*'

But Molly was walking towards Hugh.

'Oreo… *Milo*…stop harassing Hugh…'

Her brother, Jack, paused in his cricket game with his son. 'You know this guy?'

'Friend of mine from work.' Molly smiled. 'And an ace surfer. You'll be impressed. Hugh, this is my brother, Jack. I think I told you how keen on surfing he used to be.'

Jack grinned at Hugh. 'Wish I could join you out there, mate. There're some awesome waves but we haven't even finished our first innings, have we, Liam?' He turned back to the impatient boy standing with his bat in front of the plastic wickets stuck into the sand. 'Come and have a beer with us when you're done.'

Molly's mother had come to get Milo and she didn't wait for an introduction.

'I'm Jill, Molly's mum. And this is Neve. It's her birthday today.'

'I'm *eight*,' Neve announced proudly.

Hugh's gaze flew to Molly's, as if he couldn't help checking to see if she remembered the significance of this. She tried to hold his gaze. To send a silent message.

I know, Hugh… I know exactly how hard this is and I'm sorry…

But Hugh was breaking the eye contact too soon. Before the most important thing Molly wanted him to know.

You don't have to do this alone. I'm here…and… I love you…

Hugh was oblivious. He was smiling at Neve. That distant kind of smile that he used with his young patients. It didn't mean he didn't care.

It meant he knew what could happen when you cared *too* much.

'Happy birthday,' he said. 'I hope you have a wonderful party. Maybe I'll be able to see all those candles on your cake from out on the waves.'

And, with that, he excused himself with another smile and strode off into the sea.

The waves *were* awesome.

It was close to a high tide and, as often happened close to sunrise or sunset, there was a decent swell and the offshore breeze was enough to smooth things out. Best of all, the swell was on an angle so that the wave was peeling off instead of breaking all at once.

Hugh wasn't the only surfer making the most of the fading daylight but it was far from crowded, in the sea or on the beach. Molly's family celebration was, by far, the biggest group of people and Hugh was acutely aware of them each time he finished a ride and prepared to paddle back out to find another wave.

He could see Jack playing cricket with Liam and even heard the little boy gleefully shout *'Howzat?'* having presumably bowled his father out. He could see Molly building sandcastles with a toddler who was happily knocking them down with her small, red spade and, after a later wave, he saw her taking the youngest child into the shallow foam of the waves to wash the sand off her hands. The birthday girl ran to join them and they both took a hand of the toddler, lifting her up to jump the foamy curl of a spent wave.

Hugh could hear the shrieks of excitement from the baby and he recognised both Molly's laughter and Oreo's happy barking.

He saw them gathering up the toys and towels and wending their way back to the family's holiday house. He knew he would be welcomed if he chose to join them in the garden for a drink. They were probably going to start cooking sausages on the barbecue and, at some point, a cake with burning candles would appear for Neve to make her birthday wish.

But Hugh paddled back to catch another wave.

And another.

The other surfers left. Daylight was almost gone and, despite the wetsuit, Hugh was getting really cold.

He told himself that each wave would be the last one but then he decided to try just one more...

Because he wanted it to be dark enough when he got out that Molly wouldn't notice him leaving.

She knew too much and he didn't want to be at her niece's birthday party and feel her understanding. Her sympathy. To know that she genuinely cared about how he was feeling. He needed some distance.

And Molly needed it too, even if she didn't realise that.

She was in the place she needed to be. With the people—and animals—she loved so much. With her whole family and those gorgeous children who loved her back. This would be Molly's future, wouldn't it? The heart and soul of a new branch of the family with the chaos of kids and dogs and big celebrations for every birthday and Christmas.

It was never going to be Hugh's future.

How hard had it been to walk into that family scene?

Molly had known that it would be another blow to any defence mechanism he had honed to learn that it was Neve's eighth birthday. That he would be reminded of Michelle. Getting to know Oreo had been enough of a pull back into his past. To where he and Fudge had been an inseparable team. They'd both adored Michelle and had been so protective of her. They'd both comforted each other on the darker days.

There were splashes of sea water getting into his eyes and blurring his vision as he flipped out of the end of the wave and dropped onto his board to paddle back out. Or were they tears?

Hugh wasn't sure. What he was sure about, however, was that he'd come closer than he'd realised to losing any of the hard-won protection he'd built for himself in the years since Michelle had died. Seeing Molly with the children in her extended family was sounding a warning that he couldn't ignore. This might be his last chance to avoid any more echoes of a pain he never wanted to experience again.

And maybe Molly had been right and he *was* creating a distance from living a life that was totally fulfilling.

Maybe it *was* only better for himself.

She'd made it so very clear that she would never want to live *her* life like that.

They were complete opposites and getting close to Molly Holmes was…well…he'd always known how dangerous it was. But it had been a risk he'd been—almost—willing to take. Until now, when he could see it might be dangerous for Molly as well as himself and he couldn't allow that to happen.

Because *he* cared about her.

One day, she would be grateful for him keeping them both safe.

CHAPTER TEN

THE SAME BUT DIFFERENT.

That was how Molly began to describe the relationship she had with Hugh Ashcroft to herself as the days slid past after that family gathering on the beach to celebrate Neve's birthday.

The day that she wished had ended so very differently.

If only they could have met on the beach with nobody else there to complicate things. Or Hugh had come and knocked on her door after he'd been surfing and they could have gone for a walk in the hills with Oreo or shared a glass of wine and watched the sunset.

As Molly replayed that evening in her head time and time again, adding the fantasy of what she'd wished had happened, it always ended up with the same kind of love making as last time. The kind that had taken everything to a completely new level and made Molly realise how much she wanted to take the next step towards a relationship that could change both their lives and give them a future.

Together.

But it hadn't happened like that and Hugh had obviously seen enough to make him back away and Molly just knew it was about her family.

About the children in her life.

He'd only ever seen her interacting with the children she worked with and their patients were part of the professional life she shared with Hugh. He'd never seen her with the children who were such an important part of her personal life—and always would be. Had it made him think that Molly saw children of her own as part of her future? Had Hugh ever got close enough to think about a permanent relationship with someone and imagine creating a family of his own? Had he made his mind up at that point that it was never going to happen? Like the way he'd decided he never wanted to have another dog?

She couldn't blame him for making the choices he had in life, but it did make her feel sad.

Maybe Hugh didn't see how good he was with kids? Or dogs, for that matter. Or that both children and dogs were instinctively drawn to him?

He was currently with fifteen-month-old Jasper, on their ward round, who was due to be discharged after the surgery he'd had on a badly dislocated and fractured elbow.

The adventurous toddler, who'd managed to climb onto a kitchen chair and then fall onto his outstretched arm, was now in a long arm cast with his elbow fixed at a ninety-degree angle but it didn't seem to be bothering him. He was grinning up at Molly as she stood beside his mother and he was trying to lift the heavy cast on his arm so that he could reach for the stethoscope she had hanging around her neck, attracted by the bright green, plastic frog head clipped to the top of its disc.

'Can I borrow that for a sec?' Hugh asked. 'Could be just what the doctor ordered for checking the range of movement and capillary refill of those fingers.'

Molly handed him the stethoscope and Jasper's gaze followed the frog's head as it got closer.

'Ribbit-ribbit,' Hugh growled.

Hugh's registrar exchanged a grin with Molly. 'We learn that in medical school,' he said.

'True,' Hugh agreed, but he didn't look up to catch Molly's gaze.

He was watching Jasper's fingers move as he played with the frog and then he quickly checked limb baselines like skin temperature and colour. Jasper's frown as he pressed a fingernail to check blood flow suggested that his ability to feel touch was not compromised, but he didn't start crying. Instead, the frown turned to a grin as he caught the frog and he gave a gurgle of laughter.

He liked this surgeon.

Yeah... Kids and dogs could sense things that people might not even know about themselves, couldn't they?

And yes, she could totally understand where his wariness of choosing to have a child—or a dog—of his own came from but wouldn't it be easier to accept having the joy of them in his life when they were someone else's? Molly had seen Hugh patting and playing with her dogs. He would be just as good with nieces and nephews and, in time, he might even be very grateful to have them in his life.

'I'm happy for him to go home.' Hugh nodded at Jasper's mother. 'You'll get outpatient appointments and we'll be looking at removing the cast and pins at around the four-week mark.'

'Are there any long-term complications we should be worried about? I've heard that elbows can be tricky with all the nerves and things in there.'

'I don't think you need to worry.' Hugh was trying to gently prise the disc of his stethoscope from a small but determined fist. 'There may be some limitation in the range of movement but we'll encourage him to work through that as soon as he's out of the cast. Elbows are the most complex joint in the human body and we're very careful about them because of how important they are for arms and hands to function but, if there *were* any long-term complications, like disruption to the ulnar nerve, perhaps, we can deal with them.' He smiled at the anxious mother. 'And there's no point worrying about crossing bridges like that when we may never get anywhere near them. Let's take it one step at a time and be happy that Jasper's doing very well so far.'

They moved on to the next patient on their ward round but Hugh got distracted on the way by the arrival of a new patient who was waiting by the reception desk.

'Michael… I'll come and see you later today. You've got a few appointments for things like a chest X-ray and blood tests to make sure we tick all the boxes before your surgery tomorrow. How did your exams go at school?'

'Good…'

'I'll bet you smashed them. We'll talk later, okay?'

Molly had been expecting the arrival of this teenager, who was being admitted for the surgery scheduled to correct his spinal scoliosis that was affecting his breathing. She also knew that when the surgeon visited later, he would be talking about what was going to happen tomorrow. The prospect of having bone grafts and metal rods and screws being put into his body to fuse his spine had to be terrifying, no matter how brave a face this lad was showing to the world right now. Michael's mother was certainly looking as if she was on the verge of tears as they waited to finish the admittance process paperwork.

'Hi, Michael.' Molly paused to smile at him. 'I'm Molly and I'm one of the nurses who'll be looking after you while you're with us.' She lowered her voice as if she were imparting a secret. 'I've earmarked the best bed for you. You'll get a great view of all the helicopters landing and taking off from the helipad on the next-door roof.'

'Cool.'

Michael's smile was tentative but at least it was there. Hugh had seen it as well and it felt like he had deliberately kept his head turned for long enough to catch Molly's gaze and send a private message of appreciation for her attention to his new patient.

And that ability to communicate silently was something else that was different even though they were still the same colleagues. Their opinion of each other had also changed and grown into something completely different from initial impressions. They were now people who could work together with genuine respect that was personal as well as professional. Trust had been established.

In fact, they knew each other *too* well to be considered simply friends, but it was a grey area when nothing had actually been said and Molly had no idea whether Hugh even wanted to see her again. She was, in fact, on the point of giving up her patient wait for Hugh to come and find her out of working hours.

It felt as if that initial distance between them that had become the most different aspect of their relationship was being reinstated.

Slowly but surely.

With kindness. The way someone who was so good

with kids and dogs might approach something that needed to be done but could be hurtful.

Someone who'd make a great father even though he never wanted to have his own children.

Someone who had probably been the best big brother in the entire world to a little girl whose heartbreaking life was the reason he never wanted to have his own children.

And okay... Molly had been trying to follow the advice Hugh had just given Jasper's mother in taking things one step at a time and being happy with how well it was going but...

...that bridge was right there in front of her and she couldn't ignore it.

Because her heart was already aching and it would be completely broken if—or when—she had to cross the bridge that might be the only way out of a dead end.

She wasn't quite there yet, mind you. And the possibility of discovering a detour came into her head as she saw Hugh walking away having signed Jasper's discharge paperwork.

What if Hugh knew that not having children of her own was not a dealbreaker as far as a relationship with him was concerned?

And, yeah...that had been a dream once but, by the time she'd moved back to New Zealand, she'd already made peace with the possibility that it would never happen, hadn't she? She'd decided that she could be happy with the children she had in her life through her family and her work. That the fur children she would always have at home would be enough.

Perhaps she just needed to find a way to let him know that? A way that didn't put any pressure on Hugh, of course, because that would send her straight across that bridge she really, really didn't want to cross.

He heard the sound of her voice before he'd turned the corner to where the reception area bridged the two main corridors in the ward.

'Show me again…? Oh, *wow*…look at you.'

Hugh could hear the smile in her words and he knew exactly what Molly's face would look like—lit up with genuine warmth that brought a glow to everyone around her. He could feel himself taking a deeper breath, his muscles tensing, as if they could form the forcefield he needed to not feel that glow.

Because it made him remember that Molly had implied he was missing out on life by keeping himself closed off and he suspected that that glow might be one of the things he was going to miss most about not allowing himself to get too close to her.

He was somewhat blindsided, however, when he did turn the corner to find who Molly was praising with so much enthusiasm. Sophie Jacobs, wearing a cute beanie with pompom ears, was standing in front of her on her crutches and, for a split second, Hugh's head was full of the image of Molly and her dog dancing for the little girl and every cell in his body was trying to remind him of how attracted he'd been to her.

He knew he would remember the physical connection they'd discovered for the rest of his life. That he was almost certainly never going to experience anything quite like that ever again.

Sophie almost looked like she was trying to dance herself, on those crutches, but then Hugh realised that was demonstrating the range of movement she had now that she was free of her plaster cast.

'And I can do it sideways, Molly...look... I can play a game where I can hit a ball with my foot. But sometimes I just lie on a mat on the floor when I do it. It's called a hip ah...ad...'

'A hip adduction,' Hugh supplied as he came up behind Molly. 'That's great, Sophie. Do you remember to keep your heel knee pointing straight up when you do that exercise on your back?'

Sophie nodded. 'And when I walk with my crutches, I have to have it pointing in front of me like it's a torch and it's shining a light for me to see where to go.'

'That's a good way to think of it.' Molly nodded. 'Did your physio give you that idea?'

'Yes. His name's Tom and he's really nice. I'm going to physio almost every day now that I've got my brace and we're going to go swimming soon when my scars are properly joined up.'

'When did you get the cast off?'

'Last week.' It was Hugh who responded. 'I saw Sophie in Outpatients that day.' He looked around. 'Where's Mummy?'

'She went to get a coffee. Molly said I could stay with her until she gets back. We're going to see somebody else after that. The man who's making my new leg that will be like the one the dancing girl has.'

'Your prosthesis?'

'Yes... I can't say that word.' But Sophie's smile was stretching from ear to ear. 'I can't wait...it feels like Christmas...'

Hugh found his own smile was feeling oddly wobbly

and he knew that Molly was watching him. He could feel the touch of her gaze on his face but it felt as if she could see way deeper than that—as if she could see how much this child's happiness was touching his heart.

'I'd better go,' he said briskly. 'I've got a patient to see who had a big operation on his back a couple of days ago.'

'Michael's looking forward to seeing you,' Molly told him. 'He wants to ask you about when he can go home. He's been in and out of bed three times already today.'

Hugh stepped towards the desk to ask for Michael's notes.

'Want to see some more of my exercises, Molly?'

'I sure do. I might even see you in the gym this week. I take Oreo in to help children with their exercises sometimes and her friend Milo is going to start soon, too.'

'Have you got *two* dogs?'

Hugh had to wait for the ward clerk, Debbie, to find Michael's notes so there was no distraction from Sophie's excited question that was an echo of one that Hugh had asked himself that day he'd found Molly in Outpatients with both Oreo and Milo and he'd been persuaded to help with training the younger dog.

'I do,' Molly told Sophie. 'Let me show you a photo of him. He's really fluffy and he's got lot of spots.'

Hugh could see her scrolling for photos on her phone. 'Here we go… This was when Milo and Oreo were at the beach last night. They found a stick they both wanted so they decided to share and, look…they're each holding one end of it…'

'Aww… They're so *cute*…' Sophie sighed.

'I'm so proud of them,' Molly said. 'They're my fur kids.'

'Best kind to have.' Debbie grinned as she handed Michael's notes to Hugh.

'Absolutely,' Molly agreed. 'The only kind *I* really need.'

There was something in Molly's voice that made Hugh look up from where he'd flicked the notes open. She didn't look up from her phone as she kept scrolling. 'Let me find some of my mum's puppies to show you, Sophie.'

'I want a puppy,' Sophie said. 'Do you have a dog at home, Mr Ashcroft?'

'No.' Hugh closed the patient file and took a deep breath. He was still trying to identify what it was in Molly's tone that had sounded like...

What...? A warning bell...?

She needed to know, didn't she? That he couldn't give her what was going to make her happy.

Ever.

This might be the perfect opportunity to let Molly know that. Before it went any further and someone—i.e. *Molly*—got hurt. And perhaps he could do it in a way that would make it her choice as well as his own to avoid spending any more time together out of work hours.

Sophie was making it easy.

'Why not?' she asked. 'Why don't you like dogs?'

'I do like dogs,' he told her. 'But only when they're someone else's. I just don't want to live with any. I spend way too much time at work so it wouldn't be fair on them, would it?'

'But...'

Sophie's eyes were wide. She couldn't understand.

Molly could. Hugh could sense that by the way she had become so still. Pretending to be so focussed on her phone but he could tell she wasn't looking at anything in particular. She was simply avoiding looking at him.

She probably needed some time to let his words sink in and Hugh was only too happy to provide it. He walked away without a backward glance.

Maybe he needed a bit of time, too.

CHAPTER ELEVEN

A DEALBREAKER.

There was no getting past that.

It didn't matter how much in love with Hugh she was. Being prepared to forgo having her own children didn't make enough of a difference, either.

Molly simply couldn't imagine not having dogs in her life. *And* in her home.

Which meant that there was no future for her and Hugh Ashcroft.

Maybe they could be friends. Eventually. They might even laugh about it over a wine or two at some staff function in a distant future.

'I had such a crush on you back in the day, Hugh...'

'Did you? You must have known it could never have worked.'

'Yeah...we both dodged a bullet, didn't we?'

'Well... I wouldn't say that, exactly, but look at you... Happily married and with those gorgeous kids of yours— and all those dogs!'

'And look at you, Hugh. Still alone...'

'Just the way I like it. Cheers, Molly...'

Molly's breath was expelled in something that sounded like a growl. Flights of conversational imagination weren't ever going to help. If anything, they had contributed to how difficult it had been for Molly to deal with the aftermath of what had felt like a significant break-up. Which was ridiculous, really. How could she have allowed herself to get in that deep when it hadn't even been a real relationship?

Except, it had been, hadn't it?

On her side, at least.

There was nothing fake about how she'd fallen in love with Hugh.

And something told her that, even if he hadn't realised it, the attraction on Hugh's side had to have been more than purely a physical thing.

They'd connected on a level on which she just knew Hugh had never connected with anyone else.

He'd told her about his sister.

About Fudge.

They'd made love.

There hadn't been any distance at all between them that night. Every touch had been as full of an emotional connection as much as anything physical. But now, the distance between herself and Hugh felt even further than it had been the first time she'd met the aloof surgeon in the radiology procedure room. Because of how close they'd been that night, the barrier between them felt...

...impenetrable, that was what it was.

Not that the solidity of that barrier mattered when neither of them were going to make any attempt to break through it because there was no point. For both of them, what lay on the other side was not something they wanted in their future and there was no compromise that could make it work.

Molly hadn't been pushed to cross that bridge to walk—
yet again—into her future alone. She had chosen to cross
it because she realised that the road she'd been on with
Hugh had been a dead end all along.

And she was going to be okay.

She'd spent as much time as she could playing with
Bella's adorable litter of pups in the few weeks since then
and she'd poured hours into stepping up Milo's training
as he settled in to living with her and Oreo in the beach
cottage. They all spent time walking in the hills or on the
beach every day but, while there were more and more
surfers there when there were some decent waves, Hugh
had clearly crossed Taylors Mistake off his list of preferred beaches.

Milo was living up to his promise to become a valuable
assistance dog and would graduate to being in work rather
than training on his visits to the hospital, but it was Oreo
who was by her side when Molly headed for the ground
floor of a wing of Christchurch Children's Hospital that
was becoming one of their regular destinations.

The state-of-the-art physiotherapy department included
a full-sized indoor basketball court suitable for wheelchair rugby to be played and a gymnasium crowded with
exercise equipment and soft mats, walking tracks with
rails on either side and even a small staircase. It also had
a twenty-five-metre heated swimming pool with hoists
and waterproof equipment that could cater for any level of
disability. Community groups and staff members had access to some of the facilities, like the basketball court and
pool, outside normal hours but Molly and Oreo weren't
here today to take advantage of that privilege.

They were here to be a part of Sophie's first session of

learning to walk with the custom-made prosthesis that she'd been anticipating with such excitement because it would represent a big step on her long journey back to being able to dance. Oreo took no notice of the children in wheelchairs and on beds who were working around the edges of the gymnasium. She was heading straight towards the small girl sitting at one end of a walking track with a small cluster of people around her.

'Hey, Sophie...'

'*Oreo...*'

Sophie's mum stepped to one side to allow Oreo to get close to Sophie's wheelchair to say hullo. Her smile was apologetic.

'We're happy to see you too, Molly—not just Oreo.'

'I'm happy that I'm allowed to be here *with* Oreo,' Molly responded. 'How exciting is this?'

Tom, the physiotherapist, was helping one of the technicians from the prosthetic department to encourage Sophie to push her foot into the first version of the artificial lower leg that would enable her to walk without needing her crutches.

That would, hopefully one day, enable her to dance again.

Sophie's face was scrunched into lines of deep uncertainty, though. Disappointment, even?

'It feels...weird...'

'It'll take a bit of getting used to.' Tom nodded. 'This is just a try on to see how it fits. And it's just your training leg so it doesn't have the brace that will fit around the top of your leg.'

Sophie's head bent further as she stared down at the leg.

'Her hair...' Molly whispered to Joanne. 'Look at those gorgeous curls coming through.'

'I know.' Sophie's mum had tears in her eyes but she was smiling. 'It's like her baby hair used to be. So soft...'

Sophie lifted her head and she was smiling now, too. 'My new foot's got a shoe the same as my other leg.'

'Of course,' Tom said. 'You can always do that with your shoes.'

'Even ballet shoes?'

'Even ballet shoes,' Tom agreed. 'Like in that picture you showed me. Now...let's see if you can stand up, sweetie.'

Sophie looked suddenly fearful but, with a determination that brought tears to Molly's eyes as well as Joanne's, she let herself be helped up to stand on her normal foot and then, very tentatively, put some weight onto the artificial foot. Then she let go of Tom's hands and held onto the rails of the walking track instead.

'Do you feel ready to take a step?' Tom asked.

Sophie shook her head. Her bottom lip wobbled.

Molly quietly signalled Oreo, who moved to where she pointed, going under the rail to sit on the track a short distance from Sophie.

'Do you want to give Oreo a treat?' Molly asked.

Sophie nodded.

Molly took a tiny piece of dried beef from the pouch on her belt. She put it on top of the rail just out of reach for Sophie.

'Oreo really wants that treat,' she said. 'But she's not allowed to have it unless you give it to her. One step will just about get you there.'

Sophie stared at the treat. Then she looked at Oreo, who

had her mouth open and her tongue hanging out and her ears down. She was smiling at Sophie. Encouraging her.

And everybody held their breath as she moved her prosthetic leg in front of her, put some of her weight onto it and then moved her other leg. She could stretch out her hand now and pick up the treat.

'It's for you, Oreo,' she said proudly. 'You're a good girl...'

'Take it nicely,' Molly reminded her dog. Not because Oreo needed reminding but because she needed to take a breath and say something so that she didn't end up with tears rolling down her face at the joy of seeing Sophie— quite literally—taking her first step into a new future.

Giving up her free time to do something like this was no hardship.

It was, in fact, inspirational and Molly knew she could channel this little girl's determination and courage to move on with her own life. She would get over missing seeing him at the beach or remembering what it had been like to have him touch her. She would learn to respect his boundaries and have no more than a polite friendship at work. There was no point in continuing to feel grief of losing what could have been with Hugh Ashcroft because it had never really been there in the first place, had it?

It took two people to want a future with each other.

Maybe her imaginary conversation with Hugh hadn't been that far off base, either. It wasn't beyond belief that she could still meet someone who would want to share her life and her dreams of a family of her own—dogs included—but, if that didn't happen, it was up to her to make sure her life was as full of joy as possible.

And, with moments like this in it, how could it not be?

* * *

Despite the fact that the physiotherapy department became like a second home for many of his patients during their rehabilitation, there was no need for Hugh Ashcroft to go into that wing of this hospital. He was very familiar with what went on in the department and he could follow up the progress his patients were making after their orthopaedic surgery by reading reports written by the physiotherapists or speaking to these experts when they attended team meetings in the ward. What was most satisfying, however, was simply observing the changes in his patients for himself during their follow up outpatient appointments.

He had to smile when he saw the way Michael was walking into the consulting room, only weeks after his spinal fusion to correct the scoliosis. Even better, the teenager had a grin that was shy but still enough to light up his face.

'Look at you,' Hugh said as he got to his feet. 'I don't think I need to ask how you're doing.'

Michael's mother looked just as happy. 'He's taller than I am now.'

Hugh clipped the X-ray films to the light boxes on the wall. 'Everything's healing very well. Look, you can see how straight things are now and where the fusion is happening between the discs in your spine. Let's get your shirt off and get you on the bed so I can have a good look at your back.'

His examination was thorough but he stopped towards the end when Michael winced.

'Does that hurt?'

'A bit.'

'Your body is having to adjust to the change in the position of your ribs. You'll find there are bits that hurt, like here in your shoulder, that didn't used to be a problem. It'll get better. Is the paracetamol enough for pain relief now?'

'Yes.'

Hugh scribbled in Michael's notes as he got dressed again and then came to sit in front of the desk with his mother beside him. 'How has the gentle exercise programme they gave you been going at home?'

'Okay.' Michael nodded.

'He gets frustrated at how tired he gets,' his mother added.

'Don't forget you've had a big surgery,' Hugh told him. 'It can take longer than you expect to recover from a general anaesthetic and blood loss. There's a lot going on in that body of yours that isn't just adjusting to a new shape—like the healing around the implants that you can see on the X-rays. That sucks up some of your energy. There are things you can't see, as well. It's a lot more work for the muscles in your trunk to be holding up a spine that's suddenly straighter and longer and that takes more energy than it used to. It's really important to pace yourself and rest as often as you need to. Full recovery can take anywhere from six to twelve months.'

'Can I start driving lessons during the summer holidays? My uncle said he'd start teaching me on his farm when I'm there for a holiday.'

'I'll leave it up to your physios to decide when you're good to do something like that but I'm happy to sign you off to start physiotherapy sessions in the department here. They've got a hot swimming pool you're going to love and you'll get some one-on-one sessions in the gym as well.'

'Cool,' Michael said. 'I like swimming. Can I stop wearing my brace now, too?'

'Not just yet. I'll have a meeting with your physios before your next outpatient appointment and we'll talk about that then, okay?' He turned to Michael's mother. 'Have you got any questions or worries about how everything's going?'

She shook her head. 'That nurse practitioner in the ward has been so great. You know Molly?'

Hugh gave a single nod of agreement. He dropped his gaze to Michael's notes again so that he could hide the way it made him feel when he heard Molly's name.

Uncomfortable, that was what it was.

As if he'd done something wrong. Or stupid. Something that he should apologise for?

Something that he had the disturbing feeling that he might regret for the rest of his life?

He had pushed her away. They were simply colleagues now. He'd made sure they didn't meet by chance out of work hours. He'd even gone as far as not going surfing. Anywhere…

Because thinking about going surfing made him think about Taylors Mistake beach and that made him think about Molly.

'She called us every day when we were first at home.' The list of things that Molly had helped with felt like a muted background to Hugh's thoughts but he nodded occasionally, to make it look like he was listening. 'And if Mike ends up being a helicopter pilot it'll be Molly's fault.'

Oh…now he could see her in the ward on the day that Michael had been admitted. Taking the time to ease his fears and to make him feel special by telling him she'd saved the best bed for him where he'd be entertained by watching the helicopters come and go.

It was only a tiny example of how kind a person Molly Holmes was.

She'd made Hugh feel special too. As if he'd met the only person in the world who could understand what he'd gone through when he'd lost both his sister and his dog.

She had really cared about him and he'd pushed her away.

Yeah...he needed to apologise...

Hugh pasted a smile on his face. 'Is that what you want to do, Michael?'

'It was pretty cool, watching them taking off and landing on the roof,' he admitted. 'And I love flying...'

'I'll tell Molly she's inspired you,' Hugh said. 'I'm sure she'll think that's a brilliant plan.'

They weren't just empty words, he decided, as he gave Michael and his mother directions to get to the physiotherapy department and make their first appointments.

He would tell Molly at the first opportunity he got. It might even provide an opportunity for that apology that he needed to make.

Molly was later than she'd intended to be leaving the physiotherapy department after sharing Sophie's first walk with her prosthesis because she'd bumped into Michael and his mum and they'd had a chat.

She was in a bit of a rush, now, to get Oreo back to the van in the hospital car park and head home. Molly needed to pick Milo up from her mother's, take some time to admire Bella's puppies and play with them, of course, and she was hoping to still have enough daylight for a walk on the beach. She had her head down, sending a text to her mother to let her know she was finally on her way, when Molly thought she heard her name being called.

She hadn't imagined it because Oreo had suddenly gone on high alert with her ears pricked and every muscle primed for action.

And there it was again, coming from behind her. *'Molly...'*

Two things happened in a tiny space of time as Molly swung her head to see Hugh coming towards her, framed by the backdrop of the hospital's main entrance.

Oreo—very uncharacteristically—did a U turn and took off, bounding towards Hugh as if he was a long-lost friend she couldn't wait to reconnect with.

And a car came racing along the stretch of road that led to both the car park entrance and the emergency department of Christchurch Children's Hospital.

Hugh's voice was much louder this time. 'Oreo...*no*...!'

Like it did in the movies, sometimes, everything became slow-mo and, to her horror, Molly could see it happen in excruciating clarity. Oreo had her focus so completely on Hugh she was unaware of the vehicle speeding towards her. A split second either way and it probably wouldn't have happened.

But it did.

Oreo ran in front of the car. She got hit square on her side and knocked flat. Even worse, the car went over the top of her and for another split second she vanished. Then she rolled out from beneath the back of the car as the driver slammed on the brakes.

And she wasn't moving.

At all.

* * *

The car screeched to a halt and the driver was starting to climb out of the car as Molly ran towards Oreo.

'Oh…my God…' The man was halfway out of the driver's seat, clearly distressed. 'I didn't see her… I've got my son in the car and he's having a bad asthma attack…'

Hugh arrived at the same time Molly did.

'*Go…*' he told the man. 'Get your son into the emergency department.'

The man drove off, his car door still swinging half open.

Molly sank to her knees. Oreo's eyes were only half open and she couldn't tell how well her beloved dog was breathing. She could see injuries that made her feel sick to her stomach. An open fracture to her front leg with bone visible. Missing skin and bleeding on her flank. A lot of bleeding. Molly's vision was blurring with tears and her breath felt stuck in her chest beneath an enormous weight.

Hugh had one hand on the wound. He put his other hand on Oreo's chest. 'She's breathing,' he told Molly. 'Her heart rate's strong but rapid—maybe two hundred beats per minute. We need to get her to a vet. *Stat…*'

We…?

Molly blinked to clear the tears in her eyes. She could feel them rolling down her face as she looked up to meet Hugh's gaze. She wasn't alone in what felt like the worst moment of her life.

For just a heartbeat—a nanosecond—Molly remembered being on the beach that evening when everything had changed. When she'd known Hugh was confronted with memories of the worst moments of *his* life, when he'd lost everything that mattered the most to him. She remembered the silent message she'd tried so hard to send him.

You don't have to do this alone. I'm here...and... I love you...

It felt as if she was the one receiving that same message right now and it was cutting through her fear and shock.

'I need to keep pressure on this wound and stop any more blood loss,' Hugh said. 'Do you know if there's a vet clinic near here?'

'Yes...there's a big one only a few minutes' drive away.'

'Can you go and get your van?'

Hugh still hadn't broken that eye contact and it was giving Molly a strength she wouldn't have believed she had.

'*Yes...*'

'Hurry...'

Molly ran. She was out of breath and her hands were shaking so it took two attempts to get the key into the lock and open the driver's door. It took less than another minute to drive down the hospital's entranceway to where a small crowd had now gathered around Hugh and Oreo. Someone had supplied a dressing and bandages—maybe from ED—and it looked as if the bleeding was under control. Oreo was panting but her eyes were closed as if her level of consciousness was dropping and Molly had a moment of absolute clarity as she opened the back door of the van and Hugh gently picked Oreo up to put her on the soft blanket on the floor.

There was no way she could let Hugh come with her to the vet clinic.

No way she could put him through possibly having to witness Oreo being euthanised because her injuries were too severe to survive with any quality of life.

She loved him too much to put him through something he'd spent most of his life trying to escape.

'We'll be okay now,' she told Hugh. 'You don't need to come with us.'

'Are you sure?'

She loved that he looked so torn. That he was prepared to go through this for her sake. But she could see the flash of relief in his eyes when she gave a single but decisive nod of her head.

'I'm sure.'

Hugh stood where he was, watching the little green van speed off.

The crowd was beginning to disperse. A couple of people helpfully picked up the wrappers from the bandages and dressings he'd used to keep the worst of Oreo's wounds covered and under pressure to help stop the blood loss. He could hear the shocked tone of the things they were saying to each other but it sounded as if it were muted. That someone else was listening to it or it was a part of a dream. A nightmare.

'I know his kid was sick but he shouldn't have been going so fast.'

'His kid was sick. He wouldn't have been thinking about anything else.'

'And why was that dog here, anyway?'

'It had a coat on. Maybe it was a guide dog.'

'Its owner wasn't blind. She was driving a van!'

'I hope that kid's okay...'

'I hope the dog's okay...'

Hugh could have added to that conversation to echo those comments and say that *he* hoped Molly was okay.

But he didn't want to share his feelings with strangers.

He didn't want to think about them, either. Maybe if he made himself move he could somehow wake up from this daytime nightmare.

For some reason Hugh turned to walk back into the hospital rather than continuing towards the car park. Because he couldn't imagine going home to stare at the walls of his apartment and think about what had just happened? Or maybe it was because he needed the comfort zone of being at work rather than in a personal space?

He got as far as the stairs he could take to get up to the level of his ward and his office but he didn't push the firestop door open. He pressed the button to summon a lift, instead, but he wasn't thinking about what he was doing or why he was doing it. His head was full of something else.

The knowledge that Molly couldn't possibly be anything like okay.

She *loved* Oreo. Adored her, even. She was able to love fiercely and without reservation and she could give everything she had—heart and soul—to the things she loved that much.

He'd been like that, once.

He'd loved Michelle like that.

And his mother.

And Fudge.

Before he knew just how destructive it could be to have your heart shattered in an instant. Or chipped away at slowly so that it felt like it was bleeding to death, the way it had when his mother had become lost for ever in the depths of her grief and depression.

But Molly knew how hard it was to lose someone or

something you loved that much and yet she was still prepared to do it again. She had no hesitation in throwing herself into everything she chose to love in her life. To her family. To her dogs—her fur kids...

He could hear an echo of her voice.

It's unbearably hard to lose dogs...but, for me, it would be even harder to live without them...

She was that passionate about her job, as well. To those children she gave so much to in and out of her normal working hours, like she had when little Sam Finch was dying.

Maybe she would love *him* that much, if he ever let her get close enough. Or maybe she would have but he'd destroyed that possibility by pushing her away so decisively.

The ding announced the arrival of the lift. The doors opened and people got out. And then the doors closed again but Hugh hadn't stepped inside.

He was thinking about Sam again.

About how he'd known Molly wouldn't be okay and how he'd had that urge to go and find her. Not to tell her that she should have heeded his warning about the dangers of getting so involved.

He'd gone because he'd needed to see her.

To make sure she wasn't alone because...

...because he needed to *be* there with her.

And he finally knew why. It was because he *loved* her. As much as he'd ever loved anything in his entire life.

Hugh turned away from the lift. He was scrolling his phone to find the address of the closest veterinary hospitals.

He was running by the time he reached the car park.
He knew exactly where he was going now.
Where he needed to be.

CHAPTER TWELVE

THERE WAS NOTHING more Molly could do.

Staff from the veterinary hospital had rushed into the car park as soon as Molly stumbled through the doors, begging for help. They had carried Oreo into one of the clinic's treatment rooms and they were doing everything they could to help the badly injured dog.

It could have been a trauma team in the emergency department of Christchurch Children's Hospital working on a child who'd been rushed in by ambulance after being hit by a car, Molly thought as she listened to them going through a primary survey. It felt like she was watching from a huge distance even though she could almost have reached out and touched Oreo.

'Is her airway open?'

'Yes.'

'Is she breathing?'

'Tachypnoeic. Breath sounds reduced on the left side. Potential pneumothorax. Feels like at least one rib's fractured.'

'What's her heart rate?'

'Two hundred. Gums are pale. She's in shock.'

'Let's get an IV line in, please, and fluids up. Forty mils per kilo over the next fifteen minutes or so.'

'What's her weight?'

'I'd guess around twenty kilos.'

Molly knew it was eighteen kilos but the vet's guess was close enough. She couldn't make her lips work in time because they, along with the rest of her body, felt completely numb. Things were happening too fast and this was simply too huge. These strangers were fighting for Oreo's *life*…

'I think we should intubate and ventilate. Her oxygen saturation's dropping.'

'Is that external bleeding under control?'

'As soon as we've got her airway secured, we need to set up for X-rays. I want an abdominal ultrasound, too, thanks. We can't exclude major internal bleeding from a rupture with that mechanism of injury…'

They knew what they were doing, this team, as they worked swiftly and effectively to get Oreo's airway and breathing secured and fluids up to maintain her circulation and blood pressure. They started antibiotics, took X-rays of the fracture in her front leg and cleaned and dressed the wound on her flank. The ultrasound showed some free fluid that could be internal bleeding but, as the head vet explained, they wouldn't know the extent of all the damage until they got her into Theatre.

Oreo was heavily sedated and dosed with pain killers so she probably wasn't even aware of where she was or what was happening but Molly had to press her lips to the silky hair on her head and whisper something only her dog could hear before they took her away to Theatre. She had signed a consent form that included a statement to the effect that if it was clear that the likelihood of Oreo surviving or that her quality of life would be unacceptably diminished, they would not wake her up again.

A nurse took her back out to the waiting room. She touched Molly's arm and her expression couldn't have been more sympathetic.

'Is there someone I can call for you?'

Molly shook her head. She could have called for her mum or her brother or a friend to come and stay with her while she waited for the call that would tell her whether Oreo was still alive but she couldn't do it.

Not simply because she was still feeling so frozen.

She knew she would need all the comfort and understanding that her family could give her soon but, right now, there was only one person who would be able to hold her hand on a level that was so much deeper than merely physical.

Only one person who could touch her soul in a way that would give her the strength to get through anything.

Even this…

But she had pushed him away. She'd put up the same kind of barrier he'd put in place himself not so long ago. Except that she'd done it for very different reasons, hadn't she? She'd wanted to protect him from pain because she loved him *that* much.

He'd put the barriers up to protect himself…

Was that why Molly felt so utterly alone?

So…*lost*…?

'You could wait here but it could be hours,' the nurse said. 'We've got your number. I'll call you as soon as we know anything. It might help to be somewhere else. Or to go for a walk or something?'

But Molly shook her head again. She didn't want to leave.

But she didn't want to stay, either.

She had absolutely no idea what she wanted, to be honest.

Until she heard the doors sliding open behind her and heard a voice that filled the air around her and she could breathe it in and feel it settle close to her heart.

'I'll look after her,' Hugh told the nurse.

And then he folded Molly into his arms and she pressed her head into the hollow beneath his shoulder. She could feel the steady beat of his heart beneath her cheek.

'I've got you, sweetheart,' he murmured against her ear. 'I'm not going to let you go…'

There was a river that meandered along the foothills on the south side of the city and it had wide enough borders to provide walking tracks, picnic tables, children's playgrounds and lots of benches for people to sit and enjoy the kind of serenity that moving water and the green space of trees and grass could bestow.

Hugh would have preferred to take Molly to a beach to watch and listen to the waves rolling in but he knew she would hate to be taken too far away from where Oreo was fighting for her life. Luckily, like Christchurch Children's Hospital—a mile or two downstream—this veterinary hospital was just across the road from the river so Hugh led Molly across a small, pedestrian bridge to where there was a bench on the riverbank—a two-minute walk at most from the front doors of the veterinary hospital and he'd told the nurse where they would be. That way they could come and find Molly to give her any news, rather than making a more impersonal phone call.

For the longest time, they simply sat side by side.

In silence.

There were ducks on the river who were diving to catch their dinner and then popping up again to bob on the surface like bath toys. People walked past, some walking their dogs, but they were too far away to intrude.

It was Molly who broke the silence.

'Thank you...' she said softly. 'For coming.'

'I had to,' Hugh said.

'No...' Molly shook her head. 'You didn't *have* to.' But her sideways glance was anxious. 'I hope you don't think what happened was your fault. I should have had Oreo on her lead. She's never run off like that before.'

'It was because I called you.'

'No...' Molly shook her head again but this time there was a poignant smile playing around her lips. 'It was because she loves you. She's been missing you.'

Hugh swallowed hard. 'I've been missing her. And you.'

Molly was staring at the ducks on the river again. 'Same...'

Hugh reached for Molly's hand and she let her fingers lace through his and be held. Silence fell again and he knew they were both thinking about what was going on in the operating room of the veterinary hospital across the river. About how much Oreo would be missed if she didn't make it through this surgery. This waiting period was more than anxiety. It felt like a practice run for grief.

'You told me once that grief is love that has nowhere to go,' he said softly. 'I know how overwhelming your love for Oreo is right now. I can *feel* it.'

Molly's voice had cracks in it. 'But you're so good at *not* feeling things like that. At protecting yourself.'

'I used to be,' he agreed quietly. 'And, if it ever got hard, all I needed to do was remind myself that grief can kill you, like it killed my mother. It didn't matter that I was there and I loved her. She just took herself somewhere else and never came back. She died of a broken heart but she never told me how bad it was.'

'Maybe she was trying to protect you,' Molly suggested. 'By shutting you away from her pain?'

'I didn't want to be shut away,' Hugh said. 'I wanted to help.'

'I know. I'm sorry...'

Hugh had to pull in a slow breath. 'I'm sorry, too...' he said.

'For Oreo?'

'Of course. But for more than that, too. For the way I've been shutting *you* away.'

'I pushed you,' Molly admitted. 'I pushed my way into things that you wanted to keep private. I said things I shouldn't about you being selfish when you were only doing what you needed to do to protect yourself.'

'When I was coming to find you, I found myself remembering the day that Shelly died,' Hugh said quietly. 'Mostly, the way that Fudge refused to get off her bed. The look in his eyes that told me he knew what was happening and, no matter how hard it was, he didn't want to be anywhere else.'

Molly nodded. And brushed away a tear that rolled down her cheek.

Hugh squeezed her hand that he was still holding.

'I remembered you saying how hard it was to lose a dog but that it was even harder to live without them. That dogs have the ability to supply limitless, unconditional love.'

She nodded again. 'They do...'

'I think you do, too.' Hugh had to swallow past the lump in his throat. 'I never wanted to become dependent on any kind of love again after losing everything I cared the most about. I didn't think that I could even get close to feeling like it could even exist for me again.'

He could feel an odd prickling sensation at the back of his eyes.

'Until I met you,' he added.

He could feel Molly's fingers tightening around his own. Looking up, he found her gaze fixed on his face.

'Until I realised that you could not only understand the kind of grief I went through with Shelly—and Fudge— but that you were still brave enough to get in there and do it all again. And...and I think that maybe you're right. That it is harder to live without that kind of love in your life. Emptier, anyway...'

'I think of love as being a kind of coin,' Molly said. 'There's lots of different kinds—or values, I guess, like real coins. There are the ones for friends and siblings and others for, say, your mum or a child. And dogs, of course. And really special ones if you're lucky enough to find your soul mate.'

She paused to take a breath but Hugh didn't say anything. He knew she hadn't finished yet.

'They have two sides, too, like real coins,' Molly added. 'There's love on one side but there's grief on the other side and if it gets dropped and spins you don't know what side it's going to land on. And yeah...there are some coins you don't have a choice to hold, like your family, but there are others where you get the choice of whether or not you pick them up and it's safer not to, because some of them are the wrong coins and some of them might lead to heartbreak again, but if you don't pick them up, you'll never know the joy it can bring if you've found the one you were always meant to find—or were lucky enough to be given.' She offered him a smile. 'Like your Fudge coin?'

'I remember.' Hugh nodded. 'The joy I felt when I came home from school and Fudge would be there, lying just inside the gate, his ball between his paws. Waiting…just for me. And how it felt when he sat on the back step with me late at night sometimes and I could put my arms around him and hide my face in his hair while I cried…'

Oh, *God*… He was crying now. For the first time since the day his sister had died, he knew he was crying.

Okay…maybe he had been crying that day in the surf when he'd made the decision that he had to stay away from Molly—and Oreo—because he couldn't risk loving them and he wasn't going to risk hurting them. But it had been easy to think it was sea water.

This time, there was no hiding the fact that his walls had completely crumbled.

'I get that feeling with you,' he whispered. 'Only it's even bigger. I love you, Molly. And, when I touch you, I think I can feel a kind of love that's so big it's…well, it's a bit terrifying, that's what it is.'

Molly let go of his hand but only so that she could reach up and brush away the tears on Hugh's cheeks.

'You can feel it because it's there,' she said, softly. 'I do love you, Hugh. *So* much. I fell in love with you ages ago. Right about the time I heard about your sister and I knew there was a reason why you had walls up to stop anyone getting close to you.'

'My walls don't seem to be working any longer.' Hugh was blinking his tears back. 'I've tried to stay away from you and it's not working.' A corner of his mouth lifted. 'Do you really love me, Molly?'

'More than I can say.'

She still had her hand on his cheek as she lifted her chin and Hugh bent his head and their kiss was as tender as it was possible for any kiss to be. And then Molly pulled back.

'When they took Oreo into Theatre, the nurse asked me if she could call someone to be with me while I waited and I said "no" because there was only one person I wanted to be with me and I didn't want to call you. I couldn't ask you to do something this hard...for *me*...'

'I will always be with you,' Hugh said. 'Today and tomorrow and for ever. No matter how hard it is, I will always be here and I will always love you.'

'Oh...' Molly was going to cry again. She tried to smile instead. 'That sounds like it could be a wedding vow.'

'Maybe I'd better write it down.' Hugh was smiling, too. 'Just in case we need it one of these days.'

They hadn't noticed the figure coming across the bridge until the nurse from the veterinary hospital was close enough to clear her throat and warn them of her approach.

Molly's heart stopped. She felt Hugh's hand close around hers and then she felt a painful thump of her heart starting again. But she still couldn't breathe. Even though the nurse was smiling.

'Oreo's okay,' she said. 'She's come through the surgery like a champion and she hasn't lost her leg. We're going to keep her well sedated and in intensive care for a while but do you want to come and see her for a minute or two?'

Molly was already on her feet.

So was Hugh.

And his hand was still holding hers as if he had no intention of letting it go.

Ever...

'We do,' was all he said.

It was all he needed to say. Because that one tiny word said it all.

We...

Molly was never going to be alone again. She had found her soul mate.

EPILOGUE

Three years later...

'WHY DOES YOUR dog walk funny?'

'A long time ago, she had to have a big operation on her leg.'

'Like I'm going to have?'

'Just like you're going to have, darling.'

'But she got better?'

'Yes, she did.'

'Does it still hurt her? Is that why she holds her paw up like that?'

'Do you want to know a secret?'

The small boy lying on the bed nodded. He was reaching out to touch Oreo's nose and wasn't taking any notice of the anaesthetist who was getting ready to inject the sedative needed for this procedure.

'I think when Oreo was getting better from her operation she learned that if people thought she had a sore paw, she would get lots of cuddles.'

The child's eyes were drifting shut. 'I like cuddles...' he murmured.

His mother leaned closer to squeeze her son, but she was smiling at Molly. 'Thank you,' she whispered.

'You're so welcome.'

'It can't be easy making the time to do this when you've got a little one of your own to look after.'

Molly adjusted the warm, sleeping bundle that was her newborn daughter, tied close to her body in its comfortable sling. 'Oh, it's easy at this stage. It's when they get mobile that it gets harder. That's why I've got our toddler in the great crèche we have here. I'm so happy that I get to use that even when I'm on maternity leave.'

An ultrasound technician had manoeuvred her equipment into place and a nurse was ready with all the instruments and other materials that would be needed, including the jars to hold the fragments of bone tissue about to be collected. Molly moved Oreo away from the table as the surgeon who was about to do the bone biopsy moved towards the table. She knew he was smiling at his patient's mother by the way his eyes crinkled over the top of his mask.

'How are you feeling, Sue?'

'Okay. You were right—it's been so much easier having Molly and Oreo in here with us. I had no idea that dogs would be allowed somewhere like this.'

'Not only allowed. We encourage it.' Hugh was smiling at Molly as she prepared to slip out of the room. A heartbeat of time that was too relaxed and warm to be entirely professional. A beat of eye contact that was even more personal. 'We all love Molly and Oreo.'

Molly paused for a moment as the room's lights were dimmed enough to make the ultrasound images on the screen clearer and Hugh shifted his focus entirely onto the procedure he was about to perform.

She just wanted to let her gaze rest on her husband for

a moment longer. To feel the sheer joy that this man was sharing every bit of this amazing life they were building together. That, so often, there was something extra special to be celebrated in the private moments they had together when their two adorable daughters were finally both asleep at the same time and Oreo and Milo just as content.

Like they had last week when Hugh had told her about his outpatient appointment with Michael, who'd come to ask him to contribute to the medical assessment he needed to gain the Class Two certificate that was a necessary part of the process of qualifying for his private pilot's licence. His parents had given him the first hours of his dual instruction in flying as his seventeenth birthday gift and, apparently, they were planning to invite Molly to his graduation ceremony.

And this afternoon, when Molly had gone to visit her ward before Oreo was scheduled to be the dogtor for this bone biopsy, she'd been lucky enough to catch a visit from Sophie Jacobs, who had been on her way to an appointment in the prosthetic department. The now cancer-free ten-year-old, who still had a smile that looked like it was Christmas, had wanted to show off the diploma she'd just received for passing her Grade Two ballet examination.

Molly couldn't wait to share that news with Hugh this evening.

No…actually, it wouldn't matter if she didn't have something interesting or exciting to share with him.

She would be just as happy to simply *be* with him.

Today, tomorrow and…for ever.

* * * * *

HER SUMMER WITH
THE BROODING VET

SCARLET WILSON

MILLS & BOON

To all the dog lovers in the world.

For my own red Lab, Max, and his partner in crime,
our Beagle, Murphy.

Best dogs in the world.

PROLOGUE

ELI TRIED TO hold his anger at bay. 'Is that it, then?' he asked his advisers in the room.

His accountant licked his lips, and his solicitor took a breath.

'You have to declare bankruptcy. There's no other option at this point.'

Eli let out the air that had built in his lungs. If it were possible, every cell in his body was exploding right now with pent-up frustration, despair, rage, and part sorrow. All his hard work. All his devotion to opening his own practice and making it a success had now all come to nothing. The countless hours he'd spent doing bone-aching work, concentrating, serving his community, had all been for nothing. All because of a woman.

All because he was a fool.

His solicitor cleared his throat. Eli knew what was coming, and he cringed. 'Your father's practice,' he started slowly. 'The last vet has put in his notice. There are two veterinary nurses. One has worked there for seventeen years. The other has been there eighteen months. The remaining vet is currently undergoing cancer treatment. As of next week, there will be no veterinary cover for the practice, unless you make a new arrangement with other existing practices.'

Eli sighed. He'd never wanted this. Never. His whole life, people had expected him to follow in his father's footsteps and take over once he retired. But that had never been in Eli's plans. No one had been more surprised than he was that he'd actually been bitten by the vet bug. Yes, he'd followed in his father's footsteps and trained as a vet. But from the second he'd started his training he'd made it clear he didn't want to join his father in the family practice.

It had caused many a cross word. But Eli had been determined. He'd served in some larger veterinary practices, gaining experience in small and large animals, taking jobs in the UK, the US, France and Spain. He didn't want to be indebted to his father. He wanted to build his own practice. Eli had always been fiercely independent, even as a child. And now, as a thirty-one-year-old adult, he was back in the situation he'd always sworn wasn't for him.

Would his stubbornness allow his father's practice to fold?

No. It wouldn't.

Being responsible for the demise of two practices would make him unemployable. The vet world wasn't as big as most people thought. Reputation was everything.

'Can you arrange an advert for the practice again?' he asked.

His lawyer nodded, but pulled a face. 'The last advert was out for four weeks. Only newly qualified vets applied. None that have the experience the practice needs.'

'Then maybe I'll need to have a rethink. I could have someone work alongside me for a few months. Get them up to speed. Then, by the time Matt is ready to come back he will be able to take over the supervision.' He pointed to his chest. 'This—me—is only a temporary solution. If we can't find a vet of the calibre we need, then I'll stay as long as it takes to supervise someone new. Get the advert back up.'

His lawyer nodded as Eli stood, staring out across the city. He did *so* not want to do this. But he wasn't too stubborn to see that if he chose to walk away his father's practice would fail, and the people in the surrounding area wouldn't have any care for their animals.

Animals. They always did better for him than people did.

And that was the simple reason he would do this—for the animals.

CHAPTER ONE

AURORA HENDRICKS TUGGED at the edge of her uniform as she juggled the puppy in one hand and her keys in the other. The little guy had wriggled so much her uniform had started to creep upwards, revealing a sliver of skin at her waist. Not exactly how she wanted to meet any potential new clients.

She gave the puppy a rub at the top of his head. 'Hold on, little guy. We'll get you in here and I'll check if you've got a chip. I'm sure someone is missing you very much.'

As she'd driven to work this morning, the car in front of her had swerved and screeched its horn. Aurora had caught sight of the terrified puppy darting across the road and had immediately pulled over.

Ten minutes of tramping through muddy woods, leaving a trail of treats and keeping very quiet, had allowed her to coax the very frightened little guy into her arms.

He didn't look quite so frightened now, and the mud on his paws, and her shoes, were leaving both a trail on her uniform and on the floor.

'Are you always late? And in such a state?' came the sharp voice to her side.

She turned her head sharply. Standing inside one of the rooms was a tall, lean-looking man, with light brown tousled hair, longer on top, that unshaven but trendy look, and an angry expression on his face.

'And who might you be?' she asked, equally sharply. All her senses had gone on alert. She was supposed to be opening up this morning. There shouldn't be anyone else here—and certainly not someone who was a complete stranger.

'I was about to ask you the same thing,' he responded.

She blinked and took a breath, trying to still her racing heart and stave off her fight or flight response. In her head, she was calculating how quickly she could put the puppy somewhere safely and find something to whack this guy around the head with. There was a broom in the corner. That would do.

'Since I'm the one with the keys,' she said sharply, 'and the uniform—' she looked down at her smudged pale pink tunic '—I guess I'm the one to ask questions. Since when did you think it was a good idea to break into my practice?'

She said the words, but she didn't get the vibe from the guy. He didn't look like some random thief. In fact, the more she looked at him, the more she was inclined to stare.

He was kind of handsome. In an annoying kind of way.

The one thing she definitely wasn't getting was a fear factor—which she could only presume was good. Because—due to past experience—Aurora Hendricks had developed a spider-sense when it came to danger, and men.

She placed the bedraggled puppy on the table near her and kept one hand on him as she shrugged off her wet jacket.

'So, this is *your* practice, is it?' Her head shot back up

as she contemplated letting the puppy go for a second to grab the microchip scanner in the nearby drawer. There was an amused tone in his words. It raised her hackles and irritated her.

She held the puppy with one hand and put a few treats in front of him as her other hand grabbed the scanner. 'Well, until someone else shows up it is,' she muttered. Then paused. 'What? You're not some other random locum, are you?'

A furrow creased his brow. 'What do you mean—another random locum?'

She ignored him, concentrating on scanning the puppy. She checked all the usual spots where microchips with the owner's details were usually inserted on puppies, with no success.

'Oh, dear,' she sighed, picking up the puppy and holding him close to her chest as she stroked him. 'You must be an escapee.'

The man moved forward. It was as if she'd captured his attention. 'An escapee from where?'

She gave a sorry shrug. 'One of the puppy farms. There's a few about here. If he's not chipped, they hadn't managed to sell him yet.' She held the puppy up and squinted at him. 'Or maybe he's not from the puppy farm. He doesn't look like a pure breed.'

The man gave a nod as he looked appraisingly at the puppy. 'Maybe some kind of collie cross?'

She blinked. 'You *are* a new locum, aren't you?' Then she wrinkled her nose. 'But how did you get a set of keys?'

'They're mine.'

Her nose remained wrinkled. He reached over and took the puppy from her hands. 'Let me check him over.'

She'd been too slow to keep a hold of the puppy, but her instincts around animals were strong. She put her hand over his. 'No, you don't. Not till I see some proof of who you are, and your credentials.'

He looked at her in surprise. 'So, you're not bothered about being in here with a perfect stranger, but I tell you I'm checking a stray and you want to see my credentials?'

She couldn't tell if he was angry, annoyed or a mixture of both. But she didn't care.

She looked him up and down. 'I think I could take you,' she said frankly. 'I've learned how to take care of myself over the years. But I'll fight you to the death before I let you near that puppy without checking out who you are.'

They stood in silence for a few seconds, looking at each other, like some kind of stand-off.

Then he gave a nod and gestured for her to follow him. He walked slowly out to the hall and stopped in front of a picture on the wall.

She turned to face it, even though she'd seen it and walked past it a million times. It was of the original owner, David Ferguson, with his fellow vet partner, and his son.

The man raised his eyebrows at her.

And the penny dropped.

She squinted at the picture and moved right up close to it. 'That's you?' she asked incredulously.

She didn't mean it quite the way that it came out. But the skinny-looking kid in a T-shirt and ill-fitting jeans was a million miles away from this over six-foot lean guy with light tousled hair, pretty sexy stubble and blue eyes. She looked even closer at the picture, and then back to his face again.

'You might have the same hairline,' she said finally.

He made a noise that sounded like an indignant guffaw. 'Elijah Ferguson,' he said. 'Son of the late David. I'm only here until Matt is well enough to come back to work, and we can recruit a new vet to take over.'

Aurora was still thinking things through. 'Matt mentioned that you were a vet.'

She'd actually felt instantly relieved when he'd said the name Matt. Because that meant that he knew who usually worked here. This wasn't just some elaborate ploy to break into a vet's and steal some drugs, or an abandoned puppy.

'Where are you staying?' she asked.

'In the adjoining house,' he said quickly. 'But I plan on including that in the advert for the new recruit.' He nodded upstairs. 'I can sleep in one of the rooms upstairs while I train him.'

'Or her,' she said automatically.

'Or her,' he agreed with a smile, before holding up the puppy and looking him in the eye. 'Now, do I have your permission to check this little guy over?'

'I suppose,' she said, unsurprised when he walked straight through to one of the consulting rooms behind him. It was clear he knew the layout of this place. He'd obviously spent a large part of his life here.

She accepted that he was who he claimed to be. But it still didn't explain him just turning up like this. She was an employee. Didn't she have a right to know what was going on? It seemed rude.

She watched him cautiously. Aurora might not have been a vet nurse for too long—only four years so far. But she was wise enough to know if someone was competent or not.

He sounded the puppy's chest. Checked its mouth, eyes and ears. He had a little feel of the tummy and ribs, standing the puppy upright to check its gait. Then he got out the scales and weighed the little guy.

Her hands were itching to take the puppy from him. She wanted to check it over herself. It wasn't that she didn't trust him to do his job, it was just that she didn't *know* him.

Why didn't he work here? Wouldn't it have made more sense to work alongside his father, then take over from him? Maybe he wasn't that good a vet—and his father, from what she'd heard, had exacting standards, hadn't wanted to work alongside him.

Or maybe this guy was one of those fly-by-night vets who locumed everywhere before it was discovered they just weren't that good.

All of this flew through her head as she watched him examine the puppy, as she filled the deep sink with warm water.

'He's scrawny,' came the deep voice.

'Well, that's obvious.' She could tell that from first sight, and from forty metres away.

'Heart murmur,' he added, and her heart gave a little pang.

'Severe?' Her skin had already prickled.

His eyes were still on the puppy. He shook his head. 'No. I'd want to recheck on a regular basis, but I suspect it might just disappear as he grows.'

She walked over and held out her arms. 'My turn. Let me clean him up, and then give him some food.'

'What've we got?'

She lifted the puppy, who didn't object as she gently submerged him in the few inches of warm water, lifting a soft cloth to remove the dirt and stones from his coat and paws. She named the two brands of food they currently had in the cupboard, and Grumpy vet scowled. 'Is there a deal with them?'

She was trying not to smile. 'Grumpy' vet had just automatically come into her head, rather than his actual name. She let out a sigh. 'I don't know. It's been stocked here since I arrived last year. We sell some over the counter.'

He picked up his keys, and it struck her that she hadn't seen a car out front. 'I don't like it. I'm going into the city to pick up some other supplies. I won't be long. Don't feed him until I'm back.'

Aurora gave a nod. Dog food could be an endless debate. Some practices had deals with brands to stock their food, and usually received some sort of incentive to do so. She hadn't been involved in any of this. There were websites and chat forums that dedicated hours to the nutritious content of every food on the market and the benefits of raw, dry or wet dog food. What she did know was the practice also had a freezer stocked with chicken and plain white fish—which they frequently used for sick dogs, alongside some rice, or sweet potato. If Mr Grumpy didn't get back in time, she would happily make something up for the little guy.

A few moments later she heard a car engine, and looked out to see a low bright red sports car emerge from the garage next to the house. The same car was in one of the other photographs on the wall. It must have belonged to Elijah's dad.

She finished cleaning off the puppy, before giving him a few more treats and settling him in a basket with a blanket in one of the secure stations in the main observation room. He was already half asleep; clearly his escapee adventure had been too much for him.

Aurora went upstairs and changed into a spare uniform, before coming back down, turning the sign on the door to open and checking the answering machine.

There were a few routine appointments this morning. Weight checks, nail clipping, eye drops and a skin treatment for a West Highland terrier. She also had a few test results to check from samples that Matt had taken last week before he'd had to stop working. Elijah Ferguson hadn't told her what exactly he was doing here, so she didn't want to make any assumptions.

As the first patient came in, she settled into her normal routine. Finding this practice on the outskirts of Edinburgh had been a blessing in disguise. At twenty-eight, vet nursing hadn't been Aurora's first job. She'd had stars in her eyes as a kid and gone to stage school, getting a few small TV roles, then a lead as a daughter in a new series about a family that had gone to Africa. Funnily enough, the main character in the series had been a vet, and her whole time in Africa had been spent among staff who had great respect for animals.

The series had catapulted her into stardom and onto social media, with pictures of her in clubs with friends, or shopping in London, regularly appearing in the tabloids. Soon after that, the stalking had started. It had taken her a little while to realise at first that the letters delivered to her agent, then the gifts that had mysteriously appeared at her rental, were actually a bit more sinister. As they'd moved into the second TV series, where staff changes made her uncomfortable, and had led to a member of the crew sexually assaulting her, Aurora had quickly realised she wasn't going to continue. Her colleagues had been supportive and leapt to her defence, particularly when the press called the incident a publicity stunt around #MeToo. Her return to London had coincided with the arrest of her stalker after an apparent kidnapping attempt and Aurora was all out of showbusiness.

Her saving grace had been the friends she'd made first time around in Africa, and one of the show's vet advisors had encouraged her to look at vet nurse courses. It had been exactly what she needed. Her course in Hertford-shire, along with some hair dye and returning to her own name, had given her the time and space she'd needed to escape the demons that had chased her. A few of her col-leagues had eventually recognised her along the way, but she'd always managed to shy away from talking about her experience, or why she'd left.

Her first year after her degree had been spent at a prac-tice on the edges of London. But when she'd seen this job advertised on the outskirts of Edinburgh, and realised the practice worked with both domestic and farm animals, it had seemed a perfect match for her.

Her old-style cottage was tiny, but she'd bought it out-right with her earnings from the TV series. The bills were reasonable, and she was able to keep saving. Life, for the most part, was good now, as long as she could continue to keep out of the spotlight.

She finished checking the weight of a cat whose owner had been told to put the cat on a diet for strict health rea-sons. It seemed it was an uphill battle. 'Ms Bancroft?' Aurora asked. 'Have you been sticking to the food we talked about?'

The older woman nodded solemnly while not quite meeting Aurora's eyes.

'And no treats?'

The woman's face screwed up and she gave a minimal shrug of her shoulders. 'She only gets a few.'

The cat glared at Aurora—actually glared at her, as if she knew exactly what they were talking about and didn't approve in the least.

'Well, Trudie's weight is still the same. She really needs to lose some. Her bones and joints are under so much strain while she's this heavy, and her heart too.'

The elderly woman lifted her indignant cat back into her arms. 'Well, I'll try my best.'

Aurora gave an inward sigh. 'The good news is that she's not put any more weight on. So, that's at least a step in the right direction. How about you bring her back in two weeks and we'll check her again?'

Aurora could almost sense that Trudie had Ms Bancroft exactly where she wanted her, and likely annoyed her most of the day for treats.

'Two weeks.' Ms Bancroft nodded, before allowing Aurora to put Trudie back into her cat carrier as she hissed in annoyance.

Next, Aurora trimmed a Pekingese's nails, clipped a hamster's teeth, gave eye drops to a young kitten with a nasty infection, and finally treated a white Highland terrier with atopic dermatitis. She gave careful instructions to the young owner. 'Around twenty-five per cent of West Highland terriers develop atopic dermatitis at some point in their life. We need to keep on top of it, as it can cause skin damage, infection and general discomfort. It's really hard to get them to stop scratching. If you treat the skin like this every day, it should reduce the itch, and help keep the symptoms at bay.'

The young girl nodded seriously. Aurora knew that she loved her dog, and would do her best to treat the condition.

By the time she'd finished with the fourth patient, Elijah Ferguson still hadn't returned. She quickly made some chicken and white rice for the puppy, cutting the chicken into tiny pieces before taking him outside to let him relieve himself. 'We need to give you a name,' she said, taking a snap on her phone and uploading it to the vet website page, asking if anyone knew the owner.

She held the puppy up. He'd cleaned up well, his black and white coat almost fluffy at this stage. She studied him for a few seconds. 'Bert,' she said with a smile. Her favourite cast member back on the show. Old enough to be her grandfather, and the person who'd stepped in when needed. It had made a big difference for her, and she'd always be grateful. 'You look like a Bert,' she said to the little guy before sitting him back on her lap whilst she checked some of the test results from samples taken last week. The first result made her close her eyes for a second and take a few breaths.

Cancer. In an older dog. And fairly advanced. The dog had recently developed a limp and the owner had brought him in to be checked. Matt, the vet she'd been working with, had been fairly sure what the diagnosis might be, and had already prepared the owner.

But Matt wasn't here. His own treatment for cancer had taken its toll, and he'd needed some rest and recuperation. Frankie, the French vet who'd worked here up until last week, had put in his notice and gone to work in Dubai.

Aurora knew the owner of this dog. He'd lost his wife a few years ago, and she wanted to make sure she dealt with this sensitively. From first meet, she wasn't entirely sure that Elijah Ferguson was the person to do that.

She picked up the phone, and kept a hold of Bert, as

she made the call. It was the one part of her job that she didn't enjoy, but she knew it was one of the most important. So she ignored her heart thumping in her chest and took a deep breath as the phone was answered.

Eli was mad. And there was no real reason for it. He was mad about puppy farms around the vet practice. He was mad about the fact his own car had broken down last night and he'd been forced to use one of his father's. Just driving it now brought back a whole host of memories. He was mad about not contacting the practice staff before he'd arrived. A novice mistake. He'd startled that woman this morning and it was hardly a good start.

He was even mad about the brand of food that Matt had obviously chosen to sell these last few years—even though it was entirely none of his business.

He could actually feel the suspension on the low-slung sports car suffering due to the amount of different feed he'd just purchased from a supplier.

And he was mad about how remarkably attractive the vet nurse was. Her dark red hair had been windswept and strewn about her face, her uniform dirty, and his first reaction wasn't entirely gracious as she'd walked in with the dirty puppy. But it seemed that she was unfazed by his bad temper.

It suddenly struck him that he hadn't even asked her what her name was and he groaned at his pure bad manners. That sent off another wave of annoyance in his head at how disappointed in him his father would have been.

Truth be told, the second that Elijah Ferguson had even glimpsed the familiar countryside every part of him had been on edge.

There wasn't even a reasonable explanation for it. And

he knew it. It wasn't as if he'd had an unhappy childhood or been abused in any way. His mother and father had both loved him. But his father had been obsessed with his job. He'd always been working long hours, tending to horses or sheep on farms at three in the morning, missing Eli's football matches because of an unexpected emergency. Falling asleep at school assemblies because he'd been up all night. Everyone had loved David Ferguson, including Eli. It was just hard to tell anyone how it felt to literally have an absent father. Always feeling second best to a job. Joining his dad as a young kid at the practice on a Saturday had been the only way to get a part of his attention.

Even as an adult he hadn't really been able to articulate it. So it just hung above his head, as words always unspoken, feelings never really being acknowledged, and a part of himself feeling resentful and stupid. He'd had a good life. His father had been delighted by his career choice. He'd been so proud of Elijah being top of his class.

And all of that had just made Eli want to run further and further away.

Today, as soon as he'd set foot in the place, he'd been jittery in a way it was impossible to describe. Again, he felt foolish. His father had been dead for six years now. But memories of him were all over the place. The photos. The colour of the walls. The layout of the practice. Matt hadn't changed a single part of it.

As he turned back towards the large country practice, he finally paid attention to the little blue car parked in front. It was covered in mud. Clearly the nurse had gone off the road to recover the puppy. He remembered the fierce look in her eyes as she'd demanded to know his credentials, as she'd clutched the puppy to her chest.

He liked that. He admired that. And the thoughts caused a gut punch to his stomach. Last time he'd had his attention drawn by a member of staff he'd practically sold his business down the river. That was the last thing he'd ever do again. The last.

He pulled up alongside the car and walked back up the stairs to the entrance. It was later than he'd planned and as he opened the door he could hear her talking on the phone in a low, sympathetic voice. 'I'm so sorry,' she was saying.

He frowned. What was going on?

Something made his footsteps slow, and he heard other parts of the conversation. Test results. A cancer diagnosis. A poor prognosis. Alarm bells started going off in his head.

Who on earth was this woman, and what on earth was she doing?

'Who are you talking to?' he demanded as he walked inside the room.

She started, and the puppy, which was on her lap, gave a little jump.

'Just one of our clients,' she said. 'They were waiting for some results from tests that Matt took last week.'

Her green eyes were wide and he'd clearly surprised her.

'And you think it's your job to do that?'

He could see her bristle. She turned her head away from him and continued her conversation on the phone. 'Mr Sannox, our new vet has just arrived. I know this is really upsetting for you. Why don't I drop by later and I can tell you everything you need to know?'

'You won't,' snapped Eli. It was all he could do not to pull the phone from her hand. She was really overstepping. And what was more, he hadn't even asked her name so he could actually demand that she stop right now.

'Finish that call.' His hands were on his hips right now. This shouldn't be happening. Not in his practice. News like this should always be delivered by a vet. She had absolutely no right.

But whatever her name was, she completely ignored him, actually standing up and putting her back to him as she continued to talk. 'Yes, I'll see you about three o'clock. No problem at all.'

If he hadn't noticed the tiniest tremble of her hand he would be yelling right now.

She put down the phone and turned to face him, eyes blazing. 'I was right about you.'

It was the last thing he'd expected her to say. 'What?'

'I actually contemplated if I could rely on you to give results like those. And guess what? I thought not. And I was entirely right. How dare you interrupt me when I'm telling someone their pet is going to die? What's wrong with you?'

She was angry now. Her jaw was clenched.

'What's wrong with me? What's wrong with you? What gives you the right to think you should be giving results like that without them being checked by a vet first? Do you even understand the results? Do you know the treatment options? Are you qualified for any of this?'

Oh, no. A horrible thought crept over him. This woman had demanded to know his credentials earlier—he hadn't even thought to ask about hers.

Not only did he not know her name, he didn't know if she was qualified in anything.

His brain was going mad. The logical part screamed, *The lawyers told you the two vet nurses were qualified.*

One of them he'd known for ever. This one...? Had she been here a year? Two? He couldn't remember.

She stepped right up under his chin. 'Let's get things straight right now, Elijah Ferguson,' she said, an unexpected accent appearing in her tone. 'You don't ever talk to me like that again.' The words were hissed. 'You left here, after appearing this morning, not even telling me where you were going, when you'd be back, or even if you were going to be working here in future. As far as I know, *I'm* the only qualified person on shift today.' She pressed her hand against her chest. 'I know these people. I know exactly how much Rudy means to Mr Sannox, and I know exactly what's happened in his life these past few years. I have a duty of care to him, and to his pet.' She flung her hand to the ceiling. 'So, you go off and worry about pet food, while I deal with the patients and tell them the news they don't want to hear.'

Her accent, which had started as a mere hint, was now pure Liverpudlian. The anger which had also started as a hint was now emanating from every pore of her body.

'Jack Sannox?' he said, his skin growing cold.

She blinked in surprise and nodded. 'Yes.'

Lead was settling in his stomach. 'I know him,' he said automatically. 'This is his dog?'

'His border collie.' Her words were careful. 'He lost his wife a few years ago. He's become quite solitary. Something happening to Rudy will kill him.' The words were dramatic. But it seemed that Aurora had learned rapidly about farmers, their livestock and their pets.

'So, you've told him,' Eli repeated.

She looked at him carefully with those calculating green eyes. 'I've told him,' she said, holding his gaze. 'Because from what little I saw of you this morning, didn't give me confidence you would treat the case with the compassion it deserves.'

Wow. She wasn't messing about. Could he really work with this woman—even if it was for only a few weeks? He was instantly annoyed and offended. But should he be?

He straightened his own back and shoulders and held out his hand towards her. 'Elijah Ferguson,' he said. 'But call me Eli. Qualified eight years ago. I might not appear a very good human, but I can assure you that I'm an excellent vet.' He let out a long stream of air from his lips. 'And I know Jack Sannox. I went to his wife Bessie's funeral.'

His hand was still hovering in midair. She hadn't moved yet.

She'd changed since he was out, and her tunic was now a pale green, complementing her eyes. Her previously scruffy hair had also been combed and pulled back into a neat bun at the nape of her neck. She looked much more professional, and what was more, she had an extremely professional air. It was something that most people couldn't quite put their finger on. But she had it.

And though he was reluctant to say it, the fierce protection he'd now witnessed for both animals and owners was actually what he looked for in a colleague.

She still hadn't shaken his hand. There was tension in the air. They certainly hadn't started on the right foot. He wasn't even sure if this situation could be retrieved.

He brazened it out. 'I'll be working here for the near future. In the meantime, we're trying to recruit a new vet. If I have to take someone newly qualified I will, then hopefully mentor them for a short while to get them up to speed until Matt is well enough to come back and work alongside them. So, in effect, for a short period I'll be your new boss.'

Her shoulders tensed at those last words. He could see a million things flash in her eyes. And he was pretty sure one of them was her resignation. Considering this practice was currently losing staff like a dandelion shedding seeds in the wind, it wasn't what he wanted to hear.

Finally, she stepped forward and shook his hand with a firm grip. 'Aurora Hendricks,' she said, her accent vanishing once more. 'I've been here eighteen months, and it's always been a team approach. I'm not much for hierarchy. And yes, I am fully qualified. I have a BSc in Veterinary Nursing, and I know exactly what those test results mean.'

Aurora. An unusual name. But it suited her. There was something else though. Something strangely familiar about her that he couldn't quite place. Had they met somewhere before?

A little quiver of something ran through him. With her dark red hair, pale skin and green eyes, she was certainly attractive. He was sure if he'd met her before she would have made an impression. So, what was it about her that was familiar?

She took a deep breath, letting the words she'd said settle before she continued. 'And I don't just mean the science of the results. What I mean is, I'll likely be going up to Jack Sannox's farm for the next year to keep an eye on him.'

And that was when he knew.

That was when he knew that he had to find a way to work with this woman.

He needed her beside him, not against him.

He nodded. 'Aurora. It's an unusual name.'

She looked surprised that this was where the conversation was going. 'Well, "call me Eli",' she said, as quick as a flash, 'Elijah isn't so normal either.' She glanced out of the window. 'My father named me. After the actual Aurora Borealis. Aurora means dawn.'

He gave her a rueful smile. 'Well, my dad named me too. And he wasn't religious, but he remembered the name Elijah from Sunday School as a kid, and just liked it. I'm probably lucky he didn't name me after his favourite breed of cow.'

'Angus or Galloway?' she quipped.

He rolled his eyes. 'More than likely something neither of us have ever heard of.' He took a careful breath. 'If you don't mind, I'd like to familiarise myself with Rudy's case, then I'd like to go with you later today to speak to Jack. He will need extra support, because it's likely there will be no treatment that will actually make a difference.'

He turned his attention to the puppy in her arms. The little guy hadn't even squirmed during their exchange, just watched everything with his big brown eyes. He leaned forward and smiled. 'What are we going to do with this guy?'

'This is Bert,' she said determinedly.

'Where did that name come from?'

She shrugged. 'A reliable friend. I've posted a pic on our website. But since he's not tagged, I'm assuming he isn't actually owned by anyone. We might need to see if the local shelter can arrange someone to foster or adopt.'

'What about any of our clients?'

'What do you mean?'

'Is there anyone that might be looking for another dog? A companion for another dog?'

Aurora looked thoughtful and then wrinkled her nose. 'We've had a few older clients die in the last few months, and myself and Anne have managed to place their pets with other clients.' She sighed. 'I think we might have used up our supply of local, willing pet fosterers.'

He reached over and took Bert in his arms. 'He looks about eight weeks. Puppies take a lot of work. Maybe he already had an owner who just wasn't ready for the work involved.'

It only took a few moments to make a decision. 'Let's give it a few days on the website and see what happens. I'll vaccinate him, and in the meantime he can stay here with me. There were kennels outside at one point, I'll go and have a look and see what state they're in.'

'You're staying here?' She seemed surprised.

He shrugged. 'I told you earlier, I could move into the house but it doesn't seem worthwhile. I want to use it as an incentive for the new vet. I'll just sleep upstairs. There's three bedrooms, a living room and a bathroom. There's even been a new kitchen put in.'

'You do know that if we take a patient overnight, either myself or Anne usually stay in one of the other rooms?'

He tucked Bert under his arm. 'You do?'

She nodded.

'It's okay.' He shrugged. 'I'm sure we can make it work. It'll only be for a few months. And I don't snore,' he added.

She arched her eyebrow. 'But I do.'

And there it was. Another challenge. It seemed that

Aurora Hendricks was someone who was going to keep him on his toes.

He leaned down and nuzzled into Bert. 'Let's go find some earplugs, kid. We've got to plan ahead.'

CHAPTER TWO

THE RAIN WAS pelting down as Aurora arrived the next morning, and the normally paved area in front of the practice was swimming in mud. She turned and frowned at the nearby hillside. There had been some slippage in the past—was it going to happen again?

She shucked off her wellies at the front door, knowing she had some flat shoes in her locker—and promptly stepped in a pool of puppy pee.

'Ew,' she said before smiling. It wasn't the first time, and wouldn't be the last.

'Sorry,' came a voice from the doorway. Eli had Bert tucked under his arm. 'We tried the kennels last night after I'd fixed them up but—' he looked down at Bert '—it seems that Bert is actually a house dog.'

Aurora couldn't help but smile. She peeled off her wet socks and walked across the tiled floor, rubbing Bert's head. 'Are you just showing him who's boss?' Bert licked her hand. 'Guess you'd better get started with the toilet training then,' she said.

He looked down at her painted toenails. 'How about I get you a pair of socks first?'

She nodded gratefully, and was pulling the thick woollen socks onto her feet as Anne came through the door.

'Typical Scottish summer,' said Anne, shaking off her

umbrella, and then stopping short. 'Eli?' she said in wonder, before crossing the room in long strides and enveloping him in a giant hug.

Aurora's gaze flicked from one to the other. Anne only worked here three days a week now. But she'd been here from the time that Eli's dad had run the practice, so it was obvious that they would know each other.

Eli, surprisingly, returned the hug with a relieved expression on his face. Had he been worried that Anne wouldn't be happy to see him?

'Who is this?' she asked, rubbing Bert's head.

'A stray, we think,' he said, glancing over at Aurora. 'This is Bert. I'll keep him for the next few days to see if anyone comes forward.'

'Sure you will,' said Anne, still smiling. She'd released him now but tucked her hand into his arm. 'Let's just go and have a cup of tea and catch up a bit. You can manage, can't you, Aurora?'

Aurora gave a nod. Eli looked a cross between still being relieved along with a mad dash of panic. 'Can you put Jack Sannox in the diary for later today, since he wasn't up to it yesterday?'

Aurora gave a nod as Anne swiftly moved Eli through to the kitchen, talking the whole time.

She checked through the patients for the day. She noticed that Eli had put a few notes next to some, mainly questions on getting some more information from owners or looking at medications or treatment plans. She took her time to read them all. He was thorough. He'd also left some notes and instructions about the surgical list for tomorrow, asking her to call all the owners to remind them of the instructions for their pets, prior to any procedure.

Aurora always did that automatically, but he wasn't

to know that so she tried not to let it annoy her and just left it for now.

She sighed as she looked at a few of the notes he'd left regarding Rudy and Mr Sannox. Jack had called back and asked them to change their visit until today. He'd said something about needing a little time.

In all honesty, she would have preferred to see Jack yesterday, if anything, just so she could give him a hug. Aurora finished what she was doing and tried not to be curious about the conversation that was clearly going on in the kitchen. She'd have loved a cup of tea but didn't want to intrude.

She'd always enjoyed working with Anne, who came equipped with a million stories and a world of expertise. She lived in the nearby village and had never even considered working somewhere else. Aurora could remember a few times when Anne had casually mentioned that it was a shame that Elijah hadn't taken over from his father, but had always backed the words with something like 'children should always spread their wings'.

An unexpected arrival—a cat with fleas, brought by a horrified owner who asked a myriad questions about her designer wardrobe and furniture—kept her attention away from the conversation in the kitchen. Aurora spent a considerable amount of time concentrating on treating the cat and emphasising how important it was to continue treatment, before covering the basics about vacuuming the home, washing all bedding and soft furnishings and spraying everything with flea spray.

After that, there were some routine appointments. Anne and Aurora shared the vet nurse appointments, accompanying Eli when required and keeping an eye on Bert.

Anne opened the store cupboard and blinked at the newly stocked food. She leaned over and checked the side label before giving an approving nod. 'This one is hypoallergenic. It will actually suit a lot of our patients with more sensitive tummies.'

Aurora smiled. She hadn't even looked that closely. 'So, what do you think of our new vet?' she asked, trying to sound innocent.

She could tell that Anne was bursting to talk. Anne had lots of skills but keeping secrets wasn't her best—although she could, when necessary, be discreet.

'I'm so happy to see Eli again,' she said with a smile. 'He's grown up to be the picture of his father.'

'Has he?' Aurora had seen the photo on the wall earlier, but didn't think they were so alike.

'Oh, yes,' said Anne with authority. 'Same height and build. Eli has his mother's colouring, but his mannerisms are identical to his father's.' She gave a soft smile. 'It brings back lots of memories.'

Aurora wondered how many questions she would get away with. 'His father and Matt were partners, weren't they?'

Anne nodded. 'Right up until David retired. He worked on much longer than he should have. But by then Sarah, his wife, was dead and Eli was away working someplace else. He didn't want to leave Matt on his own.'

Aurora looked out over the Scottish countryside. Right now, it was difficult to get a good view, with the sheeting rain and small mudslide from the hills nearby. But usually this view was a wild array of green, a dash of some heather and a few spots of white sheep.

'Why on earth is it so hard to recruit around here?'

Anne gave a sorrowful shrug. 'I'm not sure. I think

for a while David was too picky, and Eli seems to have inherited his father's traits. When the practice passed to him, he constantly didn't think any of the applicants were good enough.' She gave Aurora a knowing glance. 'You know the thing—he didn't want to work here, but no one else was good enough?'

Aurora frowned as she tried to make some sense of her new workmate. 'Interesting.' She paused, looking in the direction of the kitchen to make sure the coast was clear, and then asked the ultimate question. 'So, why did Eli never come back to work with his dad, or take over?'

Anne wrinkled her nose. 'He'd opened his own practice for a while on the outskirts of London. Not sure what happened there. I guess right now it's just about timing. Matt's sick and Frankie's left. What other option did he have?'

And that answer left Aurora with an uncomfortable feeling. Anne was going to retire soon. But Aurora had another twenty years or more to work. If they couldn't recruit another vet, this practice might fold. She didn't want to end up out of work. She loved her cottage and where she lived. She didn't want to have to move. But if Eli was only there on a temporary basis, she might need to consider other options.

Anne nodded towards the car park as another car pulled in. 'Recognise them?' she asked.

Aurora shook her head, 'No idea.'

Eli met her at the front door. As soon as he stood next to her, she got a waft of his aftershave. Fresh but woody, it made her breathe in even deeper. Darn it. The last thing she needed was to be attracted to someone she worked with. Particularly when he could be occasionally snarky. Mixing work and pleasure was never a good idea.

It didn't help that he glanced sideways at her and gave her a half smile.

A couple in their twenties entered the practice with a cat carrier. Although they didn't have an appointment, there was a short gap where they could be seen. Eli showed them through to one of the examination rooms. Aurora instantly had a weird feeling. She watched the interaction between the couple as they removed their cat from the carrier and placed him on the examination table.

Eli asked them some details as he examined the cat, which was called Arthur. Again, as she watched him, she appreciated how thorough he was. But something about the couple seemed off. It was that niggling feeling right between her shoulder blades that she really couldn't explain to anyone. Aurora had had this before—it sometimes caught her by surprise.

The man seemed to continually talk over his partner. He also kept glancing towards Aurora, even though she was not speaking to him directly. She was merely making notes on the computer as Eli examined the patient. His continued glances made her nervous and uncomfortable; he even hinted at a smile a few times towards her when he knew his partner was looking elsewhere. There was just something creepy about him.

She could sense that Eli caught something in the air. He gave her a curious look but continued with his examination, and after a few careful questions Aurora knew exactly where this diagnosis was going. Eli looked at them. 'I think I can say with some confidence that Arthur has diabetes. All the symptoms you've described—the weight loss, the excessive drinking and excessive eating—all point in that direction. I only need to run a few minor tests to be able to confirm it.'

The women looked pale. 'Is this serious?' she asked.

Eli nodded. 'It can be. But diabetes in cats is not uncommon and it's a condition we can treat.'

'Will he need injections?' asked the guy. 'My gran has diabetes and she requires injections.'

Eli nodded again. 'That's very likely. Why don't you leave Arthur with us for a few hours, and when you come back we can confirm the diagnosis and make a treatment plan?'

The guy shot another few glances in Aurora's direction and she shifted uncomfortably in her seat. She hadn't spoken a word to him during the consultation, so knew that she had done nothing to attract his attention.

'Is everything all right?' asked Eli as soon as they left.

Aurora gave her shoulders a little shake. 'Just something about that guy. He made me uncomfortable.'

She didn't want to go into any details. Being assaulted, and then being stalked, had a huge influence on her life. The outcome of these had affected both how she lived her life and her decision-making. It had been built into her TV contract that she would be covered for any consequences from being in the TV series. She knew that essentially had been around any possible accidents or injuries but, thankfully, her assault had also been covered—and not for a short period of time. Now, all these years later, she still attended counselling sessions when she needed them. They'd started intensely but now happened as and when Aurora ever decided she needed them. She had that odd prickly feeling that she'd be making contact with her counsellor some time soon.

She stood up and walked over and picked up Arthur. 'How about I get started on those tests for Arthur and you can prescribe his insulin?'

Eli gave a nod and started taking more notes. Aurora half hoped that only the woman would come back. She would need to spend some time with Arthur's owners to explain his new diet plan, and how to do his injections. They'd already left insurance details, so she knew Arthur would be covered, and it would likely take another few visits to get his condition stabilised.

It had been a strange start to the day. Eli had been nervous about seeing Anne again and wondered how she might act. But Anne had been warm, friendly and professional. He just had a sense, deep down, of a slight feeling of disappointment that emanated from her. It could all be in his head—maybe it was just old feelings being rehashed?

Anne had been well aware of the underlying hostility that lay between Eli and his father. But she showed no hard feelings towards Eli, and seemed happy to see him.

He still wasn't entirely sure about Aurora. She'd seemed a little off in the earlier consultation, but maybe he was just misinterpreting things.

He was still trying to get to grips with how the practice was run. It seemed that Anne and Aurora shared the variety of roles, and he wondered if that was the best use of their time. Aurora had mentioned the practice being a team approach. It was hard to get a sense of that when he was the only vet. And he wasn't sure how much time and energy to invest in finding out, when he would only be here a short space of time.

But Aurora intrigued him. He could sense something from her earlier when she'd been uncomfortable in the consulting room. He'd almost felt a shift in the air. He was slightly annoyed that he hadn't picked up on anything, but would pay better attention in the future. He still wanted to find out a little bit more about her and her experience. His eyes were continually drawn to her, no matter how hard he tried for them not to be. His brain was constantly wondering about her. And it was odd, but he could sometimes swear there was a buzz in the air between them. But maybe he was just imagining it.

He wondered if he would get that opportunity to find out a bit more about her when they visited Jack in a few hours' time. But in the meantime, he had other things to concentrate on.

Bert was showing no interest in toilet training. It had been so long since Eli had looked after a puppy that he'd forgotten how hard it was. He cleaned up a variety of puddles and took Bert back outside with some treats to try and encourage him to toilet outside and reward that behaviour. No matter where Bert eventually ended up, he would likely need to be toilet trained, so it was worth the extra time and effort. More people were likely to adopt a puppy if they knew the toilet training routine had started.

Anne shouted them all through to the kitchen, where they all prepared lunch. She looked at the visits for the day. 'What is going on at the Fletchers' farm?' she asked.

Eli looked up. 'What do you mean?'

Anne put her hand to her chin and looked thoughtful. 'It's in the book for today but there's no notes next to it. I'm sure that Matt has already been there a few times. I think some of the cattle have been poorly—but I don't think there was anything specific.'

'I have no problem going back up there,' said Eli. 'Has Don Fletcher phoned down again?'

Anne shook her head. 'The writing in the book is definitely Matt's. He must've put a note on here a few weeks ago that he wanted to go back.'

Eli was thoughtful for a minute. 'Put it forward a few days, please. I want us to spend a bit of time with Jack Sannox this afternoon.'

Anne nodded and changed the diary. Lunch was quick, and Eli spent a bit of time checking off everything he would need for the few surgical procedures that were scheduled for the next day. One lesion to be biopsied. One cat, and one dog to be neutered.

Aurora's answers were swift to each query. 'Done, done, and done.'

He got the hint that she was getting annoyed with him. But this was basic stuff. He didn't know Aurora, and had no idea what her capabilities were. Last thing he wanted was for an animal to present tomorrow who hadn't been properly prepared for surgery. Then it would require cancellation and would be a waste of time for all concerned. He was only ensuring every box was ticked. It was what any good vet would do. If Aurora didn't like it? Too bad.

The afternoon passed quickly and soon it was time to do the home visits. For farms, it went without saying that the vet had to visit. For domestic animals, home visits were much fewer. Occasionally when an animal had reached the end of their life span, and was clearly in pain or desperately unwell, some owners would ask for them to be put to sleep at home, rather than in the practice. Eli knew that Matt and his father always respected the client's wishes in these cases, and he would do the same. He pointed at a name on the list that had been scored out. 'What's happening with this one?'

Aurora took a deep breath. 'Mrs Adams wants another day. She says she's not quite ready.'

He took a quick glance at the notes. An elderly cat, signs of dementia, untreatable cancer, now being incontinent, and its back legs weren't functioning. 'Are you sure she can cope?' When an animal reached this stage it was like being a full-time carer. It could take a lot out of owners.

Aurora pressed her lips together and gave a tight nod. 'She'll cope. She'll phone us back when she's sure she's ready.'

'Does she have pain relief for her cat?'

'Of course, we would never leave any animal in pain.' There was a tiny bit of defensiveness to her words.

'Okay then, ready?' he asked as they made their way outside to head to Jack Sannox's farm.

'We can't go in that.' She smiled, pointing at the low-slung sports car. 'Have you seen the farm roads?'

He pointed to the garage. 'Don't you know my dad was a bit of a car fiend? He's got another three in there. There's an old eighties Land Rover. It's built like a tank and it's fit for any farm road. He used it for most of his visits while he worked here.'

The car wasn't modern enough to have a key fob press-button lock, so Eli had to do the old-fashioned way of opening the doors with the key.

Aurora climbed in. Part of him wanted to get to know her a little better. He couldn't deny how attractive she was. And she didn't wear a ring. But that meant nothing these days. After his previous experience, the last thing Eli wanted to do was have any kind of relationship with a member of staff. So why was he even having these thoughts? He couldn't deny how attractive she was, but she was prickly at times.

As the thought entered his head, he almost laughed out loud. Prickly? So was he. More than prickly. But he couldn't help it. Being back at the family home and practice was conjuring up a whole host of past feelings—ones that he really hadn't wanted to deal with. And now? When, if he didn't recruit another vet, the whole place would be under threat didn't seem like the best time to deal with things.

As she sat in the Land Rover next to him, the scent of her perfume drifted towards him. Hints of amber and musk. Quite distinctive. Her hair, which had been tied up earlier, was now down around her shoulders. The long, dark red bob suited her, and looked more sculpted that he would have expected.

'What?' she asked unexpectedly.

His stare had clearly been noticed. He decided to play things out. 'How long have you been here?'

'Eighteen months,' she answered easily.

'And what brought you to Scotland? Was it family? Or did you get married?'

She gave him a distinct side-eye. 'I'm not married. No partner. This practice brought me to Scotland.'

So, the fact he'd been asking if she had a partner had not been lost on her, and he pretended not to be secretly relieved.

'You came here for the job?'

'Of course I did.'

'Where did you train?'

'Hawkshead.' The Royal Veterinary College. The most prestigious place to carry out vet training, or vet nurse training.

'Outside of Edinburgh is a long way to travel.'

She shrugged. 'I don't have family ties, and I'd worked already in outer London, I wanted to move to a place where there was a chance to work with both domestic and farm animals.'

He gave a smile as they continued along the winding country road. 'Not a lot of people want to work with both types of animal.'

She waved a hand at the clothes she'd changed into. Big green wellies and a large, dark waterproof coat. 'I don't like to be caught unawares. We're going to talk to Jack about Rudy, but if there's another farm issue he wants us to look at, I like to be prepared.'

Eli couldn't help but be a little impressed. He'd stashed his own stuff earlier in the back of the Land Rover. It was nice to know that Aurora was prepared too.

'What about your accent?' he asked. 'I've noticed it tends to come and go.'

For a moment there was silence, and he wondered if he'd stepped over a line he shouldn't have.

'My accent?'

He swallowed. He'd started the conversation. He couldn't back out now. And, for some reason, he wanted to know. His head flooded with thoughts about his past experience. Could Aurora be pretending to be someone she wasn't? Was there a reason she changed her accent at times? He needed to be able to trust those he worked with.

But as she brushed a length of her hair behind her ear, and he caught a glimpse of her pale skin, his stomach clenched. She was anxious. Anxious he found out something she was trying to hide?

'Yes,' he said firmly. 'Most of the time you don't seem to have an accent at all. But occasionally the odd twang seems to slip in.'

'The odd twang?' she repeated. This time he could see her eyebrows raised. She looked as if she were about to roast him.

'Yip,' he said with a smile in his voice as he turned onto the road towards Jack's farm.

'My accent does come and go,' she said carefully. 'I grew up in Liverpool. But when I worked in London some of the clients appeared to have an issue with my accent, so I tried to tone it down.'

It was an odd kind of explanation. London was one of the most diverse populations in the UK, with a multitude of accents. But he did concede that certain parts of London had old-fashioned clients who might be a bit haughty towards a Liverpudlian accent.

'No excuse for behaviour like that,' he said promptly. 'I've worked all over the world. I get that my Scottish accent can be quite broad, and I've had to repeat myself on numerous occasions, but I wouldn't try and hide my accent.' He shot her a glance. 'If I'm in another country, I usually get mistaken for Irish instead of Scottish. But I can live with that.'

They pulled up outside Jack Sannox's cottage. The word cottage was a bit of a stretch. The farmhouse was much more impressive as it had been extended over the years, but the original parts of the cottage were still there. He obviously took pride in his home.

Eli took a breath. 'Wow... Haven't seen this place in years. He's extended—it looks great.'

Aurora climbed out of the Land Rover. 'I've only been here once before, when there was an issue with the pigs. Matt said the work had just finished and Jack gave us a full tour. He was very proud.'

'So he should be.'

They moved to the front door and Jack opened it with a solemn expression on his face. He led them through to his sitting room, where Rudy was lying on a rug on the sofa. Jack sat down next to him.

'How's he been?' asked Eli, bending down so his face was next to Rudy's and stroking his head.

'He was up last night whimpering. I don't think the painkillers are working.'

'I can increase them,' said Eli instantly. 'But it may make Rudy drowsy.'

'He's so used to being by my side, walking the fields with me, riding the tractor,' said Jack, a definite waver in his voice. 'He's just not going to be able to do that.'

'No, he's not,' said Eli reluctantly. He wanted to give Jack a realistic expectation for what happened next.

Jack sighed and stared out of the window, one hand on Rudy.

Aurora moved and sat beside him, taking his other hand in hers. 'It's not fair. And we know that. None of us deserve the dogs that we have—they're all just too good. I know this time of year is difficult. I know it's around the same time that your wife died.'

Jack's eyes widened in surprise; he turned to look at her. 'But you never got to meet Bessie.'

'I know, and I'm sorry about that. But you're the one I need to worry about.'

Jack blinked and Eli could see the wetness in his eyes. 'No one left to worry about me,' he whispered, and Aurora leaned over and gave him a hug.

'That's not true.' She looked over at Eli. 'I'm sure we can make Rudy comfortable, and give him another few months.'

Part of Eli wanted to be annoyed. But the way she was looking at him with those green eyes was almost sending him a secret message. He had written in Rudy's notes that he thought he could make the dog comfortable for the next few months. Maybe she was just letting him know that she was following his lead?

Jack turned to him. 'I don't want my dog in pain. Are you sure there isn't anything else that can be done?'

Eli spoke in a low, serious tone. 'His cancer has spread. Some of the organs that are affected could give him other symptoms. But most of these we can control. I can certainly control his pain. There's another medication we can try—a cancer medication that can also shrink some of his tumours and give him a better quality of life.'

Jack gave a sniff. 'A few months, you say?'

Eli nodded. 'I'll talk you through the medications. I brought them with me.' He moved back over and kneeled in front of Rudy again. 'I think you'll do okay as a house dog, Rudy.'

Rudy looked at him with his big brown eyes, and Eli remembered why he was a vet. For this. To take care of animals that had brought joy to families and give them a comfortable end to their life.

He looked at Aurora, who still had one hand in Jack's, her other arm around his shoulder. She was squeezing it. It struck Eli that he didn't know who might have hugged Jack since his wife had died a few years ago. This could be his first hug since then.

He also wasn't sure how Aurora had found out about when his wife had died. Maybe Matt had told her? But however, she'd found out, she'd taken the information into consideration when here. He liked the fact that she'd thought about the whole situation, and not just the immediate circumstances.

They left Jack nearly an hour later. They were quiet. It was always sad when discussing plans for a terminal pet.

Aurora leaned her head against the window. 'I'm not sure if Rudy will want to be a house dog.'

'I'm not sure either,' admitted Eli. 'But we'll just have to play it by ear, and give Jack the support he needs.'

She turned her head towards him and locked her eyes on his. 'This,' she said quietly. 'This is part of the reason I wanted to move. You get to know these patients. You get to know what matters to them. In the city, it was just a constant stream of French bulldogs, dachshunds, cockapoos, cavapoos and chihuahuas. Most of the time we never saw them on a regular basis. We didn't get to form any kind of relationship with people. The turnover was incredible.'

'And you decided that wasn't for you?'

She gave a nod. 'Or maybe I just like cows,' she said with a smile.

There was something in that smile. Something that made him know that she was being entirely honest.

But as soon as he had that thought, something else flashed into his head. But was he really a good judge of character? After all, he'd thought his last practice manager, Iona, was honest. He'd been sucked in by everything she'd said. They'd even started dating. Then the bills had started to arrive. It seemed that money from the practice had been funnelled off into places it shouldn't go—mainly Iona's bank account.

She'd offered to take over the wages system, the banking, the accounts. In other practices, it was a fundamental part of the practice manager's role. She'd come with excellent references—which he'd later found out had been faked—and he'd been thankful for the assistance.

It wasn't until another vet in the practice had taken him aside about an unpaid bill, that he'd found one day when he came in early, that Eli had any understanding at all that something was amiss.

And as the world had come crashing down around him, and his staff had been forced to find other jobs, and Iona had disappeared just as quickly as she'd appeared, Eli Ferguson had been left feeling like a complete and utter fool.

It seemed that fraud was harder to prove than he'd first thought, particularly when it seemed that it was his signature on some of the accounts. He'd had to dig into what little of his savings he still had to engage experts to confirm that he hadn't signed for certain things. Loans and credit cards had been the most popular. But that was the reason for his earlier visit to his accountant and solicitor. He'd had no option but to file for bankruptcy.

He wouldn't be able to be a real financial partner in his father's practice for a number of years. Instead, he would have to be an employee. And if he was embarrassed about that it was just too bad.

So maybe his judgement couldn't be relied upon at all. Not when it came to business or financial matters.

And any thoughts of how attractive Aurora Hendricks was, how cute her smile, the shine of her hair, or the fact she was feisty, with a warm heart, he had to put clean out of his head.

He was only here on a temporary basis. And he would do well to remember that.

CHAPTER THREE

AURORA STILL HADN'T quite got a handle on her new boss. She didn't want to admit she found him a little intriguing. He was handsome, there was no denying it, with his tall frame, his tousled light brown hair and his blue eyes. That darn designer stubble made her palms itch to touch it. If she'd met him at a bar somewhere she would definitely be interested. But their initial meeting had been a bit unusual.

In a way, she was glad that he'd caught the sharp side of her tongue and how protective she was of her work space, and any animal in it. That was important to her.

Then there was the fact she'd been uncomfortable around that cat owner the other day. He didn't need to know why. But her spider-sense never tingled without good reason. She'd learned to trust her instincts. It had been part of the reason she hadn't really panicked at their own first meeting. Eli might be a bit untouchable, but he wasn't intimidating or threatening.

She was still unsure about her job security though. Whilst vets might be hard to recruit in this part of the country, it seemed that the population around Edinburgh had veterinary nurse as a first career choice. Jobs were usually sought after. She'd been lucky when she'd interviewed for here. Both Anne and Matt had been in the middle of an emergency surgery—a dog who had developed a blockage in their bowel. It was a surgery she'd been involved in before and she'd offered to roll up her sleeves and assist so to speak. They'd hired her shortly afterwards and she'd been happy here.

The outskirts of Edinburgh was also a good place to hide. But hiding? Was that what she was actually doing?

Half of her hoped that no one remembered her fifteen minutes of fame. But, like any TV series, the show had ended up streaming on some of the satellite services and gained new fans. Every now and then she saw a social media post about *Where are they now?*

No one had ever got her location right. But there had been a few sightings—particularly when she'd qualified as a veterinary nurse and started working just outside London.

She wanted a private life. She didn't want to be dragged back into the #MeToo debate. She'd stood up for herself at the time, and now wanted to just get on with the rest of her life. She no longer had an agent. She'd drifted away from the fellow cast members on the series, and most of the crew. She'd changed her mobile number, and since her Equity card was under her acting pseudonym she'd felt relatively safe.

Of course, there was the inevitable person she'd gone to school with who occasionally commented on her disappearance from the TV screens, but most people thought she'd headed to find fame and fortune in the States, and failed. She was actually happy for that rumour to continue. It meant that life was safe, in this little part of the world.

The world didn't really understand the damage she'd suffered. The assault had left her feeling vulnerable and frail. The stalking had left her feeling unsafe. She'd had to build herself back up, take advice, attend regular counselling. Self-defence classes with regular refreshers helped too. But, most of all, she trusted her instincts. She would make sure she was never alone with that new client on any occasion. It didn't matter what reason she gave to Anne or Eli—she might even just tell them the truth. She'd learned to believe in herself, and that was what she'd do.

Today was going to be a bit different. She'd told Eli that she was interested in working with farm animals, and today they were doing several visits to farms.

'Are you really ready for this?' asked Eli as he climbed into the old Land Rover.

'Are you?' she asked, glancing at their list. She wrinkled her nose. 'Have you met all these farm owners before?'

He shook his head. 'I only know one out of three. I've been on two of the farms before, but one of them has changed hands.'

She gave him an amused glance. 'I've checked the notes. We have mysterious cows at the Fletchers' farm, temperamental pigs at the Sawyers' and a possible lame horse at Jen Cooper's riding school.' She gave an approving nod. 'It's going to be a good day.'

He gave her an amused sideways glance. Maybe he hadn't quite believed she did love farm work. Well, he would soon find out.

They ended up going to the Sawyers' farm first as it was closest. Shaun Sawyer took them to his pigsty, where two of the pigs had been separated out from the others.

It was clear that neither of these pigs were happy. They were grinding their teeth, were listless, with lots of abdominal kicking.

'Any vomiting?' asked Eli, as he prepared to go into the sty.

Shaun shook his head. 'Only minimal. And not for the last few hours.'

Aurora prepared herself too, and Eli gave her a sideways glance. 'I don't suppose they've escaped at all?' she asked as she swung her leg over the fence. The field around the pigsty had some straw but also a decent amount of mud. Aurora wasn't bothered at all.

Shaun pulled a face. 'They did a few days ago. Five of them did. But we managed to get them back relatively quickly.'

She jumped down, just as Eli did, and moved over to the nearest pig. She followed his lead and they both checked for any obvious bloating or signs of intestinal blockage. 'This one is a bit tachycardic,' she said.

'Mine too,' said Eli. They both checked the pigs' temperature, and Eli walked back over to Shaun. 'My gut feeling is this is colic. You've got an automatic feeder in action to stop gorging, plenty of water and plenty of space for the pigs to move around. There's no sign of obstruction at present—but you know that can be rapid. It could be they've eaten something that doesn't agree with them when they escaped. There is always a higher risk of twisted gut as we come into the summer and temperature fluctuates. But I don't think that applies right now. If we think there's an obstruction we might need to X-ray or ultrasound them.'

Shaun frowned and shook his head. 'Can I watch them a bit longer?'

Eli nodded. 'You can call me if you have any concerns. I'll give you some non-steroidal anti-inflammatories for them both.'

'Where did they go when they escaped?' asked Aurora.

Shaun inclined his head. 'Over the field and into the school playground.'

'Ah,' she said with a smile. 'Any chance they raided the school bins and overdosed on some sweet treats?'

Shaun pulled a face. 'My pigs? More than likely.'

They stayed a bit longer, observing the pigs for any signs of something more serious, before finally getting ready to leave. As Aurora went to swing her leg over the fence, there was a loud squelch and her foot came over, leaving her welly boot stuck fast.

The momentum carried her, and she landed on the other side of the fence with a laugh.

Eli shot a careful glance at Shaun and then they both burst into laughter too. Eli was still in the pen, so made his way over to her boot. He had to grab with both hands to finally free it, and nearly landed in the mud himself.

By the time they'd rinsed their wellies and got back into the car they were still laughing.

'What's next?' asked Aurora.

'You choose,' he said. 'Horse or cows?'

'Cows are my favourite farm animal,' declared Aurora. 'So let's leave them to last and go and see the horse first.'

The journey was only fifteen minutes and as the countryside sped past Aurora settled a little more comfortably into her seat.

'Where did you work before?' she asked.

As soon as the words were out of her mouth she realised it might not have been a good idea. He bristled. He actually bristled. Then he took a breath and said quickly, 'I've worked all over. I worked in Madrid for a while, then in Brittany in France, three months in Italy, then in the US in Florida and Maine, and in Lincolnshire in the UK.'

'Wow!' said Aurora, feeling part admiration and part envy. 'That's a huge range of countries.'

'I went for the experience with the animals.' He gave a smile and raised one eyebrow, as if he was just admitting something. 'In Madrid I worked in a practice that specialised in horses. Brittany was mainly farms. Florida—'

'Tell me it was alligators!' she interrupted.

He laughed. 'I did encounter one on a golf course, but not through work.'

'Darn it,' she muttered, then frowned. 'So, what was it in Florida then?'

He gave her a sideways glance. 'Turtle rehab.'

Her eyes widened. 'You're joking, aren't you?'

He shook his head. 'Are you telling me you don't think turtles should have care too?'

She stuttered for a moment. 'Oh…of course I don't think that. It's just such a change.'

'Working with sea life was such a great opportunity. I jumped at the chance. When I moved to Maine it was a real mix again. I was part of a practice with forty vets. I saw domestic animals and dairy and beef cattle, equine and poultry.'

Aurora couldn't take her eyes off him. 'It's like you stuck one finger in an atlas to decide which country to go to, and one finger in Pasquini to decide what animals to look after.'

He waggled a finger. 'Not all animals are in Pasquini.'

'True,' she admitted. Then she gave him a sideways glance. He seemed much more relaxed around her now. Less defensive. She wondered why he'd bristled at first. 'That must have been a lot of exams.' She knew that vets had to sit country specific exams to get the licence to practice.

He groaned. 'You have no idea. Thankfully, exams have never really bothered me.'

'Just as well,' she said as they turned into the riding school and pulled up outside the stables.

Jen Cooper stuck her head from one of the stalls and walked quickly over to meet them, getting straight to business. 'Thanks for coming. It's Bess. I noticed this morning her gait was different. It's her right leg. She was fine yesterday, and there's been no accident.'

'No problem,' said Eli as he held out his hand. 'Eli Ferguson. I've got a bit of experience with horses, so let me have a look.'

'Where did you get your experience?' said Jen casually as she opened the stall door.

'Jerez,' he said simply.

Aurora stopped walking—as did Jen. 'Jerez?' they both said in unison.

The school was renowned for the world-famous Andalusian horses that danced in shows.

Both heads turned towards him, and Eli held up one hand. 'What I'll say is that those horses are kept in pristine conditions, have the best veterinary care and some of the best facilities I've ever had the pleasure to work in.'

Aurora hid her smile. She knew exactly why he might think they would comment. Some people didn't like animals used in a show, or sport for that matter, and queried the conditions and attention.

Somehow, she knew every word he said was true. She might have only known him a few days but she already had a real sense of the man and his values.

'What about the bulls?' asked Jen, her gaze narrowing.

Eli shook his head. 'I had no involvement with any of the bulls in the vicinity. My sole area was the horses.

The equestrian school was very clear to make sure all who dealt with them knew they had no part in any of the bullfights or any of the bull runs that happen.'

Jen gave him a careful look. 'Okay, let's go and have a look at Bess then.'

Eli worked steadily, using the scale that some veterinary surgeons used to grade lameness in horses. He wasn't afraid to get up close and personal and once he was sure that Bess was steady and not upset he waved them over as he examined one of her hooves, picking it out with a hoof pick, checking for foreign objects, sharp stones or nails. 'Tell me a bit more about this morning,' he said to Jen.

'No problem. Out in the paddock as normal. Then out for a gallop late morning. She was fine until lunchtime yesterday.'

'Hard ground or soft ground?' His head was still dipped over Bess's hoof, his blue eyes peering carefully at her as he gently examined her.

'There's a very slight purplish-red spot,' he said. 'I think this might be a stone bruise. Do you have any pads you can use while this heals?'

Jen gave a swift nod and headed towards a large box in the stables. 'It goes without saying Bess will need to rest, and I'm happy to come back and take another look in a few days.'

Aurora looked over at Jen, who she hadn't met before. 'Do you know what to look for? Inflammation, formation of a haematoma or an abscess?'

Jen gave her a serious nod. 'I'll get our farrier to come over and balance the hoof and remove the shoe for now.'

They talked for a few minutes more as Aurora stood on the sidelines. It was interesting to watch how Eli worked.

It was true, he did have a good deal of knowledge about horses, and for a few moments she wondered if Jen and he were testing each other.

But then she quickly realised he was just trying to get a feel for how experienced Jen was, and what kind of treatments he could recommend to her, knowing she could carry them out safely.

The batting back and forward between the two was interesting, and Aurora started to have a good sense about his experience. At first, it had seemed all flash, sitting so many exams, working in so many countries, with such a range of animals; he'd seemed a bit like a child in a sweetie shop who couldn't decide which to try first.

But now she wondered if it was just a genuine thirst for knowledge. And what made it even more irritating was that she admired him for it. Why did this guy have to be so darn attractive?

By the time he was finished he gave her a nod and they headed back to the Land Rover.

They were certainly starting to get more relaxed around each other. Aurora took some notes from her bag. 'I checked through the computer and the diary next to Matt's desk to see if I could find out any info about the Fletchers' farm.'

She turned her head towards Eli, who was looking at her curiously. He wrinkled his nose. 'We haven't met before, have we? Because I think I would remember.'

Aurora's skin prickled. 'No,' she said as easily as she could manage.

He shook his head. 'You just seem a bit familiar.'

'I can't think how. I'm sure our paths haven't crossed.'

She could tell him. She could ask him if he'd ever watched the show. Most vets she'd come across since she'd changed profession usually said they'd tuned in to see what the show had got wrong. That didn't really surprise her. She had some friends who were nurses or medics who regularly watched some of the medical TV series to see if anything was remotely familiar.

But somehow she just couldn't get the words out. Was she embarrassed by her previous job? No. She wasn't. But it was all the repercussions from being in that show that played on her mind. It still sometimes gave her sleepless nights. The assault. The stalking.

She just didn't want to talk about all that any more. She'd put it behind her for a reason.

'Do you have a brother or sister that I might have come across?'

Darn, he was persistent.

'Only child,' she said, pasting a smile on her lips. 'I must just have one of those faces.'

She took a breath, and started on the notes again. 'I have to be honest. Matt isn't a great diary keeper.'

She held up her hand as Eli looked at her in surprise. 'Let me finish. What I mean is, the diary on his computer he didn't actually use as a diary. I think he might have started, but then he used it to just take notes, or write lists for himself. So it was almost impossible jumbling through to find out what he'd written about the Fletchers' farm.'

'Did you find anything?'

She gave a small shrug. 'Some scribbles about further tests…phoning Dave, but I have no idea who that is. And checking symptoms.'

'Symptoms of what?'

She pulled a face. 'That's just it. He didn't write that part. It must have been all in his head.'

Eli gazed out onto the road ahead of them and pulled

out. 'I just don't think I can phone Matt to ask him about this right now. I'll just have to go to the Fletchers' farm and get a feel for the place. Matt's wife texted me last night to say that his veins weren't standing up to the chemo drugs and they were putting a central line in today.'

Aurora inhaled sharply. 'So it's definitely not the time to call about work.'

'No,' he agreed, giving her a smile. 'It absolutely isn't.'

Aurora pointed to the road ahead. 'Just up on the left. This is the family that you know?'

Eli nodded. 'Well, I did when I was a kid. I mean I would have recognised them in the nearest village, but we didn't hang around together. I knew Dad was their vet, and every conversation was to do with the animals on the farm.'

'So, any clue what it might be?' she asked as he turned onto the farm road.

'Not a clue until I get there' he admitted, and she actually quite liked that about him.

When they approached, the farm seemed strangely quiet. Eli had already made his way to the nearest cow pen, but Aurora knocked on the cottage door. There were some farm vehicles around, but no actual car.

The door opened to a pink-cheeked woman. Aurora put her hand to her chest. 'I'm Aurora, the vet nurse. I'm here with Eli, our new vet. We're looking for Don Fletcher.'

The woman shook her head. 'Barb,' she said, putting her hand on her chest. 'It's taken me two weeks to persuade him to go the doctor, and his appointment is in ten minutes.' She lifted one finger to Aurora, 'Don't dare call his mobile and give him an excuse to come back.'

Aurora lifted both hands. 'I wouldn't dare. Would you mind coming and speaking to Eli?'

Barb shook her head and lifted a thick jacket from a peg near the door. She was already wearing boots so led Aurora back to where the cows were.

Eli was already checking over one cow. It was slightly scrawny-looking and in the space of time it took them to reach him he'd checked the eyes, ears and listened to the chest.

Barb held out her arms. 'Hi, Eli,' she said. 'Long time no see.' Like many farmers, she moved onto business. 'They're just generally sickly. Nothing too specific. Matt came about a month ago and said he'd come back. They're eating and drinking—maybe not as much as before. And we've been careful. It's just one herd that's affected.'

Eli stood up. 'How many herds?'

'We have beef and dairy. Three separate herds.'

'All kept in separate places?'

She nodded. 'Mainly, except for a few escape artists.'

Eli looked thoughtful and gave her a nod. 'Let's take a walk around,' he said.

They were at the farm for more than two hours. Eli looked at the layout of the fields, the dairy sheds, the pens, the hay/straw store and so much more. He examined seven different cows, all with a variety of symptoms. There were a range of coughs, some minor, some more severe, some cows were more tired than usual, and some had lost their appetite. After a long conversation, Barb agreed to keep the cows separated who were showing any symptoms, while Eli consulted about tests.

'It's a bit of a mystery,' he said as they climbed back into the Land Rover. 'None of these cows are really sick.'

'But there are enough symptoms for you to ask her to isolate?'

He nodded. 'You just never know. Lots of animals are similar to humans. Things spread. I'd like to do a bit of research and get back to the farm for more testing.' He frowned as he drove. 'I'd also like to get a chance to see Matt's notebooks to see if I can make any sense of them.'

Aurora was instantly offended. 'You mean when I couldn't?'

'If I meant that I would say it,' said Eli promptly. He continued, not giving her a chance to break in. 'I do similar things to Matt. I doodle, I write when people talk to me. And I don't always do it on the same page. If I'm writing animal notes, that's entirely different. But if I'm on the phone, and scribbling while listening, I doubt anyone would make much sense of what I've written. But it makes sense to me.'

He heaved a huge sigh, as if he knew she was still trying to make out whether to be offended or not. 'Believe me, I've driven fellow vets and nurses to despair in the past. My clinical notes are clear. But my own? Never.'

Aurora kept her mouth closed. It would be easy to pick a fight right now, but it wouldn't really serve any purpose. Today had been interesting. She'd got to see Eli Ferguson in a variety of settings, talking with a whole host of owners. He was new to most of them too, and it was fascinating watching them all try to get the measure of him, and decide if they trusted him or not.

Would she trust him with a pet? Likely. But as a person? She was still unsure.

She was certain there were sides of Eli she hadn't seen yet. He could be snappy at times—as she knew could she. His good looks were distracting. But Aurora had never been the kind of person to rely on looks alone. She always looked much deeper. And Eli's depths were still clearly hidden.

As were her own. At some point she would tell him she'd been in a TV series. It should make absolutely no difference to their working relationship, or how he saw her. But she'd sometimes felt that her previous vet colleagues had looked down on actors. Even though they shouldn't. Some of the smartest people she'd ever worked with were actors.

And whilst she could feel herself occasionally warming to Eli, she wasn't ready to reveal that part of herself. It would lead to questions, and uncomfortable memories.

And he didn't need to know that. Not yet anyway.

CHAPTER FOUR

THINGS IN THE practice settled down over the next few days. It was almost as if they fell into an easy routine, with Bert easily being the star of the show.

Aurora and Anne hadn't tried that hard to find somewhere to place him as yet. There was no urgency about the request, and he and Eli seemed suited to each other. Granted, there were occasional puddles in the hall, and even something else one day, but a vet's practice was used to animals having accidents and they all took it in their stride. It probably helped that they all frequently took Bert outside to try and imbed some toilet training rules with him.

So Aurora was surprised when Eli appeared in the doorway with a car harness for Bert. 'Will you come in the car with me? I have a potential home for Bert.'

She felt a little jolt of sadness but leaned over to grab her jacket. 'Okay, but who is it? Is it someone we'll know?'

Anne looked up from her desk. Aurora couldn't quite read the expression on her face. 'You'll know if it's the right place,' she said, looking steadily at Eli. She waited until he met her gaze, then gave him a nod. She picked up a piece of paper beside her. 'There's a message for you, Aurora. A...' she wrinkled her nose '... Fraser wants you to call him back about his cat, Arthur. The cat was recently diagnosed with diabetes. Quite insistent, actually. I did offer to speak to him, but he only wanted to speak to you.'

Aurora had an instant chill. 'They're not actually registered as our patients. And I'm sure it's the woman's name we had, not his. We saw them as an emergency.' She was silently praying that Eli would tell her not to call back.

But he was too busy with Bert. 'You can call later,' he said, not really paying attention.

Aurora gave a wave of her hand. 'Just leave it for me. I'll get to it later.' She pressed her lips together. A telephone call she could manage, but if the owner wanted to come in she would have to mention things to Anne or Eli.

As she went out to the car with Eli, she expertly manoeuvred Bert into his car harness, clipped him in, then climbed in the back seat next to him.

'What is this?' said Eli as he sat in the driver's seat.

'Last time in a car was traumatic,' said Aurora. 'I'm going to keep him company.' As Eli started the car, she continued. 'Or we're just going to sit in the back and plot against you.'

'That sounds more like it,' agreed Eli as they pulled out onto the road.

Aurora softly stroked Bert. 'So, no one has contacted the website about the picture we put up. How come you think you've found him a home?'

Eli turned his head to glance at her. 'This is just a meet and greet. I met a family the other day who said they wanted another dog. I told them we'd found a collie mix puppy who seemed healthy and they said they were interested.'

'Do you know these people? Where did you meet

them? Are they patients of ours? What kind of dog do they have?'

'Whoa!' Eli laughed as he lifted one hand from the steering wheel. 'This feels like the third degree.'

'Actually, it's the fourth. I'll be telling Anne about this. If you think I'm bad...' She let her voice drift off and shook her head. 'You have absolutely no idea.'

She could see his face in the rear-view mirror. He was watching the road ahead but frowning. 'That's right. She used to give Dad a real hard time about rehoming pets.'

'And you know why that is?'

She saw the spark as the thought landed in his head. 'A dog should never be rehomed more than once.' They said it in unison and both laughed out loud.

He groaned. 'I'd forgotten about that. That's why I got the Anne stare before we left.'

'It sure is.' Aurora was smiling now as they turned into one of the nearby villages on the outskirts of Edinburgh. 'Where do they live?'

'Here, in Stockbridge. I met them at the farmers' market, and that's where they'll be today.'

Aurora sat a little straighter. 'You're not even seeing their home? We're going to the farmers' market?' She groaned. 'Give me your whole vet background again, please. Because I'm having trouble believing any of this.'

The village was already busy and it was clear the farmers' market had already started. He pulled into a car park and turned around to look at her. She'd moved Bert onto her lap and was holding him protectively.

'Do you honestly think I haven't done due diligence? I went to their house a few days ago. I met their teenage son, and their other dog. They work every day at the farmers' market, and I suggested we meet here in case the dogs aren't sure of each other. I'd hate for the other dog to be snappy because another dog came into their home.'

Aurora narrowed her gaze. She couldn't keep the ironic tone from her voice. 'You have concerns.'

Eli sighed and took a breath. 'They want a puppy to help socialise their other dog.'

'No,' said Aurora, pulling Bert closer. She was only partly joking.

'Their other dog was fine,' he said, and she was sure he was trying to sound reassuring.

'But?' she asked.

He took a breath. 'But they bought their dog at the beginning of Covid and didn't have much chance to socialise it. It's definitely a people person dog. I'm just not sure it's another dog dog.'

Aurora nodded. 'So we take Bert along, and see how the meet goes?'

The expression on his face tightened slightly. 'It's just... I won't be here for long. I don't want Bert to think he's found a home, and for me not to give him a chance of another. I like the little guy. But I will move on soon. It's selfish of me not to try when an opportunity came up.'

Aurora licked her lips. She knew it was inevitable Eli would move on. He'd said so right from the start. 'We don't seem to have any vets beating down the door.'

It was probably out of order. But she knew he'd put another advert out.

A dark look crossed his eyes but he didn't respond, just turned back around and opened the door. Aurora climbed out, clipping a lead onto Bert's collar.

The sun was rising high in the sky. Scottish summers could be unusual. It wasn't strange to have a few perfect weeks in June and then four weeks of rain for the whole of July—just when the schools closed. But today was just perfect.

She slipped her jacket off and tied it around her waist. 'It's going to be a scorcher,' she said, and turned abruptly when Eli burst out laughing.

'What?'

He shook his head. 'Your accent. It's like you have a gift for them. You sounded as though you came from Glasgow then.'

Aurora felt her cheeks flush. Accents had always been her speciality. Even though she'd stripped her own right back, with certain phrases and words, her brain seemed to automatically mimic the way she'd initially heard them used. She hadn't even thought as she'd spoken out loud.

He clearly noticed that he'd embarrassed her and pointed along the footpath. 'This way to the market. Let's have a stroll around before we go to meet the Kings.'

Aurora was grateful for the distraction and encouraged Bert as he walked well beside her. The market was busy and after a few moments' hesitation Eli bent down to pick Bert up. 'He might get overwhelmed by all the feet, and the food smells,' he said.

Aurora nodded in agreement. 'Let's go over here.'

They moved over to a large array of flowers and plants and Aurora picked some orange gerberas. 'These have always been my favourite. My gran had these in her garden when I was a child.' The seller wrapped them in some paper for her, and they moved on.

Next, they sampled some cheese. But Eli pulled a face when the one with chilli clearly hit the wrong spot. He started coughing and Aurora couldn't help but laugh, before she pulled a bottle of water from her bag. 'Stop coughing around my dog,' she murmured as he took a sip.

His eyes were watering now, and the stall-holder was laughing appreciatively. 'Always one that gets caught out,' he said with a broad smile.

They moved onto some craft stalls, bakery, bread and fish. Aurora paused for a moment. 'I wonder if I should get some for dinner.'

Eli looked at her, then licked his lips. For a second she wondered if he was nervous. 'Why don't you just let me buy you a big lunch once we've met the Kings? You might not even want a dinner.'

She looked again at the fish, wondering if she even had the ingredients in her house to make the sauce she'd want alongside. 'Okay, then. Deal,' she said.

They moved to a fruit and veg stall, where a couple in their fifties were serving and a brown cockapoo was hiding under the table.

She noticed that Eli kept Bert in his arms. 'Hi,' he greeted them, tucking Bert under one arm as he shook both their hands. 'This is Bert, the dog I told you about.'

Mrs King came out from behind the stall and started talking to Bert. 'Aren't you a wee beauty,' she said, giving his ears a rub.

Mr King came out too, and they both fussed over Bert, who seemed nonplussed by the whole event.

Mrs King eventually went to bring out their cockapoo, who was obviously shy. 'Tyler, come and meet Bert.'

Eli put Bert on the ground near Tyler, staying close. Aurora watched carefully. She'd met lots of anxious puppies and dogs. It was far more common than most people realised. Tyler was clearly one of those dogs.

There was sniffing. Bert, being a pup, was more boisterous and Tyler retreated under the table. But Mrs King

persisted kindly, trying to encourage the dogs to inter-
act. Mr King still had a few customers to serve but he
was keen too, and Aurora quickly realised they were a
kind couple, and true dog-lovers. She could see why Eli
had considered them.

After nearly fifteen minutes, when Tyler had come out
a few times, and retreated on each occasion, they finally
agreed the first meeting was over. Eli shook both their
hands again and picked up Bert, threading through the
busy market with Aurora following.

'I know a place,' he said over his shoulder, leading her
away from the main market towards a pub with multiple tables outside in the garden. There was also a little
fenced-in section that was called a puppy play park, and
they were right next to it.

'This place does quite a lot of fish options. Thought
you might like to try, after wistfully gazing at the
salmon,' he teased.

She reached over to swat his arm. 'I was not wistfully
gazing at the salmon,' she said in mock horror.

'You were,' he teased, nodding at Bert. 'Wasn't she?'

It was almost as if Bert nodded too.

'Traitor,' she muttered, unable to keep the smile out of
her voice. The waitress appeared, handing them menus
and taking a drinks order. There were no other dogs currently in the puppy play park.

'I'll let him have a runabout,' he said as he filled up
one of the water bowls. 'Let me know if anyone else ap-
pears.'

Bert was happy to play and when the waitress came
back to take their food order he was jumping in and out
of a stationary tyre in the play park.

She gave Eli a stare as she ordered. 'I'll have the sea bream, please.'

He raised his eyebrows as he handed his menu back to the waitress. 'I'll have the Cajun salmon,' he said sheepishly, and they both laughed as the waitress laughed.

The sun was beating down, although their table was a little shaded by a parasol. Aurora automatically took some sunscreen out of her bag and put some on her arms, before handing it over to Eli. 'Danger of being a redhead,' she said with a smile. 'Always have sunscreen.'

Eli nodded gratefully as he slid some on too. 'What did you think of the meet?' he asked.

'I think it's a no,' she said simply, holding up her diet Coke towards him. 'Tyler isn't ready for another dog in the house. He's too shy, and I think there might be a good chance he'll retreat further into himself.'

Eli tipped his head to one side and looked at her curiously. After a second he lifted his soda and blackcurrant too. 'I completely agree.'

'What will you tell the Kings?' she asked curiously.

He looked thoughtful for a moment. 'They adore Tyler,' he said. 'I think they'll know themselves. They would never do anything to upset him.'

'Here's hoping,' she said, glancing over at Bert. 'Oh, look, he's got the zoomies.'

They laughed as they watched Bert run around in circles at a hundred miles an hour.

'Do you have any other visits today?' she asked.

He shook his head. 'I'm going to do some more reading about cows,' he said with a sigh. 'Something is definitely bothering me.'

'It'll come to you,' said Aurora with a smile as her sea

bream was put down in front of her. 'Usually in the middle of the night, and completely out of nowhere.'

Eli looked a bit surprised. 'Is that when things come to you?'

'Always,' she said as she sampled her fish. 'Like, if I've met someone that day but can't place them. And it annoys me all day. Then, in the middle of the night, I'll remember it was Sally from school's Auntie Jean. Or it was a patient from Hawkshead who has moved miles away, and because I'm not there any more I couldn't place them.'

'Do you ever sleep?' he asked with a smile on his face.

A memory flitted across her brain, and she pushed it to one side. Sleep at one time had evaded her for months.

She gave him a smile. 'I sleep like a log. It's the one reason I've got a cat and not a dog.'

Eli looked momentarily confused. She waved one hand. 'Because at the beginning you have to get up with a puppy in the middle of the night. Them waking because they need the toilet would generally wake a person. But...' she sighed '... I have slept through an alarm in the middle of the night before. Cats can use a litter tray. Not useful if you're trying to toilet train a puppy.'

'Where were you going that you needed an alarm in the middle of the night?'

It was a natural question, but it made her stall. She'd been going to catch a flight at Heathrow for filming in South Africa. She'd ended up with a taxi driver hammering on her door to wake her. But she just didn't want to get those words out. 'I was going to a festival,' were the words that came out. From nowhere, from absolutely nowhere, and she was cringing before she'd finished the sentence.

'Do you like festivals?' Eli asked, his eyes brightening. 'Where have you been? I love festivals. Used to do them all when I was a bit younger.' He gave her a broad grin. 'Remember the famous year at Glastonbury when it turned into a mud bath? That was me.'

Her brain was now on overdrive and it was entirely her own doing. 'Isle of Man,' she said as a little bit of her died inside at the continuation of her work of fiction.

His brow furrowed for a second. 'What one was that?'

'Can't remember,' she said quickly. 'I just realised sleeping in a tent was not for me.'

'Not a camper?'

She shook her head. At least this was true. 'Not a chance. I like comfort. I like electricity. I like heating. I want a comfy bed. A kettle. And the last thing I want to do in this world is have to squat in a forest to pee.'

He started laughing again, and Aurora started to relax. 'You're a five-star hotel girl, then?'

She held up her glass to him again. 'Without a shadow of a doubt.'

Part of her was a little sorry. If she'd been honest about her previous job, she could have told him about the wonderful lodges she'd stayed in while they were filming the vet series in South Africa. The lodges were in the middle of the Kruger National Park and were amazing. She could have been honest about the animals and wonderful vets. But again, it would lead to memories of the not good parts. The assault. The stalking. She'd worked so hard to put all that behind her. The spider-sense feeling had led her to have another online session with her counsellor the other day, and she was taking comfort from some of the outputs of the session. There was no quick fix. Not for what she'd gone through.

She just didn't want to let those memories in, not on

a gorgeous sunny day like this. Not when she was currently watching Bert jump around a dog play park having the time of his life.

It hadn't gone the way he'd wanted. But, then again, Eli wasn't entirely sure how he'd wanted it to go. He'd meant it entirely when he'd said he wanted to give Bert the chance of a good and permanent home. But it had felt too easy to say that the Kings wouldn't be a good fit.

He could feel himself becoming even more curious about Aurora. There was that familiar feeling around her. Anne had mentioned casually that there was no other half in her life. The more he spent time with her, the more the walls he'd built up around himself seemed to relax a little. Or maybe it was the setting. Being back at his father's practice hadn't been quite as bad as he'd thought it might. The work was interesting.

But he still worried about trusting those around him. It was ridiculous. He wasn't responsible for the accounts at the practice. That was still Matt's domain. But whilst he was off sick Matt had given him access to the practice credit cards, and told him that 'one of the girls' would likely handle the salaries.

It made him naturally jumpy. He wasn't sure how things normally worked around here. Last thing he wanted to do was interfere with the normal. But didn't he also have a responsibility to keep an eye on things? He couldn't deny he still had trust issues when it came to money—and especially for the business. He'd already let one business go to the wall; he couldn't let it happen to another. He pushed the money aspect from his head.

Because Aurora had hit a nerve earlier. He'd only had one enquiry so far about joining the practice—and it was from someone who wouldn't qualify for another six months. Eli spent his nights scouring the internet for other vet jobs—so why would he imagine anyone else wouldn't do the same? Did the outskirts of Edinburgh compare to the heat of San Diego, or the learning curve of working in the bush in Australia?

Bert gave a short yap—not quite a bark yet—and Eli turned his attention back to their puppy.

The thought stopped him hard. *Their* puppy? The practice's puppy, of course. He gave a little shudder.

'Cold?' asked Aurora innocently. Her dark red hair had fanned around her shoulders, and he could see her attracting glances. He was trying so hard not to notice just how attractive she was, or how the casual drift of her perfume instantly caught his attention.

Had he learned nothing from his last experience?

He set down his knife and fork. 'Not at all,' he said quickly. 'Want another drink?'

Aurora shook her head and nodded behind him. 'I think there's another dog about to come in.'

Eli caught sight of the black Labrador entering the pub grounds with her owners. He picked up Bert from the play park and slipped him back on the lead next to them. 'I'll just settle the bill,' he said, signalling to the waitress. 'Is there anywhere else you'd like to go?'

Aurora leaned back a little, stretching out her back and looking thoughtful. 'There was a bookshop along the street. It had stacked tables outside. I wouldn't mind having a look.'

'Sure,' said Eli, scanning his card to the machine the waitress brought over. 'It's a bit less busy down there. Let's see how Bert does.'

They walked casually down the picturesque street.

There was no traffic as this part of the road was cobbled. All the shops had old-fashioned frontages, painted in a variety of colours. Some had window boxes on the upper floors filled with colourful flowers.

'This place is like a picture postcard,' murmured Aurora as she walked alongside him.

'It's a lovely town,' said Eli, stopping and looking through the glass of the butcher's shop.

After a few moments Aurora bent closer, her hair brushing against his face as she joked, 'Eli Ferguson, are you wistfully gazing at a steak?'

He burst out laughing and shook his head as he walked away. Two minutes later, Aurora stopped walking as she stared in the front window of a clothing shop.

She held up one hand as he opened his mouth. 'Yes, Eli Ferguson, I'm wistfully gazing at a pink shirt.' Her hand went to her back. 'In fact, give me two minutes.'

Eli watched in amazement as she ducked inside, had a conversation with the woman behind the till, who crossed to the other side of the shop and looked through a few hanging shirts before pulling out a pink one and carrying it back to the counter. Aurora leaned over to look at the tag and nodded in agreement as she pulled out her purse.

Literally, two minutes later, she was back by his side, bag in hand.

'You just bought that.'

'I did.' Her smile reached right across her face. It was the first time he'd noticed her eyes sparkle. She clicked her fingers. 'This is the way I shop. I see something, I like it. I check my size and I buy it.' She shrugged and laughed. 'Boyfriends in the past have loved it, but my girlfriends all hate it. They like to spend hours in shops.'

'You don't need to try things on?'

She wrinkled her brow. 'I know what size I am. Unless the shop is unusual and runs bigger or smaller than normal, it's never an issue. And the people behind the counter know that about their clothes. They do generally let me know.' She smiled and held up her shirt. 'Fastest female shopper ever?'

He gave a short laugh. 'I'm sure there must be some kind of medal for that.'

She rolled her eyes. 'Guess what? That medal is made of either books or chocolate.'

In a lightning move, Aurora ducked into the next shop, a bakers, and came out carrying a white box. 'Don't ask—' she smiled '—it's a surprise for the journey home.'

They moved to the next shop, which was stacked up with books on the tables outside. People were browsing casually. 'Why don't you go in?' said Eli. 'Bert and I will wait outside.'

She shook her head. 'Oh, no. I love to rummage. The best and most obscure stuff is likely to be out here.' She started sifting through the stacks and Eli joined her. It only took a second for him to see something that interested him. He pulled out a dog-eared hardback with a faded blue cover.

She moved closer. 'What is it?'

He flicked it open. 'Just a book about an old shipwreck.' He gave a rueful smile. 'This is my weakness.'

She looked at him with a broad smile. 'Not old musty vet books?'

He had the tiniest inkling of something again. But he pushed it away. 'Oh, no, that was my father's weakness. I spent my life surrounded by them, and inherited most of them.' He held up the book. 'Shipwrecks is my go-to non-fiction.'

'Egypt is mine,' she countered, and he couldn't help but be intrigued.

'Really? Why?'

'So much history, so much unexplained, so many interesting people. And how did they build those pyramids?'

He smiled. 'You don't go for the conspiracy theories?'

Her eyebrows raised. 'Oh, I love those. I half believe that thirty-year-old film about gates made of stars that said the aliens brought the pyramids down and they are secretly spaceships.'

'That would be kind of cool.' He held her green gaze. She studied him in return, and for a few seconds he was frozen. Stuck in that place that made the sounds and colours fade around them, and for Aurora to become his only focus. She was captivating. Her perfume aroma drifted near to him on the breeze, sparking his senses. For a moment there was nothing else. Just her, and him. He could already imagine her in that pink shirt she'd just bought, and how it would bring out the red in her hair even more vividly.

And then a little body nudged against his leg and broke him out of his momentary spell.

He blinked and shook his head, licking his lips. 'Think there's any Egypt in amongst this lot?' He nodded to the stacks of books.

'Give me a minute,' she said, and he watched as she took a few steps, her eyes scanning up and down the books like a true shopping professional, moving a few stacks before stepping back with a sigh. 'Nope, no Egypt.'

'You did that in under a minute.'

'Told you. I don't waste time.'

'Want to go inside?'

She glanced down at Bert, who had tucked himself

under the table. 'Let me go and grab a thriller. I need something to read tonight. I'll pay for yours too.'

She went to add something, but Eli held up one hand, laughing, 'You'll only be a minute.'

True to form, she came back out holding a new release. 'Set on a cruise ship,' she said with a grin. 'A woman wakes up and everyone else is gone.'

'That does sound good,' said Eli. 'I might borrow it when you're done.' He held up the book she'd bought him. 'Tell me how much I owe you.'

'Don't be silly,' she said. 'You bought lunch.'

'Then thank you.' He looked down at Bert. 'Come on, little guy, that's enough walking for today.'

Bert seemed quite happy to continue, but the heat was building and Eli didn't want to walk him on the pavements any longer than necessary. He bent down and picked him up, tucking him under one arm.

Aurora leaned over and stroked Bert's head. 'We're going to find someone for you, little guy, don't worry.'

'Have you ever had a dog before?' He was curious.

She nodded. 'Yes, and no. My parents bought a red Labrador when I was a kid, but couldn't handle it. My gran ended up taking Max and since I went there after school every day I was always with him.'

'So, it worked out well?'

'It did. He was a great dog, and my gran was just too old to handle a puppy again when he finally passed away. It leaves such a gap in your life—you know, when you lose an animal.'

He looked at her carefully as they reached the car. 'So, if you could bring your dog to work every day, would you think about it?'

Her steps slowed. 'What do you mean?'

He opened one door to strap Bert in. 'I mean, I've fixed up the kennels outside now. Bert is quite happy running around in the enclosure during the day.'

'You want me to take Bert?'

He was trying to find a delicate way to put this, but was clearly failing. 'Well, maybe.'

'But what about in winter? There's no way I'd leave a dog outside in the snow we get.' She climbed into the car, but kept talking. 'And what about when you leave and there's a new partner? They might not take kindly to staff bringing their pets to work.'

'Or they might love the idea.'

She pulled a face. 'Not when we have to go into emergency surgery and might be stuck in there for hours.'

Eli sighed and nodded. 'Okay, so you've got me there. But if that happens in the next few weeks, Bert will need to go in the kennels out back. At least I know he's safe there. It was just a thought,' he said as he started the car.

He pulled out into the traffic and Aurora opened the white box. 'Iced raspberry doughnuts,' she said, offering him one.

'These match your new shirt,' he said as he took a bite.

'So they do.' She smiled as she took a bite of her own. 'I didn't even think of that.'

As they pulled out of the village and onto the country road he shot her a glance again. 'At least tell me you'll think about it.'

She gave him a hard stare. 'About Bert?'

He nodded.

'What if you decide you want to keep him yourself and take him wherever you decide to go?'

Eli shot a glance in his rear-view mirror at the puppy

sleeping on the back seat. 'It would get too complicated,' he said. 'Particularly if I decide to go abroad again.'

'You're not done running away yet?' she asked.

The words prickled, and his hands tensed on the wheel. 'I'm not running.'

'Okay,' she said simply as he shot her a sideways glance. But the expression on her face made it clear she didn't believe him. 'But why would your next job be far away again?'

He swallowed. He could tell her the truth. He could say he'd opened up a practice for the last few years in England, and ended up going bankrupt because he'd been conned. But somehow, telling that story didn't have a huge amount of appeal.

'You could always just stay a bit longer at your dad's old practice,' she said, as if it were the easiest thing in the world. 'Or stay for good.'

It was like throwing a bucket of water over him. 'I won't be staying,' he said firmly.

Aurora opened her mouth again. It was clear she had a million arguments around this. But she must have caught sight of the expression on his face because, instead of speaking, she gave half an eye-roll and took another bite of her doughnut.

He glanced at his own expression in the mirror. It wasn't pretty. His jaw was clenched tight, just like his hands on the wheel, and his own doughnut was currently languishing in his lap.

He took a breath and let his shoulders relax. This had been a good day. Probably the first he'd had in a long time.

He wasn't going to let anything spoil it.

'Just promise you'll think about it,' he said again.

A hint of a smile appeared on her lips. 'You're going to get my new boss to sack me, aren't you?'

He winked. 'Don't worry, we'll write it into your contract that you can bring your pets to work.'

Aurora sighed and leaned back in her seat, 'Okay, I'll think about it.' She wagged her finger at him. 'But that's all. *Think* about it.'

And as the countryside sped past, Eli smiled too.

CHAPTER FIVE

AURORA WASN'T TOO sure how to feel about anything.

Her afternoon with Eli Ferguson had whipped up a whole host of strange feelings. She hadn't expected to enjoy herself so much. She liked sparring with Eli. She liked finding out more about him.

And she couldn't pretend she wasn't a little disappointed when he'd said, categorically, that he wouldn't be staying at his father's practice. There had been a definite edge to his tone. One that made her understand there was likely a whole host of things she didn't know about.

Anne hadn't been too free with information. It was obvious she had a deep loyalty to David Ferguson and, in turn, to his son.

As for Bert? She'd love a dog. But, due to the nature of her job, it just wasn't practical. If Eli had actually meant what he'd said...

The phone rang and she answered automatically. 'Ferguson and Green veterinary practice.'

'Can I speak to Aurora, please?'

There was something about the voice. It instantly made her defensive.

She was hesitant with her reply. 'Who is calling, please?'

'It's Fraser, Fraser Dobbs. She was supposed to phone me back about our cat, Arthur.'

Aurora straightened up at the implication. 'You were called back, Mr Dobbs. A message was left for you yesterday at four-twenty p.m.' She could remember precisely when she'd called because she'd been relieved to get an answer machine.

There was a humph noise at the end of the line. Another thing that pressed her dislike buttons.

'Well, I want to speak to her now.'

'You are speaking to her, Mr Dobbs.'

He went into an immediate tirade about the cat, and how essential it was for him to come and see Aurora, and when could he get an appointment. She tried not to let her past experiences affect her. Maybe this gentleman was just concerned about his animal, and wasn't coping with the long-term condition.

She asked some questions, explaining things as best as she could. But everything always came back to the same thing—he wanted to bring Arthur in, and see her.

It made Aurora distinctly uncomfortable.

It wasn't entirely uncommon for some patients to prefer to see the same individual in a vet practice. It helped with continuity of care, and with maintaining therapeutic relationships. Occasionally, some pet owners became a little possessive over staff members, but this was usually when a pet was severely ill.

Aurora looked at the appointment calendar. Her spider-sense was tingling again, and while she wouldn't refuse to see a patient, she would make certain she wasn't going to be in the practice alone.

She asked a few questions around his partner, to see if she would be attending too, letting him know it was best to see them together, in case his partner had any questions of her own. He made some brush-off excuse to let her know that he would be attending alone, and that his partner didn't really understand anything about it.

After another few minutes they agreed on an appointment the following week, when Aurora knew that Eli would be around. She would talk to him about this later.

She replaced the handset, wondering what on earth she would say to him about this. As an employee, she should let him know that the individual made her uncomfortable. But, on the other hand, she didn't want him to think that she was unwilling to work with difficult clients, or when a pet owner had anxiety over their condition.

Bert trotted around the corner towards her, and she bent automatically to rub him behind the ears.

'Naughty, naughty,' came the sigh from the corridor.

'What?' Aurora looked up, amused, and surprised, with her eyes wide.

Eli had a cloth in his hand as he rounded the corner. He almost fell over them.

'Oops,' he said. Then his face coloured.

'Bert,' he said quickly, 'I was talking to Bert.'

Aurora glanced down the corridor, where a small puddle glinted in the sunlight. 'Really?' she teased. 'Because I'm not sure you're allowed to talk to employees that way.'

She picked up Bert and stood up, walking into the nearby consulting room.

'And doesn't our good vet know that our dogs don't get into trouble when they pee indoors? We just take them outside and clean it up without a fuss.'

'Well, this will be non-fuss number four this morning,' said Eli as he grabbed the mop and bucket from the corner.

She looked at Bert. 'Come on, son. Let's go outside for a bit.'

She left Eli mopping as she took Bert out to the run next to the kennels and set him down. Almost immediately, he did another pee. 'Good boy,' she said as she gave him a tiny treat.

'He does it to play me,' sighed Eli behind her. 'He pees inside, I bring him out. He pees outside, I praise him, take him back outside and he looks me in the eye, and does another.'

'Have you forgotten how hard the puppy stage is?' She smiled.

'Oh, I think you could say that.'

'When was the last time you had one?'

He shook his head. 'Honestly? Years ago. I've adopted or rescued mainly.'

'The old boys and girls?'

He nodded. It was common practice that vets or shelters were frequently left elderly pets, particularly when costs became more difficult for owners. Older dogs and cats in shelters were often overlooked when people came to find a new pet.

'There's something nice about giving an old dog or cat a great last few years,' said Eli, a wistful look on his face. 'Sometimes it's only a few months, but just devoting yourself to their care and attention for that period of time, letting them know they're settled and loved, is worth it.'

Aurora straightened in surprise. 'Eli Ferguson. You almost sound as if you have a big melting heart.'

'With animals?' he said. 'Every. Single. Time.'

'And with people?' She couldn't help herself, and as he turned to look at her she had a wide smile on her face.

He wrinkled his brow and looked a bit sorry about life. 'When you're concentrating on your animals there isn't much time for people,' was how he answered the question.

But Aurora wasn't going to let him get away with that. 'Come on, you mean to tell me that in all the time you stayed in—' she swiped her hand '—Florida, Spain, France and Maine, you never dated?'

He raised his eyebrows and the edges of his mouth tilted up in amusement, 'Good memory.'

'I'm a stickler for details. You'll learn that.'

He was still amused. 'Will I?'

'Only if you answer the question.'

It was like a standoff, but Eli was too quick. 'I will if you will.'

She tilted her head and put her hands on her hips. 'What?'

'Your other half? Or exes? You haven't mentioned anyone.'

There were a few seconds of silence.

'You first,' said Aurora.

Eli licked his lips. 'I dated a few people casually in each of the places you mentioned.' He took a slow breath, and then said rather slowly, 'I've kind of learned I shouldn't mix my personal and professional life.'

Wow. That was saying something. It was like a slap on the face. And though her first thought was to be offended—particularly when this had definitely seemed a bit flirtatious—she kind of got the impression there was more to this. Eli Ferguson actually looked a bit hurt, and a bit wary.

And he would never realise this, but his words actually resonated with her.

'I dated someone at work once, and it didn't work out particularly well.'

'Really?'

She wrinkled her nose. 'I was a bit younger, and it was

just kind of awkward, when you split up and still have to work together.'

He let out a long, slow breath, along with a kind of ironic laugh. 'You have no idea,' he said.

She stared at him, curious. 'Well, that's kind of cryptic.'

He paused for a moment, as if he was actually going to give her more information—fill in some of the blanks that she was conscious were still there. But he just put his hands on his hips and stretched his back. 'That's for another time, and likely a lot of beer.'

She blinked and pressed her lips together, because she hated where her head had automatically gone. Straight back to the pub they'd had lunch in, but there at night, on an actual date. Her brain did that in a few milliseconds, and she was cursing it.

She didn't want to think about Eli Ferguson like that. One, he was her temporary boss. Two, he wasn't staying. Three, there were still some things he wasn't sharing. And four, she hadn't been honest with him about herself. None of these things could add up to a healthy fling or relationship.

She gave an amused smile.

'What is it?' he asked.

She shook her head. 'Daft memories. Mainly around a very bad date and falling into a table full of beer that, unfortunately, was all in pint glasses instead of bottles.'

He shuddered. 'Messy.' Then one eyebrow arched. 'But was it you that fell on it, or your date?'

'Oh, it was my date. He was a friend of a friend, and had gone to the pub early as he was nervous and drank himself blind drunk. When I arrived, he got up to buy me a drink and went straight back down again.' She bit her bottom lip to stop herself from smiling too hard.

'Poor guy probably never recovered.'

'Oh, he did. I danced at his wedding last year. You know the mutual friend? They got married.'

'She set you up when she liked him herself?'

Aurora smiled. '*He* set me up. One of the best weddings I've ever been to, and the part about the almost date made it into the wedding speech.'

Bert had finished his toileting and made a beeline for them both, catapulting himself at Eli, who had to reach out his hands to catch him. 'Whoa, little guy.' He held him up to his face. 'How can someone so small jump so high?'

The phone started ringing inside and Aurora darted in to answer it. Eli followed her in, carrying Bert. She gave him a careful look as she spoke on the phone. 'Hey, Marianne, how is Matt? He is? Okay...' She paused. 'Yes, I'm here with Eli now.' She mouthed the word to him. *Visit?*

He immediately nodded.

'Yes, we'd love to. Today?'

Eli nodded again.

'No problem, we'll see you in an hour.' And then she paused for a moment. 'Is there anything you need? Anything you want us to bring?'

Marianne started to immediately say no, then there was a small noise at the end of the phone, and Aurora knew she was crying.

'Marianne, ask me for anything. It's absolutely no bother and we're happy to do it.' There were a few more sniffles and something about not wanting to be a bother. 'You're not a bother. Send me a wee text, and we'll pick up whatever you need on the way there.'

'Everything okay?' asked Eli as she replaced the receiver.

Aurora shook her head. 'She phoned because Matt's concerned he didn't get to do a proper handover and wants to see you.' She gave a sad smile. 'He's conscious that not all his notes are up-to-date.'

Eli pulled a face. 'His notebook—I haven't even had a chance to look at that yet. Where is it?'

'In your desk drawer,' she said, not taking pleasure in the fact he hadn't looked yet. She'd begun to actually wonder if she might have missed something he could spot.

He opened his drawer, pulled out an A5 green-covered notebook and started flicking. His smile was broad. 'Matt is exactly the same scrawler and doodler as I am.'

Aurora watched him as her phone sounded with a text message notification. 'Marianne said that he's sleeping loads right now while he's mid-treatment, so might not be awake for too long.' She gave a soft smile. 'She's also given me a list of girl's things that she needs. She's clearly been running about for Matt and forgot about herself.'

She looked out of the window as Eli kept flicking, writing a few random notes himself. 'I wonder...' Her voice tailed off.

'You wonder what?' His blue eyes met hers.

She pulled a face. 'It's just that on the way there we'll pass their favourite restaurant. I've been there with them a few times. I know what they like.' She glanced at her watch. 'It's nearly five o'clock. How do you feel about us getting them some takeout dinner?'

'Sounds like a great idea.' He glanced down again and his hand froze over a word. 'Oh, no!' He let out a sharp expression.

'What?' Aurora was genuinely startled. She moved

behind him to bend over his shoulder and see the word that had stopped him.

Badger. With a question mark next to it.

It was on the bottom corner of one page. The corner had creased upwards so it was almost hidden. But the top of the page held information about the Fletchers' farm.

Eli closed his eyes for a second. 'Don't suppose we know the last time the Fletchers' cattle had their TB tests?'

Aurora instantly felt her mouth go dry. Bovine TB was serious. Herds could be wiped out. Farms could be ruined. Badgers were a protected species, but could also have TB and carry it, and secrete it in their urine, faeces or any wounds. If cattle had direct contact with infected badgers, or if cattle feed or water was contaminated by badger excretions, then TB could pass between the species.

'Is that what Matt suspected?'

Eli flicked another few pages. 'It could be. It's not clear. The symptoms could match, but it could also be a host of other things. Darn it.'

'Maybe that's what Matt wants to talk to you about?'

He nodded solemnly. 'Could be.' He looked up again. 'Do you want to get changed before we go visiting? And, apart from the restaurant, where do we need to stop off?'

'A supermarket,' she said quickly. 'And yes, I will get changed. Is it okay to use the shower upstairs?'

'Of course,' he said, settling back down at the computer to keep checking some files.

By the time Aurora came down the stairs she'd changed into the pink shirt she'd bought the other day and jeans, and her hair was combed loose. Eli had made a few notes with questions to ask Matt, but he was also conscious his father's old partner might not be up to it. He'd dashed upstairs to change his shirt and brush his hair and was ready to go. He hadn't been sure of what Matt's relationship had been like with the newest member of staff, because there hadn't been an opportunity to have that conversation, but from Aurora's expression on the phone today it was clear she was close to both Matt and Marianne.

Her suggestion of buying them dinner from their favourite restaurant was thoughtful and a nice touch.

The drive was just over half an hour, and whilst thoughts of TB were flitting around his head he tried to push them away.

'Didn't take you long to wear your new shirt,' he said.

Aurora looked down at herself and brushed the shirt. 'This is actually the second time. It's soft and really comfortable. I might go back and try and get it in another colour.'

He smiled, doing his best not to notice how good it looked on her. Her dark red hair was stunning against the pastel pink of the shirt, and it seemed to complement and enhance the green of her eyes. His eyes couldn't help but linger on her lips. Her make-up was always light, but she'd clearly put on some extra lipstick when getting ready. That, with her long lashes, made her look like some kind of film star.

He had a weird jolt again. Just like he'd had before around her. The wave of strange familiarity that he just couldn't put his finger on.

They chatted easily about books, films and a few of the farms along the way. Eli started telling her about cases Matt and his father had dealt with when he was a boy. It was odd how easily the memories flowed. But these ones weren't dimmed by feelings of neglect. When anything had been happening in the practice, his father had welcomed any interest or assistance.

'The stoat ended up where?' laughed Aurora, tears streaming down her face.

'In our pipes. First under the floorboards in the staff kitchen. Then inside the wall upstairs. He was like a magical Houdini. It took seven days to finally catch him again.'

'What did his owner say?'

'Oh—' Eli waved his hand '—that was old Gus Bryant. He just laughed and said to bring him back when we found him.'

They pulled up outside the supermarket and Eli joined Aurora inside. She hovered near the tower of baskets, then changed her mind and grabbed a trolley. 'You know what. I'm just going to buy them some things. Food, household stuff, toiletries.'

'I'll grab some crime books,' said Eli. 'Matt always loved those.'

Aurora didn't scrimp. She bought chicken, fish, steaks, some fresh fruit and vegetables, alongside milk, cheese, crusty bread, and a whole array of women's toiletries. As they neared the checkout she stopped at the chocolate aisle and ran her eye along it. 'There!' she said happily. 'Marianne's favourites.' They packed the food into the boot of his car and she directed him to the local restaurant.

Eli couldn't help but look at the menu as Aurora ordered Matt and Marianne's favourites. He put his hand on her arm. 'Once we've seen Matt, we'll come back and eat here. We might as well. No point driving back and making food at home.'

For a second she didn't say anything, and he realised his hand was still on her arm and she was staring at it.

'Sorry,' he said instantly, pulling his hand away.

'It's fine,' she said briskly, but he noticed her rub the spot with her other hand.

It only took five minutes for the kitchen to put the meals together, and Aurora carried them in covered plates. As they pulled up outside Matt's house, Eli felt a wave of nerves. He had spoken to Matt on numerous occasions, but he hadn't actually seen him in person since his father's funeral.

Everything about the house was familiar, from the six grey steps leading up to the pale blue door to the front window that spilled out warm light. He got the shopping from the boot as Aurora climbed the steps, balancing the plates and ringing the bell.

The familiar ringtone of the ancient bell made his face break into a smile. A few seconds later, Marianne opened the door and ushered them both inside. Her eyes filled with tears when Aurora explained what they'd brought.

'You're an angel,' she said, sweeping Aurora into a careful hug, then taking the plates from her. 'Let me put them in the oven to stay warm. Matt's just taken his anti-sickness meds, and we need to give them time to work.'

'He's not keeping things down?' asked Eli, concern lacing his voice.

The small, grey-haired woman met his gaze. It was almost as if she hadn't heard what he'd said. 'So like your father,' she said with a smile, before holding him in a long hug.

His awkwardness vanished in an instant, with the familiar smells of the house, and warmth from Marianne. 'I've missed you both,' he said quietly. She would know.

She would know exactly what he meant, and how he felt, because Marianne had been witness to it all. She was too kind to ever say a bad word about her friend—his father—but that didn't mean she'd been blind to his shortcomings.

They padded quietly through to the sitting room. Even though it was a warm summer evening, the fire was lit and Matt was covered in a dark red blanket. His treatment was obviously making him feel the cold.

His skin was translucent, and he'd lost a lot of weight since the last time Eli had seen him. He was shocked by Matt's appearance. But Aurora didn't miss a beat, she crossed the room in a few steps and dropped a kiss on Matt's cheek.

'It's so good to see you. We're missing you so much.' She quickly mentioned a list of patients who'd enquired after him and wanted him to come back soon.

Warmth spread through Eli's chest. This was the benefit of being a long-term vet somewhere. The patients and people knew you. They noticed when you weren't there. Had anyone noticed when Eli had left any of his previous posts?

He hoped so, but it wouldn't be the same as this. He moved quickly, first shaking Matt's hand, then kissing his cheek too, and automatically sitting on the little footstool at the bottom of the chair.

Matt bent forward and cupped his cheek. 'It's so good to see you again.'

Eli's hand covered Matt's. He had so many good memories of this couple. So many times he'd stayed at their house, or had their support for school or sports events.

'You too,' he said slowly, hoping his voice wouldn't break.

There was a chance he wasn't going to have Matt much longer. He didn't need to ask questions. He didn't need to focus on scans or treatment plans. One look at Matt, plus the expression on Marianne's face at the door, told him everything he needed to know.

They didn't have children of their own. Marianne had nieces and nephews, but Eli had been the one to whom they'd shown undying support.

He settled on the stool as Matt started talking about the practice. It was clear he wanted to get things in order. As Eli pulled Matt's notebook from his back pocket he wished this didn't need to happen. But he had to respect Matt's wishes.

Aurora caught his eye and nodded towards the kitchen. 'I'm going to help Marianne unpack,' she said.

Matt quickly went through some patients, including a planned complicated surgery that Eli would have the skills to take over.

'What about the Fletchers' farm?' he asked cautiously.

But Matt was still sharp as a tack. 'Cows still sick?'

Eli nodded. 'I found some of your notes, but they weren't exactly in order.'

'It's the badgers,' said Matt without hesitation. 'Check the badgers.' Then, as if he could read Eli's mind, 'The bovine TB testing is due next month.'

Eli's heart dropped like a stone. He'd half hoped it had recently been scheduled and bovine TB could have been ruled out. But not now. 'I'll deal with it,' he said quietly.

Matt looked as if he wanted to say a whole lot more, but sagged back against the cushions on his armchair. 'Okay,' he replied simply.

He glanced to the door and back to Eli. 'So, you've put all that stuff behind you?'

Eli knew exactly what he was referring to. He sighed. 'It's resulted in bankruptcy. Iona will face criminal charges if she's ever found, but the practice property was repossessed and I was left with a whole pile of debts.'

'The staff?'

'I used my savings to pay their salaries. I did that as soon as I realised what had happened, and knew there was much more to come. So, I prioritised their salaries and notice periods, gave them all references, and closed the practice doors while the fallout happened.'

'You could have come to me!'

'For my stupidity? For trusting someone who took my livelihood? She got enough from me. I would never have come to you for something like that. It was my mess. I had to sort it.'

'I would have helped you,' Matt said shakily, and Eli's heart squeezed inside his chest.

'I know you would have. But I can start again. I just need to sort things out with yours and Dad's place, and then I'll take myself off somewhere else, and decide what comes next.'

'You have a practice. You have staff. You have a community where some people have known you since you were a boy.'

Eli couldn't get a reply out. He wouldn't hurt this man for the world. He couldn't explain how the practice brought back memories he found hard to push away. He just gave a shake of his head. 'I just can't do it. Not now.'

Matt tilted his head a little as laughter could be heard from the kitchen. 'What do you think of Aurora?'

Eli gave an embarrassed laugh. 'We've exchanged a few words, but she seems to be a good vet nurse.'

'She is. Smart as a whip. I'm worried someone will try

to steal her. When she started I had a few emails from another vet who had met her down at Hawkshead. They were impressed by her. I think a few had given her alternative offers, but...' he smiled broadly '...she chose us.'

Eli was curious about that. 'She's young to move up here by herself. Does she have family around here?'

Matt shook his head. 'She's from Liverpool. No family up here. As far as I'm aware, her mum and dad are still in Liverpool.'

Liverpool. He was getting used to hearing the remnants of the accent when it emerged.

'No husband?' Eli queried.

Matt leaned forward. He had a grin on his face, and a sparkle in his eyes. This. This was the way he'd always remembered Matt. 'And why would you be asking that? Has Aurora Hendricks caught your eye, Elijah?'

Eli gave a fake shudder. 'Don't. You only call me Elijah when things are serious.'

'And they are. She's a beautiful girl, with a big heart and...' he narrowed his gaze on Eli '...possibly too good for you,' he finished with undisguised relish.

Eli laughed. Matt had always teased him like this. All good-heartedly.

He glanced at the open doorway again. 'She's...nice,' he said. 'Thoughtful. And passionate about the animals.'

There was a noise and they both looked up. Marianne was carrying in the steaming hot plates of food on a tray. The smell was delicious. 'Look what Aurora and Eli brought us from Eldershaw's restaurant. Our favourite.'

Eli stood up, pulling over the nearby table so Matt's food could be close to him. He leaned over again and kissed Matt on the cheek. 'It was lovely to see you—enjoy your dinner and we'll catch up in a few days.'

Matt's frail hand caught his and squeezed it hard. 'Love you, Eli,' he said with a glimmer of a tear in his eye.

'You too,' was as much as Eli could manage, before hugging and kissing Marianne too, then heading to the door.

When they got outside, they both stood on the top step for a few moments. He could hear Aurora's shaky breaths; his own weren't much better.

'Okay?' he asked.

'I could really use dinner about now,' she answered.

He was grateful. Neither of them wanted to admit how sick Matt was. There was time for that later.

They climbed down the steps, into the car and drove back to the restaurant, where they were seated at a table at a window looking out over the back terrace and gardens. The sun was just beginning to dim, sending streaks of orange and red across the darkening sky.

'Do you want me to drive back?' she asked as they looked at their menus.

'Why would you ask that?'

Her eyes shone with sympathy. 'Because you've known Matt all your life. I saw the shock register on your face when you saw him. I just figured you might like to sit here and have a beer with your dinner.'

He was struck by how considerate she was being. 'I've driven the car before on visits to farms, so I know I'm covered on the insurance,' she added.

He hadn't even thought of that. Thank goodness she had. 'You know, I'd really appreciate that,' he said.

Eli's head was all over the place. The swamping memories, being back at his dad's practice. The mixed emotions of the love he still felt for his father, added to the

adult perspective now, where he could see he'd been ne-
glected in some ways. The anger that still simmered on
a daily basis at being conned so thoroughly, and so well,
that his only option had been to use his savings to pay
the staff wages before declaring bankruptcy. That deep
down regret that he'd lost the ability to trust people, and
it now affected his everyday life.

And yet he looked at Aurora and felt…something.

He didn't want to, and he shouldn't. But he couldn't
help it. Something just seemed to radiate between them,
to spark. Whether it was the too-long glances or the occasional flirtatious chat, he wasn't imagining this. He
just wasn't.

The waiter came and took their order. 'Is there some
kind of irony that I'm ordering the same things we got
for Matt and Marianne?' he asked as he sampled the beer.

'It's one of the best things on the menu,' she said simply. 'And I'm getting the other.'

There was a quiet ambience around them. People at the
tables chatted in low voices. There were no loud boisterous parties and Eli was grateful.

'What do you normally do on a Friday night?' he asked
her.

She was thoughtful for a few moments. 'Watch TV,
allow my cat to make a fool of me, or read a book.'

'What about parties, or nightclubs?'

'I did that when I was a bit younger. I'm past that. I
don't mind the occasional wine bar. Or I went to one of
the observatories at night, on a tour where you can see
all the stars and realise just how small this planet is. I
liked that.'

'I did that Night at the Museum thing when I was

younger—when you sleep next to the dinosaur bones in a museum.'

'Oh, wow,' she said enviously. 'That must have been great.'

'It was. But my friend snored, and another friend had an accident. Kind of spoiled the mood.'

She leaned back. 'I would have so loved that.'

'The snoring, or the peeing?' he teased.

'Don't be silly. Just the experience. Lying there, looking up at the dinosaur bones and wondering what life would have been like if we'd lived at the same time as the dinosaurs.'

'Only a mere sixty-five million years in between.'

She took a bite of her salmon. 'You're nit-picking now.' She tilted her head. 'But you're a bit like that, aren't you?'

He put a hand to his chest, feigning mortal offence. 'You wound me. Just because I pay attention to the details doesn't mean I'm a nit-picker.'

She looked up from under her thick lashes. 'That's exactly what it means.'

The conversation flowed easily. The food was delicious, and as two hours slipped away, Eli finally started to find some peace.

As they walked out to the car, he turned to her. 'I guess I need to face the fact that Matt isn't likely to get to work to train a new vet any time soon.'

She held his gaze as she opened the driver's door. 'So where does that leave us?'

Us. That was what she said. And he knew she meant the practice. But it didn't stop a good percentage of his skin from prickling. Would he ever be ready for another *us*?

The roads were quiet. Aurora turned on the radio and selected a channel that played soul music as they made their way back to the vet practice, where her own car was.

Eli contemplated all the things he could do next. None of the options made him happy—at least he didn't think they did.

'I hadn't planned on staying, but if I want the practice to successfully continue, I'd need to stay for at least a year after I recruit a new vet—maybe even longer.'

'You make it sound like a prison sentence,' she said simply.

The words made him cringe. 'I just have mixed-up memories about this place. After my mum died, my dad was juggling things. I know that he loved me but, to be honest, I think he loved the practice more. He missed out on a lot of things that are important to a kid.'

She shot him a glance while she drove. 'Did he have any help?'

'Matt and Marianne. He and Matt shared the work-load but—' he shook his head '—it seemed like whenever there was something important for me: a football final, a school concert, a big exam—' Eli sighed '—there just always seemed to be an excuse for him not to be there. Always an emergency, or a planned surgery, or he'd forgotten to put it in the calendar. And the thing is, I know Matt and Marianne reminded him. I know Matt always offered to do whatever the vet thing was at that point.' He closed his eyes tight for a second and scrunched up his face. 'I can even remember a conversation I wasn't supposed to hear, when he asked Matt to swap with him, so he didn't *need* to come.'

'Oh, Eli,' she said softly.

He opened his eyes again and gave another soft shake of his head. 'So, Matt and Marianne would come. I'd stay there if he was called out in the middle of the night. And they were great. I think, in truth, they were as frustrated with him as I was.'

'Do you think you reminded him too much of your mum?'

He turned to look at her, watching how the final remnants of purple light cast a glow across her skin and hair. 'I wondered that at one point, but I don't really resemble Mum at all, I have much more of my dad's features.'

'Maybe you have your mum's mannerisms, or habits. Apparently, I've inherited some of my gran's traits, and even sometimes, when something comes out of my mouth, I cringe, because I can almost hear her voice in my head saying it too.'

'I guess I might have. I just still have a deep-down feeling that I had a dad who loved his work and the animals more than his family.'

'Do you ever wonder if you might get like that?'

He leaned his head against the window. 'Don't miss anything with those punches, Aurora,' he said, a light tone still in his voice.

She shot him a worried glance. 'Sorry, I really should think before I speak.'

'One of your gran's traits?'

She gave him a grateful smile. 'Absolutely.'

They pulled up outside the practice and both climbed out of the car. Eli walked around the bonnet and met her halfway.

Now, she was lit up from the back, streaks of silver,

purple and deep navy behind her. She sensed it, and glanced over her shoulder and laughed.

'I guess someone thought we needed good lighting,' she said easily.

They locked gazes, and Eli took a step forward. It seemed entirely natural.

'Thank you,' he said in a low voice. 'For this afternoon, and tonight.'

She stepped forward too. Now, they were only inches apart. She lifted her hand and put it on his arm. 'It's fine. I was glad to be there. I don't think you should have gone alone.'

He focused on the hand on his arm. And all the sensations that were shooting along his nerve-endings. His eyes moved slowly from her hand, up her body and to her face.

Their gazes locked again. Green eyes. Big green eyes with dark lashes. Dark? She must be wearing mascara.

As they stood in silence, Aurora licked her lips. This time she took a mini step forward. Eli's hand lifted and rested on her hip, just as her own palm tightened on his arm, almost as if she was willing him even closer.

They moved in unison, lips brushing for the briefest of seconds before they locked entirely. Her hands wrapped around his neck, the length of her body pressed up against his.

He didn't want this kiss to stop. He refused to let any memories of the last person he'd kissed invade his mind at this moment. He refused to let himself be swayed by the fact Aurora was a workmate.

He was wise enough to recognise the different circumstances. There were no similarities here. He could concentrate on this.

The feel of her lips against his. The pressing of her hands around his neck and back. His lips moved to her face, her ear and her neck and she let out the tiniest groan. He could taste her perfume on his lips, feel it with every inhale.

She let out a breath and stepped back, nervous laughter filling the air between them. Her pupils were dilated, the green of her eyes nearly invisible.

'Whoa,' he said, trying to catch his breath.

'Whoa,' she repeated, a broad smile across her face.

She blinked for a second, obviously letting the cool night air clear her head. 'Not how I expected the evening to end,' she said.

He wasn't sure about her tone. Was it regretful? Was she questioning herself? Did she have doubts about their kiss?

'Me neither,' he said. He couldn't be untruthful. 'But I'm not sorry.'

She licked her lips again, and he wondered if he should invite her in. But Aurora was too quick for him.

'I have a cat to get home to, and you have a puppy to attend to.' She let her shoulders relax, and she swung her bag over her head. 'I'll see you Monday?' she said.

'Sure,' was all he could reply. Was she dying to get away from him?

She gave a wave of her hand as she headed over to her own car. ''Night,' she called as she climbed in and drove away.

''Night,' the reply came on his lips. But he stayed

where he was and watched as her car headlights finally faded into the distance.

What on earth would Monday bring now?

CHAPTER SIX

ANNE WAS MANNING the phone with an annoyed look on her face. Aurora was immediately on edge. Did Anne know that she and Eli had kissed the other night?

She immediately stuck her bag in her locker and came through to the main reception. 'Want me to take over?'

Aurora had learned that although all tasks were supposed to be shared, there were some things that Anne just didn't enjoy doing. She had a pad and a calculator and a spreadsheet open on the computer. Aurora recognised the software immediately. Wages? Was there an issue?

The wages software was usually easy. Hours entered. Checked by the accountant, salaries paid.

'I think I made a mistake. Matt should still be getting paid sick leave. Eli is on the payroll now, you and I have our hours inputted, but Frankie called to say he hadn't been paid for his final week's notice. He had holidays owed, so he should still have been paid. But I can't find the glitch in the system.'

Aurora nodded. 'That's right, I remember us having that conversation. Do you want to swap? I've got Mrs Pringle coming in to get some information on getting her cat spayed. Do you want to have the chat, and I'll have a look at this?'

'Perfect,' said Anne, out of the chair like a shot.

Aurora smiled. She really didn't mind. She was sure she would figure things out.

Half an hour later, Bert sniffed his way around the corner towards her. 'Hey, little guy,' she said, picking him up and setting him on her lap.

She was still petting him as Eli came around the corner. 'Hey,' he said easily.

'Hey,' she replied, unable to help the smile on her face. She hadn't slept a wink the other night. Too many what-ifs had floated through her mind.

It had been spending the afternoon and evening with him that had just drawn her to Eli, stronger than ever. She'd seen him vulnerable at Matt and Marianne's, the love they all had for each other very apparent. The meal had been delicious, but the conversation in the car?

It had felt as if she was finally getting to know Elijah Ferguson for real. There were some real mixed-up feelings about his dad. She could tell he was doing a lot of unpicking himself. But he'd been honest with her. Now, whilst she might not really understand the resentment he felt deep down, at least she could empathise. Coming back here was tough for him. And the realisation on the same evening that he would likely have to stay here for at least the next year—was that what had done it for her? Knowing this flirtation and attraction might have a chance of lasting more than a few weeks?

It had certainly helped. She'd never been the kind of girl to look for very short-term. She liked a chance to get to know someone and be part of their life on a regular basis.

And the kiss? The kiss had taken her breath away. Literally.

She'd wanted to get in her car and drive away? Absolutely not. Had it been the right thing to do, for him and for her? Absolutely yes.

She'd needed that space. She needed to work out how things would be at work between them. Some people couldn't handle a relationship with a workmate, but she certainly hoped that she and Eli were adult enough to work this through, because she actually wanted to see where it might go.

It honestly felt like something was sparkling inside her. She hadn't really wanted to attempt any kind of real relationship in the last few years, since her assault on set, and the stalking fiasco afterwards. The long-term counselling had given her the rational grounding that she needed. She'd learned to forgive herself, and respect that she wasn't responsible for either incident. She'd learned to apportion blame appropriately. She'd started to trust herself again. She'd been so cautious ever since both incidents—probably to the point that she recognised she pushed people away, and likely hadn't given anyone much of a chance in the last few years. But she was getting there.

And this was the first time she'd *wanted* to give someone a chance. She'd felt the buzz, the connection, that she hadn't felt in years. But this time she was older, more confident, and surer of where she was in life, to take it and grab it with both hands.

But would Eli grab it with her?

'Are you up for going back to the Fletchers' farm today?'

'Of course,' she said as he moved over, closer to her.

'I know you were planning on talking to Matt about it. Did you get a chance?'

His face was serious. 'Yes, he's definitely thinking

it could be a risk of TB due to the badgers. He said the farm was due to do their bovine TB testing next month. We need to get up there, find out as much as we can, and see what we can do next.'

'Want me to get changed?'

He nodded then glanced down at the screen. His gaze narrowed. 'What are you doing?'

She was a tiny bit surprised at the edge in his tone. 'Wages, swapped with Anne. She said there was a flaw somewhere, and Frankie hadn't been paid for his last week. I've just checked, amended it, and forwarded it on to the accountant to check.'

He blinked, nodded and said in a low voice, 'Okay, go and get changed and I'll meet you back down here.'

Was that slightly awkward? She wasn't sure, because her head was so full of the potential consequences of finding bovine TB on one of the farms they served. It was massive and would involve a huge team of professionals to work through the issues.

'I've phoned Don Fletcher to let him know that Matt suspected there potentially could be an issue with the water or food supply transferred by badgers. He's devastated at the potential threat to his herd, but happy to do everything he can.'

'We'll need to check the cows, isolate them, contact the authorities and arrange testing.'

He nodded. 'It's going to be a long day. Let's go.'

If she'd expected some lightness today, Aurora knew she wasn't going to get it. A flirtation at work was nothing. This was someone's livelihood and herd. She had to be completely focused on work, and play her part to gather as much information as possible.

It was late evening by the time they got back to the

practice. They'd spent hours at the farm, talking to Don, checking the cattle, making sure they were sufficiently isolated. It did look as though the food supply could have been compromised. Some badgers were either ingenious or sneaky, and potentially could have infected the food or water supply. Since there was more than one herd, there had been long discussions about making sure there was no crossover of usage of areas. Plus, ensuring that no cattle, equipment or milk could leave the farm. In amongst all this were the huge array of phone calls to Defra, the government agencies and departments who dealt with potential bovine TB, Public and Environmental Health and the Animal and Plant Health Agency. It was exhausting.

They'd followed all the personal cleansing and disinfection rules on entering and leaving the farm as a precaution, and the testing was arranged for the next day, along with one of the specialist vets. But both of them still felt grubby. Aurora was pulling at her tunic top and jacket.

'Want to grab a shower?' Then he looked at her again. 'How far away is your place? Do you want to just stay here, rather than drive home tonight, since we need to be back at the farm early?'

She hesitated, but only for a second, because it did make sense and she was already feeling too tired to drive.

'Okay, thanks.'

Aurora was familiar with the layout of the rooms. The place had previously been some kind of small family estate, the downstairs mainly converted to house the practice, with upstairs occasionally used by visitors or staff.

She understood Eli had been staying there rather than use the vet's house next door, which he hoped would attract someone to the new job, but she hadn't really seen much of how he was living.

By the time she came out of the shower, she could smell something cooking in the upstairs kitchen. She knew this one was rarely used and, as such, was immaculate, or at least it had been until Eli arrived.

He had white flour on the tip of his nose. Bert was in the corner of the kitchen, drinking from his water bowl then making short work of his food.

'Making pizza,' he said, clearly a bit frazzled.

She changed into new scrubs, which she always kept at the practice. This pair were older and well worn, so more comfortable than usual. 'From scratch? You didn't have anything frozen?'

He gave a shrug. 'I lived in Italy. I know how to make real pizza.'

'You know how to make a mess,' she joked.

He looked around the kitchen and nodded in agreement. 'I certainly do. Let's hope it's worth it.' He opened the fridge and pulled out a bottle of white wine. 'Want some?'

'After today? Abso-blooming-lutely.'

He poured two glasses and kept peering into the oven, checking on the pizzas. After a few more minutes he pulled them out and put them on wooden boards. Instead of sitting at the small table in the kitchen, he gestured with his head. 'Want to go through to the sitting room?'

'Sure.'

The sitting room window was wide open, letting the warm summer evening air filter into the room. Eli set the boards and pizza cutter down on the low table in front of the grey sofa, then flicked on the TV. 'Football, football or football?' he asked in a jokey manner.

Aurora glanced at the clock. 'One of the history or mystery channels, please. I'd like to hear about Machu Picchu, the Pyramids, the Rosslyn Chapel or the Titanic, please.' She gave him a quick wink. 'I'll even watch something about an old shipwreck if you can find it.'

He walked swiftly through to the kitchen, grabbed their wine glasses and sank down beside her. 'Do you know how long I've wanted to hear those words from someone else?'

'I guess I'm just permanently nosey and curious,' she said. 'I'd love to work on one of those shows.'

It was a throwaway comment. And she had considered working in the background of TV, rather than as an actor or presenter. But for a second she froze, wondering if she'd just revealed too much.

But Eli clearly didn't take too much from the comment. 'Me too,' he said with a spark in his eyes. 'Can you imagine how much more doesn't reach the screens? It must be fascinating.'

He grabbed a slice of pizza and took a bite and she did the same.

'Wow,' she said as the flavour hit her tongue. 'That's amazing.' She stared at the pizza base suspiciously. 'It's got a bit of bite to it.'

He nodded. 'The tomato base sauce has a hint of chilli—more like an Arrabbiata sauce? I think it makes it tastier.'

She nodded in agreement, her brain swirling. This was the time. This was the time to mention her previous job, and why he might think that he recognised her. She could just do it casually, ask him if he'd ever considered a different career before training as a vet. But now she knew the answer to that would be no. It wouldn't be an easy subject to introduce that way.

There was a noise from the corner, and they both turned their heads. Bert had snuggled down in his basket and was comfortably snoring. They started laughing at the same time.

'A snoring puppy?'

'Lucky me,' said Eli. 'I'll sound his chest tomorrow, but I think it's just how he's lying with his little head tucked in.'

He took another breath. 'There's two extra bedrooms across the hall. You can pick whatever one you like to sleep in.' The words came out so quickly that they almost ran together. Was he nervous?

She picked up her wine and took a sip. 'Perfect, thank you. I'm just glad I didn't need to do that drive home. I might have fallen asleep.'

'What about your cat?'

'Miss Trixie will be fine. I already texted my neighbour to feed her and go and check on her.'

'You called your cat Miss Trixie?' There was scepticism in his tone.

'She's a rescue, she came with the name. But I have to say, The Queen would probably suit her better. She thinks the rest of the world is there to do her bidding, and I swear she looks at me with disdain most of the time.'

'The world of cats,' he sighed. 'One day, scientists will be able to understand a cat's thoughts, and I genuinely think we will all be horrified by how badly they think of us all.'

She laughed. 'Oh, I can almost guarantee it.'

He reached out and touched her arm and she flinched. She hadn't even had a chance to have a single thought. It was just slightly unexpected, and it was her body's automatic response.

Eli's face changed instantly. 'Aurora, I'm sorry.'

She reached for the spot on her arm and shook her head. He'd shared so much about himself in the car. Wasn't it at least time she shared a little bit in return?

'It's me,' she said. 'I had an experience when I was younger that came as a shock.'

He was sitting very still on the sofa next to her.

'It makes me nervy. I feel as if I have a spider-sense that tingles sometimes.'

'With me?' he asked, looking horrified.

She gave him a soft smile. 'No, not with you, Eli. But if anyone touches me and I'm not expecting it, my body just reacts.'

He closed his eyes for a second and just breathed. 'I am so sorry,' he said. 'That should never have happened.'

'No,' she said calmly, 'it shouldn't. But sexual assault happens to women all over the world. And I was, like most, shocked at the time, blamed myself, and didn't want to report or complain.'

'So, what happened?'

'I finally admitted things to a much older member of our team, who had much more direct methods. He reported him, and when others heard, other women stepped forward to say he'd grabbed them, or cornered them too.'

She gave a sigh. 'Actually, just knowing that made me feel a whole lot better. It wasn't just me. He'd been the same with other women, and I absolutely wasn't to blame.'

Eli gave a careful nod. She could tell he was treading warily, but she'd noticed he'd stuffed a clenched fist under his leg on the sofa.

'Did he get sacked?'

'Yes, and no reference.'

'Did the police do anything?'

She'd been in South Africa at the time. But police forces the world over weren't much different.

'An alleged sexual assault is difficult to prove. Unless a grab has been particularly forceful it sometimes won't leave a mark. I didn't want to put myself through a trial, where some might have doubted me, or thought that I deserved it.'

'That's awful.'

'It was. But I survived it.'

And a lot more too, she thought.

'I had no idea,' he said earnestly. 'I'm sorry I alarmed you.'

The screen flickered in front of them and the titles for a documentary on the *Marie Celeste* appeared. Aurora felt partly relieved.

'Do you know what I could do with?' she asked.

'What?'

'A hug,' she said simply. 'Refill my wine glass, let me slump on the sofa next to you, watch some interesting TV and not worry too much about what tomorrow will likely bring. I need a few hours of nothingness.'

'I can do that.' He picked up their glasses, walked to the kitchen to refill them, and when he got back to the sofa he relaxed down as Aurora leaned against his side. His arm went easily around her shoulders and she just rested against him.

'Perfect,' she murmured.

Eli's head was spinning, as his body would quite like to react in a normal way to having a woman he was extremely attracted to this close. But he concentrated hard to try and dampen all his desires.

The documentary passed the hour easily. They sipped their wine, and he enjoyed the heat and feel of her next to him. The curves of her body against his. The clean scent emanating from her hair and body.

As the credits started to roll, she looked up at him with those too green eyes. She didn't even speak, just lifted her mouth to his.

He was tentative. He was wary. Because now he was in new territory. Now, he was conscious of his every move and not wanting to give her any reason to feel nervous. So he let Aurora lead the way entirely.

And she did. As their kisses deepened, and hands brushed against each other's skin, it was Aurora who made the move to swing her leg over and sit astride him, letting him run his hands up her back and touch her smooth skin.

It was Aurora who tilted her head back to give his mouth access to the delicate skin on her neck.

And it was Aurora who positioned herself where she could clearly know the effect she was having on him.

'How about I don't sleep in one of the spare rooms?' she asked.

He tried not to let out a groan. 'You want to steal my bed now too?' he joked.

Her eyebrows lifted. 'I want to steal your bed with you in it,' she replied.

He thought they might take things slow, but she stripped off her clothes on the way to the bedroom and turned to face him as he entered.

'Always so slow?' she teased as she climbed into bed.

Eli had never shed clothes so quickly in his life as he joined her on the bed.

'You sure about this?' He had to ask. He had to make sure they were both on the same page.

'Absolutely,' she replied with a big smile on her face as she pulled him towards her.

CHAPTER SEVEN

TESTING A HERD of nearly one thousand seven hundred would have been a nightmare. But, thankfully, the Fletchers kept their herd segregated, and it was only two hundred cows that could have been exposed.

The seven who were considered symptomatic were tested first, with their tuberculin skin tests to be read in seventy-two hours. In the meantime, Don Fletcher wasn't looking too good himself.

'Don,' said Eli, already knowing what the answer might be, 'do you drink unpasteurised milk on the farm?'

'Every day,' he admitted. 'Public health are sending someone out to test me later today. Me, and Jake, the herd boy. He has breakfast here every morning and we both drink unpasteurised milk.'

'Any symptoms?'

'GP already asked me a few questions days ago. He's ordered a chest X-ray, but the public health person said they will need to look at that and the TB test together to consider a diagnosis. Chest X-ray is booked for tomorrow.'

'What about Jake?'

Don frowned and shook his head. 'Not sure who his doctor is.'

'I'll let the team at public health know and they'll arrange a chest X-ray for him too.'

Don sighed. 'We've reinforced around all the stores and water supply, but it's really too late now. Once bovine TB is in the herd, the cow-to-cow transmission can be high.'

'Let's just wait and see what the tests show.'

Don nodded as Eli finished up all the things he needed to do on the farm that day.

It had been a strange morning. Nice to wake up with Aurora in his arms. Reassuring to notice how comfortable she felt beside him. Unusual to discover how in synch they were in the kitchen in the morning, where both of them had refused to even function before they had coffee.

There had been a serious atmosphere this morning. Because they knew the day ahead was going to be tough. To her credit, as soon as they'd arrived at the farm and after taking one look at Don, who was pale and thin, Aurora had gone with the vet from the Animal and Plant Health Agency, along with one of the farm hands to get things started.

Eli had assisted where he could, then gone back to chat with Don in the farmhouse for a while. Don could already have tuberculosis, which was impacting on his health. But Eli was also conscious of the immense amount of stress and pressure an event like this would cause to a farmer. The health and wellbeing of the farming community was always at the forefront of his mind.

'I'm surprised you're still here,' said Don, in between coughs.

'You are?'

Don nodded. 'I thought you'd cut and run as soon as you could.'

Eli decided to be honest. 'I wanted to, but Matt is sick. I'm not sure if he'll be well enough to come back, and I'm still advertising for another vet. Until all that happens, I have to stay.'

'Do you think you'll get someone?'

Eli raised both hands. 'It's difficult. I might be able to attract someone newly qualified, but even then I'd need to stay and oversee them for at least a year. So, my plans have had to change.'

Don looked at him for a few moments. 'I'm glad to hear that.'

'You are?'

'Of course I am,' he replied. 'If you close, the nearest vet practice is twenty-five miles away. And I don't know those people. Your practice—Matt's? I've known you both for years. I trust you both. If Matt hadn't been sick, this would all have happened probably some time last week. But I'm grateful that as soon as you both had that conversation you picked up the phone to let me know what you were thinking, and what would happen next.'

'It's what every vet should do.'

'But not all do. I've heard tales from other people that other agencies have just turned up at their farm after the vet has left.'

'I'd never do that to you, Don.'

'I know, son.' He reached out and placed his hand over Eli's. The gesture was small, but meant so much for an old guy like this.

Eli's eyes fixed on their hands. This. This was part of why he was here. He'd never want to let the farming community down. This was part of why he loved his job so much. Working in all parts of the world was great. Learning and getting experience with other kinds of animals was also great. But farming was the backbone of so much in Britain.

He'd always known his father had completely loved it. And that, in turn, had made him want to invest his time and energy in different ways, and in different places. But the reality was that he, Elijah Ferguson, loved working on the Scottish farms. And for some reason it seemed as if he was only truly realising that now.

Aurora appeared at the doorway. 'Everything okay?'

Don pulled his hand back and gave her a nod. Aurora walked over to the stove in the kitchen and turned the hob on. 'Barb phoned with strict instructions I was to make sure that you ate, Don. She's left this pot of soup, and said it was big enough for us all.'

Eli moved over to join her, cutting bread from a thick loaf. 'He is looking thin, and pale.' He glanced at Aurora, who was pulling out bowls and had found a soup ladle. 'I'm glad Barb phoned you.'

They exchanged a small smile. He liked how resilient she was, and how she wasn't afraid to jump in and help. One of the farm hands went to round up all the others and plates of lentil and ham soup, along with thick farmhouse bread, were served to all.

'I need to get the recipe for this,' Aurora whispered in Eli's ear. 'I am absolutely rubbish at making soup.'

He smiled in surprise. 'The first thing you're not good at. I learn something every day.'

'The second thing might be pizza,' she freely admitted. 'I've never made pizza from scratch before. Some might say that last night you were just showing off.' There was a glint in her eyes.

'What part?' he immediately joked and laughed as colour seemed to spread up her cheeks. But no one else in the room had noticed. It was as if they were in their own private bubble.

When everyone was done, Eli loaded the dishwasher as Aurora made Don a coffee and cut him a slab of gingerbread that Barb had left.

Something was dancing around in his brain. He liked her. He liked her a lot. But he'd been down this road with a colleague before. Someone who had pulled the wool over his eyes.

Yesterday, he'd noticed that Aurora had been in the practice's accounts. Granted, it was a small place, and everyone might do more than their role. But neither his solicitor nor accountant had mentioned that the wages were done by the staff themselves. Matt had mentioned it. But to Eli, with his naturally suspicious mind, it all seemed a bit strange.

It wasn't as if Aurora had tried to hide it. She'd been upfront and said Anne had been struggling, the last employee hadn't been paid and she was helping. Was it really normal for a vet nurse to do the wages?

Maybe it was because he'd been working in other countries. Most other practices had been much bigger than this one at home, and there had been finance offices to deal with all the wages. He couldn't remember what had happened in the past. He'd been too young to care and then, as a teenager, he'd only been interested in the animals, not the running of the practice. This could be entirely normal.

But he'd need to check.

He hated he felt like that. But he couldn't push it away. It was just too important. If he was going to be around for the best part of a year or more, he really needed to get a better handle on the day-to-day running of the practice. He should have done it before now.

'What's wrong?' Aurora asked.

'Nothing,' he said quickly.

'Are we ready to go then?'

He nodded and they followed all the cleansing and disinfectant rules before they left the farm. As they drove along the road Aurora gazed at the scenery.

'You know, I was thinking. You could make some improvements to the practice.'

'What do you mean?' He wasn't sure why he was instantly alarmed.

'It's just that, last night, I noticed upstairs has clearly been renovated in the last few years. Downstairs, the practice looks a bit tired by comparison.'

'You think?' He hadn't really thought about it at all. He'd worked in some state-of-the-art practices, and some middle of the road. His father and Matt's practice had never really entered his thoughts at all.

'It's just, as you're advertising and looking for someone new, if you brightened the place up a bit, got some new equipment, it might attract some new candidates.'

Okay, what she said made sense.

'And you've already made a start on the kennels out back.'

He nodded. She was right. The kennels at the back had been used during the good weather to sometimes monitor pets or keep them until their owners returned to collect them. They'd been pristine in years gone by, but had obviously been less of a priority in recent times. It had taken some blood, sweat, tears and some timber to resurrect Bert's playpen, but he could take some time to do the rest, particularly when it was nice weather.

'I could do the rest of the kennels,' he said slowly.

'Then we could think about the two treatment rooms. The doors could do with replacing, and maybe a new sink in one. The floors in both could be replaced and they could do with a coat of paint each too.'

'Are you turning into one of those house shows on TV, where they throw you out for a couple of days, then the owners come back and find they've turned a library into a disco?'

She gave a small laugh. 'Not quite. I just think it might help things. And I'm happy to help. I can put a few things through the accounts.'

It was like a chill going through his veins. He tried to be rational. But being a victim of a crime, and realising how many tiny tells there had been that he'd missed, had imprinted on his brain.

Last night had been the best night he could remember. Aurora's lips on his, her skin against his, and that feeling of connection that he'd always been seeking but had never found before. All of that was currently skewing his rational thoughts.

Aurora must have noticed the way his hands had tightened on the steering wheel because she gave him a strange look. 'Forget it, don't worry. It was just a suggestion. Why don't you wait another few weeks and see if you get any applicants?'

His heart ached. She was trying to help him. And if this was genuine she might think him ungrateful. But if this was something else—something cold and calculating that he'd missed before—then there was still a chance to stop things.

As he drove along the last mile to the practice his mouth was bone-dry. He couldn't pick up the phone to

Matt. It wasn't fair. He couldn't ask him the questions he wanted to ask. Like how well he knew Aurora. If he'd checked her references and qualifications.

Then, cutting clean through those thoughts, was something else. Was this it for him? Was this how he was going to spend the rest of his life? Second-guessing. Never trusting, always questioning what anyone told him.

He wanted to believe not. Maybe it was just timing. Maybe it was just because this was the first time he'd really let someone close since Iona. It could be that he would always have been like this next time around—and Aurora was just caught in the emotional crossfire.

He hated the way that sounded. He hated more the way it felt.

'I'll think about it,' he said, knowing his words might sound a bit abrupt. 'I'm still thinking about a lot of things with Don Fletcher's farm. Let's deal with that first.' He looked sideways. 'And, there's some other things to pick up. Jack Sannox and Rudy for one.'

She turned to face him. 'Do you trust me to do that?' There was an edge to the question.

'Of course I do,' he replied.

'Then I'll go tomorrow if we're not back at the Fletchers' farm all day.'

He licked his lips, trying to be rational and calm. He was a vet. There were a number of crises right now for his clients. Some huge in volume, and some smaller— but with equal emotional value.

'I would really appreciate that,' he said steadily. And he realised he meant it. Jack Sannox and his wellbeing mattered to him. From everything he'd seen of Aurora in her professional capacity, he had absolutely no reason not to trust her. If she was worried about Jack, she would let him know.

Aurora's phone buzzed and she pulled it out of her pocket as they reached the practice. She frowned. 'It's Anne, saying that patient with the diabetic cat is insistent on talking to me again.'

Eli's head shot around. 'Are you worried?'

He watched as she took a deep breath and focused on the practice building instead of him.

'Let's just say that my spider-sense tingles around him.'

'Then we don't see him. I'll ask Anne to tell him that our books are full, and to divert him to another practice.'

He could see the wave of relief wash over her, not just from the visible welcome slump of her body. This had been hard for her—hard for her to admit. If they hadn't connected last night, might she not have told him?

That was the last thing he wanted for staff that worked for him.

'Thank you,' she said, her voice a little shaky.

He reached over and took her hand. 'Any and every time,' he said firmly. They sat for a few minutes while she collected herself, then she gave a big sigh and fixed a smile on her face.

'Let's go back inside.'

They were met by Bert at the door, who looked as if he'd been up to mischief. Anne simply raised her hand from the desk. 'Don't ask,' she said.

Eli smiled and walked over to her. 'The man you texted Aurora about, the one that's been insistent about dealing with her?'

Anne nodded.

'Can you phone him back and say unfortunately our

books are full, and refer him on to another vet practice, please?'

Anne met his gaze. She was one of those characters that didn't need things spelled out to her. 'No problem, I'll do it now,' she said, picking up the mobile handset and moving into another room.

'What have we got this afternoon?' asked Eli, as Aurora walked back through to Reception.

'Two dogs. Both are being considered for breeding. Eye checks done. DNA tests completed with no concerns, but both need to be sedated to get their hip and knee X-rays completed for grading.'

'What kind of dogs?' Eli asked. This was routine work for this practice. Not every practice had the qualifications or skill to do these kinds of tests, but it was something both Matt and his father had insisted on continuing. Mainly because it helped keep up the quality of dogs being bred, and it was profitable.

'One Labrador, and one dachshund,' said Aurora.

He gave a nod. 'No problem. I'm going to spend some time writing up the notes from the Fletchers' farm, then I have a video call with some of the other agencies at five o'clock tonight. Give me a nudge, will you? I might forget.'

'We'll be finished the X-rays long before then, and I'm happy to stay later if either of the dogs takes some time to come out of their sedation.'

'Thank you,' he said, meaning it. She really was an excellent staff member.

Anne came through once he was settled at the computer. 'Anything you want to tell me?' she asked.

Eli felt heat rush into his cheeks. How on earth could Anne already know that something was going on between him and Aurora? His father had always said not to underestimate how astute she was, but that was usually in relation to owners who didn't quite tell the whole story about something.

'Er...' he started, stuttering over his words. 'I might have started dating someone,' he said.

It was like being a fourteen-year-old again. Anne had just started at the practice then, and used to leave him tongue-tied. But he was a fully grown adult now. Should he really tell her this stuff? She didn't have any right to know.

She'd just blindsided him.

A smile appeared around her lips. 'Anyone I know?'

He took a breath. 'Maybe,' was his response as he straightened himself up and got ready to explain that this really wasn't something to discuss.

But Anne rested a hand on his shoulder, the smile disappearing from her face. 'I was talking about Matt,' she said sadly. 'Marianne said you visited last night.'

His face fell, and he inwardly cringed. Of course she'd meant Matt.

'But I welcome the other news,' said Anne, in a way that only she could.

He moved his hand and put it on hers, looking up. 'He wasn't great, Anne. Much sicker than I realised. His colour was almost translucent, and he's lost so much weight he hardly looks like Matt any more.' He sighed and looked down for a second, before he had a moment of realisation. 'But you knew that, didn't you?'

She gave a slow nod. 'I would never have said anything to you, until I knew you'd been to visit.' She paused for a moment, her face the most serious he'd ever seen it.

'You have to think carefully about the future, about what makes you happy, Elijah.'

'I know,' he admitted. 'And I still don't know what that is.' He put his hand on his chest. 'I still don't know if I have the heart to be here.'

Anne stayed silent for a few moments. 'Only you can answer that question.'

'I know,' he sighed. 'But there's so much going on right now, and so much to think about.'

'You're right. There is. But at some point you have to take some time to stop and think. Just promise me that.'

He gave a nod and Anne slipped her hand from his and disappeared back through to one of the treatment rooms.

Aurora was feeling odd about things. One part of her was fizzing with excitement. She'd only ever experienced telling one potential partner in the past about her sexual assault. The reaction had been confused, with a real reluctance to try and reach out to her. She got that. It scared some people. But Eli's reaction last night had been different.

He'd accepted what she'd said. He'd been angry—even though he hadn't said anything. He'd been sorry she'd had that experience but had been supportive. Then he'd still reacted to her touch. With caution, maybe. But his touch had been just what she'd needed.

It had revitalised her. It made her feel real again. Parts of herself that she'd kept hidden had been unleashed. She'd also felt good about revealing a part of her history with Eli. He'd taken it well, and she knew she still had to tell him about her past career.

She was just worried that he would think less of her. The reactions of colleagues at university and in placements had made her so glad that she'd worked as an actress under another name. Even those colleagues who'd said they admired the TV show had still treated her as a bit less. It was actually shocking how the world seemed to assume that anyone who was an actor wasn't clever. She hated that.

She could already tell that Eli was beginning to trust her professional judgement and competence. She didn't want that to be compromised.

Then there was the stalking. It was another horrible dark hole in her mind, and if she really wanted to have a relationship with someone it would have to be revealed.

She didn't want to think about any of that right now. She wanted to live in the moment. Let the electricity continue to spark between them. See where things led. For a few moments today she'd wondered if something was off. But then again, when was the last time she'd been in a relationship? Maybe she was just rusty. Maybe she should make more of an effort?

They worked closely together the rest of the afternoon. Both dogs were sedated and X-rayed without any concerns. The little dachshund took a bit longer to recover completely and Aurora was happy to stay with him until he was wide awake and his owner came to pick him up.

Once she handed him over, she walked back through to one of the offices, where Eli was still working on the computer.

'Ready to finish?' she asked.

He looked up. 'Nearly—why, is something wrong?'

She shook her head. 'I just wondered if you want to do something.'

He must have got a hint she had something planned. 'Like what?'

'Well,' she said slowly, not trying to hide her smile, 'I know it's summer. But there are two options. We could head to Portobello Beach for chips and ice cream, or we could head into the city and catch one of the last tours of the graveyards and the dungeons. It should be dark enough by then.'

He leaned back in his chair and folded his arms. 'Wow. Two great suggestions.' He looked out of the window. 'What time is the last tour?'

'About eleven,' she said, 'and they last about an hour. We could grab dinner some place first.'

He closed his eyes for a second. 'Or we could take Bert with us and go for a walk on the beach. It's years since I've been to Portobello Beach,' he said with a smile.

'How long?' she queried.

'Maybe eighteen or nineteen years. I wonder how much the place has changed.'

'Chips and ice cream it is, then?'

He nodded. He seemed genuinely happy. 'Let me go and get changed. Do you want to get changed too?'

She nodded but said, 'My house is on the way. Can we stop there and I'll run in and grab some clothes, and check on Miss Trixie?'

'No probs,' he said. 'Give me fifteen minutes. I'll finish this, jump in the shower and grab Bert.'

Bert could clearly sense something was going on as he started to get excited. Aurora wrestled him into his harness for the car journey, and Eli appeared a few minutes later in jeans, a white T-shirt and brown leather jacket.

All it did was remind her just how handsome he was. He looked like something from an aftershave ad.

This time the car that Eli pulled from his dad's garage was an old-style silver Aston Martin.

'You have to be joking,' she said.

He shook his head. 'Perfect for a wee drive to the beach.' He laid a blanket over the back seat and secured Bert in place. 'Let's go.'

She had to give him directions to her house. It was slightly odd for her. After her stalking experience, she'd been careful about what name she used, and how many people actually knew where she lived. She'd kept it to a minimum. She directed Eli through her village and to her cottage. She loved her home, was proud of it. Her garden was immaculate. And although the house had new windows and shutters, it had a traditional wooden red front door.

'Your place is lovely,' said Eli as he pulled into the driveway.

'Thank you,' she replied with a smile. 'Do you want to come in while I get changed?'

He gave a nod, then glanced at Bert and changed his mind. 'I'll just take Bert for a walk around the garden first.'

Aurora nodded and got out of the car, leaving her front door open behind her and dropping her bag on the table near the entranceway. She ran up the stairs, took the quickest shower in history and grabbed some clean clothes out of her bedroom, while Miss Trixie watched her with apparent indifference from the top of the bed.

The temperature was still warm, so she grabbed a pair of white capri pants, flat shoes and a white-and-green-striped T-shirt. As she went back along the corridor she noticed Bert and Eli still outside. Her eyes caught sight of a pile of mail from the day before that she hadn't even looked at. But the thing that caught her attention was her stage name—Star Kingfisher—on one of the envelopes.

Not only that, it was addressed to her stage name, with the actual house address. It hadn't come via her agent like most mail did.

Her skin chilled. Had someone tracked her down? She swallowed hard. Her stalker had gone to jail but had been released less than a year later. She hadn't heard anything from him in years. Could he have tracked her down again?

She felt sick.

'Ready?' came Eli's voice from outside.

She stuffed the letters into her bag. She'd look at them later. Eli was outside, as Bert sniffed around the garden.

'Didn't you come in?' she asked.

'We got as far as the sitting room,' he said. 'Like your purple sofa, by the way. But Bert was sniffing around too much. I was too scared he'd relieve himself on your nice purple rug.'

She smiled, because she couldn't quite laugh yet.

He held up one hand as she stepped outside. He hesitated a second then gave a little shrug of his shoulders. 'Just wondered if you wanted to bring anything for tomorrow.'

Now, her smile broadened. 'Are you asking me to stay overnight?' she teased.

'Only if you want to.'

She stood for a few moments, letting him think she was considering things, before turning and going back in, putting tomorrow's food out for Miss Trixie. She grabbed another few things, flung them in another bag then went back out to lock her door.

As she turned around, something about the car flashed through her head. 'Has that car been in a film?'

Eli gave a bashful smile. 'One nearly the same was in

one of the James Bond films. I'm not sure how or where my father ever got an Aston Martin from, but he only took it out on special occasions.'

'So, is that what I am,' she asked as she climbed in, 'a special occasion?'

He laughed as he started the car. 'Of course.'

The drive down to Portobello Beach was beautiful. The sand was a dark yellow and the tide was currently coming in with blue waves and white peaks as they found somewhere to park.

'Will the car be okay here?' asked Aurora, feeling a little worried.

'It's a car,' said Eli easily. 'And—' he spun around, holding his hands out '—the people here are good. They're not going to make off with a James Bond car. Remember what happens to any villain that tries.'

She frowned for a moment, trying to remember what did happen to people in those films, but her mind was a blank. And she was secretly pleased that he liked her home, even though he hadn't got to see much of it.

They moved along the street, which was filled with locals and holidaymakers. She could hear an array of different accents and even though it was late in the evening there were still some children down on the beach, playing on the sand.

Eli lifted Bert up into his arms. 'Right, little guy, let's see what you make of the sand, and the sea.'

They made their way down onto the beach. As the tide was part way in, they didn't have to walk too far. Bert loved it. There was no other way to describe it. He looked at the sand between his paws for a few moments then had a dig, sending sand flying. Next, he rolled in it.

Then, when they moved closer to the sea, he didn't hesitate to run straight into the waves.

'He loves it!' declared Aurora as he splashed her again and again. She took off her flat shoes and walked through the waves with him, grabbing the lead from Eli. 'This is freezing though,' she yelled over her shoulder as Eli crossed his arms and stood laughing at them both.

A crowd of twenty-somethings walked past, with one nudging the other and then all turning to look at them. Were they looking at him? Or her? Nope, they were definitely looking at Aurora, with her dark red hair flying madly about and her laughter as she interacted with Bert.

'Your feet will take an hour to heat up,' he said, shaking his head as they both made their way back to him.

'They won't. These shoes, they're actually made from a kind of recycled material. They can be washed and are waterproof.' She gave him a wink. 'What's more, I have them in twenty different styles and colours.'

He groaned. 'I knew there had to be a flaw somewhere beneath that perfect smile.'

She moved closer, cutting out the wind between them that was blowing briskly. 'You think I've got a perfect smile?' she said.

She was trying to pretend to be cool, but the man in front of her was one of the most handsome guys she'd ever seen. A few other women had glanced in their direction. With his blue eyes, scruffy styled hair and designer stubble, he was attracting lots of admiring looks. She almost wanted to make sure everyone knew he was with her.

He put his arms at either side of her hips as she moved closer. 'I think your smile is pretty great,' he said. Her hair, which was whipping around her face, was caught by him, with a strand tucked behind one of her ears. 'And I think the colour of your hair is stunning.'

'You do?' They were chest to chest now. She decided it was time to tease him again. 'So, last time you were at Portobello Beach, did you kiss a girl?'

He threw back his head and laughed. 'I wish. But I'm doing it this time,' he added, before putting his lips on hers.

And for the first time in a long time Aurora thought she might get a chance at happy ever after.

CHAPTER EIGHT

THE FIRST LETTER seemed almost like a mistake. A fan apologising for sending a letter to her address, which was more of a query to ask if Star Kingfisher would be returning to the vet series. The second letter asked why she was living her life under another name, and if she was trying to keep her identity a secret.

Aurora tried to phone the police officer who'd dealt with her stalking case—but he'd moved on, and no one else could really help.

She was left jittery and unnerved.

In the meantime, work was getting busier by the day. Bovine tuberculosis had been confirmed in some of the Fletchers' herd, which sent a huge chain reaction of next steps. All the other cattle were tested, with no milk or beef allowed to be sold or moved from the farm.

The impact on Don Fletcher's farm was huge, along with the repercussions for his workers. He himself had been diagnosed with TB, as had his younger farmhand. The system was designed to recompense farms affected by bovine TB. However, all things took time.

In the meantime, all the surrounding farms had concerns, and testing was arranged for them too. Aurora and Eli spent huge amounts of time on virtual meetings, coordinating with all the agencies involved.

Eli himself was clearly stretched. He was doing the work of two vets. There had been contact from a French vet who was interested in coming to Scotland, and there had been a few enquiries by those due to qualify. Two had arranged to come and see the practice, but Aurora was already convinced that working alongside one vet wouldn't appeal to a new graduate. They usually wanted to find their feet in larger practices with bigger support networks.

With all this happening around them, it seemed as if there wouldn't be any time for Aurora and Eli. But, strangely, this wasn't quite true.

There was a consistent and ongoing connection between them. When a pet had required overnight care after surgery, Aurora had volunteered to stay over. It happened on rare occasions, when animals had a slower recovery from their anaesthetic, or their owner wasn't quite equipped to take care of them.

Eli had waved his hand. 'I can do it. I'm here anyway.'

'But you have a million other things on, and you need to get some sleep,' she'd insisted. 'I can set the alarm and get up a few times in the night to check. It's fine.'

And she did. Of course, she hadn't minded at all that they'd decided to take the little cat upstairs and held it on her lap as they watched TV on the sofa, his arm around her shoulders and her head on his neck.

It was such a comfort. She was just trying to get her head around the fact she could actually have something real. Seven years ago, she'd been the apple of a number of guys' eyes—but it was hard to separate who was interested in her, Aurora, as opposed to who was interested in tabloid fodder and headlines about the latest popular actress.

She didn't have to worry about that with Eli. He only knew her.

The next week passed easily. They continued to work together, supporting the members of the farming community around them, learning how to create a new team. Anne watched with the permanent hint of a smile on her face. She said very little about it, but occasionally remarked on how the practice was beginning to run smoothly again.

They were making plans to head into Edinburgh for the evening when the doors of the practice burst open and a teenage girl ran in, clutching something in her arms.

'I can't believe it. I am so sorry. I never even saw him.'

Aurora and Eli were on their feet in seconds, Aurora wrapping her arm around the girl's shoulders as Eli eased the little animal from her arms.

It was a dog—a puppy, and almost a carbon copy of Bert. One of its legs was clearly broken and the only sound it made was whimpers.

Aurora steered the girl to a chair. 'Tell me what happened.'

'It just ran in front of me.' She crumpled and put her hands on her face. 'I hit it with my car. I've only had my licence for six months. I didn't have time to stop.'

'Where on the road were you?' she asked gently. She was trying to be patient, but knew she had to assist Eli urgently.

The girl explained. It was near the spot that Aurora had climbed through the woods to find Bert.

'Phone your mum or dad,' she said. 'Ask them to come and get you, and let us take care of the puppy.'

She hated to do it, but she had to leave the girl in the waiting room to go and look after the puppy. She dialled

Anne on her mobile as she took the few steps into the treatment room. It was likely they would be busy for the next few hours and the practice would be left uncovered. Anne answered immediately, and said she would be there in ten minutes.

Eli's head was bent over the puppy as she entered the room, washing her hands and grabbing a trolley with IV supplies.

He spoke gently. 'He's so scrawny,' he said, then pressed his lips together.

Her heart ached. 'She knocked him down near where I picked up Bert. Do you think they could be from the same litter?'

'Highly likely. Can't imagine how this one has managed to keep going.'

The little dog's ribs were clearly visible. Eli had his stethoscope out and was listening to the puppy's abdomen. 'Sounds okay.' His eyes flickered to the back leg. 'It's badly broken.'

She knew what he was going to say. The little puppy was so scrawny and thin; he had to contemplate if it could withstand an anaesthetic.

They worked together, shaving the hair on one of his front legs, inserting an IV to give fluids for the puppy's too fast heart rate and low blood pressure. Aurora put some oxygen on, and drew up some pain relief for Eli to insert.

'What do you think?'

The little guy's whimpers started to die down. Eli took the opportunity to draw some blood and handed it to Aurora. She knew automatically what to check for. This was another way to ensure the puppy would be fit for anaesthetic.

The practice had been able to screen their own bloods for a number of years and it saved time on the more regular tests. Complicated blood tests still needed to be sent to more specialised labs, but in times like this the ability to check for themselves was crucial.

'He's a little bit dehydrated,' Aurora said, showing him the blood results.

He nodded. 'I'd like to weigh him,' said Eli. 'I need to know how much anaesthetic he could tolerate. This could be touch and go.'

'Let's give the opioids another minute to kick in,' said Aurora. 'I'll need to lift him onto the scales.'

Eli was gently stroking the little dog's back. 'There, there,' he said. He met her gaze. 'Operating might not be a good idea. There's a chance he won't tolerate the anaesthetic. And we already know he doesn't have an owner. Not when he looks like this.'

Aurora gave a nod, but pulled the scanner from the nearby drawer to check for a microchip. Of course, there was none.

Eli looked her steadily in the eye. 'We'd need to look after this guy ourselves in the rehab period before we hand him over to a rescue centre.'

'We can do that,' she said steadily. 'I think we have to give him a chance.' Their gazes remained locked. 'Why have one Bert, when we can have two?' she said with a smile.

Eli had been upfront to begin with about not wanting to stay. But since their visit together to Matt's, it was as if all parameters had changed. They both knew he'd have to stay for at least a year. Recruitment was still open. Another vet had yet to materialise.

Before that visit, he'd asked her to consider adopting

Bert. But nothing had been mentioned since. Maybe she was jumping to a whole host of conclusions here. Maybe the fact they were in a relationship was clouding her judgement. But she didn't think so. He'd revealed part of himself to her. She understood why he struggled with the memories of his past here. And he, in turn, had been a good personal support about her assault. It gave her faith that she could continue to move past that and form a meaningful relationship.

There was a noise as the front door opened and Anne bustled in. She was her usual reliable self, her eyes catching sight of the young girl in the waiting room and their own situation in the treatment room.

She gave them a wave of her hand. 'Go and do what you need to do,' she said.

They disappeared into the theatre. The little dog was anaesthetised, his leg area prepped and draped, with the theatre lights adjusted to give Eli the best possible view.

Before cutting the skin, he took an X-ray to see what he was dealing with.

'It's broken in two separate places. I'll need to plate and pin.'

Aurora knew that would take a few hours. They worked together steadily, her assisting where required and monitoring the little dog's breathing and vital signs. There were a few scary moments, when the little dog had a burst of tachycardia during the procedure. But things settled down.

Eli kept a close eye on the puppy's blood pressure, ensuring adequate IV fluids were given, since he was already a little dehydrated. 'Thank goodness there's not much blood loss. I'm not sure his body could take it.'

He leaned back, arching himself to stretch out his

spine. As he finished his delicate work he looked at Aurora. 'Do you think there's any chance there are more of them?'

'Don't say that.' She shuddered. 'It's bad enough I missed one. I'd hate it if there were others.' She licked her lips under her mask. 'Do you think we should go and check later?'

He paused for a second, then looked down again. 'Let's wait and see how this little guy does first. We need to get him through this before we worry about anything else.'

After a while, Anne stuck her head through the door. 'The young girl was picked up by her mum and dad. I've to give them a call to let them know how the puppy is.'

As Aurora gave her a nod, Anne paused for a second. Even from the other side of the theatre, Aurora could see the flash of concern in her eyes. 'There's another query about the wages that I can't answer.'

Aurora didn't hesitate. 'That's fine, leave it for me. I'll sort it later.'

Eli gave her a fleeting gaze, and for the briefest of seconds she thought she saw something strange in his eyes. But, next second, the alarm sounded and they both turned their attention back to the puppy.

'We should give this guy a name. We can't keep calling him dog, or puppy.'

'Why don't you pick the name, since I picked Bert?'

'You picked Bert because you said it was someone good that you worked with?'

She nodded.

'Okay, in that case, this guy can be Hank.'

Aurora couldn't help but smile. 'Hank?'

'Yes, when I worked in Maine, I worked with a vet

called Hank. He was one of the good ones. Great accent. Great values. I really admired him.'

Aurora looked down and stroked the little one's head. 'Okay, Hank. Here's hoping you can wake up soon and we can introduce you to your brother, Bert.'

Finally, the surgery was finished and the wound stitched. Anne came into the room. 'I'd made scones at home, so just brought some when you phoned. I knew you'd be here a while. Go and have something to eat and I'll monitor him while he recovers.'

'Hank,' said Aurora. 'We've called him Hank, and think he could be Bert's brother. The accident was in the same kind of area.'

'Oh, dear,' said Anne, stroking his head. 'He does have the same distinctive white flash on his head.' She gave a little nod. 'Off you two go.'

They walked back through to the kitchen, where the plate of scones sat, along with the kettle boiling. Eli pulled off his cap and sighed as he sat down. 'We'll just need to wait and see how things go.'

Aurora went to sit down, then changed her mind. She walked through to the back kennels and shouted Bert in, picking him up and cuddling him while she sat at the table.

'You okay?' Eli asked, pouring the tea.

'Yeah,' she sighed. 'Just wishing that the day I found Bert, I found Hank too, and all of this never happened. That little guy has been foraging for himself for nearly a month. It doesn't bear thinking about.'

Eli carried the tea over and reached across, rubbing Bert's head. 'You can't think like that. At least you found Bert. He's doing great, aren't you, guy?'

Bert lifted his head into the air and sniffed. 'Is that the

scones you smell, or is it your brother?' asked Aurora, giving him another cuddle.

Eli split the scones and spread them with butter and jam, putting them on two plates, and she continued to hug Bert.

'What will we do with Hank over the next few days?'

'I can ask Anne to do some extra hours. I'm sure she'll be happy to.'

'Okay then.'

'Because…' he met her gaze with a smile '…we will need some time off.'

'We will? What for?' she asked with a smile, warmth flooding through her like a comfort blanket.

'I've booked us onto something.'

'That sounds mysterious.'

'There's a graveyard tour in Edinburgh, by bus. Does the underground stuff too. But also some drinks and snacks as we do the tour. Thought we might give it a try.'

'That sounds like fun. You thinking about the Scottish weather again?'

He gave a shrug. 'You know what it's like. The graveyard and vault tour are probably best in October and November. This seemed like a fun added extra, and it doesn't leave until eleven at night.'

'Why do I have a feeling there's something you're not telling me?'

He gave a wide grin. 'It might be billed as a horror comedy tour.'

She laughed. 'Is the horror the actual comedy?'

'I guess we'll find out.'

'When are we going?'

He pulled a face. 'I'd booked for two nights' time. That

was before Hank though. I'll check with Anne, to see if she can cover or not. If not, we can change it.'

Aurora nodded and, as she ate her scone, lifted the pile of notes that Anne had written this afternoon while manning the desk and answering the phone. Most were for repeat prescriptions. Anne had already printed them, and was just waiting for Eli to sign. She and Aurora would dispense and phone the owners back to let them know to collect the medications. There was another with some follow-up details Aurora had asked about a dog's diet. One query about a sick parrot. And a final one that made her stop cold.

Caller on the answering machine asking to speak to Star Kingfisher? Quite insistent. Must be wrong number.

A chill swept over her entire body. *No, not here too.*

She closed her eyes for a second and tried not to throw up. Could this be her stalker again? The kidnap attempt hadn't been a physical kidnap attempt, but the police had got wind of it, and foiled it. There was clear evidence of the stalking. Aurora had texts to her phone—even though she'd changed her number a few times. Letters sent to her house. And emails to her agent, and to her own private email account. All of them bombarding her to continue in her role, when it had been announced she was leaving the series.

She hadn't actually had to appear in court with her stalker. She'd been protected from that. And she'd never seen him in person. Just his police mugshot, and a picture of him entering court seven years ago. Would she even recognise him if she saw him now?

That actually scared her more than she wanted to admit.

She had to tell Eli. She had to tell Anne. It made her

insides curl. Not only would she be letting them know she'd had a past career she'd kept from them, but now she was potentially bringing trouble to their door. What on earth would they think of her?

'Aurora? You okay?'

She opened her eyes and took a quick gulp of tea to soothe her bone-dry mouth.

She tried to be rational. Matt knew about her past career. When she'd applied for the job—although she hadn't written it on her submitted CV—she did tell him what she'd done in her late teenage years. He'd brushed it off easily, asked a few questions about the animals she'd interacted with on set, and what she'd learned about them. But once she'd answered his questions she'd said she was just trying to have a new life, and he'd said he respected that, and wouldn't mention it again.

So she hadn't been totally dishonest.

She took a deep breath. 'Yeah, there was just something I was going to mention—'

But she got cut off. Anne appeared in the door way. 'Eli, I need you.'

They were both on their feet in an instant. Animals could crash after anaesthesia. The most common signs were tachycardia, low blood pressure—both of which had been borderline for Hank—and hypothermia, which he was exhibiting now. Anne had wrapped a silver blanket around him.

'I'll give something else to reverse the anaesthetic again. Can you increase the rate on his IV fluids please, Anne?' asked Eli, checking the wound, then taking out his stethoscope to listen to Hank's chest again. They were all silent for a moment, before he pulled the stethoscope from his ears. 'No fluid in his lungs. No heart murmur, just a consistent tachycardia.' He touched Hank's head tenderly. 'Just a little guy who might not have the pull to get through the other side of surgery. Maybe we shouldn't have done it. Maybe this was cruel?'

It was the first time she'd ever heard Eli doubt anything he'd done as a vet. No practitioner was infallible. There were always times they had to weigh the odds and hope they worked in their favour. Had she pushed him to do this?

She put her hand over his. 'This wasn't cruel. This was us doing our best and trying to give Hank a chance.'

Anne gave a slow nod. 'There's the human side too. If I had to tell that teenage girl that we'd had to put the puppy down, I doubt she'd get over it. Hank had a chance, and he still does.'

Eli gave a slow nod and sighed. 'I just hate these parts of the job. He's just so scrawny. I've used minuscule amounts of drugs on him, as I have to be so careful about what his body can tolerate.'

'I have an idea,' said Aurora. 'Give me a minute.'

She ran through to the kitchen and picked Bert out of his basket, holding him firmly in her hands as she walked back through to the recovery area.

Bert made a little noise, as if he picked up the scent as soon as he came in the room. He started to scrabble a bit, but Aurora held him firm. 'No, honey. Hold still, let me take you over to him.'

Hank murmured too, coming around a little more from the anaesthetic now the drugs were kicking in, and sniffing the air.

Eli and Anne smiled as Aurora brought Bert nearer, talking quietly in his ear the whole time. She held Bert close enough to rub his head next to Hank's. Bert desperately wanted to get closer, but she didn't want him to knock Hank's leg, so she manoeuvred around, allowing them to see each other, to lick each other's face, and to touch with their paws.

'It's probably a million times better than any drug,' said Eli, giving her a smile that warmed her heart.

It struck her just how much she wanted this to work. She'd never met anyone like him before. And although she needed to tell him about her alternate identity, she was still glad that he just knew *her*. And liked her.

What had started out as rocky had blossomed very quickly into something special. And as she watched him lean over Hank, stroke his head and talk to him, she realised she loved this man. She actually loved him.

His too long, scruffy hair that she could run her fingers through. The stubble on his face that would scrape her cheek. The feel of his muscles flexing under the palm of her hand. That look from those blue eyes that made her insides want to melt.

She could do this. She could stay here. She loved this place already, but had never really considered it for ever. But now? With Eli? It could be.

But could she be his for ever too?

Trust for her had been so hard since her past experiences. But trust with Eli had always seemed unquestionable—even when she hadn't liked him those first few hours, she'd never felt unsafe. She'd never been worried.

But there still seemed to be an edge to Eli. Something that lay deep down beneath the surface. She wondered sometimes if she really knew everything about him.

But then, he didn't know everything about her.

That would have to change.

But as she watched him take care of Hank, while still holding Bert close to her chest, she knew there was a time and place for everything. And this wasn't it.

CHAPTER NINE

'I THINK I might fall asleep,' said Eli, as they climbed onto the decorated bus.

'Me too,' Aurora whispered as they were led to a table on the bus where a skeleton was in one of the seats.

'Guess this guy won't mind,' joked Eli, as he slid in next to the skeleton and slung an arm around its shoulders.

'Maybe that's what we all look like when we get off the bus,' joked Aurora, as one of the attendants approached with a tray of cocktails, all smoking and bubbling.

Eli picked something green and Aurora something peach-coloured and they both took a sip. 'Ouch,' laughed Eli, his cheeks drawing together. 'Well, that one is a bit strong.'

Aurora's eyes started to water. 'Mine too.' She gave a little choke. 'One of these will definitely be enough.

The last few nights had been tiring. Hank hadn't settled well. They had no idea where he'd been sleeping in the woods, or how long Bert and he had been separated from their mother, but he was difficult to get to sleep.

Both of them wished Bert could be in beside him. But Bert still had jumpy puppy traits that meant he could unwittingly hurt his brother, so they were waiting until he'd healed a bit better. They'd also spent a whole afternoon tramping around the woods to ensure there were no further puppies abandoned, but had found nothing. It had been a relief.

As the other passengers loaded and the guide gave an overview of what would happen, Eli studied Aurora.

He didn't mean to. He just did it every opportunity that he got.

She was beautiful, with her skin slightly tanned and a few freckles across her nose, her dark red hair and bright green eyes, he actually couldn't believe he'd got this lucky.

More than that, she had a good heart. She was feisty. She didn't put up with any nonsense. She had a real understanding of the farming community that actually put him to shame.

He'd underestimated her in the first few seconds of meeting her—but he'd never been that foolish again since.

Every day he spent around her, he learned more about himself, and more about her. Part of him felt as if coming here had been cathartic. Part of him felt as if seeing Matt had been a wakeup call, to be grateful for life, and all that was in it.

But meeting Aurora had been the icing on the cake.

He'd never experienced a spark like this. He'd thought he had. But now, with hindsight, he realised he'd been fooled. Every time he looked at her, he had a fresh wave of emotion. She affected every part of him. His senses seemed to go into overdrive around her. Just one whiff of her perfume was enough to send goosebumps across his skin and blood rushing to other parts of his body.

It was time to talk. Time to feel his way to seeing if he could make this more permanent. He still had questions.

He still had trust issues. He wasn't sure they would ever go away. But those were his issues, not hers.

Aurora hadn't given him reason not to trust her.

He wondered if things had just moved too quickly between them. How he felt certainly had. He loved her. He was sure of it. He wanted to work next to her every day. He wanted to take her for a drive in every car in his father's garage. He wanted to replace some of the photographs in the hallway with some newer ones—one of them together, one of them with their dogs. But how would she feel about that?

The bus pulled out. The journey would take a few hours, with some pitstops along the way. They'd go on a visit to Greyfriars Kirkyard and walk to the statue of Greyfriars Bobby. They'd pass Holyrood Palace and go along Grassmarket and close to Edinburgh Castle. They'd go back down the Royal Mile, learning ghastly and ghostly history wherever they went, and finally finish with a visit to the underground vaults.

He leaned back into his skeleton friend as they listened to the comedian. The mood on the bus was light, jovial and the drinks seemed to be going down well.

He took a breath. 'About the practice,' he said.

'Yes?' She looked up straight away.

'You've probably guessed this because you were with me when we visited Matt and Marianne, but I'm going to stay.'

'For good?' There was an edge of hope in her voice. And he cringed inside. His answer should be yes, but he still couldn't honestly say that.

He swallowed. 'I'm going to stay for at least a year, then take it from there.'

'A year?' Was that disappointment in her voice?

'At least. One of the potential applicants looks like a good candidate. You met her—Cheryl Wood? She, her husband and children are keen to move here. Her husband's a school teacher and they know there are plenty of jobs in the area. She's had some maternity leave during her studies, so qualifies in September.'

'The school term here starts in August. Won't that be too late for her husband?'

'He can work on the teaching bank. Apparently, there are lots of hours, and it will give him a chance to get to know the area, and where he might want to work permanently.'

'Only a year?'

He blinked and put his hand on his chest. 'I'm still not completely sure if I want to take over Dad's practice. Working here has been better than I thought. I'll always be known as David Ferguson's son, but I'm beginning to feel as if I can put my own stamp on the place.'

'Does that mean you'll let me decorate?' She'd already shown him some plans and given him some costs to update parts of the practice.

'I showed them to Matt, and he likes the idea.'

'You did?'

'I did.'

'But you still can only say you'll stay for a year?' Her voice had softened slightly.

'Aurora,' he said softly, 'I don't want to make false promises. I think this could work out. I think I might like to stay. But, until I know for sure, I only want to promise that I'll stay for the next year.'

She looked at him steadily and he continued.

'You have to know that a big part of why I want to stay is you.'

She sucked in a breath. 'Me?'

He gave her a smile. 'Absolutely.'

The bus jolted and both their drinks slid across the table, Eli barely catching them with one arm.

She let out a laugh, then leaned forward, her face serious as she reached out and touched his hand with her fingers. 'I'm glad you want to stay because of me, but you have to want to stay because of you too.'

'And that's the part that's getting there. You just have to give me a little more time. There are a few other complicating factors that mean I can't take over the practice completely. I have to let Matt and Marianne look after my dad's share for now.'

'But Matt's...' She let her voice tail off and pressed her lips together.

His other hand met hers. 'And I'll cross that bridge if I need to. For now, I don't.' He took another breath. 'And if I do decide I don't want to stay, I'll talk to you about it first.'

Her brow creased. 'So you can say goodbye?'

'No, so I can ask you if you want to come with me.'

She stayed very still. 'That sounds serious.'

'I am serious.'

'We've only known each other for a short time.'

He gave her a level look. 'I know that, but I know how I feel.' His insides were doing somersaults. It struck him that having this conversation on a bus, where both of them were essentially trapped for the next few hours, meant things potentially could go horribly wrong.

'How do you feel?' she asked, her fingers clenching under his.

He kept his voice steady. 'I feel like I've met someone that I can picture myself spending a lot of time with.'

Her voice was equally steady. It was almost as if she was challenging him. 'Spending a lot of time with, as in a fling? Or spending a lot of time with, as in something else?'

The question was close to the bone.

He didn't hesitate. 'Definitely something else.'

A slow smile started to spread across her face, and she leaned over and rescued her peach cocktail. 'Is that something we should drink to?'

'I think it is,' he said, picking up his green cocktail and clinking it against hers.

The two of them were smiling, and Eli had to untangle himself from the skeleton to lean across the table and put a kiss on her lips. Her lips were cold and sweet from the cocktail, and he instantly wished there wasn't a table between them.

'When can we get off this bus?' he groaned.

Her eyes gleamed as she pulled her lips from his. 'I have to see Greyfriars Bobby. I have to do the unthinkable thing of touching his nose.'

'I don't think we're allowed to,' he whispered. The act of touching Greyfriars Bobby's nose by visitors was frowned upon, and had caused the paint to have to be restored on numerous occasions.

'You can distract everyone else,' she said.

He shook his head in mock horror. 'I'm a Scotsman. I don't think I can do that. It goes against the grain.'

She rolled her eyes and signalled to the waiter on board for another drink. 'It's just your luck—' he grinned as the waiter plonked a blue glass down in front of her, again with smoke pouring from it —to end up with a patriotic Scotsman.'

She raised her eyebrows at him in disdain, then looked

warily at the cocktail. 'I have no idea how they do this, but I like it. Okay, if you're going to fail me at Greyfriars Bobby, then we need to talk about our dogs.'

It was that little word. *Our.* It struck him straight in the gut and he liked it more than any other word on the planet.

'What about our dogs?'

'They're brothers. I don't think we should separate them. They've been through enough trauma.'

'Ah.' He lifted his own glass, which was looking remarkably empty. 'You're going to play the trauma card, are you?'

She smiled. 'To be honest, I don't think I need to, do I?'

He shook his head and smiled. 'What kind of vet would I be if I didn't have a rescue dog?'

'And what kind of vet nurse would I be if I didn't encourage you to have two?'

He raised his glass to her anyway. 'To Hank and Bert?'

She clinked his glass and lifted the still smoking blue liquid to her lips. 'To our boys.'

CHAPTER TEN

THEY COULDN'T HAVE timed things better. Aurora had called the pet hydrotherapy pool this morning and there was a cancellation. Things were quiet today, so they'd left Anne at the practice with Bert, and she and Eli had brought Hank to the treatment centre.

Hank was improving slowly. His wound had healed perfectly but he was walking with a slight limp. Eli had X-rayed him again to check the position of the plate and it was perfect. But a visit by a pet physio had told them that his back leg muscles were imbalanced and needed building up and the best way to do that was in a pool with hydrotherapy.

Since their colleague knew they were professionals, she'd agreed to set the programme and teach them how to assist Hank, with only a few check-in sessions with herself. The one thing she had been clear about was that the first time they immersed the little guy in water they both went in with him.

Neither of them had objected to this, and Aurora had changed quickly into her red one-piece swimsuit and tied her hair up in a ponytail, before emerging and meeting Eli, in his dark swimming shorts, at the door.

'Shouldn't we be in Ibiza, dressed like this?' he joked.

'If only,' she sighed. 'But then I would need a shed-load of sunscreen, so I can live with this.'

Hank was sniffing the air, obviously smelling the chlorine.

'Does this count as a date?' She smiled as she took her first few steps into the small pool.

The treatment centre was perfectly equipped. There was a small pool that could be used for any pet that needed immersion or swimming therapy. Then there were smaller set-ups with treadmills underwater to allow the dogs to exercise without the full weight on their legs.

'This would have to be one of the weirdest dates in history,' said Eli as he stepped into the water, let his shoulders go under and then held out his arms for Hank.

He whispered in his ear as he took Hank from her. 'Check out the beginners. All the others have wetsuits on.'

Aurora looked around and pulled a face, realising they were the only people with actual swimsuits on. 'Well, we're new to this. And, let's face it, we'll do anything to help our boy build up his muscles. If I have to come here every week and put on my swimsuit, I will.'

Hank's front legs were paddling in the water. He seemed to be a natural.

'Hey,' she said, 'did I ever tell you about my red Lab, Max?'

"You mentioned him."

She raised her eyebrows. 'Well, one day, Max and I went for a walk around the boating pond back home. I took him regularly along a river walk and he would bound in and out of the edges of the water, actually skipping, but he'd never really swum. Then one day we walked around the boating pond, and I swear he took a look and then just soared.' She made a motion with her arm. 'He actually soared through the air and landed straight in the middle of the boating pond.'

Eli looked at her. 'I take it he swam?'

'Oh, no.' Aurora shook her head. 'He sank like a stone.'

'But all Labradors can swim.'

'No one told Max that.'

Eli started to laugh. 'What did you do?'

'What do you think I did? I jumped in to save him. Pulled him up, and my boy, he hadn't jumped in at the edge of the boating pond where there were reeds and sand. No, he'd jumped in at the end where there was a concrete wall. I had to push him up over it, then try and haul myself up.'

Eli started to laugh. 'That must have been fun.'

She gave him a hard stare. 'I was like a giant squid. It's safe to say it was not the most elegant moment of my life.'

Eli couldn't stop laughing and Hank looked up in surprise. 'Don't worry, little guy,' he said. 'You look like you can definitely swim.'

They both watched Hank, who seemed to like the water and didn't seem fazed by it at all. Aurora gave him a kiss on the head. 'Who's a good boy then?'

They stayed in the pool for another ten minutes, making sure Hank was fine, before moving over to one of the standalone set-ups that had an underwater treadmill. One of the treatment centre staff came over and set things up for them, following the plan that had been laid out to strengthen Hank's muscles and improve his range of movement.

Once the tank was full, the treadmill started gently and he walked along with a bewildered expression on his face, licking the dog peanut butter at the front of the tank that was there to keep him focused.

'We'll never get out of here.' Eli smiled. 'If peanut butter is the standard treat, he'll never want to leave.'

'As long as his leg gets better, that's fine,' said Aurora. She was looking around at all the facilities available. 'I've never been in this place before. It's such a great set-up.'

Eli nodded in agreement. 'I've referred clients to similar places before, but I'm glad we've had the chance to come along and try this out for ourselves.'

They spent the next half hour in the treatment centre, then took turns getting changed, dried Hank off, then moved outside to the attached coffee shop.

Hank was happy to lie at their feet while they sipped their coffee.

'Matt's looking a bit better,' said Aurora. 'He had some more colour yesterday when I dropped off some things for Marianne.'

'He messaged me,' said Eli. 'Said he felt as though the treatment might actually help him rather than kill him now.'

'Chemo is just horrid,' said Aurora. 'I've a few friends that have gone through it. Things are always better when they come out the other side.'

'He has another few rounds still to go.'

'I know. Is there anything else we can do to help them?'

Eli looked at her. He took a breath and reached out and took her hand. 'And that's what I love about you.'

She blinked. 'What?'

'That you think about other people. And you genuinely mean it. You thought about them right from the beginning, to get Marianne's shopping, and both of them dinner.'

Aurora gave a little shrug. 'Don't think I don't know about you helping them set up new smoke alarms the other day.'

He shrugged too. 'But you know how big a part they played in my life when I was a boy. You've only worked at the practice for the last eighteen months.'

She gave a smile. 'But that doesn't matter. When you meet people—inherently good people—you just know it. And the length of time you know them doesn't come into it. What's important is that you know if you needed help they would give it. And it's why you're happy to step up and do things for them.' She gave a smile. 'Anne bakes for them every week. I don't have that skill set, so I'm happy to do other things.'

Her mind flashed back to first meeting Matt. She smiled. 'You know, when I came for my interview, they were both in the middle of an emergency surgery. I offered to scrub in and help.'

'You did?' Eli's eyes widened. 'Matt never told me that.'

Her brain was currently spinning. He'd used the word *love* a few moments ago, and her heart rate had instantly started racing. A few nights ago, he'd told her he'd stay at least a year, and would ask her to go with him if he left. All the barriers that had been in place in her head were now simply falling away.

Was Eli Ferguson going to be the guy she could take a chance on, and hope for a happy ever after?

Her brain flashed to the interview with Matt afterwards, when she'd told him about her past career, and he hadn't been judgemental at all. He'd actually just wanted to know about the animals and her experience. Maybe Eli would be exactly the same.

She opened her mouth to tell him just as Hank decided to wake up and nudge her leg.

'Oh—' Eli smiled '—that's the toilet training nudge. We'd better go outside.'

She nodded and smiled too. It could wait. It wasn't urgent. It had waited this long after all.

And as they strode out into the Scottish sunshine he slipped his hand into hers and a warm glow flowed through her. Perfect—everything was just perfect.

CHAPTER ELEVEN

IT WAS BUSY. He had to go to Don Fletcher's farm today, as some of the cattle were going to be destroyed and he knew that Don was upset. Public health had also decided to screen the other farm workers who weren't currently displaying any symptoms as a precautionary measure, and Don was upset about that too, thinking he'd put his workers at risk.

Eli checked on Bert and Hank. Bert was running up and down the run, and Hank was nestled in some bedding, catching a little sun. Hank was healing slowly, but well. He was eating and drinking and gradually gaining a bit of weight—his muscles a little stronger every day.

He waved to Aurora, who was on the phone to someone, to let her know he was going, and grabbed the mail on the way out. Matt had warned him the practice insurance was due to be renewed and he wanted to keep on top of it.

As he reached the farm his four-by-four slid a little on a slight build-up of mud. It was a typical Scottish summer with occasional flashes of monsoon type rain. As his car drew to a halt, the mail landed in the footwell.

He groaned and leaned over to pick it up, noticing for the first time that one of the letters was in fact a credit card statement. He frowned, not remembering using the credit card, and tore it open. The total amount made him stop. Four thousand pounds? What? He scanned quickly, not really recognising the names of any of the places where money had been spent.

His mind jammed with a million thoughts—all of them panicking, none of them good. He glanced at the farm, knowing he had a job to do.

This would have to wait.

No matter how much he didn't want it to.

Aurora hadn't gone to the farm today. She was catching up on filing some notes and going through the plans for the updates, making sure she had ordered everything she needed. Two of the deliveries were arriving today and she wanted to make sure she was here to receive them—living out in the middle of nowhere meant having a failed delivery was always an issue.

The practice officially had shorter hours today, with the afternoon off for staff training. But Anne had gone out to see Jack Sannox and Rudy this afternoon, and Aurora was still keeping an eye on Hank.

The front door jangled, meaning someone had opened it. Her delivery? Maybe. She walked through to find the owner of Arthur standing in the hallway.

'I'm sorry. We don't have any appointments this afternoon. Is something wrong with Arthur?' She looked around him, expecting to see his partner walking up the steps behind him. But they were empty.

And so was the practice. She was alone right now, with the exception of Hank and Bert, and a small rabbit in the back who was recovering from surgery.

Her spider-sense didn't tingle, it yelled.

The man gave her a strange smile. 'Yes, I just need

you to go over some of the principles of diabetes again. We're struggling with Arthur.'

'Didn't our vet say we were oversubscribed right now? Didn't you manage to find another vet?'

She was trying her best not to panic.

'We couldn't find another vet locally. Our cat is sick. He needs treatment. He's very lethargic.'

Now, that could be truthful and could happen with newly diagnosed animals.

She gave a small smile, a good vet nurse wouldn't turn a sick pet away. 'I thought you said your gran was diabetic, and you understood things?'

Was that cheeky? Maybe.

'I understand the injections, but that's about all.' There was something about his facial expression, as if it was fixed in place and he was playing a part.

'Would you like to make an appointment to come back and see the vet?'

'He isn't here?' It was a pleasant enough question, but it made Aurora feel as if a million caterpillars were currently trampling over her skin.

'He's out back,' she said automatically.

'I didn't see his car.' The man kept smiling. What was his name again—Fraser?

'He has a lot of cars. His father was a collector.'

There was a long silence as the man kept looking at Aurora. His eyes swept up and down her body, making her feel even more uncomfortable, then fixed on her face.

'I can give you some reading material about diabetes in cats. It's probably best you start there.'

She moved to the computer at the reception desk, searched in the files and started printing things off.

'I think I'd prefer a chat,' he said smoothly. 'I have lots of questions.'

Aurora might not have been in any bad movies, but she'd seen her fair share. This was like one of those, where the creepy guy cornered the heroine.

This was not happening to her. She'd taken self-defence classes a number of years ago, on the recommendation of the policewoman in charge of her stalking case. But right now, all those moves seemed to have vanished from her brain.

'I'll start,' he said easily. He moved his hand and clamped it on top of hers, which was on the reception desk. 'Like, why did you change your name?'

Every cell in her body screamed. Her instincts were telling her to pull her hand away and get out of there. But she actually froze. It was as if something icy chilled her entire body and stopped her from moving.

'I mean, Aurora is nice too. But it's not like Star. And what about the TV series? Nothing has been good since you left. The ratings have tanked. You have to go back. I've even thought up a whole scenario for your character, Tara, so she can get back in the thick of things. And don't you think it's time Tara was the main character, instead of a supporting one?'

Her mouth was dry. She could barely speak. 'I want you to leave,' she said. The words came out strangely. Not like her voice at all.

'That's not very friendly.' He didn't even blink an eye.

Everything she'd hoped for. Everything she'd thought she could finally have. And he was here. Spoiling it.

'Your name isn't Fraser, is it?'

He smiled, pleased to have some recognition. 'Anyone

can change their name after a few years. I like Fraser. I think it suits me.'

'You are supposed to stay away from me. There's a restraining order against you.'

He shrugged. 'Different country, different laws.'

'I'm done asking, now I'm telling you to leave.' Her voice had got just as icy as her body felt. But she was angry. She was angry at him for invading her private life and ruining her chance of happiness. She'd run away from this guy once. Now she'd have to run away again. Leave the job that she loved. The home that she was happy in. And the man that she'd told herself it was safe to love now.

He looked around. 'But Star, we've finally got a chance to chat. Let's take it.' He went to move around behind the reception desk, and she reached out and grabbed what was nearest. That was the thing about working in a vet practice—constant cleaning—and the nearest thing was a mop and bucket.

She swung around with the wet mop and directly hit him in the face with it, grabbing the length of the broom like a weapon across her chest and pushing him square in the chest. He was already staggering backwards, caught off-guard by her movement, as Eli came rushing through the door.

'What the...?' he said as he took one look at the situation and put a foot on the guy's chest to keep him on the floor.

She'd never been so glad to see him.

'Eli, this is Brandon Rivers. He was convicted of stalking me a number of years ago and has decided to come and pay me a visit, even though there is a restraining order against him.'

Eli looked down at the floor. He squinted. 'I thought this guy's name was Fraser.'

'Apparently he's changed it.'

'You didn't recognise him?'

'We never came face to face in the past. And I was protected from seeing him in court. This is the first time we've met in the flesh.'

Eli reached down and grabbed the guy by the scruff of the neck. 'Call the police,' he said.

Brandon turned his head and started yelling at Aurora. 'But Star, you've got to come back to the *Into the Wild* series! They need you. We need you. Tara needs to be reunited with Owen!'

Eli looked completely bewildered as Aurora called the police. She explained the situation in a few short sentences, and they promised to send someone immediately.

Eli had taken Brandon into another room and closed the door, so he couldn't see or shout at Aurora. She had no idea what was being said in there. But even though Eli was here, she still didn't feel safe with Brandon in the same building as her.

Had he followed her home some time? Was that how he knew her address?

It was all so overwhelming, but she was determined not to crumple. Not to sink into the corner like she really wanted to and cry her heart out.

The beautiful life that she'd made for herself was over.

Eli's head was on a perpetual spin cycle. He'd been mad driving back to the vet practice. Mad about the amount of money put on the practice credit cards, which he wasn't entirely sure had been discussed and agreed.

For all he knew, she could have added a million personal things into the purchases and he wouldn't be unable to unpick it. This wasn't how a successful business was run, and he knew that better than anyone.

But when he'd walked in the door to see Aurora fighting off some man, all thoughts had gone out of the window. His instinct to keep her safe had gone into overdrive. Now, he was stuck in a room with a man who didn't seem rational or reasonable, who kept calling Aurora by another name, and she said she already had a restraining order against him. Was this the man who had sexually assaulted her?

It was all he could do to keep his hands to himself. Brandon had made a few shouts about wrongful imprisonment, but Eli couldn't care less. He'd attacked a member of the practice, apparently had history for it, and the police had been phoned.

They could sort it out, and take this piece of trash with them when they did.

He desperately wanted to go into the other room to check Aurora was okay. But that wouldn't be wise right now. He could tell from the look on her face that she wanted to be as far away as possible from Brandon or Fraser, or whatever this guy's name was. Who changed their name?

There was a sharp knock at the door, and a uniformed officer walked in, assessing the situation. 'We can take this from here, sir,' he said to Eli. 'My colleague outside would like to speak to you.'

The rest of the afternoon passed in a daze. There were conversations about Scottish and English law. A large purple bruise had started to appear on Aurora's hand. She'd been looked after by a female police officer, who'd been sympathetic and ruthlessly efficient. Both he and

Aurora had been asked to go to the police station the next day to make formal statements, but for now Brandon Rivers was taken away in the back of a police van.

Eli ran his fingers through his hair as he walked back through to the practice kitchen, where Aurora was sitting, a cup of tea—which looked cold—between her hands.

'Want to tell me what just happened in here?' he asked.

She sat very quietly for a moment.

'Do you at least want to tell me what your real name is?'

He could see the hurt in her eyes. But he had to know the truth. The woman he loved hadn't been truthful with him. In more ways than one. He just couldn't believe he was in a situation like this again.

'My real name,' she said, her jaw tight, 'is Aurora Hendricks.' She was glaring at him now. 'My acting name was Star Kingfisher. I was in a show about vets, ironically. It was called *Into the Wild* and filmed in South Africa.'

As she said the words his mouth fell open. Pieces of the jigsaw puzzle were falling into place. He didn't watch many TV dramas but he had seen snippets of the show— mainly to see them dealing with lions, tigers and giraffes.

'That's why you looked familiar,' he said, not quite believing this.

She kept talking. 'It was the show I was sexually assaulted on, by one of the grips. I left shortly after, but as soon as I came back to England I started to be stalked. It happened over the course of a few months. The police became involved as they uncovered a kidnapping plot, and Brandon Rivers was arrested, convicted and jailed. Part of his bail conditions were that he knew I had a restraining order against him. In the meantime, I wanted a new career. I retrained as a vet nurse and haven't looked back. At least not until today.'

Her voice was quite flat. It was almost as if she was scared to let any emotion out because she was trying to hold things together.

'Are you okay?' he ventured. He had to ask—no matter what else was going on in his head—because it was the right thing to do.

'I don't think I'll ever be okay again,' she said simply. 'I thought I'd put all this behind me. I thought I could forget about it all. But it seems like I'm never going to shake him off.'

Eli sat very still. He had questions. He had multiple questions. Most of all he felt betrayed by the fact she hadn't trusted him enough to tell him who she was. This was the woman he loved. This was the woman he'd planned to spend the next year with—and maybe even more. But after his previous experience, trust was everything to him. How could he even imagine a life for them without it?

'Why didn't you tell me who you were?'

'What did it matter?' she shot back angrily.

'Because trust matters to me. A lot.' He left it there and she sighed, running her hand through her hair.

'You don't get it. At university, some people recognised me from the outset. They treated me as if I was stupid, not clever enough to pass the exams, and they certainly didn't take me seriously. As time went on, I managed to shake off Star—partly because I went back to my natural hair colour. I found out that if someone realised later I'd been on the 'vet TV show' as everyone called it, their opinion of me seemed to fall. It's a thing about being an actress.

For reasons that are totally invalid, people seem to think an actress can't be serious about having another career.'

Eli let his head hang down as he tried to take all this in. He understood that Aurora had been targeted and attacked today. That had to be terrifying. What he wanted to do was give her a big hug and tell her that everything would be okay. But for reasons he couldn't quite explain, the vibe between them had changed.

He took a breath. 'Can I ask you something else?'

'What?'

'The accounts. The credit cards. I got a bill today I wasn't expecting.'

She screwed up her face. 'Wh…what?' It was as if the question had totally thrown her.

'It's thousands. I wasn't sure what had happened.'

She shook her head. 'What's happened is the plans you looked at, and agreed to—the plans that I billed out for you, I've ordered all the supplies. The paint. The new sink. The plumbing. The worktops. The facing. The supplies. It all arrives in the next few days then we can sit down and plan where to start.' Her voice had become quieter as she continued. 'Or at least I thought we would.'

Eli blinked. 'I looked at the plans. I showed them to Matt and told you he liked them. But I hadn't okayed them yet.'

'You had.' She was clearly annoyed now.

He shook his head. 'I wanted his overall approval before starting the work. Then my plan was to get into the details specifically. It wasn't a signal to go ahead.'

The furrow in her brow increased. 'But it was. I have receipts for everything I've ordered. The lists were detailed already. I haven't gone away from them.'

'But you used the practice credit card without talking

to me first.' He was trying not to sound angry. He was trying to keep it locked down inside.

'But I thought you'd said yes. I thought you'd know.'

He took a long slow breath as he watched the last part of the life he'd thought he was getting finally crumble around him.

'My last practice went bankrupt. It went bankrupt because the practice manager—who I was dating—ran up tens of thousands of debt, and also took out loans against the practice. I had no idea she was doing it. And I found out too late to save the practice.'

There. He'd said the words out loud.

'But… I haven't done anything like that,' Aurora said. 'I've ordered supplies to update the practice. There's no loan.'

He closed his eyes. So much was whirling around inside his head. He wanted to find the right words. But for now, he actually didn't know what they were.

'This is why trust is essential to me, Aurora.'

She stared back at him. 'What I left out was minor. A small part of my past. I told you about the sexual assault.'

'You think someone being jailed for stalking you is minor?' he asked incredulously.

'No, of course I don't!' she shouted back. 'But you can't judge me, you can't judge us, on your past relationship. A relationship that *you* kept hidden. I'm not her—whoever she is.' She took a breath, and then added, 'And having a practice that went bankrupt? That's a big deal, Eli. That's something you should have been honest about. You know the arrangements here are simple. Anne or I do the wages, send things to the accountant. If you'd said there had been issues in the past, and you wanted to oversee that stuff yourself, we would have understood. At the very least, I could have copied you into every email that was sent so you had a record.' Her voice was shaking, along with her whole body. 'It seems we've both not managed to be entirely truthful with each other.'

There was silence. They both stared at each other, then Aurora stood, the chair scraping on the floor behind her.

'I can't stay anyway. Now that he's found me. I'll never have peace. I can't be here any more. I have to start over.' Her voice still trembled. 'I thought I'd found something here. Something that gave me a chance of a whole new world.'

He couldn't help but speak too. 'I thought I'd found something too. But trust is the most important thing to me, Aurora. I'll always wonder if there's something else you haven't told me. I don't want to doubt you. I don't want to doubt this relationship. But when you've been in the position that I have, this makes things almost impossible.'

He should stop her. He should try and convince her to stay. But right now, he just couldn't. His brain was still telling him to stop and think. He had to take time to discover how he felt about all this. If he could ever trust her again.

She reached the door and stopped, her hand on the doorframe. 'I'm sorry, Eli,' she said.

He looked at her. 'I'm sorry too.'

It was true. He was. For this. For her. For them. And for this whole situation that neither of them had asked for, or wanted.

And then he let her walk away.

CHAPTER TWELVE

AURORA STARED AROUND her house. She loved this place. She'd made her mark on it. Decorated with plain staples with lots of splashes of colour. She loved her garden. The neighbours. Even the drive to work.

And now? Because Brandon Rivers had this address she would never feel safe again.

But that wasn't the thing that was making her sick to her stomach. Not at all.

It had been the expression on Eli Ferguson's face when he'd been asking her questions. He hadn't cared about her past life as an actress. That hadn't made him think any less of her at all—her fears had been completely unfounded.

But the simple fact that she hadn't told him had been her undoing.

She'd always known there were more layers to Eli. She'd thought—a bit like herself—they had time to strip them back, bit by bit, at a pace they'd both be comfortable with.

She hadn't expected everything to come crashing down around them.

But then the money questions. She'd spent last night tossing and turning, trying to remember the exact conversations. She'd honestly thought the conversation on the bus had been the signal to go forward. But the more and more she took things apart, she realised that she might have got things wrong.

She was horrified when Eli had revealed what had happened to him in the past. But she was even more hurt by the fact he had obviously considered that it might be happening again.

Aurora had always been meticulous about money. It was why she'd been able to buy herself a house outright, when some of her previous co-stars had spent thousands on designer clothes and pricey wines.

The very fact he might have thought… It just made her cry even harder.

She tried to be reasonable. She tried to remember that he felt as though she'd broken his trust. And then he'd found a credit card bill, with items he felt he hadn't authorised.

She'd blown it. She'd blown everything. The best thing she could do right now was get her house on the market and try and find another job.

And while it was easy to consider the job, and acknowledge the mistake she might have made there, what wasn't easy was the ache in her heart. Eli Ferguson's face would appear in her head for a long, long time. She loved him. She hadn't told him but she did. He was the first man in a long time she'd had faith in, and she'd thought he would keep her heart safe. She'd even started to imagine a future together, no matter where that might be.

She brushed the tears from her face and stood up, looking around her house and realising she would have to get it ready to start viewings.

It didn't matter how painful it was. It was time to move on.

* * *

It had been a long night. Matt had been rushed into hospital with sepsis due to an infection in his central line, and Marianne had made a call to Eli.

But things had turned during the night. He'd started to respond to the antibiotics, and his heart rate and breathing had settled back down. Eli had taken Marianne home, made her tea and toast and sent her to bed. It was easy to see exactly how much of a strain this was all putting on her.

He went back to the hospital to check on Matt again and was pleased when the consultant arrived at the same time as he did. The consultant stayed for a while, talking about the fact that the central line had been the route of the infection, and suggesting its removal and another method of delivering the chemo. He'd clearly got the impression that Eli was Matt's son, and neither of them stopped to correct him.

Once he left, Eli sat down and took Matt's hand.

'You should know,' said Matt, 'that I named you as my other next of kin. In case it all got a bit much for Marianne.'

Eli squeezed his hand. 'I'm honoured to be named as your next of kin, and I promise to keep an eye on Marianne.'

Matt leaned back against his pillows. 'You look terrible.'

Eli laughed. 'Thanks. Someone kept me up all night.'

But Matt shook his head. 'It's not that. What is it?'

Eli sighed. There was no point in lying, and if he didn't tell Matt the truth he would then just worry about what might be wrong. So, as succinctly as possible, he told him the truth.

Matt gave him a soft smile. 'It's just a mix-up. A mis-understanding. You're adults. You can talk about that. And hurry up and give the place a facelift. Just be glad Marianne wasn't in charge, she would likely have spent five times as much.'

Eli opened his mouth to object but Matt held up one hand. 'I get to do the talking today.' His face was serious. 'Tell me honestly—how have you felt about being back at the practice?'

Eli took a few seconds to answer. He put his hand on his heart. 'I've enjoyed it in a way I never thought I was capable of.'

Matt smiled, and that meant more to Eli than anything. 'And what's helped you enjoy it?'

Eli threw up his hands and sat back in his chair. There was no point in answering. They both knew the answer.

'Then you have to fight for it.'

Eli shook his head. 'I can't. She wants to leave. She needs to move to get away from this guy.'

'Then find a reason to make her stay. Get a lawyer. I'll give you my friend's number. He's a criminal lawyer and he'll be able to help her. Find a way to keep the woman you love safe, Eli. Because there's nothing else so important.'

His skin prickled. 'I never told you I love her.'

'You didn't have to. I could see it.'

Matt took his hand again. 'Don't make your life just about work, Eli. That's how you'll end up. There's more of your father in you than you like to think. Reach out and fight for the person you love.' He smiled wryly. 'I don't even have to tell you this. You already know. Aurora is a gorgeous girl. Full of fire. Just what you need.' He lay back against the pillows, clearly pleased with himself.

He waved a hand. 'Now, hurry up. And be sure to tell Marianne I told you off. She likes to be good cop; I'm supposed to be bad.'

Eli stood up and smiled, kissing Matt on the side of the face. 'You'll never be bad cop,' he said.

CHAPTER THIRTEEN

His heart sank like a stone when he saw the estate agent board in the garden. She'd been serious. She was leaving.

He sat outside the cottage for a few moments, telling himself to stop planning everything. He'd spent all of the drive over thinking of all the ways he could say he was sorry, and ask her to stay.

He had the number for Matt's solicitor and had stopped to pick up a few other things before he'd got here. But he wasn't sure that any of them would work.

She opened the door on the second knock, and he blinked. Her normally immaculate hair was tousled and she had her pyjamas on.

She sighed. 'What do you want, Eli?'

'To talk to you.'

'I'm not sure there's anything left to say.'

'Can I come in?'

'Are you a viewer? Are you offering to buy my cottage?' Her words were sharp.

She licked her lips and paused for a second, so he took a chance and pointed to the car. 'And can I bring our boys in?'

Her bottom lip quivered. 'Hurry up,' she said, before turning and walking back inside.

He collected Hank and Bert from the car, putting them

on their leashes, but carrying Hank instead of letting him walk.

When he went inside the house and closed the door, he could see Aurora through the patio doors that led out to the sheltered garden. Toilet training was still a work in progress for the puppies and she knew that. He walked through towards her, and she held out her hands for Hank. He nestled in her lap while she patted him and looked him over.

'I've missed you,' she whispered to him, as Eli let Bert off the leash to run around the garden while he settled in the chair next to her.

'I've missed you,' he said.

She looked at him. He handed her the phone number. 'Matt asked me to give you the name of his friend, a criminal lawyer who will help you.'

She reached out and took the paper. He could actually sense a little relief from her. 'Thank Matt for me.'

He nodded. 'He also told me off.'

'He did?'

'Said our argument was a misunderstanding. And he's right.'

'The money part?'

He nodded.

'I've gone over and over that in my head. I honestly thought you'd told me to go ahead.' She shook her head. 'But that's not the part that bothers me. It's the fact you thought I could be like your ex.'

He winced because he knew she was entirely right. He put his hands up. 'You're right, and the truth is I know you're nothing like my ex. But the experience jaded me so much that I had trouble seeing past it. I was duped. And I have felt such a fool ever since. For the last year

I've had trouble with any new friendship because I always wonder if someone's aim is to con me.'

Aurora looked at him with pity. 'That's no way to live a life. You were unlucky.'

He looked her in the eye. 'But me being unlucky affects the life I can lead for the next few years. I can't take over the practice, I can't be a partner. I can only be an employee.'

'And why's that bad?'

'It's not. But being bankrupt is a stain that will hang over my head for years. I won't be able to get a mortgage in the next few years.'

'I don't need a mortgage. I own this place outright,' she said easily.

'I'm just trying to be honest with you,' he admitted as Bert came up and nuzzled at his knee. 'Not only am I a crap boyfriend, I'm also not a very good catch.'

There was the hint of a smile around her lips. 'You're not the only one who let the past affect them.'

His gaze met hers. She took a deep breath. 'I hated that when I told vet colleagues in the past about being an actress—or even if they found out on their own—they just seemed to think less of me. I hated that. I was serious about my job, and didn't want every question about when I was going back to South Africa.' She shook her head. 'Then there was the other stuff. I guess I was trying to forget all about it, to distance myself from it. It was reported in the press at the time, but two weeks later it was all forgotten about.'

She leaned her head on her hand. 'Except by me.' She looked truly sad. 'When the police told me about the kidnap threat I was terrified. You have no idea the thoughts that went through my brain.' She gave him a sad smile and shrugged. 'I'm an actress. I have a vivid imagination.'

'I can't imagine,' he said, a wave of sympathy flooding over him. She must have been terrified. How on earth could he even understand that?

'So when he appeared again...' She swallowed, and he could sense she was struggling. 'I felt like a fool—because I'd never seen him in person, and then he'd already been in the practice, and was that deliberate or am I just the unluckiest person in the world that he turned up where I was working?' A tear slid down her cheek, and he reached over and took her hand.

'If you hadn't appeared...' She shook her head. 'I don't know what I would have done.'

'Aurora Hendricks, you were doing a *spectacular* job,' he said. 'You were like some kind of kung fu fighter. I don't think the guy knew what had hit him.'

'It was pure adrenaline,' she admitted. 'I vomited later, and slept for hours.'

'Well, I'm glad I did appear. You don't deserve that. No one should treat you like that. You deserve, and are entitled, to feel safe.'

She sagged a bit further into her chair. 'But where does that leave me?'

'It leaves you with a sorry excuse of a boyfriend who made a mess of things, but loves you very much and wants you to stay.'

Her bottom lip started to tremble again.

'I will do anything I can to keep you safe.'

'But you don't want to stay,' she said in a cracking voice.

'What I want is to be where you want to be,' he said without a moment's hesitation. He leaned towards her. 'I started to love this place again,' he admitted. 'But a big part of that was you. If you want to stay then I want to stay. If you want to start afresh somewhere else then I'm happy to do that with you.'

'But you would be leaving behind your father's practice.'

'And I'd find a way to make my peace with that. My priority is you.' There was a nip at his ankle and he bent down and picked up Bert, who licked his cheek.

'I am the man who was so shameless that he brought our children with him to help him plead his case. That's how desperate I was.'

Aurora looked down to where Hank was still on her lap. She kept stroking him. 'If I honestly can't feel safe once I've spoken to the lawyer, you'd be willing to move somewhere else with me?'

'Absolutely. I love you, Aurora. Your happiness is what counts.'

'What about our boys?'

'If we need to get them passports, we can.'

She smiled. 'I love you too. And if can, I want to stay. I love working here. I love the community. I love the job.'

He moved in front of her, kneeling and resting his forehead against hers. 'It's you, me and our boys against the world. How does that feel?'

'That feels like for ever,' she said as her lips brushed against his, and he kissed her and didn't let go.

EPILOGUE

THE GUESTS LET out gasps of surprise and gave a round of applause as Hank and Bert trotted proudly down the aisle towards the groom. If dogs could smile, they were currently smiling.

'I can't believe you trust your dogs better than me with those rings,' Eli's childhood friend and best man whispered in his ear.

Eli kept his gaze on his dogs as he spoke out of the corner of his mouth. 'You lost your front door keys seven times in school. How many times have you had to replace your driving licence? And tell me right now where your car keys are.'

John looked momentarily panicked then shrugged his shoulders as he gave a casual smile. 'Oh, go on then, trust the dogs.'

Eli bent down to pat each of his beloved dogs on the head as they arrived at the top of the aisle, each with a bow around their neck, with a ring attached.

They looked very pleased with themselves, and sat eagerly at Eli's feet, waiting for treats.

The music changed and Eli stood up, watching as his bride emerged at the bottom of the aisle. Her dark red hair was pinned at the sides but cascaded down her shoulders. He took a breath, trying to remember to keep going

She beamed as she whispered in his ear. 'Not another puppy. But let's just say our family of four is expanding.'

Eli picked up his bride and whirled her around as his puppies barked in excitement and the wedding guests applauded.

And it truly was a perfect day.

* * * * *

If you enjoyed this story, check out these other great reads from Scarlet Wilson

Cinderella's Kiss with the ER Doc
A Daddy for Her Twins
Nurse with a Billion Dollar Secret
Snowed In with the Surgeon

All available now!

COMING SOON!

We really hope you enjoyed reading this book.
If you're looking for more romance
be sure to head to the shops when
new books are available on

Thursday 15th August

To see which titles are coming soon, please visit

millsandboon.co.uk/nextmonth

MILLS & BOON

MILLS & BOON ®

Coming next month

REUNION WITH THE ER DOCTOR
Tina Beckett

Her whole being ignited.

It was as if Georgia had been waiting for this moment ever since she'd come back to Anchorage. Eli's mouth was just as firm and warm as she remembered. Just as sexy. And it sent a bolt of electricity through her body that morphed into some equally dangerous reactions. All of which were addictive.

And she wanted more.

Her hands went behind his neck and tangled in his hair as if afraid he might try to pull away before she'd gotten her fill of him. Not that she'd ever been able to do that. No matter how many times they'd kissed, no matter how many times they'd made love, she still craved him.

Despite the three years she'd spent away on Kodiak, that was one thing that evidently hadn't changed.

She pulled him closer, relishing the feel of his tongue pressing for entrance—an entrance she granted far too quickly. And yet it wasn't quick enough, judging from the way her senses were lighting torches. Torches that paved the way for an ecstasy she could only remember.

How utterly heady it was to be wanted by a man like this.

Continue reading
REUNION WITH THE ER DOCTOR
Tina Beckett

Available next month
millsandboon.co.uk

FOUR BRAND NEW STORIES FROM
MILLS & BOON MODERN

The same great stories you love,
a stylish new look!

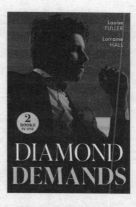

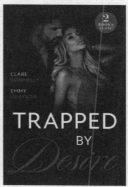

OUT NOW

MILLS & BOON

afterglow BOOKS

Afterglow Books is a trend-led, trope-filled list of books with diverse, authentic and relatable characters, a wide array of voices and representations, plus real world trials and tribulations. Featuring all the tropes you could possibly want (think small-town settings, fake relationships, grumpy vs sunshine, enemies to lovers) and all with a generous dose of spice in every story.

♪ @millsandboonuk
⊙ @millsandboonuk
afterglowbooks.co.uk
#AfterglowBooks

For all the latest book news, exclusive content and giveaways scan the QR code below to sign up to the Afterglow newsletter:

SCAN ME

as Aurora moved down the aisle towards him, her father beaming proudly.

Her dress was stunning. Cream, and off the shoulder—Bardot-style was what she'd told him—with a fitted waist and stunning satin figure-hugging skirt. Although she wore a veil, it didn't cover her face, but instead framed it, letting him know just how lucky he was.

But he already knew that.

Their wedding was a little unconventional. All pets had been invited to the outside ceremony. The Scottish weather was behaving today and blessing the guests with some bright sunshine. Jack Sannox was there with his new rescue dog that Aurora and Eli had found for him. After the sad loss of Rudy, they'd kept a careful eye on him for a number of months, and when a mixed breed rescue had been dropped at the practice it hadn't taken them long to know where to match her. Isla was on her best behaviour, sitting next to her owner.

Matt and Marianne were guests of honour in the front seats. Aurora and Eli considered them family. One year on, Matt was on the road to recovery, and was back working two days a week in the practice. Their newly qualified vet, Cheryl, had shaped up better than anyone could have hoped for, and she and her family loved their move to Scotland.

The Liverpudlian half of the outside ceremony seemed to be in competition around who could wear the most spectacular hat. Aurora's mother was winning, her bright pink and navy hat obscuring some people's view of the ceremony.

Eli met the green gaze of his soon-to-be wife and mouthed one word. *Gorgeous*. Her face lit up. She glowed. He'd heard people say those words about brides before, but now he could see it with his own eyes.

As she moved alongside him he slid his arm around her waist and kissed her cheek. He just couldn't help it. They'd been through so much this year. The court case had taken its toll. Aurora had continued her counselling, and Eli had joined her when appropriate.

Even though Brandon Rivers had been convicted again, and given a much sterner sentence, there was still a sense of disquiet around them. It had led them to their latest decision to return to one of Eli's previous roles with the horses in Jerez in Spain for the next year. Hank and Bert were ready to go with them. They all needed a break—a chance for some space to let Aurora heal fully, and for their relationship to blossom into the beautiful marriage it was about to become. It was likely they would return to Scotland the following year to take over from Matt when he would finally retire.

The ceremony started and, as planned, at one point Aurora bent to pull the satin ribbon around Bert's neck that held Eli's ring, and he did the same move with Hank, to reveal her ring.

She'd never looked so bright. She'd never looked so radiant.

And as they said their vows and slipped on each other's rings Eli knew he was the luckiest man on earth.

He pulled her close to him for their kiss. 'Love you, Mrs Ferguson,' he whispered as his lips touched hers.

She wrapped her hands around his neck. 'Love you, Mr Ferguson,' she responded. Then, with a glint in her eye, she leaned back.

'I might have some news to share.'

His eyebrows raised. 'You've adopted another puppy?'